Outstanding praise for the novels of V. S. Alexander

The Irishman's Daughter

"Skillfully blends family ties with the horrors of a starving country and the hopefulness of young love." —*Booklist*

"Written with hope for a better tomorrow, V. S. Alexander gives readers an intimate heart-wrenching account of the unimaginable suffering of those who clawed their way through Ireland's darkest years." —*BookTrib*

The Taster

"Alexander's intimate writing style gives readers openings to wonder about what tough decisions they would have made in Magda's situation. The 'taster's' story adds to a body of nuanced World War II fiction such as Elizabeth Wein's *Code Name Verity*, Anthony Doerr's *All the Light We Cannot See,* and Tatiana de Rosnay's *Sarah's Key*. Book clubs and historical fiction fans will love discussing this and will eagerly await more from Alexander." —*Library Journal*

"A totally gripping and credible imagining of how a young German woman was affected by the building chaos and cruelty during the late stages of Hitler's rule. It gains its power through the very special perspective of its main character, who is also the narrator. . . . Through her, Mr. Alexander creates an impressive and engaging novel that humanizes historical events and provides the rich texture of a life meeting momentous challenges in momentous times." —*Florida Weekly*

The Magdalen Girls

"A haunting novel that takes the reader into the cruel world of Ireland's Magdalene laundries, *The Magdalen Girls* shines a light on yet another notorious institution that somehow survived into the late twentieth century. A real page-turner!" —Ellen Marie Wiseman, author of *The Life She Was Given*

"Alexander has clearly done his homework. Chilling in its realism, his work depicts the improprieties long condoned by the Catholic Church and only recently acknowledged. Fans of the book and film *Philomena* will want to read this." —*Library Journal*

Books by V. S. Alexander

THE MAGDALEN GIRLS

THE TASTER

THE IRISHMAN'S DAUGHTER

THE TRAITOR

THE SCULPTRESS

Published by Kensington Publishing Corp.

The SCULPTRESS

V. S. ALEXANDER

KENSINGTON
PUBLISHING CORP.

www.kensingtonbooks.com

KENSINGTON BOOKS are published by

Kensington Publishing Corp.
119 West 40th Street
New York, NY 10018

All Kensington titles, imprints, and distributed lines are available at special quantity discounts for bulk purchases for sales promotion, premiums, fund-raising, educational, or institutional use.

Special book excerpts or customized printings can also be created to fit specific needs. For details, write or phone the office of the Kensington Sales Manager: Kensington Publishing Corp., 119 West 40th Street, New York, NY 10018. Attn. Sales Department. Phone: 1-800-221-2647.

The K logo is a trademark of Kensington Publishing Corp.

ISBN-13: 978-1-4967-2042-9 (ebook)
ISBN-10: 1-4967-2042-3 (ebook)

ISBN-13: 978-1-4967-2040-5
ISBN-10: 1-4967-2040-7
First Kensington Trade Paperback Printing: March 2021

10 9 8 7 6 5 4 3 2 1

Printed in the United States of America

To Alyssa Maxwell—thanks for your support and guidance

PART ONE

VERMONT and MASSACHUSETTS

1905–1917

CHAPTER 1

He was forbidden and Emma Lewis knew it.

They met by chance on summer vacation, before a horse-back riding expedition in the wooded hills near Bennington, Vermont. He was the cousin of a friend; she the daughter of an upper-middle-class merchant turned gentleman farmer in the mountains of western Massachusetts.

Kurt Larsen appealed to the sense of the wicked in her, the expectant thrill of some primal taboo not yet fully realized. She thought him "darkly romantic," a phrase borrowed from her "classics" reading as she told her friends that evening, although he was tall, fair, and blond. Emma, only two months past her fifteenth birthday, was eager for new experiences and willing to take her place among friends who knew more about the world than she. Two glorious weeks on the farm with three girlfriends—two from Boston, and Charlene from the Vermont farmhouse—plus the visiting male cousin, who settled in a few days after the young women had arrived.

"My handsome cousin," Charlene said, as Kurt strode into the kitchen when the young women were finishing breakfast.

He wore jodhpurs, polished black boots, and a loose, white summer shirt. A cotton rucksack, sporting a tartan plaid, was strapped across his back. He flipped it easily from his shoulders before settling into a vacant chair.

Charlene flicked her red hair from her shoulders and paid

little attention to him, as the others, including Emma, making eyes and stealing looks, swooned over him like a Greek god—one pictured from the descriptions in her studies. By her standards, Kurt was new and fascinating, more grown up than the provincial boys she knew who lived near her farm outside Lee. None courted her—her mother wouldn't allow such activity yet—those boys were friends, only school chums.

Jane and Patsy, the two friends from the city, who might have been sisters they looked so much alike with their tied-back brown hair and pert noses, tried every manner of small talk to capture Kurt's attention. They asked his age, where he went to school, where he lived, and the most important question, did he have a sweetheart? Kurt answered their questions in professorial style: Seventeen; his father wanted him to attend law school after college, preferably Harvard; he was from Swampscott, a resort town north of Boston; and, no, he had no sweetheart. What young man looking to further himself, with long, preparatory years of schooling ahead, could afford a serious attachment to a girl? When he said this, he looked straight into Emma's eyes with an icy determination that frightened her, yet somehow left her awed by the strength of his character. She had never seen such mature resolve in a boy.

The girls noticed Kurt's attention to Emma and teased her: "Emma has a new beau," Jane said with a flirtatious grin.

"What color is your hair, Emma?" Patsy asked, with a look of nonchalance. "Dark brown or black?"

"It depends on the light," Emma answered, her cheeks reddening. She had no use for such childish foolishness.

Shortly before noon, the five riders set out from the farmhouse with a picnic lunch. The sun had risen above the peaks, flashing between the billowing white clouds, showering golden light upon the whitewashed house nestled against the hill. The wind murmured in the pines. The sunlight, when wrested from the forest shade, warmed their backs, a perfect day for riding.

Emma, attired in her own riding clothes, noted that Kurt had no trouble with his horse, another point in his favor as far as she was concerned. He sat erect, attentive, and confident on the gelding. She was his match as an equestrian, having ridden for years on the horses that her father raised, but at one point Kurt took the reins of her chestnut mare and led the animal down the trail, past the swiftly flowing expanse of a greenish-brown river, into a valley filled with pines, maples, hackberry, and the misty veil of a waterfall. They stopped by the water and the horses drank.

"Go ahead, we'll catch up," Kurt urged the other girls as he jumped easily from his horse and offered his hand to Emma, although she needed no help with her dismount.

"There's a cleared area about a quarter of a mile ahead," Charlene said somewhat testily from her saddle. "Don't be late for lunch." Jane and Patsy pursed their lips and passed by, as Emma watched with muted amusement.

As she and Kurt stood by the river, the water gurgling over moss-covered rocks, he touched her hand.

The sense of his fingers upon her skin shocked Emma more than she could have imagined, never having felt anything like it before—at once fascinating and astonishing—an electric thrill racing up her arm straight to her heart.

She understood innately from the pounding in her chest, the rush of blood to her face, that Kurt's innocent touch might lead her elsewhere eventually—somewhere that her mother and father, in their disapproval, would never allow—that she, in this ecstatic moment, might have opened her own Pandora's box. Something flowered inside her, like a crocus poking through the snow, as urges yet unleashed signaled that the world of men would never be the same.

"Don't pay attention to my cousin or those other girls," he said. "Your hair is beautiful. I'd say it's black, but with shades of red when you step into the light—almost the color of your cheeks when you blush."

His fingers, like a satin glove, brushed up her arm toward her shoulder. A surge of nervous excitement blossomed inside her, setting her limbs trembling and her mind hurtling, urging Kurt onward with his exploration, perhaps to her breasts. However, not to be ignored, her mother's voice popped into her head like a protective saint, admonishing her to stop the fiend's hand.

"No," she said, brushing his arm away. "I don't want to disappoint Charlene—she has planned a perfect picnic." It was the only excuse she could think of.

"You're young aren't you?" He took the reins of his horse and led it from the water.

"I'm fifteen," she said, assured that she was a woman enough.

"Oh, but by the grace of God! Saved by the mouth of innocent truth." He mounted his horse and left her standing by the river.

Her heart sank and she wondered if she had done something wrong by not letting him continue his exploration. Was it so bad to be close to a boy, perhaps intimate? The feelings of warmth and tenderness flowing through her body had been wonderful. Had she read the same in him, or had she been fooled?

At the picnic, on a blanket spread upon the lush summer grass, he avoided her and spent his time teasing Jane and Patsy, winking at them, laughing at their trivial jokes, stroking their uncovered arms warmed by the sun.

At one point, Charlene snatched a gold-banded ruby ring from Kurt's finger and slid it over the fourth on her left hand. "Look," she said, her eyes wide, her pouty mouth screwed up in haughty victory. "I'm married to my cousin. Isn't that the way it used to be in the old days . . . marrying your cousin?"

"That's disgusting," Jane said. "Give him back his ring."

Kurt lay back on the blanket, his slender form ablaze like white heat in the sunlight, a smile poised on his lips. "Oh, she'll give it back or pay dearly for it, won't you, cousin?"

Laughing, Charlene ripped the ring from her finger and flung it at Kurt. It bounced off his chest and landed near his neck. He lifted the gold band, positioning the ruby toward the sun, where it flashed crimson in the brightness.

His attention to her friends brought out a feeling in Emma—

jealousy—one she had read about and pondered, but never experienced on this level; but, there was a new, deeper, darker, feeling that she couldn't shake as Kurt left the farm the next day.

She could have sworn that it was love, but somehow it had twisted into something heated and full of longing, as if she couldn't live without him; and, there would be no life in her lonely body if he deserted her.

Several days later, after bathing at home in tepid water in the washroom's stone tub, Emma gathered her pad and charcoal pencil in her bedroom, much as she had done since her father had presented her with drawing materials when she was six years old. She sketched Kurt's form lovingly, the curve of the jodhpurs on his legs, the breadth of his chest, the lean muscles of his arms. The face was another matter: the forehead arched too high, the nose was too thick, the lips too sweet. She noted her trouble with faces, and in Kurt's case, after his departure, she could only admire and hope to recreate the memory.

"Emma, sit up straight. Pay attention to your posture. It's not attractive for a young woman to slouch."

Emma picked at the peas on her plate with her fork. Sunday lunches—the large meal of the day after church—could be torture. "I'm not slouching, Mother. I simply bent over to get to my peas."

"Your mother is right, Emma," her father said. "Posture is everything . . . appearance and presentation, my dear."

It had been two months since she'd met Kurt in Vermont, and she could think of nothing else but the lean young man who occupied her dreams. School's coming, the end of the New England summer, Sunday mornings at the red sandstone Episcopal Church, meant nothing to her, as did the few other boys who filled her days.

Her father had purchased the farm near Lee, south of Pittsfield, when Emma was five. A neighbor in Boston had teased her about the move to the country, saying, "The Indians will get you if you don't watch out," and for weeks she feared being alone in the vast, empty yard, or sleeping with the windows open in her second-floor bedroom.

Her mother, Helen, ate her lunch in mannered movements while stretching as little as possible, arms moving like a mechanized toy. She hadn't changed after church, still wearing the somber black dress accented by a high satin neck that wrapped almost to her chin. The only accessories she allowed herself were a gray sash that fell from her waist along the length of the gown to her calves and a diamond-cluster stickpin attached to the bodice for the utilitarian use of holding down her hat.

Her father, George, ate in a more relaxed manner in his brown suit, shirt with rounded collars, and striped bow tie; but, much to Emma's irritation, he bowed to Helen's wishes and parroted her feelings except, it seemed, in one past instance: the decision to move from Boston to the fifty-year-old farmhouse near Lee. That came about from the sale of the Lewis Tea Company, which he had inherited fifteen years earlier from his father. When it came to buying the property he had not succumbed to his wife's pleas or tears. "I'm finished with Boston," he told her. "I want to raise horses and live a life unfettered by crowds and worries. In Lee, we can think—we can be ourselves."

Helen rang the small silver bell beside her. Matilda, a middle-aged domestic from Lee who cooked and cleaned for the family on weekends, hurried to the table. In the still spry but prematurely gray-haired Matilda, Emma found an ally—a woman, it seemed, who appreciated mistakes, the follies, joys, and fullness of life.

"Please clear the table, Matilda," her mother ordered. "We have an appointment this afternoon we must meet."

"I'm not through with my dessert," her father said with a bite of wild-blueberry pie rolling in his mouth.

Helen shook her head. "You know better than to talk with your mouth full. Hurry up . . . we mustn't keep Mr. French waiting."

Emma placed her fork on her plate and looked toward the open dining room window. The day, even though it was late August, had the look of fall. A dense overcast had rolled in from the west, covering the hilltops and coating the still-green grass with a layer of mist. The early morning breeze had dissipated, and the curtains lay limp with humidity against the white window frames. Charis, the Lewises' tabby cat, had squeezed between the sheers and the screen, appearing as a diaphanous shadow as he surveyed the side yard for mice and squirrels.

Emma was in no mood for an afternoon trip, or company, especially a visit to Mr. French, a man she didn't know. "Must I go? I have reading to do for the upcoming year." She had no intention of studying; in fact, she was screwing up her courage to write a letter to Kurt after receiving his address from Charlene.

"Of course, you must go." Her mother placed her folded hands on the table and stiffened her back. "One does not refuse an offer from Mr. Daniel Chester French, the great sculptor."

"Who?" Emma asked.

Matilda winked at her from the other side of the table and nodded as if to say, pay attention to your mother.

"The world-renowned sculptor of the American patriot of Concord, the man who honored John Harvard at his own college, the artist who has brought so many famous faces of the past to life."

"What an honor," Matilda said, continuing her almost private discourse with Emma. "I think a young lady would be thrilled to meet such a famous man."

Helen sniffed and said, "Quite right, Matilda. You *do* have a good head on your shoulders."

George finished his pie and set the plate aside so Matilda could take it away. "Allow me to attend to myself and the carriage horses."

Following Helen's lead, they all rose from the table.

As Emma started for the stairs to get her hat, Matilda whispered, "Mr. French's a famous man, known about these parts for years. Maybe you'll learn something."

"What can I learn?" Emma replied. "I'd rather stay home. Mother's always been attracted to money and fame."

"Shoo. It'll be good for you to get out of the house and stop pining over that boy. It's not healthy . . . you'll find out when you get older."

"All right," she said, ascending the stairs, but her mind was far away from Mr. Daniel Chester French.

Secretly, her father had encouraged Emma to draw when she had displayed an early interest; not so her mother, who found a woman's artistic desires to be distasteful. "One can never attract a worthwhile husband through such pursuits," she had admonished George one time with Emma within earshot.

However, Emma's practice of drawing, at first relegated to the barn, allowed her to go inside herself, to lose track of time, to fill the vacant hours in her room with something that amounted to fulfillment. Drawing gave her pleasure. She stashed finished sketches under her bed where her mother would never condescend to look, leaving Matilda to find them and compliment her on her talent.

"You mustn't tell Mother," she told the housekeeper. "It will be a secret between us." Matilda was more than willing to keep secrets as long as no one, most of all Emma, was harmed.

The dense clouds still hovered over them by the time they boarded the carriage shortly after one in the afternoon. Their legs covered by a wool blanket to stave off the damp, Emma and her mother sat in back while George took the reins in front. On the hour trip to the French home, they passed hills clothed in green, stony blue lakes, and tilled fields.

Emma grew more excited as they neared their destination, thinking that perhaps Matilda was right—meeting such a famous man might be an honor—and that the experience of a new artistic form awaited her. They arrived at the imposing stucco residence to find the sculptor waiting for them in the lane behind his home.

"I've never seen so many windows in a house," Emma whispered to her mother. "It's very grand."

"Don't be gauche," her mother shot back. "You've seen plenty of magnificent homes in Boston. Remember your breeding."

The horses whinnied to a stop and George jumped down from the carriage to shake Mr. French's hand.

Emma studied the sculptor's face as if she would sketch it. What struck her most about Daniel Chester French was his affability, a kindness she gathered from his countenance despite his preference to keep his lips distant from a smile, as if some spiritual level of artistic seriousness guided his consciousness. He was balding, with the hirsute remains of his youth covering only the sides of his head, along with a few wispy strands crossing his pate; a full, brushy mustache streaked with gray covered his upper lip to his nose; the eyes were cleanly set, dark and reflective; the ears large with pronounced lobes. He wore a gray jacket and pants and a high-collared white shirt fastened with a striped bow tie.

"Welcome to Chesterwood," Emma heard the sculptor say above the chatter of introductions.

George opened the carriage door, releasing the footsteps, and assisted his wife from the vehicle. Emma followed, holding on to her hat, as she descended the steps.

"A pleasure to meet you at last," her mother said as the sculptor extended his hand. "Thank you so much for your invitation to tea."

"I've always been fond of Lewis Tea," he said, "so when the occasion arose that we might meet, I had no hesitation." He paused and pointed to a large building not far from the house. "My studio. We often entertain visitors there, on the porch; unfortunately, on days like today we must keep inside. . . . I'm sorry my wife won't be able to join us, but I'm afraid the damp weather has brought on a summer head cold. She conveys her regrets."

The luster in Helen's eyes faded a bit at the news. "I was so looking forward to meeting her . . . perhaps another time."

"Of course. I'm sure there will be other opportunities."

He led them across the spacious yard and through the tall studio doors into a room that towered over Emma's head. Never had she seen such grand space, such sculpture in abundance: plaster casts, bronze works, animals greater than life-size, cupids, marble busts, mythological figures, all on display before her eager eyes. An ecstatic excitement buzzed inside her; she wanted to shout. How wonderful it must be to bring the lifeless materials of bronze and marble to life, a kind of divine magic akin to birth!

The sculptor noticed the look of wonder in Emma's gaze and leaned toward her. "After tea, I want you to do something for me."

Helen's eyes widened, while Emma's heart beat fast in anticipation of the mysterious request from the great man.

He led them to a room at the north end of the studio. They sat in Chippendale chairs at a table near the marble fireplace and drank Lewis Tea and ate iced cake and vanilla cookies. The conversation veered from her father's history with the company, to their purchase of the Lee homestead, to her mother's activities as a wife and homemaker.

"I would like to do more for the church," her mother told the sculptor.

Emma suppressed a smirk, for her mother had never once indicated a liking for the church members, their groups, or their activities. Helen was content to sit at home and think of things for George to do while complaining about the lack of conveniences since leaving the city, the paucity of cultural life, and the absence of any intelligent friends.

The sculptor appeared to pick up on the meaning beneath her mother's words. "We often get wrapped up in our own lives." He turned to Emma. "I hear you're good with a pen, young lady. That was one of the reasons I invited your family here."

Her mother flinched and her father stiffened in his chair.

"Wherever did you hear that?" Helen asked.

"News travels in the Berkshires like lightning on a stormy day," he replied.

Emma knew there could be but one answer. *Matilda.*

George's cheeks puffed out, his face blanching with the exposure of his secret encouragement.

"I'd like you to draw for me," the sculptor said. "I urge young people to learn about art. I sometimes teach . . . and if you display talent, you might study with me."

Her mother stopped in mid-sip and put her teacup down. "I'm sure Emma has no such interest, Mr. French, although it *would* be a great honor to study with you."

"We should let the artist decide," the sculptor said, his eyes alighting on Emma.

Her father nodded.

Helen tilted her head in defiance. "George, really . . . Emma is much too young—"

"Never too young to learn," the sculptor said and turned to her. "Are you interested in sculpture?"

Emma looked down at her teacup, then at her mother, and, finally, at her father. "I've seen statues before, but, until today I didn't know how beautiful they could be. I'd like to learn."

"Will you favor me with a drawing? I have a sketch pad and pencil in the casting room. Let your parents enjoy their tea."

Emma heard the hurried whisperings of her mother directed at her father as she got up from her chair. The sculptor took her hand and they walked to a large wooden table near the studio doors.

"Look around, decide what interests you, let your muse run free." He turned in a broad circle, and she followed him, taking in the sculptures around her. "Sit or stand, do as you wish, but pick the subject and let it fill you. Create." He pointed to the pad and charcoal on the table. "Let art become part of you."

Emma drew in a breath—being here was like being in Alice's Wonderland—and, at last, someone—someone of note—appreciated her for who she was. She picked up the pencil, the wooden shaft shaking in her hands, and sat at the table.

"Don't be nervous," he said. "If you'd like, I'll return to your parents. It seems your mother may need some calming down.

Give me a quick impression in twenty minutes. We can go into the fine details later."

As the sculptor returned to her parents, the marble bust of a man, a soldier wearing a helmet, caught her eye. French positioned his chair to sit again, its legs scraping against the floor, the conversation beginning anew.

The face reminded her of the drawing in her classics book of Perseus holding the severed head of Medusa.

The helmet flowed easily from her hand, the charcoal outlining the curved form swelling in pleasing lines around the face. She sketched quickly, finishing a rough likeness of the head, as well as the addition of a body defined by muscular biceps, abdomen, and legs. The figure was nude, but, except for the head, turned to the side to conceal any features that might be embarrassing to her parents.

The minutes evaporated, and she looked up from the pad to see the sculptor studying her from across the room. Her mother and father stared at each other across the table.

She went back to the face, but no matter how hard she tried, it looked nothing like the bust. The nose lacked the delicacy of the sculpture; the eyes, though rather lifeless in white marble, had even less vitality on the page than on the form. The chin was too angular and displayed none of the smoothness of the bust. Even she could see this as she trudged back to the table. She glanced at one of the shelves crammed with plaster figures and sketches. There, on top, was the nude figure of a woman, and angled beneath it, the nude form of a man. Her mother would have turned her eyes away and offered recriminations at the sight of both drawings, but Emma found them pleasing, particularly the man, whose frontal figure displayed every part of his anatomy. She thought of Kurt and wondered what it would be like to draw him.

"Let's see what you've created." His lips parted in a half smile. He was sitting like a judge at the end of the table.

She handed the pad to him, only its back visible to her mother's inquisitive eyes, and waited for his pronouncement about her effort. Emma shuffled her feet, until Helen shot her a look that shouted, "Sit down."

The sculptor took his time, and after a few minutes of intense study, placed her drawing faceup on the table. Her mother squinted at the form, closed her eyes, and leaned back in her chair. Her father seemed interested, but subdued, in what she had created.

"Very nice . . . respectable work. . . ." He lifted the pad between his hands and showed it to her parents. Shaking her head, Helen looked away.

"I don't mean to distress you, Mrs. Lewis, but the human body is the bread and butter of the artist . . . unless you're a master of landscapes only, like the French of late. But, even then, you can't be a *true* artist unless you understand the form, which the French have already demonstrated."

"I find it perverse," Helen whispered, her gaze still turned from the pad.

"Mother?" Emma pleaded. "Did you hear what Mr. French said?"

Helen nodded. "I don't want to speak of it."

"Do you think my sculpture perverse, Mrs. Lewis? Look around you. You'll see the naked breast of womanhood, the unadorned form of man."

Her mother pursed her lips and stared at her husband. Emma feared that the worst was to come, perhaps in the carriage ride home.

"Your daughter has raw talent," the sculptor said to her father. "If you agree, she could study with me over the next two summers before she goes off to higher studies. The preparation would do her good. Would you like that, Emma?"

She looked at her immobile mother and, seeing nothing but resistance, nodded. "I've never attempted sculpture, but I'd like to try . . . if you feel I'm good enough."

"Of course. The work will be hard, but worth your while. Over the winter, continue with your sketching, but begin to think in three-dimensional terms, not only on paper, but in space—in your mind." He looked again at the drawing. "The body is fine, but we have some work to do with the face. Do you agree?"

"Yes. Faces seem to be my weakness."

"When you're done here, you'll have no weaknesses." He rose from his chair. "Let's have a tour of the garden before you depart. It's lovely in any kind of weather."

Emma got up, her legs wobbling with excitement from the news. She would be studying with one of the country's best sculptors. She couldn't wait to tell Charlene—and Kurt.

Her mother rose stiffly from her chair and followed the sculptor while Emma and her father walked behind. As they left the studio, she and her father exchanged a look that meant they both understood the trouble ahead. George smiled as if to say, "We'll get through this," and proceeded to his wife, who brushed him away with her arm.

The carriage ride home was as frosty as the chill that had crept into the air.

Nothing was said that night, but a silent, ever-building tension between her parents grew with each passing day until the living room exploded when Matilda left for the evening the following Sunday.

Emma had never heard an argument like it, and the heated and hateful words exchanged downstairs left her shivering and crying in bed, afraid that she had created a terrible and unalterable rift between her parents. Even after pulling a pillow over her head she heard shouted snippets of the conversation:

"How *could* you encourage her?" her mother railed.

"Emma's talent is art—she should be encouraged!"

"Art is fine for men of means—not women . . . a girl working as a *sculptress?*"

"You would doom her to a life of servitude in the kitchen?"

"Better *that* than a life of poverty with miscreants."

The argument burst not with a bang, but with an unendurable silence that left the house cold and hushed as if the lonely meanderings afterward were sounds created by melancholy ghosts. Her father moved into what had been a guest room, leaving Helen alone in the marital bedroom that had been theirs since they'd moved in. In the following weeks, cold greetings were exchanged between them, even extending to Emma, while her father took refuge in his own sad counsel. A separate living arrangement might linger until spring, Emma believed, when the land, and possibly hearts, thawed. In her loneliness, she wrote several letters to Kurt—none of which were answered.

Daniel Chester French sent periodic letters to her parents throughout the winter encouraging Emma's studies. At first, Helen ignored them until an invitation to meet another well-known neighbor in Lenox, Edith Wharton, was issued by the sculptor. The chance to meet the writer of *The House of Mirth* was too much for her mother to brush aside. Helen spent many days in Wharton's company in the spring and also in the months when the novelist wasn't traveling abroad. Their unexpected friendship seemed to usher in the long-awaited reconciliation between her parents Emma had hoped for.

"She seems so sad for a talented woman," Helen told them one night at the dinner table. "Both she and her husband . . . no married couple should suffer so." She reached out her hand and for the first time in months touched her husband's arm and the next evening they reconciled, moving again into the same bedroom.

Throughout the summer, Emma rode her horse three times a week to Chesterwood to receive instruction. As the sculptor worked on plans for his outdoor statuary, he looked over Emma's shoulder and critiqued her work with the modeling clay, noting her innate ability to create the form, but fail in the details. She created maquettes of clay and plaster, and even learned techniques for carving marble under French's guidance. Emma learned to love the process of bringing an idea, a drawing, to full form, and marveled at the process of creation.

Although thoughts of Kurt lessened during her tutelage, he

was never far from her mind, especially after receiving an invitation in the autumn from Charlene to spend time between Christmas and New Year's at the Vermont farmhouse. Emma learned that Kurt also was invited and arranged for an immediate positive response.

"You never answered my letters," Emma said, fiddling with the red sash of her robe.

Kurt, reading a magazine, sat in the overstuffed wingchair in front of a dying fire of birch logs, his long legs stretched across an equally plush ottoman, trying to feign indifference to her attentions. Charlene and her family had already retired, leaving Kurt to keep watch on the fireplace until the embers died. There were four bedrooms upstairs: Charlene and her parents each occupying separate rooms on the front of the house; Emma's and Kurt's rooms faced each other, at the end of the long upstairs hall. Patsy and Jane were not at the farmhouse; instead, they were at home in Boston.

Frustrated, Emma pulled a chair near the fire, blocking Kurt's view of the flames and the warmth emanating from them.

"I will be very cold and cranky if you don't move," he said and drew up his knees, exposing his gray wool socks extending down from the cuffs of his pants. "It was twenty-five degrees outside when I checked the barn thermometer two hours ago. It's colder now."

"You might as well spend the evening with the horses, for all the attention you've shown me."

He leaned forward, the magazine crinkling in his lap. "What would you like me to do?" He rested his hands in his lap. "We can't play the Edison—we'll wake the family and Charlene's father would be angry. We can't dance because we don't have music. We can talk but I suspect you're tired, as it's nearing eleven, past your bedtime I'm sure."

"I'm not a child, Kurt," Emma huffed. "It's been a year and a half since we've seen each other. At least tell me what you've been doing." She took in his form. He had lost none of his attractiveness since she'd seen him last; in fact, the last vestiges of his boyish good looks had been replaced by the features of a handsome man: his shoulders had broadened, the beard darkened to a noticeable stubble, the chin and cheeks firmer, the eyes still a lively and lovely sky blue. She hoped to draw him.

He sighed and sank back in the chair. "Studying, studying, and more studying in order to get into law school. My father will disown me if I don't get into Harvard. I consider it an almost impossible task, but *he* won't take no for an answer. There are more things to life than putting one's nose in a textbook. I couldn't wait to come here to get away from home . . . and books."

Emma turned her head toward the fire and looked at the red embers that glowed so evenly across the stone hearth. "So, you haven't had the time to write? I thought I might at least get a letter."

"Well, my studies got in the way." He paused and with a casual motion grasped the wingchair's arms. "Also, my father beat it into my head that you should never be too attentive to a woman. They lose interest if you are. 'I've got a tip,' he's told me more than once. 'Never get married. You'll be much happier.'"

Instinctively, she objected to that reasoning, but the thought of her parents' arguments caused by their clash of wills flashed into her mind. "Your father sounds like he's unhappy."

Kurt thought for a moment. "I wouldn't say he's unhappy. He makes his own way."

Emma wanted no further explanation of what that happiness might entail. "You pay attention to your father, don't you?"

"Yes. Do you pay attention to yours?"

Emma looked toward the Christmas tree in the corner, silver beading glinting, the starched crocheted snowflakes and fragile glass ornaments shimmering in the fading firelight, the fragrant aroma of pine needles filling the room. Her parents had gone to great trouble to get her to the Vermont farmhouse, even going so far as to rent a carriage for the round-trip. She wondered if they were resting comfortably at home, or whether another argument had broken out. Were they happy beside each other on this cold night?

"I pay more attention to my father than my mother," Emma replied, looking back at Kurt. "No one makes me happier than my father. He has encouraged my art while my mother, at first, was less supportive."

"Art?"

"I'm studying with Daniel Chester French?"

"You don't say," Kurt said with enthusiasm.

Emma nodded.

"Who's he?" A sly grin broke out on his face.

She would have thrown a book at him had one been available. Instead, she plucked the magazine off his lap, whacked him across the shoulder with its rounded form, and tossed it back. "He's the most important sculptor in America."

Kurt's grin faded. "Really. . . ." He scooted closer toward her as if his interest had been piqued. "He must be a very rich man."

"Is that all that matters to you?" she asked. "Money?"

"Money's important—probably more important than anything else. How can you be happy without it? Who wants to be poor? I'll have to support a family, make a good living, but I'm not sure law is the way to go. I'm eighteen now and able to make my own decisions." He cocked his head. "You must be over sixteen."

"Yes, and able to make my own decisions."

He guffawed and then covered his mouth with his hand. "Don't make me laugh—I'll wake up Charlene's parents. You're lying. Your mother rules the roost."

Kurt was right—her mother did make most of the family decisions. In the past year, Emma had begun to realize that having a mind of one's own was a useful characteristic for a woman. She only hoped that when the time came to fully utilize this trait she would use it in a more positive manner than her mother. If nothing else, she had learned from her mother and Daniel Chester French that a woman was not to be trifled with.

"I've been studying anatomy as part of my instruction," Emma said casually.

Kurt's eyes flickered. "Another surprise."

"I'd like to sketch you before we return home."

He smiled and extended his feet until the tips of his toes touched her legs.

She didn't back away.

He moved his hands to his waist as if he was about to remove his sweater.

"Not tonight . . . when I'm ready."

He stopped. "Sure. I'm game."

"On my terms." She rose from her chair and returned it to its place. "When the time is right."

His eyes flashed and the grin returned, as she left him sitting in front of the fire.

I have him exactly where I want him. The thought occurred to her, as she trod up the creaky wooden stairs, that perhaps she was more like her mother than she realized. That idea didn't encourage sleep. Even as she was buried under the covers to fight off the frosty air, she found herself thinking of her parents and her art, looking past the open curtains, through the glass to the brilliant winter stars and slivered moon that cast a soft, pale light on the snow gathered in the eaves.

The sketching session that Emma envisioned never occurred in the way she'd hoped—privately, with Kurt acting as her model in some form of undress. The days and evenings were taken up with Charlene and her parents. Finally, the last night of the stay, as they all sat around the fireplace, Emma was able to draw them in an informal pose and setting. She was somewhat reluctant to show them the finished charcoal sketches for fear that her inability to completely capture their faces might lead to disparaging remarks, but Daniel Chester French had told her that she would never be an artist unless she opened herself to critical barbs no matter how hard they stung.

She passed the first of her drawings to Kurt. He was somewhat amused, but from his careful scrutiny there must have been something on paper that pleased him.

Charlene was the most effusive of the group. "Oh, it's wonderful," she said, holding her portrait in her outstretched arms.

Charlene's father said he would find "three nice frames" and mount the drawings "prominently" on the staircase wall. After a brief initial look, the subject was dropped for other topics until everyone grew tired and said good night.

Emma departed the Vermont farmhouse before New Year's Day, 1907, with Kurt still on her mind. One of her Christmas presents was a small diary given to her by her father.

"You can draw in it and give free rein to your thoughts," he told her.

Emma loved the rich smell of the green leather case, the gloss of the brass lock that kept the diary's contents hidden, and the small golden key that unlocked its secrets. She always kept the book secured but in sight upon her desk. The key, when not in use, was tucked behind a fitted panel in her closet. The concealing seam was so flawless and unobtrusive, Emma knew her mother would never find it, even if she dared to search her room. In the cold months of January, February, and March, Emma started the diary and fell in love with the peace that filled her as she poured out her feelings. Writing became a habit as constant as the rising sun. She also corresponded with Kurt, writing mostly of schoolwork, her interest in art and sculpture, and her hope to see him again. Never did the words, "miss you," or "lacking your affection," enter the letters. Two could play the game of muted interest, she decided. Surprisingly, he managed to send a few letters in return, which, upon their receipt, elicited her mother's scowls.

"Who is this boy?" Helen asked one March afternoon as the sun, weakened by high clouds, shone upon the still snow-covered yard. Emma sat on the living room couch reading a schoolbook, Charis stretching across her lap. Her mother waved the letter in the air in a threatening manner. "This is the second one from K. Larsen that you've received."

"He's Charlene's cousin," Emma said, looking up from her book. "I told you he was visiting in Vermont when I was there."

"How *well* did you get to know him?" her mother asked.

"Mother . . . really . . . I know how to behave." How often would she have to resort to such an argument?

"Don't toy with me. I was against this relationship with the sculptor from the beginning. Your father has allowed *ideas* about the *body* into your head. And now you're seeing boys. I can't imagine what you're thinking and what you've been taught. Taught, indeed! We will have to have a talk soon."

Emma sighed, not wanting to anger her mother, but also acknowledging that her mother's scolding contained some kernels of truth. The human body was much more familiar to her now, and she enjoyed it, not only the beauteous curves of the female that Daniel Chester French taught her to appreciate, but the firm, muscular, hardness of the young male—referenced by the gods of Greek and Roman mythology. She now considered herself advanced beyond her years in those areas of learning. There was no need for a talk with her mother. She already had learned everything good, bad, pleasing, and disgusting about sex through anatomy books, conversation, or titillating innuendo with her girlfriends. Charlene was particularly adept at making innocent jokes that had a dirty feel to them.

"We're friends—that's all," Emma replied.

Helen tossed the letter to her, and it landed upon Charis, who sprang from Emma's lap as if touched by fire. Emma laughed to herself—not at the cat's misfortune, but at the surely innocuous and noncommittal contents of Kurt's letter that would shock no one.

Daniel Chester French returned to Chesterwood in the late spring, some weeks after Emma's seventeenth birthday. The time to renew her training had come again upon school's dismissal for the summer.

"I'm coming with you," her father said on the first day she could visit the sculptor.

Emma was happy because the time they spent together was rare. As her father worked with the horses, she sat on the porch admiring the last of the fragrant lilac blooms and the first buds of the summer roses; the lawn and nearby hills shimmered in coats of lavish green.

The carriage horses hitched, they departed for the ride to Chesterwood. Emma knew something must be on her father's mind for him to make the trip—one she normally made alone on horseback.

She sat uneasily for a time waiting for him to speak. When he finally did, they were well away from the house. "Mr. Ford has a marvelous new invention and I've put one on order."

Emma turned to him unsure of what he meant.

He saw her confusion. "It's a horseless carriage—an automobile—one of the first in the county. I haven't told your mother yet, but I think it will make life easier for all of us."

"An automobile!" She clapped her hands, her excitement pouring out. "Mother probably won't like it. It'll be too hard to operate, or too confusing, or make too much noise. She's not in favor of anything new unless it's something she wants."

Her father scowled and adjusted the reins. "Be fair. I've noticed a rift between you and your mother lately. God knows, we've had our differences, but she's a good, decent woman—just a little headstrong. You've inherited some of that from her."

The day was warm and Emma took off her hat. The wind blew through her hair and ruffled her dress. The sun striking her face and the heady scent of the fresh grass made her skin prickle with life. "Papa, sometimes I want to scream she smothers me so. A little headstrong? She is *always* right—no one else is—with the possible exception of Mrs. Wharton, whom she slobbers over."

"The move from Boston was hard for her. She's never gotten over it, but it was the right thing for us to do as a family. I will tell you this, dear one, because you're old enough now to understand—your mother will deny it—but she doesn't have the constitution for the city. It was consuming her and would continue to consume her were we still living there. For your mother, life was all about possession and accumulation. I think we would have gone broke had we stayed. Fortunately, Lewis Tea was prosperous enough for me to take us away from Boston."

Emma laughed. "I'll never forget the first day when we moved in and Mother found the bathtub in the kitchen. I've never seen her so angry or mortified. Remember what she said? 'I'm not taking a bath here. This is obscene!'"

Her father chuckled but beneath the veneer of amusement sadness bubbled, a despair born of ever hoping to satisfy his wife, Emma sensed. "Yes, for six months we had to heat water and bathe behind the screen. I became a water boy and bathing attendant until I completed the heated bathhouse outside." He urged the horses forward with a few clicks of his tongue.

The heated bathhouse still was not enough for her mother. The small wooden building was subject to variations in the climate—often too hot or too cold in the winter, the same in the summer. Still, it was private and relaxing when the weather was good.

They passed between two hills rising near Chesterwood. "There's another matter I have to discuss with you," her father said, his gaze drifting toward his feet. He looked there, then at the wooded countryside and the horses before speaking. "Your mother should have a talk with you now that you're a woman. I would do so myself, but I feel it's a mother's place to handle such matters." Wrinkles furrowed on his forehead below his flat cap. "Do you understand what I'm talking about?"

"Yes," Emma said, "but I know the facts of life. Isn't that what they're called these days?"

"The facts of life."

"She needn't worry. With my studies, I've learned all there is to know about the anatomy of both sexes. And, if you can keep a secret from Mother, the girls at school talk about it all the time."

Her father kept his concentration on the reins and the horses. "That's the problem, Emma. There's much more to it than anatomy and talk—sex and love are separate and distinct, but it's best when it meshes. Emotions are part of it, too. Sometimes love is confused by sex, and vice versa, and tragedies can result. We—your mother and I—don't want that to happen to you."

She fell silent knowing her father was right, but feeling confused by his words. Were the emotions she felt when she saw Kurt—excitement, desire, and longing—wrong? Was there so much more to be learned?

"Yes, Father, I know," she said, hoping she spoke the truth.

Chesterwood with its gleaming windows appeared. The time for conversation was over until the ride home.

After a volley of handshakes and exchange of greetings, Emma and the sculptor walked to the studio, as her father went off to spend time in the garden.

"I don't need to be entertained—this beautiful day is joy enough," George told them. Emma thought he looked flushed and out of sorts, but her father had always enjoyed his nature walks and horseback rides, and his time alone in the beautiful Chesterwood gardens would be no different.

She, under the sculptor's tutelage, spent two hours drawing and working with clay. He complimented her on her progress, although she felt the face she was working on was still too crude to commit to bronze or marble.

"It will take time," he said, pulling a gold pocket watch from his jacket. "It's nearly four and I must be getting back to the house. We have guests coming for dinner." He returned the watch to its resting place. "I'm surprised your father isn't here." His face crinkled with concern.

"I'm sure he's lost in thought. I'll find him." She walked past the broad studio doors, left open to let in the air, and into the nearby garden. She called out for her father, but there was no answer. To her right, the carriage stood near the barn where the horses rested. Ahead, the lovely garden, with its flowering trees, geraniums in standing vases, marble columns, and bubbling fountain, extended north from the studio.

She spotted him, sitting in the sun on a circular stone bench across from the fountain, his head slumped against his chest in sleep, his hands clasped together in his lap.

"Papa, it's time to leave," Emma said gently for fear of startling him.

He did not move.

She drew closer, and, as she did, her anxiety grew. Her father didn't look well: parts of his face and hands had turned a bluish-purple, his body rigid against the bench.

"Papa!" She ran to him, grabbing his shoulders, shaking him, grasping his hands, the skin cool to the touch. Her efforts to awaken him were of no use, no breath went in or out of his body.

Emma cried out and fell to her knees in front of him.

She had no recollection of how long she was in front of her father, or of Daniel Chester French lifting her from the ground and leading her away from the corpse.

Emma wanted to blot the whole afternoon from her mind: the parade of men who arrived at Chesterwood; the minister, the police officer, the undertaker; the tiring explanation of how she found her father, the long ride home with the clergyman after the body had been taken away, the house growing larger in the twilight as her mother stood nervously on the porch wondering why they were so late.

Before anyone else could, she told her mother that her husband was dead. Helen hissed at the news, the sound reminding Emma of a scared animal as likely to bite as to flee from danger.

Her mother's eyes turned as dark as the indigo sky in the east. "Leave me."

The minister attempted to say a few words, but he was ordered away as well.

Full of fear and pain, Emma plodded up the stairs to her

lonely room, where she placed her head on the pillow and cried as she had never cried before. Her father's face floated behind her closed eyelids, more a ghost than a comfort, and Emma wondered how she could go on living with a mother whose love was doled out by whim—when it suited her. This was the pattern that Emma had grown up with, arbitrary affection at holidays and special occasions, a calculated coldness when her mother's demands weren't met.

I will make my own love.

I will make my own love.

Entry: 24ᵗʰ June, 1907

My father's funeral was a disaster, thanks in large part to my mother and the weather. The day started off cloudy and then what little light remained was obscured by clouds so gloomy and thunderous that the dark seemed to overtake the earth. My mother stood in black, a like-colored umbrella in her hand, rigid in her grief and anger. A sudden downpour turned the dirt she was to throw into the grave into mud. Somehow I felt this symbolic act of nature appropriate and I had little sympathy for her. Her words to me, after my father's death, outside of a snarl, have been hateful and belittling. She's never blamed me directly for his death (a heart condition most likely, according to the coroner), but from her looks and actions I know that I'm to take the full brunt of her rage. I'm sure she thinks his death never would have happened if my father and I hadn't traveled to French's home together. Knowing her propensity for anger and coldness, I doubt my mother's forgiveness will be quick to come.

Matilda, Charlene and her parents, even Patsy and Jane who traveled with Jane's parents, attended the funeral, but the gathering after, at the house, was so uncomfortable Charlene asked me how I could stand to live here. All of my friends were bored under the watchful eye of my mother. Of course, I have no choice but to stay here until I can make my own way. I have no money to pay rent since everything was left to my mother until I'm twenty-one, when only a small portion will come to me; thus, no money for art school. My life has been decided by ill fortune. Even Matilda agreed with me that I'd had "a streak of bad luck."

My thoughts have often swung to Kurt and the hope that he might, like a knight in shining armor, rescue me from this miserable existence, but that is only fantasy if I'm any judge of his character and situation. Still, I think of him often.

How I wish I could escape this prison! My mother's footsteps on the stairs, although she has no desire to enter my room or say anything to me other than to order me about, remind me that I should end this entry and lock it safely away.

Emma dropped her studies at Chesterwood, primarily because of money, although her mother found the time and funds to make several trips to see Edith Wharton. "Mr. French must be paid from funds that are now too dear," Helen said with no hint of irony in her voice.

During those times alone, for the most part without Matilda's company, Emma read and drew as if they were acts of revolution, tended her father's horses, and sat with Charis on the sofa, staring at the lawn as if looking through a prison window.

Only through the urging of Charlene's parents was Emma allowed travel to the Vermont farmhouse one weekend in mid-October. Her mother laid down strict restrictions: the family must pay for Emma's transportation there and back; she was to be picked up on Friday afternoon and returned no later than eight on Sunday evening; no men, outside of Charlene's father, were to be allowed in the house unless supervised. Emma gladly agreed to the rules in order to leave the confines of home. She had been nowhere except to classes.

The carriage arrived after her dismissal from school. Emma

gave her unsmiling mother a peck on the cheek before the horses pulled away.

"Remember what you've agreed to," Helen called out, standing stiffly on the porch like Lot's wife turned to a pillar of salt.

Emma stuck her head out the carriage window, waved, but said nothing. A forty-mile trip lay ahead, between the mountains, through the river valleys, past Pittsfield and Williamstown, until she'd arrive at the farmhouse south of Bennington. A sudden exhaustion struck her like a blow as the team proceeded northward at a brisk pace—relief poured in as the miles between the carriage and her mother lengthened and the heavy feeling of being suffocated in a coffin lifted. She thought of pulling the shade down and sleeping, but the transformed lightness of her soul, combined with the excitement of being away for two days, kept her awake. After a change of horses halfway through the journey, she settled back in the seat and watched the dark hills and the metallic glint of the nearly full moon on black waters glide past the carriage.

Shortly after ten, she arrived at the farmhouse. The windows shone with lamplight, the wide porch held wooden rockers, pumpkins, and fall chrysanthemums—the whole appearance gave her the warm feeling of a *home*, in contrast to the cold starkness of her own life. She alighted from the carriage to the open and embracing arms of Charlene and her parents.

The hour late, Charlene's mother and father excused themselves for bed, leaving her alone with her friend and the admonishment not to stay up too late for a full day of shopping lay ahead the next day in Bennington.

After hearing the door close upstairs, Charlene drew Emma aside to the farthest reaches of the living room away from her parents' bedroom.

"I have a surprise for you," her friend whispered, "but you must say nothing about it to anyone or we'll both get the switch."

"What? A surprise for me?" Emma couldn't believe that her stay could get any better than what she'd expected.

"You *can't* go to Bennington with us, tomorrow." Charlene's eyes sparkled in the lamplight. "You must stay here in order to receive your surprise—at noon—and you must be done by two."

"Done?" Now she was intrigued but also somewhat frightened by Charlene's deviousness.

"You have a cold—or don't feel up to travel—make up an excuse. Then we'll return later in the afternoon for dinner and afterward you can tell me all about it." Charlene smiled broadly, her feet planted firmly on the floor, hands wedged into her waist. "Let's extinguish the lights and get to bed. See you at breakfast."

They did so and soon were off to their rooms after a quiet embrace. The upstairs tall clock ticked in its stately, monotonous tone, and soon Emma was asleep, but dreaming of opening presents, like an excited child on Christmas morning.

Emma spent the morning complaining of a minor sore throat and a headache, enough so that Charlene's father threatened to call off the journey—until his daughter's tears took over.

"You can't, Father," her friend said in her best whiny voice. "I've been looking forward to this trip for so long and I want that new dress for Christmas." She took out her handkerchief, turned her head toward Emma, blew her nose, and gave her an artful wink. "I'm sure Emma doesn't mind spending a few hours alone."

"Not at all," Emma replied. "I don't want to spoil the weekend. You go ahead. I'm sure I'll be fine by tonight."

"See? Emma doesn't mind."

"Well . . ." her father said, sounding unconvinced.

"Please. . . ."

"All right, all right," he said, "stop acting like a petulant child. You're behaving like this to get your way." Frowning, he turned to Emma. "But you must rest and get well. Your mother will be as mad as a wet hornet if we send you home sick."

Charlene smothered her father with hugs and the matter was settled. The hours were set: They would be gone from ten until about two in the afternoon with lunch in town. Emma was welcome to help herself to bread and the soup on the stove, if she was hungry.

As planned, the family left and she was alone again in a farmhouse. The surprise wasn't scheduled to arrive for another two hours, so she sat in the living room and tried to read but couldn't, her anticipation growing as the minutes dragged by like hours. She attended to herself in the mirror, applying powder, rouging her cheeks, and combing her hair. There was no harm in being presentable when the family returned. She sat on the porch for a time, enjoying the warm morning sun, and taking in the brilliant oranges and reds that blazed upon the hills.

She was about to sit down for lunch when the screen door opened behind her.

Shortly after eleven thirty, Kurt Larsen stepped inside.

Emma had considered that he might be the "surprise," but had discarded the thought as an impossible fancy believing Charlene would never devise a plot that dangerously crafty and deceitful—unless she and Kurt had dreamed up the scheme together. Perhaps he really did want to see her! Her breath caught and she dropped the napkin she was holding into her lap.

There could be no mistaking her thrilling attraction to Kurt, that pulled at her stomach and heart like a yearning—a butterfly attempting to burst forth from its cocoon—and the mixed sense of liberation and peril that the feeling generated. She was aroused by and, at the same time, terrified of his presence. He stood in the doorway, framed in the dazzling fall light, in a dark jacket and pants, seeming more confident and mature than he had the previous Christmas. The breeze had mussed his hair; he smoothed it back with a strong hand and took a seat at the table.

He took her hand in his and smiled in a way that Emma thought kind and sincere.

Her heart pounding, she fought the urge to pull away. Instead, she leaned close to him. "Charlene told me about the 'surprise,' but I didn't think it possible." A jolt rushed from his hand to hers and raced up her arm—the same as when they had first touched by the river such a long time ago.

"I wanted to be here," he said. "We planned it together, knowing . . . I'm sorry about your father. Charlene said your mother has made your life miserable, even getting angry because I dared write to you."

"Yes. I've been crushed. She blames me for my father's death. I wasn't even allowed to study with Mr. French over the summer."

"Have you had any enjoyment since he died—any chance to recover?"

"Hardly a day."

He released her hand, pushed back in the chair, and crossed one leg over the other. "Things haven't been going so well for me, either." His eyes dimmed for a moment and he lowered his gaze. "My grades aren't up to par—at least Harvard's idea of par—so I'm rethinking where I might go to law school. My father's furious. My mother is keeping the family together at the moment."

"I'm sorry," Emma said, reaching for his hand. "You're smart. I'm sure things will work out."

He flinched, jarred by her touch.

"I think about you all the time," she said.

"I wondered." He leaned toward her, even closer, until his lips neared hers. "I think about *you* all the time."

The heat from his body reached her, the fresh scent of his skin enveloped her, as their lips met. She flushed with desire, as if she could sink into him and never return. The lonely hours in her room, the feelings of guilt and betrayal that had dogged her since her father's death, vanished with his kiss.

"We don't have much time," he said, caressing her face with his hands. "Would you like me to model for you?"

She nodded, unable to speak because of the images coursing through her mind.

He lifted her from the chair and carried her like a princess to her bedroom on the second floor. The sun splashed outside the windows, the day relatively warm even for mid-October. The crimson maples shook in the breeze and an undulating fiery light shimmered across the walls.

Emma felt as if she were consumed by a fire ignited by youth, the warmth of the dying season, and Kurt's kisses. There was no pretext for modeling now as they both explored each other's body. The room fell away as her passion exploded.

He disrobed by the bed, the first time she had seen a man, other than her father, naked. She took off her dress and undergarments. He spread her legs with his hands, enjoying her moistness with his fingers and then his mouth. Then, he pulled a rubber condom from his jacket, put it on, and straddled her, pushing his erection into her. She cried out as an unexpected slickness permeated her insides. Eventually she relaxed into his rhythm, but soon—too soon for Emma—he moaned, shuddered, and withdrew from her body.

He said nothing as he washed himself in the basin.

The breeze filled the curtains like billowing sails and ran pleasant, cool streamers over her heated body. Her breath waned as the light fell in dappled patches on her stomach and breasts. She expected him to return to bed, to thank her for making love, and to cover her with kisses. Instead he muttered, "Shit," and looked down at the white sheet. She shifted her legs and saw a reddish-brown spot where their bodies had joined.

"That's done it," he said. "Now they'll know. Charlene's parents will suspect a man was in the house and the trail will lead to me. My father will disown me if he finds out. He thinks I'm on a study weekend."

"Don't worry," she replied, still unsteady from the experience. "I'll say I had an accident—my time of the month."

He stood naked at the foot of the bed and smirked. "I never for a moment suspected you were a virgin."

She sat upright and pulled the sheet over her breasts, shocked at his presumption of her promiscuity, after such boisterous lovemaking at his initiation. "Of course I was a virgin. Why wouldn't I be? I've lived with my parents all my life. I don't sneak around with men." She got off the bed and grabbed her slip. "I can't put this on. I'm bleeding."

He sighed and sat on the bed. "Wash yourself off. I wouldn't have gone through with it had I known. A gentleman doesn't deflower a . . ."

"Deflower a *virgin*? What kind of girl *does* a gentleman deflower?"

"The virtuous woman he's just married," he snapped.

Emma's body tightened, as if a blow had been aimed at her gut. "I see. So, obviously, I'm not that kind of woman?"

He started toward her and she instinctively drew back.

"I'm sorry," he said, his voice dropping. "I got caught up . . . in the passion of the moment." He placed his hands on either side of her face and pushed his fingers back through her hair. "Help me, Emma. Please don't tell anyone about this—not even Charlene. If anyone found it, it would ruin me . . . and you."

"You don't love me?" she asked, falling back on her innocence as she walked to the basin.

"I adore you, but we have our lives ahead of us, as well as my career. We have to think about the future."

"According to my mother I have no career other than as a wife—the collector of the scraps a man sees fit to throw my way." She wiped a washcloth between her legs. "Or as a mistress."

"What about your art?" he asked, resting his hands on her shoulders. "You have your studies as well." He sighed and turned away from her. "This is a strain. I was wrong to do this. Please, help me out of this jam—don't say a word."

"What will you do for me if I promise?"

"Anything you want."

"Make love to me as often as I wish." She drew in a sharp breath. Because her virginity was gone she would have him whenever she wanted; she *could* control him if she used her sex. She would no longer be lonely. He would pay attention to her and tell her she was beautiful, and maybe even take her away from her mother and her miserable home.

Kurt left her alone in the bedroom for a few minutes and

returned with a pair of scissors from the kitchen. "You accidentally cut yourself trying to mend your slip." He handed her the scissors.

She took the instrument from him, ran a finger along the sharp silver blade, and gritted her teeth. With a quick slash, she opened a cut on her left index finger. The blood pooled in a red patch and when the quantity was sufficient, she turned her hand over, let the flow drip onto the stain, and smeared it across the sheet.

"We have a pact," he said. "I must get back to my friend's house before they return." He kissed her and pulled on his pants as the leaves' crimson reflections flashed against the walls.

"She doesn't live far away?" she asked, baiting him.

"He. I've known him for years through Charlene. The house is just over the mountain—I can walk from here."

"When will I see you again?" she asked, forgetting that she sought to control him. She walked to the basin and wrapped the washcloth around the cut.

He smiled, kissed her once more, and walked quietly down the stairs. She fell back on the bed, knowing that she should take a bath and tidy up the room, preparing her story for the reason behind the bloodstained sheet. As the warm breeze played over her, a strange sadness filled her and she felt as if she had lost much more than she had gained.

"Well?" Charlene asked after dinner.

Wrapped in sweaters, they sat on the porch steps, drinking in the cool night air, watching the flash of stars rise in the east, hearing the flutter of moths around the oil lamp, thinking of nothing but the present and little of the future.

"Why did you do it?" Emma's voice seemed lost in the void, the words empty and meaningless.

"What happened?" Charlene turned to her with a concerned look in her eyes.

"Nothing . . . nothing at all." She bowed her head.

"I don't believe you . . . I'm worried, Emma. You've seemed distant—far away from me—since we got back from town."

"All I want to know is why you did it?"

Charlene pursed her lips and exhaled. "Because I know you like him and he likes you . . . and you've been under such strain since your father died. You need to break free from your mother's talons. She's reduced you to a servant. You deserve some happiness and Kurt was willing to come. He likes you."

Emma rose from the steps and leaned against one of the white porch columns at the top of the stairs. "I guess he does. He was very nice, but I was glad to see him go."

Charlene got up and stood beside her. "Why? I thought you'd be happy and that you might even share a kiss."

A chill ruffled her body. "No . . . no. We talked and then he was gone. Now I feel lonely again and all I see is his *face*." She wondered why everything in her life seemed to revolve around the face.

"It sounds to me like you're in love."

"Maybe. I'm not sure."

"Well, you can see him again. I'll invite him back any weekend you want—maybe on the up-and-up. If your mother goes on a trip and leaves you at home—he could visit. That would be nice, wouldn't it?"

Her voice rising with each word, Emma said, "Oh, I'll see him again, when and where I want to."

Charlene shook her head. "Sometimes I don't understand you."

Emma looked at the weather-beaten planks that made up the porch, feeling like it was hard to stand. Then, she turned her eyes to the sky, allowing the blackness to seep in. "I don't understand me either," she said, walking to the door. "I'm tired. I'm going to bed."

"Okay." Charlene trudged behind her. "I'm sorry you cut your finger. I hope you see Kurt again."

* * *

She saw him several times during the next nine months, having him when and where she could arrange it, as they had agreed. Of course, she acquiesced to her mother's terms for visitations to Vermont—but broke the rules repeatedly. Kurt appeared to play along with her desires at first but became increasingly irritated and disinterested in their "sport," as he termed it, because it drew him away from his own life.

"There can be nothing between us," he said after making love one late summer day when they had ridden into the hills to be alone. His words were meant to cut and sting. Had Emma not been jaded by their lovemaking they would have struck with more force. The thought of revenge flitted through her mind, but she blotted it out, knowing that the consequences to her would be just as devastating as to Kurt.

Shortly after that meeting in Vermont, she wrote that her mother would be away for several days at the Wharton household in early September and that he must come to the farm to keep her company. She also had important news affecting him.

On the day of his arrival, she drove the carriage to Pittsfield, hoping that she wouldn't be seen by anyone she knew. He departed the train looking somewhat tired, probably from having risen early, to arrive in western Massachusetts at a reasonable hour. They said little on the trip back to the house, Kurt being more interested in the eventual delivery of her father's Model T than in Emma's well-being.

"I'd love to take it for a spin," he said.

"Absolutely not."

"Why?"

"What if there was a crash? What would we do then?"

"Pretend it didn't happen?"

Emma sighed.

After lunch, they sat in the living room, where she told Kurt her news.

"No," he said, after she was done. "This is an absurd joke. Don't torture me like this."

"It's true," she replied, her strength hampered by her own

guilt. "I've been sick from the changes in my body—ill in the morning, along with unfamiliar occurrences of a personal nature." She stared at him. "I'm going to have a baby—your baby."

"That's impossible." He sat on the sofa and, for a time, buried his face in his palms. When he finally lowered his hands, his eyes were stricken with panic, not tears of joy. "How could this happen? We took precautions."

"Don't ask me," Emma said, her voice coated with irritation. "A condom isn't foolproof." She looked down on the silvery scar on her left index finger—a constant reminder of their first sexual union. "This whole affair has been a mistake. I should have turned you away when you came to the door in Vermont as my 'surprise.'"

Charis sauntered into the room, his snakelike tail swishing behind him. He swiped at the curtain as it curled in the warm September breeze. Emma walked to the window and looked out at the verdant lawn scattered with maple and spruce trees, past the meadow, to the hazy line of blue peaks on the horizon.

Kurt came up behind her and she felt his presence.

He placed his hands on her shoulders. "Are you sure the baby's mine?"

Emma wheeled and slapped him hard.

He reeled backward, stung by the pain.

"How dare you! There's never been another. . . ."

He rubbed the red welts on his cheek left by her fingers. "You're a child. You can't have this baby."

"I'm eighteen, two years younger than you. You can't tell me what to do."

"For God's sake, Emma, what do you *want*?"

She balled her fists, stopping short of brandishing them at him. "To have our baby."

He shook his head violently. "No. This child will ruin both of us—can't you see that? Do you want to be saddled with it before you've even had a chance to begin your studies?" He stepped toward her, his eyes burning like fire. "What about your art? You want to be a sculptress, don't you? How can you fulfill your dreams while changing diapers and raising a child? I have two more years of studies left and then law school. It'll be another four years before I can even earn apprentice wages. I can't afford to have this child . . . or a marriage. It will break both of us."

He sat on the sofa, his arms stiff at his side. "What about your mother? She'll throw you out of the house. What will you live on—certainly not the little money I make? She'll send you somewhere to have the baby and then put it up for adoption. I'll be a pariah. We'll live our lives in utter disgrace."

She watched a patch of yellow sun drift across the meadow, all the while considering how easily she had lost control of her life. Rooms full of emptiness opened before her: she alone in a dreary Boston apartment; alone in childbirth, the baby yanked away by a scowling nun; she and the child in a bare room, with no heat and little light, wondering where their next meal would come from. She shivered despite the warm day. "I suppose we should have thought of that."

"*You* should have thought of that," he replied. "You were the one who wanted me at your pleasure. *You* demanded that I have sex with you."

The truth of his words pierced her. She ached with hurt, but wanted him out of the house, out of her life forever; however, she realized that Kurt controlled her life now. Although she carried the child, his decision was the one she must abide by for she had no other choice.

"I should slap you again," she said, her voice icy, "but I won't." She walked to the front door and opened it. "You're lucky my father is dead—if he were here, I'd have him thrash you. Get out!"

He walked past her, onto the wide porch filled with white wicker furniture, and down the steps before looking back. "I know you too well, Emma. You'd never have your father thrash me—you're stronger than that." He put on his cap to ward off the sun. "I'll walk to the Lee train station. The exercise will do me good." He shouted from the lane, "If you need money, let me know. Think of your reputation." He strode away and soon disappeared, his body concealed by a wooded bend.

Charis meowed and rubbed against her legs.

She collapsed on the sofa, reluctantly picked up the cat, and stroked him until he decided it was time to jump down from her lap. The curtains swirled in the breeze; moving in and out from the window as if they were breathing.

A half hour later, the sky darkened under the threat of an afternoon storm. The clouds obscured the sun on the meadow and the breeze suddenly stilled. Past the neighboring farms, behind the distant mountains of blue, lightning speared the ground and thunder cracked in echoes across the valley. Emma bowed her head, uncertain whether to cry or pray. What she thought of as love, so certain, so assured, had crumbled around her.

The end came with tomb-like finality. Alone. Complete and utter desertion. Bitterness and hatred accompanied her dissolution, Emma blaming herself and then Kurt, and, ultimately, deciding both were at fault. Her mother was ignorant, never knowing her daughter had conceived a child outside of marriage. Emma hid her pregnancy and physical ailments well with clothing and medicinal stomach powders, and found the deception easier because of her mother's cold lack of interest in her life.

Still, the feverish hours alone in the house stung her. She wondered what Kurt might be doing in Swampscott, or at school in Boston, while she languished in the Berkshires with a child growing inside her. Why couldn't he be more considerate? Why had she pushed him away when he was all she had? These and a hundred other questions plagued her as September drew to a close. She was able to send one letter to Kurt, asking to meet on a specified date.

Emma convinced her mother that she must travel to Lowell Normal School, a teachers' school for women, on the pretext that she might start a new course of study—a respected one that would allow her to earn an independent living. Her mother showed more interest in her than she had in months, apparently thrilled that her daughter would be abandoning the less honorable world of art.

She spent a day on the train traveling to Lowell, not knowing whether Kurt would be at the station. If not, she had decided to make the trip to Swampscott to find him.

He was there, sitting on a bench, looking grim and dissatisfied, as if she had torn him from an early bed after a late night. They left the station and walked near the steep banks of the Merrimack, past the river's watery boulders and adjacent redbrick textile factories that puffed smoke into the air.

"I want no more to do with you," he said when no one was near, his face turning crimson.

Emma flinched, hearing the dreaded words. "So, there's nothing more to discuss? I came because I thought you might change your mind, but I see you haven't." She struggled to speak over the river, its white foam splashing over the embedded rocks. "I can't believe you would desert us. Leave me and the baby to fend for ourselves."

"You have your mother and the funds your father left the family," he said. "I have nothing but my name and the promise of a career. If I fail my studies and can't enter law school, I fail at life. I won't risk my future because of a child and family commitments. I have no money, only my brain and nothing more."

"Certainly you have no heart—only for yourself," she said.

His tone softened. "Face facts. What can I offer you?" He stopped, snapped off a maple leaf from a tree in the first blush of crimson and crushed it like paper in his hand.

The chill of fall, not fully arrived, hovered in the air and almost overpowered Emma with its prescient smell of death. "For months we've kept up this façade," she said. "I went to bed with you in Vermont because I love you, not because I want to control you. I was so afraid of losing you—that's why I cut myself. It was a stupid, girlish, thing to do. Can't you understand? I loved you, needed you. . . ." Emma looked at the swirling brown water, frothy after a recent spate of rain, and thought how easy it would be to sink into its murky depths. One slip on a mossy rock and the nightmare of the pregnancy would be over. There would be no confrontation with her mother, nor a child to rear in a lonely home. How quickly the horror would end. She turned toward the river and tears filled her eyes.

He withdrew behind her, like a skulking animal.

"This is useless. You haven't answered my question. What can I possibly give you?"

"Nothing. If not love, nothing." She laughed, turned to face him, and looked into his eyes, their color transformed to a hard, icy blue—a shade so frigid it froze her to the spot.

"First tears, now laughter," he said and reached for her.

She slapped his hands away. "I'm laughing at the absurdity of the situation. For a moment, I actually considered throwing myself into the river—maybe not *here* in front of you—I suppose any body of water would do. If there's no love between us, there's nothing. 'Think of *your* reputation,' you said the last time I saw you. *You* should have thought of the consequences to *your* reputation as well; after all, *your* life would be ruined by a child you couldn't possibly love."

"Emma, stop. Don't be cruel."

"Cruel? I'm only thinking of what's best for both of us. Why bring a child into the world if it would negate the opportunity to further my career and my art? Why bring an unloved baby into the world if it would destroy his father's chance at law school? Yes, we're better off without such a hindrance to our *reputations*."

He stared at her.

"I can see behind your cruel eyes," she said. "If the eyes are the window of the soul, I've looked into hell."

He glared at her and then reached into his pocket. "Here's fifty dollars. It's all I have to give you—more than I should—but I knew it would come to this. Use it as you see fit, but never call upon me again. Perhaps, someday you'll understand the trouble you've caused."

He turned and walked away, leaving Emma shivering by the river.

"I *will* see you again," she yelled after him, "and it *will* be on my terms."

He looked back, scowled, and then continued up the sloping bank to the street. At the top he shouted, "How you get home is your affair."

Emma collapsed on the bank, lifted a rock, and smashed it against the earth. Mud splattered her hands and arms and she wiped away the dirt, a finger grazing the silvery scar left by the scissors in Vermont.

She found her way back to the station and, catching the last train west, found a vacant berth near the back of the car. She cried quietly, and cursed the man whom she thought she had loved, knowing that she would never see him again.

Her father's automobile arrived in early October and she now had a driver's license despite her mother's objections to the vehicle. As she had surmised, her mother hated it and would have sold it immediately if not for Emma's assertion that she would now be able to drive her about the countryside in one of the few, if not the only, Model Ts in the county. Helen quickly adopted it as a symbol of their wealth, despite their diminishing funds. The car was stylish in its way, a deep forest green with a black convertible top and spoke wheels. Everything about it conveyed the modern, as if the excitement of a new age and century had borne fruit, but there was more to the automobile than style.

Secretly, Emma had visited Dr. Henry Morton in Pittsfield before the car was delivered.

Now, her mother's trip to Boston, and the new vehicle, made a return trip to the bustling town easier. The day had arrived when Kurt's money would be put to use. She cranked the car. It sputtered before the engine kicked in with force, dust rising from the rumble.

She arrived after a short trip and parked a safe distance from the doctor's office. She stretched, stifling a yawn that verged upon a shiver. How often her mind had brought her to this point, picturing an outcome she neither wanted nor desired.

Now that she was here, she hoped only to sit in the sun and daydream rather than leave her father's new automobile and enter the office of Dr. Morton, a purveyor of services to women. She had heard about the infamous physician through whisperings at school. He was rumored to be a man with a reputation—a secret practice obscured by an otherwise legitimate office and sterling credentials: a degree from Columbia College in New York City, medical studies completed at Harvard. She wondered why such an esteemed doctor had taken up practice in Pittsfield, Massachusetts, on the far western fringe of the Commonwealth between the Berkshires and the Taconics.

Had he done something wrong to impede his career or, perhaps, been ostracized from New York or Boston, seeking refuge in a town of thirty thousand people? Was he paying off those who might have him arrested for violating the law of "procuring a miscarriage"? Whatever his background, he was the doctor Emma sought, after making a prior appointment and examination at her own risk. The earlier trip to Pittsfield to arrange the procedure had filled her with terror, but her options were few—either have the baby and, most assuredly, be tossed out penniless from her home, or end the life that grew inside her. Both choices filled her with despair.

She looked at the brick buildings with similar façades lining the street, but each one so different inside, filled with the trappings of an energetic community: an apothecary with glass vials of colored water shimmering in the window, a millinery shop sporting hats adorned with egret and pheasant feathers, a dressmaker displaying gowns of silk and other comely fabrics, a bakery exuding delicious, warm-baked smells through its door.

The midmorning crowds sauntered down the brick sidewalk as the sun, cascading its warmth over her, poured onto the automobile seat. The gentle rise of Mt. Greylock, emblazoned with scarlet maples and green patches of pines, presided over the northern horizon.

She took a deep breath and forced herself to leave the car's comfort, assuming her place among the pedestrians, knowing full well Dr. Morton's address, but wrapping her dark hair in a scarf and lowering her head as people passed, to avoid being recognized so close to home.

The brass plaque, glinting in the sun, was the only indicator of the office, which occupied the first floor of a corner building. Her hand hesitated at the door, but she screwed up her courage, thinking she was already damned so why not go through with it. Her mother had told her many times that women who had sex before marriage were shameful harlots who would never enter the Kingdom of Heaven.

As she entered the quiet office, she took a last look down the street. A white church steeple punctured the cobalt sky, a stark vision that stung her eyes.

A nurse, attired in a uniform the color of the steeple, sat behind a desk. "Good to see you again, Emma," she said, looking up from the papers in front of her. The woman forced a smile— an attempt to put her at ease, a technique used with more success by the down-home ministrations of the older, gentleman doctor who visited the family farm when needed.

Emma nodded and the nurse invited her to sit.

"Did anyone come with you?" the woman asked.

She gazed at the framed diplomas on the walls before answering. "No, my mother took the train into Boston for several days and left me with the automobile—that's why I wanted this appointment time. I told her I was staying with a friend in Vermont."

The woman studied her like a curious cat. "Then you've made your preparations and you're committed to the procedure? We are, of course, *prepared* for you. You should be fine by tomorrow—unless there are complications." She awaited Emma's response.

Emma stared at the woman, unnerved by the word "complications."

"Fill out these forms," the nurse continued, handing the papers and a pen across her desk. "After that we can begin. Oh, and please . . . use your real name and birthday. You are certifying that you are over eighteen years of age. You've done everything he asked? No meals since last night?"

She nodded and signed the documents, paying little attention to what they read, having never considered falsifying her name and age. The pen felt thick and leaden in her hand.

"Your privacy as well as Dr. Morton's will be assured by these documents." The nurse returned the papers to her desk. "It's important that you realize the gravity of your situation and the procedure practiced here." She rose from her chair, looking down upon her. "There now, don't look so glum . . . everything will be fine. You can change and then the doctor will see you."

Emma found herself in a small room at the back of the building that smelled of rubbing alcohol and medicinal salves, tepid light filtering in through two frosted windows, allowing her to see only shadowy outlines outside. She wondered what lay beyond the glass—the street, an alley, perhaps a glimpse of the church, or a view of the mountaintop with its patches of scarlet and green. The room was dominated by a wide metal table covered by a white sheet. Two oak chairs sat against a wall, framing a wooden bureau laden with medical instruments and glass bottles.

The nurse handed her a gown. "Put this on. Leave your clothes on the chair. I'll collect them after the doctor has seen you."

"If I . . ."

The nurse looked at her, expecting Emma to finish her sentence, but then completed the thought for her. "Don't worry—you won't die. The doctor has never lost a patient. You'll be fine."

"Oh, my overnight case—I left it in the car."

"I'll get it for you. You won't need it until after the procedure."

Emma told her where the automobile was parked and the nurse left the room. She undressed and, shivering, pulled the gown over her head. Dutifully, she folded her clothes and placed them on one of the chairs. After a few minutes, a soft knock sounded at the door.

Dr. Morton tugged on his wire-rimmed spectacles as he entered, a frizzy mop of white hair crowning his head. His features were bucolic, Emma thought: a doctor more comfortable treating children for colds than for performing abortions.

"Good morning, Emma," he said, and a smile unfolded. Holding a medical folder in his left hand, he extended his right for a handshake.

"Will I die?" Emma asked as she grasped his fingers.

His smile faded and a scowl a cross father would give a naughty child formed on his face. "Not in my office, young woman. I won't let that happen. You should eradicate such morbid thoughts from your mind. If you're like most, you've already punished yourself enough for deciding to seek me out."

Emma looked away for a moment, shame filling her.

He cocked his head, released her hand, and turned to the bureau, where he opened a drawer, and took out a bottle filled with small white pills. "Take one of these." He poured a glass of water and shook a pill into her hand.

Emma placed the white tablet on her tongue and drank.

Dr. Morton asked questions about her home life and her interest in art. After some time, she found herself flat on the table with her legs apart and her knees pointed toward the ceiling, the effects of the pill making her feel as if she were a drowsy actress in a slow, unfolding play.

"How are you feeling?" he asked, talking under her gown, his warm breath flowing against her legs.

She found it impossible to answer, her lips feeling sticky and rubbery. Soon, a strange pressure forced itself against her cervix, as if pointed sticks were holding her apart.

"You're coming along," he said.

A white blur opened the door, gathered Emma's clothes and disappeared, then reappeared next to the doctor. The two stood like towers over her, uttering soft, soothing words, as he placed the wire-mesh ether mask and cloth over her nose and mouth. The drops fell onto the cloth and the world spun away in darkness.

She awakened to find herself covered by a blanket, her head swimming with confusion because of her strange surroundings. The light in the room had faded to a dull gray. Emma rolled on her side as nausea clawed at her stomach. Thrusting her head over the edge, she spotted a gleaming metal pan on the floor filled with a whitish liquid. With great effort, she swung her legs off the table, but her knees buckled when her feet touched the cold tile. Her stomach jittered as she clung to the table and lowered her gaze.

A pair of arms lifted her from the floor while words that sounded like a hymn she used to sing in church poured into her ears. The arms positioned her on the table and covered her with the blanket.

"Get my baby," Emma pleaded as she clutched the cold metal, her words hollow and echoing in her head as if spoken in a cave. "Show me my baby!"

The white figure left, but soon returned with a bundle wrapped in a white cloth. "Here." Emma couldn't make out the face or where the voice came from—the room blazed with an intense light.

Her head swimming, she sat up, took the baby in her arms, and uncovered the infant, revealing an oval mass of pink flesh where the face should have been—a slight crease marked the unopened mouth, two small indentations buttoned the skin instead of eyes. The mass wriggled in her arms, and, screaming, she fell back on the table.

The nurse rushed in, followed by the doctor.

"My God," she wailed, half out of her mind. "It has no face! No eyes, or nose, or mouth!"

The doctor bent over her, stroking her arms and repeating, "Just a bad dream . . . a bad dream . . . a bad dream. This can happen when you've been under. Everything's all right." He lifted her shoulders from the table. "Take deep breaths, in and out, for a few minutes—you'll calm down."

After a time, she relaxed and felt the heavy weight of sleep upon her. Before drifting off, she sobbed and thought of her

baby and what it might have looked like had it been born—
what it might have become.

The room faded.

When she awoke the next morning, she was flat on the table,
a pillow under her head. Someone had changed the sheet and
her gown and covered her with a fresh blanket.

Light burst through the frosted windows, but she felt cold
and unable to move except to turn her head. The pain had disappeared, but the haunting memory of the faceless infant hung
over her, along with the feeling that somehow she had come
back from the dead.

The tears that fell before and after the termination were a
testimony to the power of the face—the one she had envisioned
and the one that haunted her—a memory more like a nightmare.

For more than two years, Emma stayed with her mother
at the house, doing little but atoning for the sin she felt she
had committed. The long summer days and interminable winter nights dragged by, with little entertainment but her books;
she even delved into an English version of *Madame Bovary* by
Gustave Flaubert. The novel, with its blue cloth binding and
gold gilt lettering, depressed her even further because she found
many parallels in her own life to Emma Bovary's.

Her drawings lay dormant under the bed, the charcoal pencil
and pad relegated to the closet along with her hidden diary.

Kurt wrote no letters, although she wouldn't have answered
them anyway; she even refused to answer Charlene's correspondence or her friend's calls on the newly installed telephone at
the farmhouse.

Only in the spring of 1911 did she emerge from her black
mood, as the depressive cloud began to lift. Even Helen had
expressed an interest in seeing her daughter, now a few months
short of twenty-one, emerge from her self-induced seclusion.

"You need to circulate," her mother said. "Time is growing
short."

Of course, her mother's interests were her own, and not Emma's, in the attraction of a husband, but only marriage with the "right man," a tenet Helen had espoused for many years.

At the personal urging of Daniel Chester French, along with a few pointed suggestions from Mrs. Wharton, whose own relationship with her own husband continued to falter, Helen agreed to send Emma in April to the School of the Museum of Fine Arts in Boston. French arranged the weekend visit with the purpose of introducing Emma to Bela Pratt, a sculptor at the school. Her hostess for the weekend would be Louisa Markham, a friend of Boston socialite Frances Livingston.

Despite her misgivings, Emma boarded the train in Lee, bound for Boston, while her mother lectured her on how to conduct herself. "Stand up straight, don't look down, be aloof but approachable, drink no more than one glass of champagne, if any."

After a time, her mother's instructions sounded like bees buzzing around her ears. She kissed Helen on the cheek and stepped aboard the heated car, settling in for the four-hour trip. The dawn had been obscured by clouds. As the train traveled east through the hills, the overcast thickened until it seemed a great fog had enveloped the landscape. Snow fell in spits through the mist, and the slick, naked branches of trees shivered in the wind.

Upon her arrival at the Boston station, she breathed in deeply, as if emerging alive from a coffin. The cutting air reddened her cheeks and forced her to quicken her step as she called out for a hansom cab. The crowded streets of suited gentlemen holding on to their bowler hats, smartly attired ladies clutching parasols, vendors shouting above the wind, and more automobiles than she had seen in her life filled her with an excitement she hadn't experienced since she'd first moved to the farmhouse. The vibrant city charged her with energy, shocking her with a new enthusiasm.

The cab dropped her off at an address on an elegant street

just a few blocks away from the Charles River, its rippling waves flashing between the brownstones, its dove-gray waters melding with the color of the sky.

A lady's maid answered the door and led her to an ornate parlor with wide windows where a blazing fireplace filled the room with warmth.

The maid took Emma's coat, scarf, and gloves. "Please have a seat. Miss Markham will see you shortly."

She took in the luxury of the room—the most opulent she had ever seen, even surpassing those she had visited in her childhood. The parlor glowed in the radiant heat from the burning logs, the light scattering from the ornate gold frames of paintings to the arms of gilt chairs, sparkling upon the metallic threads in the curtains. The painting over the fire depicted a grand sitting room in splendid detail—not the same as Miss Markham's but certainly one of similar taste. Living here was like living in a golden cocoon, Emma decided.

A sudden case of nerves brought on by the unfamiliarity of her surroundings struck her. What would Louisa be like? The arrangements had been made through Daniel Chester French, and although she trusted his judgment she had no idea whether she would enjoy the next few days. She grasped the silken arms of her chair and focused on the street. A few automobiles chugged by. Teams of black and white horses pulling carriages clopped past, but she found herself staring at a landscape of brick buildings that, despite her childhood, seemed as foreign to her as any place she'd ever visited.

"Enjoying the view?" asked a confident and relaxed voice.

Emma rose from her chair to face Louisa Markham, a young woman not much older than she. Her hostess was tall, elegantly thin, with dark hair coiffed in waves around her head. She wore a gold silk dress, cinched at the waist and accented by a red stripe that circled just above the knee. A braided black-and-gold, waist-length sweater complemented her ensemble.

"Please, sit." Louisa glided into the room, never taking her eyes off her guest, lowering herself into a chair opposite Emma. "So you are Emma Lewis—of the Lewis Tea fortune."

Emma blushed, feeling as if she had been ambushed by a woman who knew much more about her than she knew about her hostess. She clasped her hands in her lap. "I'm afraid I'm at a disadvantage. The 'fortune,' as you put it, was used to purchase our house in Lee and the horses. My father died several years ago, so my mother and I—"

Louisa leaned forward, signaling Emma to stop. "My dear, if there's one thing you need to learn about Boston society it's that everyone dissimulates about one's personal circumstances." She waved her hand in a circle near her head. "Everything you see here is artifice. It's paid for, but the paintings, the furniture, are trappings—used for impression. They sparkle, they shine, but they are lifeless . . . dead, really." She adjusted a curl near her face. "So from now on—at least in the time you are with me—you *are* the heiress to the Lewis Tea fortune and a student of Daniel Chester French—that's all anyone needs to know." Louisa smiled, showing perfect white teeth, and reached for the bell pull hanging near the curtain. "You must have tea before we're off for the evening."

Refreshment came, served in a gleaming silver pot, accompanied by an assortment of finger sandwiches and cookies. Having eaten nothing since breakfast, Emma devoured as much as she dared without seeming to be a glutton. She studied the woman across from her as they talked about a variety of topics, including Emma's love of horses, the few friends who made up her world, her studies with the sculptor, and her desire to be a sculptress. Something about her hostess struck Emma as they conversed—a liveliness, the mark of an unpretentious soul under the richness that led Emma to believe they could be friends, if she could just break down the glittering façade.

"If anyone can assure your future it's Mr. French," Louisa remarked after Emma had finished her fourth finger sandwich. "Tonight you're going to meet the cream of Boston, but don't be intimidated or swayed by anything you see or hear. Remember, it's all artifice, people desperate to make an impression."

Emma stiffened in her chair, her nerves kicking in again. "Can you tell me who's going to be there?"

Louisa leaned back, and lifted her arm casually. "Well, for one, my good friend Mrs. Frances Livingston, who lost her husband not that long ago. She's a devoted patroness of the arts—get on her good side and your success is assured. Singer Sargent and Mrs. Jack may be there, but I'm not sure—both of them travel so much."

Emma was amazed. "John Singer Sargent—the painter?"

Louisa nodded with a smug look.

"Who is Mrs. Jack?" Emma asked.

Louisa cocked her head. "Why, Mrs. Jack . . . Isabella Stewart Gardner . . . she makes Frances Livingston look positively bourgeoise. I mean no offense to Frances, of course." She grinned like the Cheshire Cat and rang for the maid to take away the tea. "I have to rest now, and you must freshen up. Lydia will show you to your room."

Her hostess left as silently as she had appeared, leaving Emma alone with the young maid, who spoke not a word until spoken to. She sat quietly as Lydia cleared the service, rearranged a few things in the parlor, and then stood awaiting her instructions.

"You're to show me to my room," Emma said uncomfortably, not used to this kind of upper-class treatment.

"Certainly, Miss." Lydia led the way up the stairs to a bedroom on the front of the house—another grand space filled with antique vases, silver candlesticks, sparkling paintings, and centuries-old English furniture. The maid placed Emma's bag on a mahogany stand. "The cab will be here at six o'clock sharp to take you to the reception. Your bath is at the end of the hall."

Louisa appeared in the doorway. "Miss Lewis . . . I forgot to tell you. I'll be introducing you to one other person tonight—someone who has a special place in my heart—a man by the name of Thomas Evan Swan."

Her hostess bounded off as Lydia closed the bedroom door,

leaving Emma alone and feeling much like she was living in a dream.

The smartly appointed carriage, with oil lamps and leather seats, arrived precisely at the appointed time to take them to a building near the Museum of Fine Arts on Huntington Avenue. As they rode, Emma tried to make small talk with Louisa, but the conversation seemed forced and stilted with the hostess much more interested in her appearance and the proper curve of the sable coat she was wearing than the fortunes of her guest.

Emma found herself fighting an anxious tide rising in her stomach, feeling much like a country girl thrust into a situation for which she was totally unprepared. Louisa, for her part, seemed unaware of Emma's discomfort and again lectured her.

"Let the staff take your coat, let me make the introductions. When the conversation runs out, look to your right or left, as if you've spotted someone you know, excuse yourself, and be on your way. I'll be there to guide you lest you fall."

The words gave Emma little comfort, for she wondered what on earth she would have to say to these people. Would they judge her when she stepped into the room? Who was she trying to influence to make a good first impression? Her clothes were presentable, but certainly not of the latest and finest fashion like Louisa's. Everything about the evening seemed wrong before it had even begun.

By the time they arrived, a number of carriages had already parked along the street. The air smelled damp—the possibility of snow hung in the air. The coachmen stayed near the rigs, their horses shaking their heads and snorting frosty breaths. The sky, still holding a feeble gray light, hid the setting sun.

Louisa, assisted by the driver, alighted from the carriage first. Emma followed. The imposing structure of the Museum, with its ionic-columned entrance and massive stone wings, towered over them. The building to the west, where the reception was to be held, was smaller and much less impressive.

The interior was rather stark and plain, and Emma was grateful that this building lacked grandeur. The simple walls, tables, and chairs, made her feel more at home. A tuxedoed gentleman took her coat while she looked around the room. Thirty people or more were in attendance, all dressed in evening wear. She looked down at her rather plain black dress and shoes and felt dowdy in comparison.

Louisa took her arm with a gloved hand and led her in a circle through the crowd. The introductions came fast and Emma struggled to keep up with the names and faces. Mrs. Livingston reminded her of a bird on a branch as she hopped from table to table in her cheerful manner. Singer Sargent and Mrs. Jack were nowhere to be seen. No sooner had she been introduced to someone, and exchanged a few words, than Louisa dragged her on to the next until she'd met the entire crowd. Her hostess explained in a whisper that no one besides Mrs. Livingston should matter. All the others were minor donors to the Museum and the School, she offered.

"I won't remember a single name," Emma said, after the introductions ended.

"You need only remember one," Louisa replied. "The rest have met *you*—that's what's important."

"I think I'm getting a headache," Emma said, swiping at her brow with her handkerchief. "It feels hot in here."

"It is, and you must strike while the iron is as well. Return to Bela Pratt and tell him how much you'd like to study here. Don't fail to mention that you know me, Mrs. Livingston, and, of course, play up your association with Mr. French." She clutched the high collar of her dress lightly and urged Emma on with dark eyes. "Go ahead . . . don't be shy."

Emma screwed up her courage, thinking she had nothing to lose. Pratt, an eminent sculptor in his own right and teacher at the school, seemed pensive, as if he would rather have been anywhere else than at the reception. He sat alone at a table, glowering at a glass of water, and looked up as Emma approached.

"Miss Lewis, isn't it?"

"Yes. I'm a friend of Mrs. Livingston and Louisa—"

He waved his hand. "No need to impress me, young woman. Who you know isn't nearly as important as what you can do. Please sit."

Deflated, Emma did so, awaiting his next words. He studied her for a moment, taking in her features with an unsettling gaze. "Daniel Chester French tells me that you have a modicum of talent that might be developed, but that you have trouble with certain aspects of the art."

"Yes, sir. Faces."

A forest of dark hair, parted near the middle, topped his head; his cheeks sagged naturally, and his eyes sunk like black stones in their sockets. "At least you're up front about it and don't prattle on about how good you are. You have no idea how many candidates build themselves up only to fail miserably— the school has been fooled before." He paused, looking her over again. "However, I trust my good colleague's judgment. I'll have to see your work, along with the applications, interviews, and other necessary processes for admittance."

"So, I may be able to study here?" Emma asked, overcome with enthusiasm.

"It's possible . . . but there is one drawback."

Emma nodded, waiting for him to continue.

"You excel at drawing, do you not?"

"Yes."

"It may be that painting, drawing, and colorization become the focus of your art . . . rather than sculpture."

Emma was puzzled and the anxiety that had plagued her since her arrival in Boston forced its way upon her again. "Why?"

"There are many men—I do not subscribe to it and neither does Mr. French—who believe that the world of sculpture is no place for a woman. They say the medium itself is the domain of the masculine; that the feminine mind cannot conceive of or create monumental works of merit."

The thought struck Emma as absurd. Her father had never

discouraged her, but her mother had done so for a different reason—not for her creative abilities, but because she believed such a career would make it difficult to find a husband.

"I say we prove them wrong," Emma replied.

Pratt smiled for the first time since meeting her. "Yes, let's. Just be aware that many men think as I've warned. In fact, a certain art critic in Boston will eviscerate you if you dare threaten his way of thinking."

Louisa arrived at the table, as if to rescue her from Pratt. Emma shook hands with the sculptor and left him to his thoughts.

"He wants to interview me," she told Louisa, her breath fleeing in excited puffs.

"Time to move on—never overstay your welcome," Louisa said, talking over her. "I want you to meet someone. There he is—Thomas Evan Swan."

Emma clutched Louisa's arm and stopped cold, as if her feet were mired in mud.

"For heaven's sake, what's wrong?" Louisa asked, perturbed by Emma's reluctance.

She found it hard to talk and even harder to explain that the man Louisa had pointed out bore a striking resemblance to Kurt Larsen. He was fair and blond like Kurt, but with noticeable differences. Their facial structures were somewhat similar, but Thomas was older by a few years and his face had begun to develop the creases of a man more careworn than her former lover. His hair was thinning on top, the pinkish scalp showing through the fine strands, his shoulders stooped a bit from too much studying, Emma assumed. A pair of reading glasses was nestled inside his tuxedo pocket. His fingers were thin and delicate unlike Kurt's stronger hands.

He turned his gaze toward her from the glass of red wine in front of him and a warm smile graced his face as Louisa pulled her forward.

"Emma Lewis," Louisa said, "this is Thomas Evan Swan— Tom to his friends."

He rose and offered his hand, which Emma took in a cordial handshake.

"A pleasure to meet you, Miss Lewis," Tom said. "I've heard about you through the grapevine telegraph—I've been told you're studying to be a sculptress."

"That's right, Mr. Swan."

"Call me Tom," he said, and asked them both to sit at his table. Louisa took the chair beside him, while Emma sat across trying to judge the pair's relationship. They seemed good friends, perhaps nothing more, with a long history and understanding of what made each other tick. Emma couldn't help but notice that Louisa looked at him with affection, almost to the point of fawning over him.

"Tom's in medical school and will be a doctor in good order," Louisa said and hooked her arm through his. He patted her hand.

"How nice," Emma said, trying to bolster her friend's conversation. "Do you like medicine?" The moment the question left her lips, she silently cursed herself for her stupidity. *Of course he loves medicine! Why on earth would he be studying it if he didn't? Oh, God, I'm making a fool of myself.* As these words coursed through her head, she thought of her diary and how she would record her "disastrous" first meeting with Tom.

Louisa laughed. "Oh, Emma, I knew we'd get along the moment I saw you. What a funny question to ask."

She inhaled sharply, hoping to keep the blood from rising to her face. "Yes, it was a stupid thing to say. I'm sorry."

Tom leaned forward, his blue eyes glittering in the lamplight. "It's not a stupid question at all; quite perceptive, really. People get into all kinds of things they shouldn't because they never ask it of themselves, 'Is this something I like—is this something *I love*?'"

Warmth connected the two of them, while Louisa sat in her chair taken aback by Tom's interest in what Emma had to say.

"Emma, wouldn't you like a glass of wine?" Louisa asked.

"You've had nothing all evening—and you've reason to celebrate."

Tom, still gazing at Emma, unhooked his arm and got up from his chair. "Allow me. Will you have what I'm drinking?"

Emma nodded.

Tom left and Louisa turned her attention to her gown, fiddling with the buttons near the cinched waist. "I do believe Tom likes you. I hope we can all be great friends." Her lips parted in a meager smile.

"I've learned not to presume anything," Emma said, thinking of her failure with Kurt and the years she had spent in seclusion since. The world she had entered for the evening was as foreign to her as if she were on the continent of Europe; she might as well have been in a reception hall in France or Germany, struggling to converse in languages she didn't understand, for familiarity had fled.

"I do hope we've not chased you away," Louisa said, her tone brightening.

"No. Everything's so different in Boston, so many miles from Lee. I'm not used to the attention. Even when Mr. French and I were working together, we were isolated in his studio with nothing but our thoughts and nature surrounding us. Here, life assaults you, comes at you from every street corner."

Louisa reached across the table and grasped her hand. "You will adjust. We'll be the best of friends."

Tom returned with the wine and placed the glass on the table in front of her. Mrs. Livingston flitted by once more, to say good night while on her way to "yet another social function." Tom rose, smiled at Frances, and kissed her hand.

If nothing else, he's a gentleman.

He sat down again, gazed at Emma, sipped his wine, and drank through his smile.

On the carriage ride back to Louisa's, visions of the evening ran through her head: the seemingly endless parade of names and faces at the reception, the meeting with Bela Pratt, her introduction to Tom, the possibility of studying in Boston. However, no matter how hard she tried, she couldn't get Tom's face out of her head. Was it because of his similarity to Kurt? *Why does everything revolve around the face?*

As the horses clopped toward the house, Louisa said little, her gaze turned toward the window, her hands clutching at her fur collar.

Feeling snubbed, Emma decided to clear the air. "May I ask you a personal question, Miss Markham?"

Louisa turned, her body clothed in sable, her face dark under the brim of her black hat, the only ornamentation upon it being the flash of white egret feathers. Her hostess said nothing, but Emma decided she was free to state her inquiry.

"What is your relationship to Thomas Evan Swan?"

Louisa stiffened and was silent a few moments before speaking. "We are the best of friends." She turned back to the window. "Please call me Louisa."

Emma watched as the large houses, their windows lit by the warm, rippling light of oil and gas lamps, slipped by the carriage. The air in the cab had grown cold, and she thought of curling up in the ornate bedroom; a fire, perhaps, blazing on the hearth; alone, again.

Louisa said nothing more about Tom for the remainder of the evening. After they had retired, Emma thought of him before falling asleep. She continued to see his face in her memory even as she returned on the Sunday train to Lee.

Emma—with the help of Daniel Chester French, Bela Pratt, and Frances Livingston, in her indirect way—was accepted to the School of the Museum of Fine Arts. At first, her mother balked at the cost of her training and the "fantasy" of an artistic career, but that was before Helen met Thomas Evan Swan in the summer.

"Such a fine gentleman," her mother said enthusiastically after Tom had spent the weekend as a guest at the farm. "I like him—he will do well financially."

Emma knew that her mother was endorsing him as a potential husband and that a doctor would offer stability to the family. "I know what you're thinking, Mother, but Tom is a man, not an investment."

Helen scoffed and turned away, muttering about the "obstinate blindness of my daughter," and "you could do much worse . . . I'll probably end up selling the horses to make ends meet. . . ."

When the acceptance letter came, Helen displayed a happiness Emma had rarely witnessed. Her mother suddenly was more than willing to accept the school's opportunity, and Louisa Markham's offer of accommodations. The prospect of having a doctor in the family overpowered her mother's objection to any artistic career. Emma also received a stipend from the school and some financial help from Mr. French.

Everything fell in place for her move to Louisa's in the fall of 1911. Her mother shed no tears when she left and neither did she. Emma felt more sadness for her cat, Charis, and the horses that might be sold, than she did for leaving home. She made her mother promise to take good care of the animals. Matilda, she supposed, might be able to keep Helen in check.

She headed to Boston with a large trunk containing most of her clothing and a few notable possessions, including her diary, and settled into the spacious room at Louisa's with more ease than she thought possible. Their first night alone, Louisa brought up the subject of Tom, a topic Emma dreaded. However, if the two were indeed to be friends everything would be out in the open soon.

"Tom tells me he's been to Lee several times over the summer," Louisa said. "You didn't mention that in your letters."

Emma once again took in the splendor of the sitting room, the cheery fire having been lit to take away the September evening's chill. As much as her father had planned for the future, nothing in the Lewis estate could ever match the opulence of the space she now occupied. If she would let it, it might become as familiar as a wonderful dream, one she didn't mind living, one that signaled a new direction in life. On the other hand, how honest could she be with Louisa—if she was indeed to be called a friend—and not compromise the opportunity that had arisen?

She hesitated to answer, but knew that sooner or later their relationship would be out in the open. "I didn't want to mention it." She stared out the broad windows for a moment as a carriage passed. "Frankly, I was never certain how *you* felt about Tom—I thought there might be more to the story than you were willing to admit. I do consider you a friend—one that I don't want to hurt."

Louisa studied her with a look of earnest candor, absent of cold or calculating intent. With her back straight against the cushion, her feet crossed at the ankles, her body exuding a relaxed confidence, Louisa presented the perfect picture of conviviality. "I would never go against a friend, no matter how much my feelings might get in the way. What you and Tom have is between you and no one else. That is all I have to say on the matter—in fact, all I should say on the matter."

Emma nodded, feeling drained by the topic. "Would you like to get something to eat? Perhaps go out to dinner?"

"Of course," Louisa answered, maintaining her composure. "I do have one question of my own."

"Yes?"

"Do you love him?"

She had to think for a moment, certain that Louisa would notice her hesitation. Did she love him? She liked Tom, found him pleasant, affable, charming, everything that Kurt was not—but where was the fire in her soul that cried out for him? She remembered the day she and Kurt had met that summer in Vermont; the first time they'd made love in the fall, the room vibrating with the crimson reflection of leaves; and the lonely, bittersweet days of obsessing about him from afar. However, never far away were the tears she'd shed over the child she'd lost and Kurt's rejection of everything she'd wanted . . . but, the question remained: Did she love Tom?

"Yes," she found herself saying, although she doubted her own word.

"And he loves you," Louisa replied. "That's all I need to know."

They dressed for dinner and left the house. Tom was absent from their conversation the rest of the night.

Classes and her new life in Boston occupied Emma for months. She saw her Boston friends Patsy and Jane a few times, but their lives were taking different directions now that Kurt was out of the picture and Charlene was miles away in Vermont.

Tom was equally busy with his medical studies and upcoming graduation. When time permitted, he became a frequent visitor at Louisa's, and the three of them shared conversation and nights out on the town. Mrs. Livingston entertained them as well, calling them the "three musketeers," with a touch of irony in her voice.

During the weekends they spent together, Emma still wondered whether Louisa harbored more than a passing affection for Tom, but her friend did nothing to challenge the relationship, preferring to act as the amiable hostess for the couple. For her part, Emma grew more attached to Tom as the days passed, the reality of making a living as an artist sinking in as she immersed herself in her studies with Bela Pratt and the other teachers. Through her letters and occasional visits to Boston, Helen continued to prod her daughter to secure a husband. The pressure from all sides of life was beginning to weigh on Emma.

Finally, in the spring of 1913, Tom proposed while they were walking on the Boston Embankment.

"Why should this marriage work?" she asked him a few minutes after she'd given him her answer.

"What a ridiculous question," Tom said, oblivious to the

crowd gathering on the banks of the Charles. He pointed to a seagull gliding over the silky water. The sun had brought out throngs of Bostonians to celebrate winter's demise.

Emma tugged on his hand and stopped their walk. The pedestrians split around them as they stood like pillars in the middle of the path.

"It is not a ridiculous question. We've known each other for two years, we're still very much unsettled—me in school and you just beginning your practice. If it hadn't been for Louisa, we would be going our separate ways and not talking about this nonsense."

"Nonsense? Emma, this is the most unorthodox marriage acceptance I could have ever imagined. One expects your betrothed to weep in gratitude, or at least to gratefully accept the blessings of it—not to question the concept from the very beginning."

"I'm being honest, Tom. Honesty is an essential quality for women because we aren't allowed to be much else."

Tom took her hand and guided her along the path. "Let's enjoy the moment. You've accepted and made me a very happy man."

"Why *did* Louisa introduce us?"

Tom sighed. "Because she's a matchmaker, and she thought we would make a handsome couple."

"No, the real reason. That's something that just popped into your head."

"I can think of no other reason."

Emma hooked her arm through his. "There's another possibility. Louisa wanted to force the issue because she's been in love with you from the beginning."

Tom veered off the walk and pulled Emma toward a dock that thrust into the river. Looking west toward Cambridge, they sat on wooden planks warmed by the sun. Emma could have dipped her toes in the brown river if she'd wanted to. He sat next to her, pulled her close, and kissed her. She primly returned the affection. After several kisses he said, "Really, Emma, you are the strangest creature, but that's one of the many reasons I love you."

"Strange is hardly a foundation for a relationship." She grew a bit cold at his reasoning. Sometimes she captured him with her eyes, the sun glinting off his wispy blond hair in a certain light, and she saw him for what he was: a moderately handsome doctor who promised much sensibility, but delivered few sparks to her heart. He was stable, though, a characteristic her mother had wanted her to seek in a man.

"Women know these things, Tom. Louisa forced her hand when she introduced us. For her, it was sink or swim with you. If you refused to seek my hand, she'd have another chance. Or, if I rejected you, she would have been in a better position than ever to pick up the spoils. At least she got you excited about the subject of marriage."

"She did no such thing. Subject? Marriage isn't a course you study in school. I think you give Louisa entirely too much credit. She's snobbish, wrapped up in her Boston circle, and is as creative as a freshly hewn oak plank—entirely the opposite of you. But if nothing else, she's pragmatic . . . and all she's ever been to me is a very dear friend."

Emma leaned back on her elbows and picked at the white flower blossoms that had been blown near her hand by the wind. "By your own admission, she's a matchmaker. However, I will ply her with kindness, and she will, of course, be my maid of honor. As our marriage matures and we grow old together, I will continue to smother her with kindness because of her influence upon our lives."

Tom laughed. "Sometimes, my dear, you can be wicked, whether intentional or not."

At that moment, the light struck him in a peculiar, unearthly way, as if a halo surrounded his head. She took in his profile from the hairline, past the searching blue eyes, the neatly trimmed mustache of recent days, and the moderate chin. There were moments, such as these, when he was serene, if not handsome.

She touched his face, hoping that her pulse would quicken,

some spark to shoot through her; instead, her hand was as calm as if she were petting Charis. Touching him was oddly unsettling—something was off kilter. She quickly pushed that distressing feeling from her mind in favor of a practical one.

He is right for me and I am right for him. This will be the best course for both of us, considering what happened to me. He must never learn my secret. I'm very lucky to meet a man like Tom—lucky a man will have me at all.

On a snowy afternoon in January 1914, Emma and Tom were married in an Episcopal chapel in Boston. The event was a small affair by choice. They had agreed not to spend money on a lavish wedding, instead saving for the home they were to move into at the bottom of Beacon Hill near the Charles River. The purchase had been aided by Tom's parents and the funds he'd been able to pull together.

Louisa was indeed Emma's maid of honor, while Tom selected a doctor with whom he'd studied as his groomsman. The audience consisted of a few of the couple's friends, Mrs. Livingston, Tom's parents, and Helen and Matilda. Mrs. Livingston and Louisa arranged a reception in the chapel, but the proceedings were rather dull, Emma thought, particularly for a day that was to be the happiest of her life. Perhaps the snow, the gray sky, the cold seeping through the stone chapel, the feeling that Boston would never emerge from winter, smothered any joy the wedding dare presume. Emma also kept an eye on Louisa, impeccably dressed in a white gown and matching fur coat, who managed to maintain a reserved smile through it all.

The anxiety generated by the day carried over to the honeymoon night on Beacon Hill. Tom had never asked her if she was a virgin and Emma had never broached the subject, preferring to stay as far away from her first lover as possible. She'd half-expected Kurt to show up on her wedding day seeking to derail it—after all, the marriage of Emma Lewis and Thomas Evan Swan did make the newspapers' society pages. She needn't have worried, he never presented himself.

She considered virginity would never be an issue with Tom considering the varieties of physical experience a woman might go through from birth to her wedding night. As a doctor, he understood the human body.

At the house, they undressed in the cold bedroom and slid under the blankets, huddling against each other for warmth. The mechanics of sex that evening were like starting the Model T on a frigid day. Eventually, some warmth grew between them, but the lovemaking was perfunctory and Tom's body felt like a marble slab on top of hers. At one point, as she eased into a rhythm that might as well have been played on a drum, she saw Kurt's face instead of her husband's and her ardor increased, clawing at Tom's back with gusto.

He withdrew as soon as he had climaxed, disposed of the condom, and fell asleep within minutes, leaving her unsatisfied and restless. This was the pattern of their lovemaking for many months before Emma finally guided him to her like a patient teacher, but by then she had little inclination to be an instructor because their sex had become perfunctory and devoid of sensuality. Sometimes they talked of having children, but the subject never went far, Emma thinking of her painful past, Tom thinking of the future. They agreed that the time was "not right" for a child—that they should focus on his practice and her art. Too little time and too many early marriage expenses would make for a worrisome pregnancy.

War broke out at the end of July, and, for a time, no one in Boston seemed affected, other than to mouth the shallow words to pity the "poor Europeans."

"It's a total scandal," Frances said one August day when Emma, Tom, and Louisa met for lunch at a Newbury Street restaurant. "I would have had you over for tea, but I felt the need to get out of the house, and, if you don't mind my saying so, not trouble my staff on a Saturday. One tends to fixate on bad news when one is alone with the help." She popped open her black lacquer fan and swung it vigorously near her face. "The heat is terrible today. Perhaps we should have lunched under an umbrella in my garden."

"Quite right," Louisa added. "Everyone is shocked by the war news, but I suppose it will blow over soon."

Tom looked at his plate of cold fish and put his fork down beside it. "I hope you're right, ladies, but I don't hold such an optimistic view."

"Tom, no one wants to hear bad news," Emma said.

Louisa leaned across the table and gently slapped Tom's hand. "Emma's right, no one wants to hear it. And besides, America's not in it. Let the Europeans sort it out for themselves—far away from us."

Frances sipped at her wine and then frowned. "Restaurant vintage is atrocious—and at such prices! I should have brought my own bottle." Her face soured as if a horrible thought had struck her. "French wines may become more expensive. How terrible!"

It was Tom's turn to frown. "You're overlooking the terrible *human* tragedy, Frances."

"Not at all," she said. "Like most Americans, I know it's there but prefer not to think about it."

"How is your sculpting coming along?" Louisa asked Emma, bringing about an obvious change of subject.

Emma leaned back in her chair, keeping an eye on Tom, whose frown still registered his displeasure about the war. "I've started a new work—*Diana*—after the huntress. Of course, it's up to me to get it done and make it work, now that I'm no longer in school. It's a smaller bronze, one that will fit on a table, but still of moderate size."

"It sounds exciting," Louisa said and beamed at Emma.

"I can always count on you, my zephyr," Emma said.

"Why do you call her that, my dear?" Frances chimed in.

"Because, like a gentle breeze, she has always been there to lift my spirits, and often guide my way. . . ." She patted Louisa's hand.

"Don't forget *me*," Frances said. "I've always been your supporter . . . and you must let me have the first look at your new creation once it's finished. There's a place in the music room that might be perfect for it."

Emma tamped down her enthusiasm, not used to praise being heaped upon her. "Yes, of course."

Tom picked at the fish with his fork and then covered the dish with his napkin.

"Is something wrong?" Frances asked. "If the catch isn't satisfactory, I'll send it back. I'm picking up the bill—my compliments for dragging you out on this hot day."

"No, everything's perfect," Tom said. "I'm not that hungry today."

Emma knew he was lying. Concern blazed in his eyes, a look that had developed when Frances began talking about the war. They left the restaurant and escorted Louisa to her home before returning to theirs.

On more than one night after that, Emma dreamed of Kurt holding her in his arms, followed by the cooing sound of a baby. She awoke in a sweat, before seeing the child's face, to find Tom lying next to her in his usual state of exhaustion from his practice. He was kind, generous with money even to the point of getting her a dog for company during the long days and evenings of his absence. Emma named the black Labrador Lazarus, feeling the name somehow appropriate for a resurrection of their relationship. Tom even hinted that it might be necessary to hire a maid to run the household so Emma could concentrate on her art.

In many ways, her husband was perfect, but during those dreams of Kurt, which expanded to unknown men who made love to her in ways Tom never dreamed of doing, she knew the foundation of her marriage had settled like an old building. Was Kurt the love of her life? Had her former lover mortally wounded her heart to the point she could no longer love any man?

* * *

For two years, life went on as normal, a gray page on which the same lines were written every day.

The only friend she could talk to was Louisa, although Emma was never sure how much to disclose, how much might get back to Tom because of their closeness. "Tom seems so distracted by his work," Emma admitted one day. They sat in Louisa's sitting room during a purple afternoon as the sun began to set. Lydia came in to light the fire.

Louisa chuckled. "All men are consumed by work . . . would you like some tea?"

Emma shook her head. "I must get home soon to feed the dog . . . I felt the need for a walk."

"You mustn't worry too much. After all, Tom is a good man, a good provider, loyal beyond belief to those who are likewise to him, and one who is building his own fortune for his family. I've always known and admired those qualities about him. Out of all the fish in the sea, he's a catch."

"Tom doesn't want children." Shame filled her, its powerful tendrils rapidly turning to sadness, as the faceless child roared into her head. She took a few breaths to calm herself. "I'm not sure I do either because . . ."

Louisa waved Lydia out of the room and sank into her chair. "I'm sorry, Emma. Tom's never mentioned anything like—"

"Why would he?" Emma blurted out. "*I'm* his wife." Tears welled in her eyes as she remembered their sporadic conversations about having children, most dying after a few minutes like their passion. "We've talked about it, but there's always some excuse not to—Tom's practice, my art career such as it is, money, the war . . . always the war."

"Of course," Louisa said, looking askance at the fire, but turning back to Emma after a moment. "He never indicated any such thoughts to me in the past when he and I talked more. . . ."

"I wanted . . . want . . . a child," Emma said, swiping at her cheek. "Perhaps that will happen someday." Of the many things working against her, she knew perfectly well what was holding her back more than anything else: the memory of the child she had lost, the depressive secret she could never tell Louisa, which left her periodically only to come racing back when she least expected it. A child on the street, the sign for a doctor's office, the way the sunlight glinted off a church steeple—any of these might trigger the emotion. The thought struck her that she held as much responsibility for the decision not to have children as Tom did. Had her relationship with Kurt so deadened her to the possibility of children, even if she believed that was what she wanted? She straightened in her chair. "In the meantime, I must count my blessings—be thankful for what I have."

"That's what all women must do—only Frances has escaped that fate because she now has the fortune left by her husband. I think she quite enjoys being a widow."

Emma blew her nose in her handkerchief. "That's unkind, I think."

"But true. She doesn't have that many years left—let her enjoy them."

"Not a word of this to anyone, especially not Frances," Emma said, getting up from her chair. "Lazarus is at home in the dark. He won't be happy."

"I envy you, Emma," Louisa said, almost as an afterthought. "You have a man who loves you, your art, a comfortable home, and friends. Whether or not you have a child, not everyone is so lucky."

"Yes, I am lucky," Emma said, stiffening. She kissed Louisa on the cheek. "I can see myself out."

She walked home by the river, the cold west wind slicing over the whitecaps, urging her to walk faster despite the shivers coursing up her legs. Bringing her hands up to her mouth, she gulped down the sobs engulfing her, for all she could picture in her mind were the intimate moments with Kurt Larsen and her appointment with Dr. Henry Morton so many years ago.

They took their places in the sitting room one rare night when Tom came home early from his practice.

Emma sat in her favorite chair across from the fire, sketching random thoughts that filled her head for new work. *Diana* was coming along nicely and would soon be done. Across the room, Tom read the newspaper and absentmindedly fingered a pipe that lay in an ashtray on the table next to him. His father had given it to him after his graduation from medical school, but he rarely smoked it.

Lazarus lay on the Moroccan rug in the middle of the room. She looked up from her sketches to see Tom's newspaper pages turn, and thought of what she would write in her diary: *The picture of contentment—that's what anyone would think of my surroundings. Me, laboring on the work I love, not yet making any contribution to the household except to act as a maid. Tom, happy with his newspaper, thinking God knows what, because I find it so hard to get into his mind these days. Lazarus stretched out between us like a god of serenity, his fur glinting in the firelight. When the dog "sighs" with satisfaction it seems as if the whole world is at peace.*

But it's not. The war rages on in Europe and Tom talks of it, but I know it occupies him even more than he lets on. In fact, it weighs on all aspects of our life. Our lovemaking has diminished to the point of nonexistence—a friendly hug, a quick good-night kiss, the best we can do. Things can change so quickly in a relationship, even in the early years. I suppose I was naïve to think that all would be rosy after my experiences with Kurt, but when one pushes something far back into the mind, away from the present, one is doomed to repeat mistakes.

I do love him and he loves me, I think, but I would expect our current state of affairs to be more like our golden years when comradeship is the glue that holds the relationship together. I think it's my own weakness that keeps me from confronting him, asking him if everything is all right, expressing my confusion about having a child, but I don't want to rock the boat because I've had enough of that. Stability is precious— something that never would have occurred with Kurt. Is there a man who can make me feel like I'm alive and *fire my passion? Is that asking too much?*

As she was looking at him, the newspaper slid down in front of his face, revealing the pinkish-white skin, the reading glasses perched on his nose, the blue eyes brimming with sincerity, the skin around his mouth creased, not a hint of a smile or happiness on his face.

"Louisa dropped by the office today," he said.

"Oh?"

"Yes, she mentioned something to me that I've thought we should do for a while—in fact, I've already taken the first step."

Emma rested her pad next to the chair. She said nothing because Tom had already decided what needed to be done—but more upsetting was his willingness to accept Louisa's advice without consulting her.

"I'm hiring a maid for the household," Tom said. "She's a sweet girl who's come from Ireland, looking for a better life. Her name is Anne."

Emma fidgeted with the pencil. "We don't need a maid, Tom. Housework keeps me busy when I'm not working on my art."

Tom folded the newspaper, placed it on his lap, and took off his glasses. "Louisa always makes a good argument. I listen to her. She's always the practical one, despite her money."

"I don't care about her money. What about *my* opinion of the matter?"

Tom leaned forward, bending over to pet Lazarus. "I knew you'd put up a fight. This is for you. A housekeeper will allow you more time for your work. You won't be chained to the stove or to the dishes."

"That's very nice, but perhaps I *enjoy* doing work around the house."

"No woman enjoys housework."

Emma's limbs grew cold and a frosty resentment churned inside her to the point that she didn't want to speak.

Tom sensed her anger and lowered himself to the floor next to the dog. "Believe me, it's for the best."

"Why is it for the best? Louisa inherited her money!" She trembled in the chair. "We have to work for ours. Can we afford a housekeeper?"

"I've saved enough, and we're doing well now that the practice has grown." He petted Lazarus and the dog rolled over on his back. "Sit on the floor with me and give him a rub on his tummy. It'll calm you down."

"Lazarus is wonderful company, but I'm in no mood to calm down. Frankly, I'm angry that Louisa Markham has an equal footing in this household. You should have talked to me first. She's like a second wife to you, and sometimes I wonder if she might not be the first." She hated the words as soon as she said them—belittling her husband and taking shots at her best friend—but Tom's action upon Louisa's suggestion rankled her. She wondered if she could ever get over the feeling that *Louisa* harbored more love for Tom than she did, igniting her own jealousy and confusion.

Tom lifted his hands from the dog, sighed, and leaned against the chair. "That was cruel, Emma. I'm surprised at you, but you've always harbored a jealous streak against Louisa. How many times do I have to tell you—she's been a friend to me for far longer than I've known you?"

She shook her head, feeling the ice in her veins thaw a little. "I've been called wicked and cruel by you, and headstrong by my mother, but I always seem to be the one who gets short . . ." Her voice dropped, ashamed of acting like an ill-tempered child.

Tom lowered his gaze. "Short shrift?"

Yes. Short shrift. I don't have the courage to tell him that I feel I've settled—that our romance is dying. Something is missing from my life that comfort can't provide. That faceless child. I see it in my dreams and when I think of Kurt.

Tom flushed and Emma wondered if he might be having some kind of attack. She looked at him with questioning eyes.

"I have something else to tell you," he said. "I don't imagine you'll be happy, but I've made up my mind."

Her mind raced as she clutched the armrests. Did he want

a divorce? Was he leaving her for Louisa or another woman? Blackness, like a veil, descended upon her.

"I'm going to Europe."

A temporary burst of relief jolted her. Perhaps it was for work, for a project, for a short time.

"I've offered my services to the Red Cross in France."

"What?"

"As a doctor. The Allied Powers need doctors. Thousands are dying at the Front for lack of adequate medical care."

She looked at him with blank eyes, barely cognizant of his words. "Why?"

He scooted across the floor, settling at her feet, his hands grasping hers. "I've told you why," he said gently. "I've felt this way for months. I don't feel right, sitting here in Boston, doing nothing while men are dying. I've a chance to make a difference for thousands of others, to contribute to the war effort. I've made up my mind."

"But what about our future? What about the practice?" Any budding anger was washed away by the shock of his words.

"We have obligations that are greater than both of us— your art and my medicine. Perhaps, later, after the war is over, when the world is a better place, we'll have a better view of the future—when things are settled. An older physician, Dr. Lattimore, will be taking over the practice while I'm gone. I'm paying him, but any income will be ours."

She thought of the years that might go by and whether, after the war was over, that future might include a child. She didn't want to raise the subject because it would only lead to more discord and, perhaps, tears. What if Tom never came back from France? What if he was injured and couldn't work? What if— a most heinous thought—he met another woman? Certainly, his decision was a noble one for humanity, but what purpose did it serve for them? The questions overwhelmed her.

"I'm tired," he said. "We can talk more about it later. I won't be leaving for a while—forms to fill out, clearance, passage to Europe—all that has to be worked out." He rose from the floor.

"Are you coming to bed? Please don't be too upset—it's for the best."

"No, I'll wait for the fire to die." *It's for the best—for you.*

For an hour, she watched the flames die, until only red embers remained among the blackened coals. The mantel clock struck midnight. She let Lazarus out on the patio to conduct his business and then treaded softly up the stairs to the bedroom.

Tom lay naked under the sheet and blankets. She crawled into bed and settled against him, tears welling in her eyes. Perhaps he was right. She was being selfish. There was a greater good, a higher purpose, for both of them than just blithely existing in Boston. A young woman around the house and the opportunity to perfect her art might be just what she needed. After all, for years she was used to being on her own: alone in the farmhouse, alone after Kurt, as solitary as a cloistered nun.

Tom faced her in sleep. She placed her right arm over him, but he snorted and turned over. The dampness slipped down her cheeks onto the pillow as she shifted to her right side away from him. They were two people next to each other in bed, but as distant as North America from Europe with an ocean between them. Nothing she could say or do would change his mind. Was it even necessary?

PART TWO

———◆———

BOSTON
MAY 1917

CHAPTER 2

The ragamuffin boy, his mouth twisted into a sneer, eyes bulging from his head in disgust, dashed from behind a building to the street corner. Then he turned, jammed his thumbs into his ears, stuck out his tongue, and wiggled his fingers at someone behind him. A woman in a drab black dress loped after the boy, shooing him forward with her hands.

From her spot across the street, Emma was unable to discern what had captured the boy's attention. She shielded her eyes against the sun and watched as a nanny, resting her hands lightly on the rail of a black-wicker baby carriage, neared the corner. Spotting the same unidentified threat coming toward her, the young woman lowered her head and stretched a white blanket tightly across the pram's opening before hurriedly pushing the carriage across the street. Her evasive actions reminded Emma of a bird fleeing a cat.

Soon, the object of their attention came into view. He was no terror, no supernatural adversary. He was a soldier attired in a tattered uniform.

Even from yards away, the scope of the man's tragedy became clear. Emma guessed the soldier to be in his early twenties. He hobbled on spindly wooden crutches patched together with bandages soiled brown by dirt. His face had been burned, partially ripped away, the right side of his head sunken like a crater, the fleshy remains of his mouth grotesque and twisted. Red patches of flesh and black strands of hair floated like islands upon his scalp. In his left hand, he carried a battered tin cup.

Men and women looked away, lowered their heads, or crossed the street to avoid him. The surprised few who happened to look upon him cringed as if confronted by a monster.

Emma crossed the street in the patchy sunlight, weaving between horse-drawn carriages and sputtering automobiles, drawn closer to the soldier, fascinated by his face. Her curiosity vanquished any urge to flee—she had never seen a human with such injuries. He was abhorrent, freakish to most, but he elicited sympathy in her and, in some manner, empathy—powerful feelings that drove her toward him.

She understood the soldier's need for comfort. His visage drew her forward, as she remembered the vision of the faceless child. If only she could heal the wounds and obliterate the anger and sadness he must feel, and, by doing so, assuage her own. Did she possess the patience and strength for such a task? The young soldier, illuminated in the sunlight, fueled a sudden bout of nerves in her, as if she were approaching a specter.

He looked up from his cup and stared, no spark of life flickering behind the one terrible, brown eye rimmed with scarred flesh. He might have been an American but he wore the unrecognizable tunic and breeches of a foreign army—Americans had not yet begun to fight in the war.

"May I help you?" Emma said as cheerfully as she could. "Do you need to cross the street?"

The man shook his head and slumped against the building's brick wall.

Emma looked into his cup. It contained only a few pennies. She pitied him even though such an emotion seemed self-serving as her own memories of loss flooded her. The soldier needed medicine, a safe place to rest and recuperate, and the attention of doctors who could restore his face, if such a feat was possible. She reached into her purse, withdrew a shiny half dollar, and dropped it into the cup.

The soldier peered at it and then lifted his head.

Questions plagued her as she studied his face. What could she do for him? Could she fill his wounds with clay, much as she molded statues over wire frames in her studio? Could she restore his face along with his chance for a normal life? She thought of Tom, serving as a volunteer surgeon in France, struggling each day on the battlefield to save dying and wounded soldiers, facing even his own death. A Red Cross banner flying over a medical camp was no defense against errant shells.

An insane idea, she thought—filling a wound with clay. The dream from her past lingered and she shuddered at the memory, one that filled her with sadness no matter how hard she tried to bury it. Nothing could displace it while she was in the soldier's company.

She managed to smile as he stared back with the brutal eye. He was dead inside and his cadaverous coldness settled over her like snow falling upon her shoulders on a winter's day. Emma turned, feeling the eye bore into her back as she walked toward home. His circumstances were too painful; his physical and emotional needs too grave for her to offer any real solace. She looked at her feet, the neat black shoes treading over the bricks as if she were walking in a dream. The soldier's disfigured face threatened to overwhelm her.

Entry: 13ᵗʰ May, 1917

I return to you, diary, whenever I am bored. And now that Tom is gone, I find solace in you for a long night alone. I wonder where Tom is in France and if he is happy. When he left Boston, he looked so gay, like a child about to get a new toy. I didn't cry when he stepped into the cab, only a slight numbness overtook me, no more than I have felt upon many an occasion. The next few days I knocked about the house with only the housekeeper for company. I even avoided our friends. When I look into my heart I know Tom's work is his real wife and I'm only an occasional mistress. This throws me into minor despair, less so now than it did in the last weeks before his departure. Perhaps a certain emptiness has become like a comfortable friend—always there, constant, and without change. And to rid one's self of a friend causes pain. Since our marriage I have been reliable, steady Emma because that's what Tom and I wanted from our relationship. Now I focus on my art: A sculptress in a world where men of like ability are held in high regard and women are often scorned.

I feel oddly enough, at 27 years, that my youth is long past. My carefree feelings have been compressed by remembrance. My work calls, but still my art and my emotions suffer from my unfortunate past.

By chance, I saw a badly wounded soldier on the street today. I gave him a fifty-cent piece, which is probably more than he collects in a week. I don't know his story and I'm sure I will never know, but he wrapped the war around me like a blanket. My fear for Tom, as well as for myself, surfaced, but for different reasons. That wounded, lonely soldier has more in common with me than he suspects. We both need restoration, and we both need love.

Emma stepped back. She stared at the creature and disgust prickled over her, filling her with darkness.

Perhaps the flute was out of proportion to the faun's hands. No, the panpipe was perfect. She brushed her hand over the clay face. The eyes, the nose, were too odd, too alien, even for a world plummeted into insanity by the war raging in Europe. Thousands died every day; yet, Tom of the gentle hands and the sharp eyes saved soldiers' lives. Here, safe at home, she tinkered with a maquette, everything seeming so bourgeois, so irrelevant, compared to the unfolding tragedy across the Atlantic.

She wiped her fingers on her white smock. In Boston, the war was as distant and remote as a tropical beach, but, whether she was working or not, her own inadequacies rushed to the fore, their sting compounded by memories. She blotted these out until they were dim shadows; but, when night drew close, or she tossed in muddled sleep, they cut into her like a scissor sliced against a finger.

A chilly breeze ruffled the newspaper covering her worktable and a desiccated edge flapped onto the brown clay. She flicked the newspaper away, then looked up, and watched the dull clouds drift over the courtyard. How long would it be until a spring downpour interrupted her work? Her first day working outside since the cerulean days of October had been frustrating—the exhilarating promise of May dashed by a gloomy afternoon. She put aside her anticipation of light and warmth even as bleak New England winter faded.

She swiped a finger through clay and softly molded the brown blob against the faun's right cheek, drawing a furrow with her nail, then smoothing it with the mound of her index finger. For her effort, the cheekbone rippled like a creased sheet of paper. Now the faun, its youth destroyed, appeared old and ugly. She blotted the face with a towel, bits of clay sticking to the white cloth. She raked her fingers over the scalp and the faun's wavy hair shifted like beach sand battling the tide.

No, it's wrong. All wrong. Perhaps Bela Pratt's warning was correct. I should spend my time in pursuits more suited to a woman. No, that's madness! What do critics know? How can they understand what I've felt, what I've experienced?

Tom appeared before her, pleasing in his soft smile, his manner gentle, his words encouraging her from thousands of miles away. He wanted her to succeed! Just as quickly as she gauged his support it faded under her apprehension. He only wanted to keep her busy; thus, her little avocation would root her to home, pleasantly occupied, while he remained at the Front, doing the job he *needed* to do.

Lazarus padded past the open French doors into the courtyard, his tail slapping her leg. As she reached down to pet him, a spit of rain splashed her hand.

The faun stood naked, unprotected, under the gray, iron sky.

"Come, inside!" she yelled at Lazarus as he circled the courtyard before following her across the threshold. She closed the doors against the wind and stood in front of the logs sizzling in the sitting room fireplace. Her young Irish housekeeper, Anne, had stoked it earlier that afternoon in anticipation of a dreary day. The cheery light and warmth of the room buoyed her somewhat as the dog settled at her feet. Yet, she couldn't help but stare through the wavy glass panes at her work sitting forlornly on the table.

"I feel sorry for the faun," she said to Lazarus.

The small fir in the courtyard thrashed in a sudden burst of wind, and rain pattered upon the walls in increasing veils. Rivulets of muddy clay coursed down the faun, onto the table, soaking the newspaper, before splashing in brown streams upon the stones. The face she had fretted over for weeks was dissolving in the downpour. She turned to the fire and called for Anne.

The faun's face was never right. Never.

Agitated, she swiped her hand across her husband's photograph on the mantel. An oily film of soot and smoke coated the glass. Tom, in a contemplative mood, stared out at her. Anne needed to be more thorough in her cleaning. Tom's picture should never be allowed to get dirty—but the thought arose more from irritation with her husband's absence than with the housekeeper's duties.

She stared at the photograph and was transported to the privacy of their bed in their first years of marriage. Trying to fire his emotions, she had touched his cheek, run a finger over the stubble of his chin, and down through the light matting of blond chest hair. Often when they had made love, even when she was thinking of Kurt, she studied the muscle and sinew of his body, the bone and cords that formed him. In a clinical way, he was a model for her. He had the gift of a surgeon; but, in the silence and the darkness, she was the artist, the sculptress who saw beyond the body, into the soul, capturing that essence for later transformation into bronze or marble.

But the early days with Tom had become long ago and Emma struggled to recreate in her mind any touch from a man, the way it had been before such tactile senses had diminished.

Anne broke the silence with her soft query, "Ma'am?"

"I'll have supper upstairs, in the studio," Emma said.

Anne nodded and then cried out.

"For heaven's sake, what's wrong?"

"Your statue, ma'am. It's melting."

The faun dripped in the murky light, the face transformed by the rain into a shapeless mass. Emma took some pleasure in watching the transfiguration, as if she were a Greek goddess mocking the folly of men.

"It's all right," she replied after some time, "the faun was a failure."

"I thought it was beautiful," Anne said.

"If only you were a critic." She pointed to Tom's photograph. "The glass is dirty. Please clean it the next time you do the room. I'd like his picture—"

"I understand, ma'am. I know how you must miss him." Anne smiled.

"I don't want things to get . . ." She couldn't finish the sentence because she didn't know how to reply. Yes, she missed him dearly at times, but her instruction was more a matter of keeping a household together.

Anne departed and Emma settled into her favorite chair across from the fire. Lazarus, needing no prodding, curled at her feet. With her every glance into the courtyard the faun's form changed—metamorphosing—the eyes washing away, the nose disintegrating to a smooth lump. The brown water pooled on the stones.

An image jolted her.

Narcissus.

After supper, she would look at her art books for depictions of the youth obsessed with his image. He was the perfect metaphor for the nations, all vainglorious, thrust into war. Why had she not considered the subject before?

Her mind drifted from her work to Tom. From a basket next to her chair, she fished out his first letter from Europe. She read the censored text again, searching for some hidden meaning or further deduction regarding his emotional state that she might have overlooked on previous readings.

10ᵗʰ *April, 1917*

My Dearest Emma (from somewhere in France):

How can I describe what I see here? I cannot, for the censor would never let my words pass. We crossed the Atlantic without incident—although our guard was always up. Several merchant ships had XXXXXXXX. Upon arriving in France, the Red Cross rushed us to a field hospital at XXXXX. The field officer, without endangering our lives, wanted us to understand what we would be up against. The medical conditions are primitive but serviceable. The tents to which the injured are carried strive to keep out the wind, the rain, and the heat. The men lie in single beds under white sheets and service blankets. The smell of bleach and alcohol permeates the tents, but the men, mostly French, seem in somewhat good spirits despite their injuries. Some of them are in desperate shape, however, with wounds so XXXXXXXXXXXXXX they must eventually be moved to a better facility.

I am traveling now and will be happy when we arrive at XXXXX. There, I hope, we doctors will not have to deal with XXXXXX conditions, XXXX, or the rampant XXXXX. My fervent wish is that these men, the most seriously injured, fighting the good fight, have lives ahead of them, and that I, doing my duty, will aid them in their recovery.

Our stop in Paris was brief, and I was absolutely enchanted by the city. I had the chance to sneak away for a few hours and visit Notre Dame. The venerable Cathedral never looked so formidable, or as welcoming, as it did on a Sunday evening when I climbed to the top, to stand amongst the eternal gargoyles and look out over the shimmering silver city. A mass was being said below. The sun was setting in the west, near the Eiffel Tower, and its rays cut through a bank of purple clouds which dripped rain over the arrondissement. The view brought chills to my spine and I wished you were here to see the enchantment as well.

I do miss you and Boston. Enjoy the spring days—you know how precious they are. Take a walk with Lazarus along the river. His name always reminds me of spring and eternal life.

I will write you as soon as I arrive at my destination and tell you as much as I can.

Give Anne my best wishes. Have her bake something special for you—something light for the warmer weather. Soon you will be able to drink lemonade in the courtyard with Louisa.

By the way, how is the faun coming along? I know you were pleased with what you had accomplished so far. I believe it's your best work to date, especially the face. I fully expect to see it in bronze by the time I return. Hopefully, deadlines will be set for both—completion of your work and an end to the fighting. Most of all, I hope your gallery showing of Diana goes well. I know it will. Have faith in your talents.

Your husband,

Tom

Emma refolded the letter and dropped it in the basket. *Not once did he write, I love you.* The thought struck her that he missed her and Boston equally, perhaps Boston more. The same feeling had filled her the night before he left for Europe. Later, as she watched the endless stars pass beyond their bedroom window, she tossed, sleepless, but still wondered, why the concern? Would separation be so bad? Their marriage was as worn as an old shoe. She was the trusty book and Tom the trusty bookend. However, one without the other would ruin the pair.

Now that he was gone, she strove to remain placid, resolved not to break under the fear of a distant and bitter war. She shook off a burst of anger about his absence and felt ashamed. Tom was a noble man performing a noble deed, she the sacrifice that he had made in the grand plan to make the world safe. At least he supported her art. For the moment, that was all that mattered.

The evening's rain passed and the next morning fled as quietly as a moth on wing.

The day was sunny and clear, but chilled by a northwest wind. In the afternoon, Emma began her preparations for the gallery opening. She and Tom had stipulated a bathroom with hot and cold running water for their home. Anne drew hot water in the claw tub, and Emma took her time, soaking up to her neck. In the bath, she paid particular attention to her hands, scraping the clay from under her nails, polishing them with a buff, and washing her fingers with a bar of oatmeal soap. After, she picked out a simple black dress, jacket, and hat from her closet and finished the outfit with a mauve scarf.

Anne ushered Louisa into the sitting room promptly at six, as Emma relaxed with a cup of tea. Louisa was dressed smartly as usual, attired in a dark coat with an ermine-trimmed collar. The few open buttons of her outerwear revealed an emerald green dress of layered folds accented by a platinum leopard pin studded with silver and black diamonds.

"Where should we eat?" Louisa asked in a chipper voice.

"I hope you won't be too upset, my zephyr, but I'm in no mood," Emma said.

"To eat?" Louisa stepped forward and placed a hand on Emma's forehead in mock concern. "I've never seen you too sick to eat. You've the constitution of a horse, and the appetite of one as well."

"Thank you, but I'm too nervous about the opening to eat. I'm worried about what the critics will say."

"Nonsense. Just a slight case of nerves. Nothing to get worked up about. You must eat." Louisa slipped out of her coat and settled into the wing chair near the fireplace.

Emma took another sip and then replaced the cup in the saucer. "When I meet a stranger, I tell them about *my zephyr*. You *are* like a warm breeze comforting me—a woman of impeccable social standing wrapped in current fashion. Everything I'm not."

Louisa laughed. "Should I be insulted? No, I think your assessment is fair—and you *have* hit upon my loyalty." She tapped her fan against her knee. "You do need to get out of the house more often, Emma. Many days, I worry about you in a practical sense. I know you're making your mark and I admire you for that; but as much as I respect your passion for art, there are other things in life."

"I'm quite aware of that. Sometimes I feel stuck in the last century and I wish I could rid myself of the classical references. I'd like to stop thinking in those antiquated terms because they are quite limiting. After all, the world has entered a new age."

"Hardly an age of genius," Louisa said with a raised eyebrow. "But *you*, my dear, are an exception, despite any outmoded conceptions you might have. Your solitary pursuits may confine you, but Boston depends on women like Emma Lewis Swan to lead the way—out of the kitchen and into the world. However, I would never ask you to relinquish the classics. Where would we be without the Greeks and the Romans?"

"Perhaps not in this horrific war, considering their propensity for battles."

"Speaking of . . ." Louisa leaned forward, rustling the folds of her dress. "Have you heard from Tom?"

"Yes. He's on the way to a hospital somewhere in France." She looked at her cup. "Would you like Anne to bring tea?"

"I do hope he's in fine form—no tea for me. I'm quite content."

"As fine as can be." Emma looked at her friend. "All in all there's not much to say about the whole matter. He can only tell me so much, and I can only go about the house, continue my work, and wish the whole mess would be over. He told me in a letter how much he misses Boston, and how you and I should drink lemonade in the courtyard."

Louisa shifted her gaze and stared into the shadowy space beyond the French doors. "Is that your faun?"

Emma rose from her chair and walked to the threshold.

"That *was* my faun," she said, "before I let nature destroy it."

Louisa waved her hands in a gesture of dismissal. "Well, I didn't much care for it anyway—something seemed off about the face."

"It was that evident?" Emma asked.

Louisa nodded. "Well, before we become too morose, I think you need a lift. Rather than hail a cab, let's be adventurous and walk to the gallery. Afterwards, we can stop at Grover's for a bite."

"I truly do have a case of nerves."

"You'll be fine. Everyone will love your work."

"Well, I see you've settled the matter," Emma said. "Let's be off." She strode to her friend and offered a hand. Louisa rose gracefully from the wing chair. After saying good-bye to Anne, they walked arm in arm out the door after Emma suggested a route by the Charles River.

Evening, like a deep-blue blanket, descended upon Boston. In the west, the sun dipped toward Cambridge, casting angular patches of light on the city across the Charles. To the east, toward the Atlantic, the Back Bay row houses formed a horizontal line against the deepening twilight. Ducks, with their young, paddled near the river's shore, while gulls soared on white wing. A stiff breeze pushed at their backs as they passed by the few walkers out for a stroll. Emma was quiet while Louisa chattered about her Commonwealth Avenue neighbors.

When they arrived at the Fountain Gallery on Newbury Street, they joined a small crowd inside. The gallery walls were hung with brightly colored paintings, many in compositional forms Emma had never seen before. Her sculpture, *Diana*, sat on an onyx pedestal near the center of the exhibition. Emma spotted Alex Hippel, the owner, talking to a prospective client by a painting on the back wall. She disengaged herself from Louisa and edged toward the two men.

"It's rubbish on canvas," she overheard the man say as she approached. "As ridiculous as what those French maniacs produced at the end of the last century."

"No, not so," Alex insisted. He repeated this sentiment over and over, each time shaking his head and wagging a finger at the man. "Wait . . . wait and see. This painting will be among the great works one day." The man scoffed and strolled off. Alex turned.

Emma forced a smile. "I'm sorry, Alex. These old-fashioned patrons don't understand what you're trying to do."

"Ah, I feel sorry for them. They're cursed in Boston." He waved a hand toward the painting. "Only New Yorkers understand true art. Someday this bold brushwork, this powerful rendering of form and color will be commonplace."

Emma studied the canvas, but squelched her desire to reach out and touch the bold geometric shapes that disturbed yet intrigued her. The odor of fresh oil paint wafted over her.

"Is there a point to this?" she asked Alex.

He sighed. "Of course. Can't you see the woman's form in the chair? Or the bouquet of flowers on the table next to her?"

"Not really, but you know what a classicist I am. Sometimes I'm afraid the world has left me and my art behind."

"I'm afraid sculpture is no different. I recognize your figural talents, but art is headed in a new direction. However, there is room for both. You wouldn't be in this show if I didn't believe in you."

She felt a finger on her shoulder.

"You must come," Louisa whispered. "A crowd has gathered around your statue."

"A moment, Alex. . . ."

"Don't be disappointed," he cautioned her.

The crowd, unaware of Emma's presence, murmured as she approached. Sniggers and muffled laughter burst forth as well. She broke away from Louisa and stood behind the man who had argued with Alex about the painting. He was listening to another man with a profuse shock of gray hair, who held a notebook and pen. She studied them both, the former a bit hunched at the shoulders, dressed in a somewhat tattered navy jacket, the latter attired in an impeccable black suit looking like a lion defending his territory.

"I must say," the lion said, holding court while he scribbled notes, "this statue is the best piece in the show—if only the artist had the talent to display emotion on any level. Look at the face." The group bent toward the bronze of a kneeling woman with the bow in her hand. "Do you see any expression? How can we tell if *Diana* is overjoyed or distraught at the prospect of killing the stag? The sculpture is devoid of true feeling. However, I regard this piece with more affinity than the other works in this heinous gathering."

"You are quite correct, Vreland," the fawning man next to him chimed in. "Of course this is the effort of a *woman*." The appellation dripped with acid. "Women should know better than to attempt an art clearly intended for a man. They can dabble, but never succeed." The women gathered around Emma's bronze tittered—only one looked embarrassed about the comment of the middle-aged man in the navy jacket who stood so close to Vreland.

The name sent a shiver down Emma's spine. Vreland—the esteemed art critic for the *Boston Register*.

Emma looked at her *Diana*. It had taken two years to complete. The bow, the grasp of the fingers on the archer's string, the knee and leg resting on the base: all took monumental effort. Despite her struggles with the work, the balance of the legs, the proportion of the hips, the abdomen's slight plumpness and the soft curve of the breasts had been easier for her than the face.

"I may be a failure as a sculptress, but I'm not a failure as a woman," she said to Louisa, while directing her comment to the group.

"Now, Emma," Louisa whispered.

The two men turned to stare.

"So, you are Emma Lewis Swan?" Vreland asked. "I'm sorry we've never had the pleasure of meeting."

"Yes. Perhaps I should retreat to the middle of the last century where I could sculpt as Ellis Bell or some other pseudonym satisfying to men of your ilk."

"My pleasure," Vreland said and bowed. The man next to him nodded stiffly. "I meant no offense," he continued, "but in my capacity as a critic for the *Register,* you *are* aware I must make artistic judgments."

"The pleasure is mine," Emma said, sizing up the man. "You are *the* Mr. Vreland, the critic who has savaged artists before me."

"Savaged is a strong word, Mrs. Swan," Vreland said, "and I honestly don't remember seeing any of your work before now. Pity." His gray eyes swept over Emma with a fierce intensity. "My newspaper pays for my artistic opinions. The editors, and the public, I might add, see worth in my judgments."

"Despite your failed memory, many have been on the poor side of your *judgments* previously. I'd hoped this opening might prove differently, but I'd been warned."

"I'm afraid not." He paused and slowly pointed a finger at the statue. "One . . . only has to look. Warned . . . it must have been someone with little artistic taste."

Emma's cheeks flushed and she bit her tongue not to mention Bela Pratt's name.

"Still," he said, "I reiterate my feeling that your sculpture is the best piece in a mediocre show."

"Damned with faint praise," Emma responded. "I shall bear that in mind when I read your words tomorrow—if they are literate." The disagreeable man next to Vreland hissed at Emma.

"And who are you?" Emma asked, barely containing her anger.

"Mr. Everett—an admirer of *good* art."

Louisa tugged at her arm. "Alex is waving to us."

"Until we meet again, Vreland," Emma said, with mock sincerity. "Good evening, Mr. Everett."

Louisa pulled her toward Alex. "Are you mad? You'll catch more ants with honey than vinegar. Vreland will rip you to shreds."

"I couldn't care less." Emma disengaged herself from Louisa and reconsidered her attitude. "Oh, that's a lie. But, really, consorting with a clod who believes sculpting is only for men . . . what nonsense."

Alex strode toward them with his hands clasped tightly. "The verdict?" he asked Emma. His light-brown eyes flashed with curiosity.

"Not good, I'm afraid. Fortunately, Louisa came to my rescue before I made a complete ass of myself."

"There are worse enemies than Vreland, but, at the moment, I can't think of any," Alex said and then kissed Emma on the cheek. "Sometimes our enemies are inside us, and if we defeat ourselves we're doomed despite what anyone else says. Art will change, society's perspective will shift, and Vreland and his associates will remain mired in the nineteenth century. I'm certain his review of this show will be positively scathing."

"I'm sorry, Alex," Emma said. "I should have controlled my feelings."

"Artists and women have done so for far too long. Don't give Vreland another thought—although I'm not sure how long I can continue to sustain this gallery in the face of unabashed criticism. Either the critics or the war will be the end of me."

Louisa sighed. "Don't be silly. You're the only breath of fresh air in Boston. Your supporters will rally. Long live the Fountain!"

"You really are beginning to sound like a reactionary," Emma said to her friend. "Come, we should leave and allow Alex to pursue his clients. I've done enough damage for one night."

Emma said her good-byes to Alex and a few others in the gallery, lingering for longer than she would have liked. When she passed her now deserted sculpture, she patted it on the head.

Dusk had deepened the shadows to indigo when they stepped onto Newbury Street. The encroaching darkness battled with man-made lights, some soft and warm, some muted by emerging spring leaves, others glaring electric white in shop and apartment windows.

"Can you imagine a world without electricity?" Emma asked Louisa.

"Of course not. Soon the world will be ruled by the automobile, electric gadgets, and the flying machine."

"Not that long ago, we had none of them. How the world has changed." Suddenly, Emma was overcome by a powerful melancholia and stopped in the recessed entrance of a milliner's storefront. "It's too easy to say I miss Tom—my feelings are much more complicated than that, but what would my life be like, if he never came back?" She looked over her friend's shoulder, above the buildings, at the sparkling pinpoints of stars and chided herself for asking such a question—of course, she wanted him to return, but the possibility of his death frightened her, leaving her feeling helpless and alone in a world ruled by men, exacerbated by her conversation with Vreland and Everett, his contentious friend.

"I'm sure the French forces and the Red Cross will protect Tom to the fullest," Louisa said and patted Emma's hand. "I'm concerned as well, but Tom probably won't be at the Front— he'll be in some comfortable hospital far away from the battle. And the war will be over quickly now that we're in it. He will be home before you know it. I promise."

Emma took a deep breath. "Would you mind if we didn't have supper out tonight? I would be happy at home with tea or, on second thought, a shot of gin. Will you join me?"

"Seeing how I'm a single woman in Boston with no better offer? Yes."

As they left the doorway, Emma glanced down the street and spotted the dim profile of the soldier she had seen days before, leaning on his crutches, hunkering against a building, his left hand shaking the cup at passersby.

Louisa sniffed as they swept past him and whispered, "This is what we have to look forward to—the horrors of war."

The evening, as soft and languid as the May air, held no comforts. She looked back several times at the soldier and wondered if he would ever find happiness. Her restless state of mind made her wonder as much for herself. First, Kurt, and then Tom. Her subdued passion ached within her like a spring bubbling to burst forth from the earth. Her obsession with Kurt, her predictable relationship with Tom, had led to disasters of the heart and she had to come to terms with both. Could she ever find peace?

She studied the drawing in front of her, brushing her hand softly over the page, feeling the smoothness of the paper against the mound of her index finger, tracing the face over and over until the lines were fixed in her mind.

If only . . . if only the process weren't so difficult—to replicate the artist's work into sculpture. Narcissus' reflection stared at her as she sat at her desk—a face filled with vacant delight, the pool shimmering around it. *The face should be sad in its preoccupation with its own beauty.*

A palpable loneliness coursed through her, she a solitary figure in the upstairs studio in the late evening. Anne had gone to bed after clearing the dishes and the pleasant odors of dinner in the sitting room had been overtaken by the oily sweetness of paint and the earthy scent of clay. Logs crackled in the small fireplace, the light distended and orange, an ember flicking now and then above the flames. The light reminded her of the war so far away—of bombs falling and flames licking at their targets. She shifted her attention from the fire and looked again at the beautiful youth in the drawing.

There was nothing more to be done on the sketches. Work on the new sculpture could begin as soon as possible. Her lips puckered as she thought of Vreland's tart *Register* review that would surely appear the next morning. Perhaps she wouldn't read it at all, for to take in the words was to risk much. *Skin is frail, but the ego is even more fragile. The slightest prick can wound permanently.* She studied the few paintings stacked against the wall, an art she dabbled in when the mood struck her—chiaroscuro studies of faces, half-finished landscapes. *How silly. All artists receive bad reviews.* She considered that recovery from such an injury to her ego might take days, months, even years. But she needn't worry about learning the outcome of Vreland's column. Louisa, without fail, would herald any news—good or disastrous.

27ᵗʰ April, 1917
My Dearest Emma (from somewhere in France):
I'm sorry I haven't written sooner. Even though the trip was long and exhausting, I was too excited to sleep. I wanted to see

as much of France as possible, unlike some of the other men who slept the hours blissfully away. One never knows when God may call, so I try to take advantage of the present. You must forgive me; I don't intend to be morose. But one sees so much—death.

The hospital is near XXXXX and is quiet for now; the calm before the storm. It is tiny compared with Boston's major hospital. I'm not sure how much I can tell you. Suffice it to say the facilities are as modern as French and American know-how can make it. I would change a few things, but I'm only a surgeon, not the Directeur *and by no means the Commanding Surgeon.*

Last night, I was able to get away to the city square just before dark. I sat on a bench under a fragrant flowering tree. I'm not sure what it was (it smelled faintly of lemon), and when the breeze stirred, it showered white flowers around me. It was like sitting in a heavenly spring rain. And, of course, you came into my reverie, my visions of you sitting by the fire or perhaps curled up with Lazarus—please give him a pat and a hug from me. At one point, I thought I saw yellow flashes in the sky and heard exploding shells, but the disturbance must have come from a distant storm.

I haven't heard from you. I assume it's the post and not that you have lost affection for me! Perhaps the Red Cross has had trouble tracking me down. I wish the same for the Germans.

I'm most concerned about your gallery showing. I hope it goes well. Remember, have faith in your talents despite what others may say. Please give my best to Louisa. I miss Anne's cooking.

Your husband,
Tom

She read Tom's letter the next morning and then dropped it on her studio desk.

You came into my reverie. I miss Anne's cooking.

His words struck her as intellectual and hollow and, in their coolness, a mirror of their marriage. Nothing would change while they were thousands of miles apart. A chilling thought struck her: *What if nothing ever changes?* The days without Tom were torturous, but so was the thought of grinding on in a marriage devoid of pleasure. She was caught between a desire to break free and the constraints of her marriage contract. What else could a woman expect but to bow to the ways of men?

A knock at the front door echoed up the stairs; Anne rushed to answer, the wooden floor creaking under her shoes.

Hearing the sound, Emma stopped drafting the thoughts she planned to put on paper to Tom, but then resumed, not wishing to be bothered by a visitor. Emma presumed Louisa might be at the door with news of Vreland's review; on the other hand, the Sunday morning disturbance might be from a salesman peddling sundries.

Two male voices, firm but pleasant, filtered up the stairs.

Not one, but two peddlers? She couldn't hear them distinctly enough to make out their words.

Emma sighed and replaced her pen in the desk notch. Distracted from her letter, she stared out the window into the milky light of morning and a sky patchy with clouds. The day was as diffuse as her mood. She fidgeted with notepaper on her desk, folding and refolding it, until she settled upon a perfect square to fit the envelope in front of her. She thought of Vreland and cursed him as the soft steps approached.

Anne opened the studio door and peered around it. "I'm sorry to bother you, ma'am, but it's Mr. Hippel, the gallery owner, with a gentleman caller."

Emma was pleasantly surprised. "Really? Show them up." Perhaps the review was palatable after all. She slid two chairs from their places flanking the fireplace and positioned them in front of her desk.

After a few moments, Anne reappeared, followed by the two men.

Alex brushed past the housekeeper, tugging at the man behind him, relinquishing his grip long enough to give Emma a kiss on the cheek.

"Emma . . . Emma," Alex said, his voice a plaintive sigh. "Have you read the morning paper?"

She motioned for the two men to sit. "I don't like the sound of that question. No, I had no stomach for it."

Alex guided his guest to a chair.

"Vreland has finally gone mad," Alex said, taking off his hat and seating himself next to the other visitor. He settled his brown-felt derby firmly in his lap, revealing the thinning black hair atop his head, and the slight graying of the temples. "The monster wants to kill me—drive me insane—he will only be happy if I throw myself into the Charles. There is no limit to his persecution!"

"Alex, you're being melodramatic," Emma said, judging the worth of his words. "Surely, the review wasn't that horrible."

"Oh no?"

Emma clutched the arms of her chair. "Well, go ahead, tell me. I've been anxious all morning. Louisa Markham didn't telephone, so I assumed the news was bad."

"Bad would be a superlative in Vreland's view." He pulled a clipped newspaper article from his jacket pocket. "How's this? 'A show of horrors . . . art created by lunatics, thrust upon an unsuspecting public . . . the Fountain's open door is too high a price to pay for these monstrosities.' Do you call that *bad*?" Alex's head sank over his chest.

"No, I suppose not. It's much worse than bad." Emma slumped in her chair, defeated by the depth of Vreland's spleen. "I hate to ask . . . but my *Diana*?"

Alex lifted his head. "You should be grateful you were dismissed in one sentence. Vreland was kind to you. He reserved his rants about lack of talent and assaults on aesthetics for others. The sum of his commentary about your sculpture was: '*Diana*, by Emma Lewis Swan, unlike nothing else in the gallery, has the soul of an icicle.'" Alex cracked a thin smile. "He wouldn't even begrudge you an iceberg."

She thought she had prepared herself for such a remark, but pain slashed across her chest—a swift laceration leaving no vis-

ible sign, but somehow bleeding from the heart. "I see," she said
weakly. She looked away from them and out the window. The
day seemed darker now even though the strengthening sun had
broken through the thinning clouds.

"I'm sorry," Alex said. "You and I know your work is beautiful. Why, even Mr. Bower has offered to hunt Vreland down—
the dog—and thrash him."

Emma chuckled, but the wound still bled.

"I've been such a boor," Alex continued, "I haven't even introduced the two of you. This is Linton Bower, the painter who
created the wonderful *Woman with Still Life* which that disagreeable *patron* with Vreland—Everett—described as 'rubbish
on canvas.'"

Linton nodded and smiled. "I'm very pleased to meet you,
Mrs. Swan. I admire your art, even though we work in two very
different styles."

Emma looked at the man to Alex's left. When Linton had
entered the room, she had avoided looking at him directly. Now
she realized why. He was blind and stunningly handsome, so
much so that she didn't want to stare at him like a freak in a
circus sideshow. A translucent film covered the pale blue irises
of both eyes. His face, however, retained the ruddy freshness of
youth—hair profuse, black, and wavy upon his head, his lips
full and tinged with red. The extent of his beauty startled her.
An instantaneous physical attraction swelled within her and she
fought back a rushing blush of embarrassment.

Linton, wearing a cream-colored suit and waistcoat, sat con-
fidently in his chair, his manner dignified yet relaxed. Emma
found it hard to keep from staring at his muscled arms and
sturdy legs, which were evident through his stylish attire.

"I believe I misunderstood your painting." She directed her
remark to Linton in an effort to draw Alex's attention away
from her discomfort.

"You wouldn't be the first," Linton replied.

"I'm . . . sorry. . . ." Emma sputtered.

"You needn't be," he said. "Most people are shocked when

they're introduced to a blind painter." He lifted his hands to his eyes. "Blind is too strong a word. When the lighting is perfect, I can make out fuzzy shapes and colors. Not much more. That's how I paint . . . I understand that you paint as well."

Emma glared at Alex, who shook his head, indicating that he hadn't said a word to Linton about her forays into other art forms. "I attempt to paint, but in a classical manner—my work isn't as exciting as the work you do."

"But wouldn't you agree, Emma, this young man has talent?" Alex asked.

"Exceptional."

"Of course, considering Linton's condition, I never took his threat of thrashing Vreland seriously."

Emma and Alex laughed after catching Linton's own contagious laughter.

"That is what I love about you, Alex," she said. "Never one to shy away from scandal—having one of your artists thrash our favorite critic! Boston would be a dreary place without you." She paused and looked again at Linton, but dared not stare long for fear of being rude. "How about tea? Anne can make a pot."

"Thank you, but we must be going," Alex said. "I'm taking Linton to look at new studio space."

"Actually, *feel* new studio space," Linton said. "Five of my paintings from the exhibition have sold. That money and Alex's support have given me enough courage to think about painting outside my cramped apartment. I'll know the moment I walk into the place whether it's right for me."

"That's wonderful," Emma said.

Alex lifted his hat. "I wanted to give you Vreland's choice words personally. I'd hoped Louisa hadn't telephoned or dropped by."

"She would never be a party to destroying my ego," Emma said. "She and Tom always build me up."

"Of course. It's as I said. We must carry on despite what others think. Beauty lives in our work."

Emma tapped her desk. "Because we aren't having tea,

would you mind if I accompanied you on your walk? It's a nice day and I'd like to get out of the house—I can't think of better companionship."

"Of course not," Linton said briskly.

Alex frowned, taken aback by Linton's quick response. "We'll be doing quite a bit of walking."

"The air will do me good," Emma said.

"Please join us," Linton said. "I love to walk—particularly in the bright light. In the sun, the world becomes a beautiful kaleidoscope of color and form. Alex is one of the few who has taken the trouble to walk with me."

"Now you have my company as well," Emma said.

Linton rose from his chair. "I would be thrilled for you to accompany us, Mrs. Swan."

Alex managed a weak smile. "Well then, let's be off. The morning is almost gone."

Emma nodded, excited to talk a walk with a handsome man by her side and to see the prospective studio. Linton was a kindred soul, she knew; that understanding coming from deep within her, as if she had known him for years; much stronger, much deeper, more passionate, than the novelty of a first meeting—this attraction, this drawing toward him, could be dangerous if she let it get out of control. *Don't be a schoolgirl, Emma. You've already allowed that to happen one time too many.* She would have plenty of time to think as they walked.

Can I look at him? Dare I walk as close as I wish? The air tingled around her. What a sense of romance—what prickles of excitement—clung to her skin. The pleasure of walking with a man reminded her of the times that she and Tom had strolled the Embankment, arm in arm, enjoying a bright spring day or a sultry summer evening. But, with Linton, the ugly specter of the forbidden reared its head again, as it had with Kurt, and she vowed to push it away, to resist its seductive charm.

Her heart beat faster when Linton's hand rested upon her arm. Ladies, attired in pleated Sunday dresses of rich greens and blues, wearing brimmed hats, sporting yellow and white parasols trimmed in black, turned their heads as they passed. She enjoyed the scandalous attention that the looks elicited. Being with Linton opened her to freedom, to a giddy expansion of breath and soul, filling her with a vitality she hadn't felt in years. The sidewalk glided under her feet, the warm sun shone more glorious than ever upon her body. May, a fickle month— one of beauty, life, and regeneration in Boston, if winter can be held in abeyance—had never seemed so beautiful.

They glided under the fresh canopy of leaves, across the avenues, past the brownstones and weathered churches, into a part of the city Emma had never seen before. Even as she enjoyed her companion and the sight of the fading blooms of a bed of red tulips, the nascent buds of the lilac, she marveled at the power of her deceit. Was she unfaithful because she was enjoying a walk with an attractive man? Of course not. But what about Linton drew her to him? In her heart, she knew. He was as forbidden, as dangerous a new love as Kurt had been. Linton's vitality reminded her of her former lover—a man she hadn't seen in many years, a man she dreamed of, but hoped not to remember. That time when they were last together in Lowell now seemed as foreign as the faun's face; yet, being with Linton brought back a strange familiarity.

The call of the illicit, the seductive danger of romance, were siren calls to her artist's soul. But her conscience reminded her that emotions should be held in check because the risks of passion were too great.

And then an equally dangerous thought came upon her. It would force Linton and her together for art's sake. *Linton is my Narcissus.* As quickly as the idea entered her mind, the matter was settled—a nod to taboo in a manner no one could question except herself.

When they crossed the triangle at Columbus Avenue, Linton wrapped his left arm gently around her waist for support. A thrill ran up her back, his intimacy enough to rock her on her feet. But the world of men was never far away—Kurt, Tom, even

Alex. They passed a war poster in a shop window that dampened her good spirits. Shame washed over her—how could she enjoy her time, even this innocent walk, with Linton, while Tom toiled as a surgeon on French soil? The reality and horror of it, like the determined doughboy in the poster, sent her plummeting from the heavens. She squeezed Linton's arm and focused on the city stretching before her—brick bowfront after brick bowfront in an undulating wave to the horizon. Life traveled that endless distance, until it could proceed no further.

"Here it is," Alex said. He withdrew a key from his pants pocket.

Emma looked at the stone building that towered over them—five stories tall, ugly, utilitarian in its uninspired rectangular architecture. It plunged the adjoining alley into darkness as it pushed back into the murky depths of the lot. A tailor and a cobbler occupied the ground floor, the wares of the trades, suits and shoes, displayed in the grimy windows.

"It's one flight up," Alex said. "I know the landlord. He was kind enough to give me the key."

Emma and Linton, behind Alex, climbed the dingy stairs lined with dust and bits of dead leaves.

"Contrary to what you might think, Mrs. Swan, I have no trouble navigating stairs," Linton said.

"Oh, I don't doubt it for a moment."

At the landing, Alex stopped at a green metal door inset with frosted glass. He slipped the key into the lock and led them inside.

A vast room, broken only by its circular stone columns, opened before them. The studio smelled of dust and the vacant odor of neglect. Greasy cobwebs dangled from the high ceiling. But the light! The room, which faced west, was already filling with afternoon sun thanks to an unbroken row of large windows that looked out upon the low buildings across the street.

"Linton, it's perfect," Emma said. "It needs sprucing up, but I could help you with that."

"Really, Emma, you go too far," Alex said, his voice bordering on censure. "Linton isn't an invalid. He knows how to handle a broom."

"Ssshhh!" Linton put a finger to his lips. "Let me walk."

He withdrew his arm from Emma's and took a few steps toward the windows. Then, he turned in a circle, his head and the cloudy eyes directed toward the ceiling. He stopped, faced the windows again, walked to them, and caressed the glass as if it were fine crystal. After a few moments, he walked back to Emma in measured steps.

"I love it," Linton said as he approached. Fire sparkled beneath the pale irises. "The light is extraordinary. When can I have it, Alex?"

"The first of June, if you wish." Alex turned to Emma. "The owner has made a very generous offer because he owes me a few favors. Linton can have the space for five dollars a month." Alex added with a wink to Emma, "The details of our business proposition shall remain undisclosed to all."

"Always," Emma said.

"Then, it's settled," Linton said. "The space is mine as of June. I already know where I'll set up my easels. Perhaps a sofa and some chairs. My table and work counter will be there." He pointed to a dusty corner on the south side of the room. "Now, I only need to retrace our steps, so I can find my way home."

"Come then," Alex offered. "I have an appointment after lunch with a potential buyer."

"I'm sure Mrs. Swan would be glad to escort me home," Linton said. He took no notice of Alex, but stared at Emma with his dim eyes.

Alex smiled curtly as if overpowered by the two and tipped his hat to Emma. "Who am I to dissuade creative minds from their artistic pursuits?" He shook Linton's hand and then placed the key in his palm. "Hold on to it. I'll deliver the good news personally to the landlord. I know he'll be pleased. Good-bye, Emma. Linton . . ." Alex brushed his hands against Linton's and then he was gone.

"I wish there was a place to sit," Linton said, backing away from Emma. He waved his right hand in a broad circle. "Is there any furniture?"

"Unfortunately, no. Not even a footstool. But we won't be here long." She hoped she didn't sound too disingenuous because, in actuality, she wanted to linger in the studio, breathe in the electric air of possibility.

"Thank you for coming today, Mrs. Swan," Linton said, and returned to the windows. "It would have been harder to make up my mind with just Alex accompanying me."

"Why?" she asked. "And, please, call me Emma." She stopped behind him as he peered through the dusty glass. He stood, his hands planted against the casement, the contours of his shoulders and back showing beneath the suit jacket.

"Because Alex would have forced the issue," he replied. "He wants me to paint—to take this space no matter what. Even though I'm blind, I'm no fool. I'm an asset to him as long as I make money."

"That's rather cold thinking."

He looked over his shoulder for a moment. "Not at all. Art is a business as well as a vocation. Think what financial straits Alex would be in if he made no sales at all. The Fountain is barely scraping by as it is. He needs artists who sell."

"Unlike me," Emma said with a touch of bitterness.

"I didn't mean to imply that. Please don't extrapolate upon my argument . . . Emma."

He turned toward her and the light created a soft sheen upon his black hair.

"*Diana* has not sold," she said. "I often wonder why I remain in this business—a sculptress unloved by the critics, with so few sales to my credit. It's hardly worth it. My husband and my friend Louisa are great supporters, however."

"You sculpt because you love it—because you were born to. It's in your blood." He faced her, and then, as if he had come too close, strode away.

"Is something wrong?" Emma asked.

He shook his head. "No, but I think we should be going. I was about to say something that perhaps I shouldn't have."

Emma came up from behind and placed her hand on his shoulder. His muscles contracted with her touch and a sudden tension filled the space between them.

"I was about to say I could be one of your encouragers as well," he said. "But that is stupid and forward of me. We've only just met."

Emma joined arms with him and walked toward the door. "I think it's very nice of you to say so. Yes, we've only just met, but we can be . . . friends."

"I would like that," Linton said.

When they reached the door, Linton opened it and Emma locked it with the key. Linton shadowed her, his hand upon hers so he could learn how the lock worked.

"By the way," he said as they descended the stairs, "when *Diana* sells, you or Alex must give it a good cleaning for the new owner. My fingerprints are all over it. I think it's a beautiful statue."

"Thank you," she said as they reached the landing.

As they stepped out of the dark entrance into the light, Emma added, "I have a favor to ask and I hope you don't think it's too forward of me." She shuddered a bit, knowing she had crossed a threshold.

He touched her hand lightly and smiled.

"I've decided to begin work on a new sculpture. You would be the perfect model for it."

"Really? Nothing that would upset Vreland, I hope?"

"Don't be ridiculous. Alex is right: we shouldn't care what he thinks anyway. The subject is Narcissus, studying his visage in a pool. I'm trying to portray the vanity of man, the preoccupations that ultimately lead him to his own destruction. It's a sculpture of its time."

Linton frowned. "Are you implying I'm vain?"

"Don't be disingenuous. How many women have told you that you're handsome?"

"A few."

"And? Did you believe them?"

Linton slowed, and as he stood before her, his face sagged under some unknown difficulty known only to him. They stood near the triangle at Columbus Avenue where bicyclists rode alongside horse-drawn carts and motorcars sputtering exhaust.

"For all my faults, I've never been accused of false modesty," Linton said. "Yes, a few women have told me I'm handsome, and I keep my body in shape to prove it. I can't really see how I look, having had this condition for nearly three-quarters of my life, but I take them at their word. I'll admit I've used my face and body to my advantage. People have been kind to me in ways I'm certain they wouldn't have been, if I had been ugly or in some other way deformed. But despite that, life has not been easy . . . I've had to work for everything I've gained."

Emma reasserted her hold on Linton's arm and continued their stroll. "I assure you I do not consider your eyes a deformity, or your looks . . . but I must admit, I was taken aback when I met you this morning. You reminded me of a man I once knew. Not so much in the physical, but in—how shall I say it?—in the realm of the romantic. He was strong willed and not without his faults."

"Then we are hardly similar, for I have no faults." He chuckled. "I take it your relationship ended badly."

"The timing was wrong for both of us." Emma stopped on the sidewalk, resisting the temptation to touch his cheek. "But you have a perfection of face he could never attain. That's why I want you to pose as Narcissus. We could start in Roman dress, if that's suitable for you. I could retain another model, of course, if you wish to decline."

"When would you like to begin?" he answered.

"Well . . . we could start as soon as possible. Shall we say in June, after you've had a chance to occupy your new studio? Perhaps you can spare a few hours a day to pose, before or after you paint."

"Perfect," Linton said.

"I must warn you—I'm not good with faces. That's why I want to do this statue—to realize the perfect face. I understand the importance of this work, its strength, its power, as surely as I can see it in my mind. After I'm finished, Vreland will beg for more."

"Please leave him out of this. It will be better for both of us."

Emma laughed. "Yes, I suppose you're right."

When they reached the Public Garden, Linton indicated he could find his way home and said good-bye. At the last moment, she remembered the studio key and took it from her jacket and pressed it into his palm. He grasped her hands firmly and his warm touch lingered on her skin as he walked away, working his way down the path without a stumble or falter.

Emma rubbed her hands together as she approached a bench near the pond and watched children playing near the water's edge. She imagined Linton looking into the pool, studying his reflection, ignoring the cares of the world, concerned only with his own thoughts. A child threw a pebble into the water and the ripples, as they spread toward the bank, destroyed the vision in her head.

Entry: 20th May, 1917

I've had a few days to think about my project with Linton. I find the prospect exciting and at the same time daunting—for a number of reasons. Our meeting was brief, but something about Linton touched me. Perhaps it was his inherent sensuality, his courage, his obvious tenacity—all qualities I admire. Our walk was refreshing and he, as we glided under the trees, opened up something in me, a vibrancy I haven't felt in years. I have given away so much of my time, my energy, and my life to my marriage and my art—and for what? To sit at home like a lump? I've wondered recently if I would ever feel again. Now, the possibility has arisen; however, I understand my situation. I'm a married woman with obligations and a husband. . . . Well, that's where the argument breaks down. A husband who wants no children because there isn't time for a "little one" in the house. A husband who provides financially for every need, including my art, but eschews the bedroom. But I cannot deny Tom his love of medicine and healing. What he does for others is beyond measure. And, for that, I love and respect him.

I must be cautious with my emotions. After I said good-bye to Linton I noticed a butterfly skimming, soaring on beautiful black and yellow wings, through the Public Garden. I have always loved them for their fragility and, at the same time, their strength. They are small with translucent wings, yet able to overcome the storm and travel thousands of miles to fulfill their destiny. I must emulate the strength and beauty of a butterfly.

"So, who is he?"

Emma smiled and settled into the wing chair opposite the French doors of the sitting room. Lazarus curved in an oval at her feet, his black snout propped upon his paws. She looked past Louisa into the courtyard, loving the play of afternoon sun, flooding the stones with light and then plunging them into shade, as the orb toyed with the scudding clouds. The late May wind swept into the room in bursts as the fir trembled in the breeze.

"Don't smile at me," Louisa scolded. "You know perfectly well who I mean. I haven't seen you beam so since you met Bela Pratt."

"You know me too well, Louisa."

Anne brought a pot of tea and placed it on the center table.

"Thank you, Anne," Louisa said. "At least there's one woman in this house with common sense."

"Ma'am?" Anne asked with chagrin, startled that Louisa would address her outside of domestic duties.

"Oh, never mind." Louisa waved her hand in dismissal. "It's not important."

"Don't move," Emma told Louisa as Anne departed. "How

do you expect me to finish this little drawing of you if you don't hold still?" She paused. "And you shouldn't tease Anne like that."

"I'm ready to take off this damnable *chapeau*." Louisa fussed with the white plume that stuck like a feathered quill out of her black hat. "And I'll speak to domestics as I please—I've had years of experience."

Emma studied her friend. She was not beautiful; however, she was elegant, refined in a way that might be termed handsome. Her hair was darker than Emma's but only by a shade. Her eyebrows were prominent and black, belying her Italian heritage, but pleasing in line. Emma had often thought of her as a model for one of her sculptures; her face, long and angular, would lend itself easily to the sculptural form. Emma considered her own too round and soft as witnessed by the several self-portrait busts in clay she had begun in past years. She had destroyed each of them, dismayed by the ugliness of the work.

"Singer Sargent will fall over himself when he sees this," Emma said. Her pencil slid softly across the pad in her lap. She concentrated on the plume, the jaunty form of the hat, and the dark hairline of the right side of Louisa's face.

"Nonsense. Mrs. Isabella Stewart Gardner has him wrapped around her matronly ring finger. It's highly doubtful we should ever see Mr. Sargent outside of Izzy's house. You would have to present your drawing personally at Mrs. Jack's." Louisa fiddled again with the plume. "Although, I must admit, he was quite respectable to me the last time we met. I think his sincerity grew from the fact that I never asked him to paint my portrait."

Emma smirked. "He passionately hates you society matrons."

"I am not a *matron*, and I will club to death any woman who dares refer to me as such. I am, and always will be, a *mademoiselle*." Louisa reached for the teapot and poured herself a cup. "And *you* are avoiding my question."

Emma threw down her pencil. "*You* are insufferable. All right . . . Linton Bower."

"The blind painter?"

"The same."

"I saw him at the Fountain the night of the opening. He cuts quite a handsome figure."

"I missed him that evening—I was so perturbed."

"Alex told me Linton has sold quite a few paintings, despite his modern style. He considers him one of his rising stars."

"I'd like to use him as a model," Emma said.

Louisa sipped her tea and then leaned forward. "You *do* know he's a homosexual."

Emma's breath caught for a moment as she stared at Louisa, flustered that her friend blurted out something so personal, so insidious, a rumor so potentially damaging to Linton. Of course, such a revelation, if it were true, would mean the end of any romantic fantasies she might harbor, quashed like a fire splashed with water. She chastised herself for letting her feelings get so far out of hand so quickly.

"Why the glare, my dear?" Louisa asked. "There are far worse things than being a homosexual. Alex will tell you so."

"Really, Louisa." Emma straightened in her chair and dropped the drawing pad beside it. Lazarus cocked an eye, snorted, and then returned to his nap. "Have you any proof? I would never take gossip at face value—I mean, Alex is one thing. . . ."

"Yes, a homosexual. Alex likes to keep his gentlemen friends. But I have no proof about Linton—after all, I'm not a man. . . ."

Emma sighed. "You are impossible. It makes no difference to me, anyway."

"I can see that it doesn't," Louisa said, lifting an eyebrow.

"Perhaps we should just ask him," Emma said with an agitated flourish of her hand. "Let's forget this dreary drawing of you and take a walk. Yes, let's stroll straight to Linton's and ask him if he's a homosexual."

"Do you know where he lives?" Louisa asked, smoothing the folds of her black dress.

"No, but I can find out."

"Now who's being impossible? You're making absolutely no

sense. No sane person would ever ask that question of another human being."

"I intend to."

"Then you will be the first—but that doesn't surprise me, considering the way you tend to stand up to men these days."

Emma was prepared to respond that her words at the Fountain were merely self-defense, but Anne appeared in the doorway with a letter in hand. "I've just picked up the mail, ma'am. This came from your husband."

"Good," Louisa said. "A needed breath of fresh air from France."

Emma took the small brown envelope in hand. It looked rather ordinary—the censor's mark on the outside, the postage meter, Emma's name, and the Boston address written by Tom. Despite the number of letters she'd received from him, each new one filled her with trepidation. What if something was wrong—perhaps he was sick, or worse yet, badly injured? She ripped open the letter, read the first page, and then dropped it into her lap.

"My goodness," Louisa said with alarm. "What in heaven's name is wrong?"

Emma heard Louisa speak, but it made no difference what her friend said. Louisa's words vanished in the air as her mind raced. She had to have time to consider, she had to think Tom's proposition out.

"Tom wants me to come to France."

Louisa looked at her with a questioning glance and then lowered her teacup silently to the table.

The fire died in the studio. Embers crackled under the grate. Emma wished she hadn't instructed Anne to make it for the evening was too warm. Normally, the flames soothed her confused mind, but this one had little effect on her nerves. She held the letter up to her face in the dim light, scrutinizing the words for every nuance.

20ᵗʰ May, 1917
My Dearest Emma (from somewhere in France):
I have such good news for you. I received your letter today and I couldn't help but write you as soon as I could. I'm sorry your opening was less than stellar, but I hope you're holding up—don't stretch the truth on my account. I'm sure Louisa will eventually fill me in on your true state of mind, if she writes me. However, like an epiphany, your letter prompted a wonderful idea on how you can aid the war effort and also utilize your skills as a sculptress.

She reached for a book on her cramped shelves. This one, in folio size by a French engraver, hissed when she cracked open its red leather binding. Near the middle of the book she found more references to her project, including a series of engravings entitled *The Three Fates of Narcissus*. The first showed Narcissus as a child. His mother bathed him in a pool surrounded by alabaster statuary as he caressed the flower that bore his name. The second portrayed him as a man standing in a Greek temple, a loose garment draped over his torso, staring at his reflection in a handheld silver mirror. The third showed him morphing into the flower, his arms and legs crackled and vein-like, his face partially swallowed by the petals of the Narcissus. Emma considered rethinking her ideas for the sculpture. The youth staring into the pool was, after all, a cliché. However, a man obsessed with his reflection in the ruins of a temple would be more to her theme. She visualized Linton in his studio, draped in an arabesque cloth, staring into a mirror—the silver one bequeathed to Tom by his father, part of his dressing set.

I have seen such horrors, I can't describe them. You can help these men. I was told of a man in England who made masks for the facially disfigured—yes, masks! Can you imagine? I want to find out how he does this miraculous work. You could do the same in France—perhaps set up a studio in Paris with the Red Cross, far enough away from the Front to be safe, yet

close enough for the soldiers to take advantage of your services.
There is such need. As surgeons, we can only do so much, but
you could return these men to the world of the living. And, best
of all, we could see each other again.

> *Your husband,*
> *Tom*

She folded the letter and placed it on her studio desk.

See each other again? Could there be more than sight?

Emma chided herself for being so blasé. How could Tom
know what she was thinking? Had she really made her feelings
known? Both had slipped into comfort without passion and accepted the consequences without objection. She had no doubt
that she loved him and he her, but how could love be measured?
Was its quality spent in days spent together, the hours of longing
while apart, or nights entwined in the bedroom? Perhaps they
loved each other equally as absence diminished their relationship, the war ripping them apart as surely as Europe was split by
the Front. Perhaps she had loved Tom more than he loved her, or
vice versa; she couldn't really tell. It seemed that fate, as a trick-
ster, had drawn them together. The thought had crossed her
mind that she was being punished by God for ending a life, but
she considered her situation. There had been no other choice.

She closed the book and drifted near sleep as Narcissus, followed by the faces of men without eyes, noses, and cheeks like
the begging soldier on the street, visages horribly broken and
torn, floated in the void.

Lazarus scratched at the door.

"Anne?" she called out while sitting in the dark room, but
the house was silent. The fire lay black and cold. "Anne, did you
let Lazarus out?"

A door creaked open from the attic bedroom above and steps
flowed down the stairs, followed by a knock at Emma's studio.
Her maid opened the door in her nightgown. "Are you all right,
ma'am?" Lazarus padded in past the housekeeper.

"Yes, just tired. Have you taken the dog out?"

"Hours ago, ma'am. Do you know what time it is?"

Emma shook her head as Lazarus nuzzled against her legs.

"It's after midnight, ma'am."

"My God, is it? I dropped off." She brushed her fingers through the dog's silky fur.

"Were you dreaming?"

"I was—of a man in a Greek temple."

"A strange dream indeed, ma'am. Was the man your husband?"

The question pierced Emma. She pushed Lazarus gently away, rose from the chair, and replaced the book of engravings on the shelf.

"We should both be in bed. I'm sorry I awakened you." Emma thought for a moment. "It must be near dawn in France."

She turned to the window, catching her reflection, as Anne called Lazarus. For a moment, in the darkness, she saw her husband dressed in his white surgeon's apron. In her vision, a young man, silent, purple in death, lay on a gurney as Tom lifted a bloodstained sheet, the wounds of the flesh raw and crimson before him.

Emma gasped and forced the image from her head.

CHAPTER 3

———◆◆◆———

BOSTON

June 1917

Emma paced herself as she walked to the Fountain, flushed with the thrill of starting a new project, yet wary of the prospect. She also found it hard to keep her model out of her mind. But despite the tamping down of thoughts some might consider indecent, she determined to enjoy the late spring in all its resplendent glory. Heady June days, when Boston emerged from its winter depths after an often dull and bleak spring, were to be savored. She noted this truth as she strode down Arlington Street admiring the purple irises, white-flowering hostas, and yellow pansies that dotted the small gardens and window boxes of the residences.

Her step quickened as she approached the gallery. Newbury Street's bustle charged her with energy, the shop doors open for business despite wartime rationing, men and women strolling down the street and taking in the sun, the smells of fresh-baked bread and grilled meats emanating from bakeries and cafés. In moments like these, in the majesty of a glorious day, the war seemed far away, almost romantic and magical, as if some distant Crusade was in progress. In many ways, the war *was* a crusade. Millions of men were caught up in the fervor— Tom being one of them—volunteering to make the world safe for Democracy. She passed a recruiting poster of a Yank, rifle in hand, pasted on a tobacco shop window and remembered the evening Tom had told her of his plans to serve. Her immediate reaction had been shock. His decision was a surprise, made without her consultation, but not unexpected, given his propensity to elevate his career over all else. That night, Emma asked herself the questions any woman would have, but only to herself—questions about his love and commitment to their relationship that she had revisited in her mind so often since his departure.

Only recently, months after Tom's absence, had loneliness and a sometimes sad desperation filled her mind like a slow-acting toxin. She had thrown herself into her work, attempting a few pieces, including the faun, but nothing came out as it should. And as the days dragged by, there were times when she wondered if her husband missed her at all, or whether she might be able to live without him. Those extraordinary feelings had taken on sharper focus since meeting Linton.

But today, she thrust those troubles aside and told herself she *was* more fortunate than thousands of poor wives, who had little means of support and sustenance, now that their husbands had been ripped from the house. No, she would remain strong, *not* because she was putting on a brave face, but because Tom's absence was of *his* making, and *his* decision had led to her current circumstances—a comforting notion when called upon. She could muster her own reserves of courage and creativity if she had to.

Perhaps *The Narcissus* could be her best project. Today, Linton would serve as her model. A thrill washed over her. She felt like working again, imbued with energy, and dared believe that she might achieve her place among the great sculptors of America.

Through the gallery windows, she saw him sitting in a chair near her *Diana*. Alex stood behind him, his hands draped over the artist's shoulders. Her heart dropped, however, when she saw the other occupant of the gallery—Vreland. The critic brandished his arms as he talked, his mouth twisted in exaggeration, the signs of someone who felt his own importance.

She opened the door and stepped inside. Linton instinctively looked her way. Alex smiled, and Vreland gave a brief nod, the first to offer a greeting.

Emma returned the salutation.

Linton, smiling broadly, rose from his chair, forcing Alex to remove his hands. "Good afternoon, Emma."

"Everyone seems in good spirits today," she replied.

Alex pulled a chair from behind his desk so Emma could sit. "Yes," he said, with an air of satisfaction. "Monsieur Vreland has agreed to do a column for his paper on none other than Mr. Linton Bower."

Vreland nodded and said, "At Alex's insistence, of course." He laughed and his joviality boomed through the gallery.

"Really," Emma said, barely masking her sarcasm, "I thought you despised his painting."

"I'm not fond of it, but money talks. Alex has made Linton's sales records available to me—quite confidentially, I assure you—and I was impressed with the attention being paid to this young painter. Of course, there is the other aspect of the story, in respect to Mr. Bower's . . . condition. . . ."

"That's despicable," Emma said, irritation rising in her. "Using a man's sales figures and blindness to hawk—"

"Emma, please," Linton said, resuming his seat. "The matter is settled and the arrangement is satisfactory to me. Alex and I appreciate that Mr. Vreland has even considered writing a column on behalf of my art and the Fountain—in light of his recent review."

"I've made it quite clear to the artist, and to Alex, that I must *love* the work in order to compose a positive critical piece," the critic responded. "However, attention must be paid to any artist who sells like this young man has sold since the opening."

"I think the whole affair is insulting," Emma said. "Linton, how could you agree to such pandering?"

Vreland sniffed. "Pandering? On the contrary, Mrs. Swan, this is business. Your attitude is exactly the reason why you will never achieve greatness as a sculptor. You, like most women, have no acumen for the business world."

Emma pushed forward in her chair. "*Sculptress.* I've had quite enough of the insults. You can label my talent small and my opportunities limited, Vreland, but you cannot disparage the whole of womankind. Men like you have harnessed the yoke for too long."

"Another suffrage argument I'm bored with," Vreland responded. "Gentlemen, if you'll excuse me, I have other business to attend to—let's reconvene for our interview at the appointed time tomorrow." The critic shook Alex's and Linton's hands and bowed slightly to Emma. "Good day, Mrs. Swan." He stopped near *Diana* and ran a finger across its face. "*Still* unsold, I see."

"Insufferable old fool," Emma said as Vreland closed the door. "His head is as big as his girth, and he throws it around in any way he can."

Alex bunched his fists in disgust. "My God, Emma, you *are* trying to ruin me, and doing a damn good job of it. Must you always antagonize him? You know he despises the work in my gallery. This is an opportunity to build good will for all my artists."

"Don't be an apologist for reprehensible behavior," Emma said.

Linton lowered his head and sighed. "I understand your concern, but the man has power. He sways public opinion. If he writes a favorable story it will help us all."

"I realize that, but we, as artists, are no longer controlled by our patrons. This is not the Renaissance. We have power, too . . . oh, what's the use. I feel as if I'm talking to myself and always butting heads with men. And men have created most of the messes in the world, including this damnable war. We women should take the lessons of *Lysistrata* to heart."

"I can vouch for your sentiments about men," Alex said, "but the world will go on despite our protests."

"I'm not going to let Vreland ruin the day," Emma said. "Are you ready, Linton? I'm prepared to work."

"What do you have planned?" Alex asked.

Emma rose from her chair and placed her hand on Linton's arm. "Sketching and preliminary modeling for a new project."

"I'm sorry I won't be able to drop by, but I have work to do here in the gallery," Alex said.

"Indeed." Emma leaned toward Linton, who shifted in his chair. "Did my supplies arrive? I paid one of the local boys dearly to haul twenty pounds of clay, my sketch pads, and tools."

"They're safe and sound on my new table," Linton said. "Well, new for me. The junk man told me Whistler had mixed his paints on its very boards. For provenance, he wanted an extra dollar."

Alex kissed Emma on the cheek, and said with true affection, "Take good care of my young man."

The sentiment unnerved Emma, considering what Louisa had revealed about the artist, but she shrugged off the gallery owner's words as a gentle admonition, preferring to believe that what she felt for Linton was matched by the painter's own ardor.

They emerged from the relative quiet of the gallery to the rush of Newbury Street. Men and women strolled on the crowded sidewalk, their sinuous movements creating intricate patterns of color and form. Surrounded by the blare of horns and the rolling thunder of carts, Emma led Linton across Berkeley Street and headed east into the South End.

As they walked in the shadow of the brownstones, Linton hooked his arm around her waist. The gesture felt comforting and familiar, his grasp automatic and without pretense. Strangers passing them on the street would have raised no eyebrows unless they'd read unlikely embarrassment upon Emma's face. Of course, Tom had walked with her many times in a similar fashion on the Embankment. But this was different. Linton was a stranger who felt, suddenly, as close to her in body and spirit— if not more so—than her husband. It had been years since she had enjoyed such thrilling companionship, and if she had to put a date upon it, possibly since her first meetings with Kurt. The electric charge of sexual attraction threatened to overtake her.

Linton turned his head toward her as they walked, and a few of his wavy locks shivered in the wind against his forehead.

"How is Tom?" he asked.

His question startled her, as if he had read her thoughts. "Fine," she replied, somewhat perplexed. She studied the handsome face, the pale fires that smoldered beneath the clouded irises.

"I wondered," he said. "You never talk about your husband. I know he exists. Alex told me he's serving as a doctor with the Red Cross in France."

"I *wondered* why you asked."

He scrunched up his nose. "Naturally curious. Are you getting along?"

"Rather personal questions, Linton. There are answers, but . . . answers I would share only with the closest of friends." A warm breeze wafted over her.

Linton unhooked his arm and stopped in the dappled shade of an elm. "I would hope I'm your friend—especially if I'm going to model for you."

"We know so little about each other." Emma took his hand and pulled him gently toward her. His coal-dark hair, the fullness of his lips, the pearly luster of his skin, nearly made her swoon. A shiver arced through her back.

"Then, it's time to learn," he said and grasped her hand firmly in his and guided her down the street. As they walked farther east, the fashionable buildings of Back Bay became more ragtag and industrial.

Emma drew in a breath. "You are persistent and you require much of your friends. Let's cross here." They strode across the Columbus triangle where a cluster of brownstones rose around them. As they neared Linton's studio, her body tightened. "I won't bore you with details, but it's fair to say my husband and I are in love."

Linton shook his head as if to admonish her. "Just in love? Nothing more?"

"What's wrong with being in love?"

"You're too coy, Emma Lewis Swan." Linton lifted a finger to his throat. "I can hear it in your voice and feel it in your soul. You may love, but your heart has taken refuge. It's buried deep inside you, like a treasure chest waiting for the lock to be opened. Who has the key?"

Emma looked away, hiding the blush crossing her cheeks. Linton had gotten far too close too quickly. She regrouped for a moment, and then tugged on his arm, while changing the subject. "Are you certain you want to model for me?"

"Yes, of course. I have nothing to be ashamed of, and I'm not afraid of what you might ask of me." The burgeoning smile, the strength and warmth of his face, aroused her. She resisted brushing her hand through his hair.

"All right then, let's proceed," Emma said. "But I don't want to take you away from your work because of a selfish interest in my project."

"Strangely enough, since I've moved into my new studio my output has been less than prolific. One could say I'm blocked. It's as if my cramped little apartment fired my imagination."

"I'm sure it's only because you're getting used to your new surroundings. Soon, your studio will be just like home."

When they arrived, Linton guided Emma up the dimly lit stairs. At the landing, he withdrew the key and inserted it into the lock. "See how well I do, even when it's gloomy?" He opened the studio door and gestured for Emma to enter.

She stepped inside, dazzled by the change from her first visit. Linton's easel stood in front of the broad windows, facing the western light, the easel's triangular form holding a broad canvas nailed to wooden stretchers. Two stone columns, on the north side of the studio, framed a pair of weather-beaten klismos chairs and a Grecian couch upholstered in faded blue silk. An array of patterned scarves in lacy Moorish design draped the couch and hung from the columns. A worn Oriental rug covered half the studio's floor. A massive bookcase, mostly empty, concealed most of the south wall. Whistler's table was centered in front of the case. Despite all its furnishings, the studio felt airy and immense, the cobwebs swept away, the sultry air of late spring pouring in through the open windows. The clay, the sketch pads, and Emma's bag containing her sculpting tools and drawing instruments lay on the table.

"Linton, I'm amazed," she said and grasped his hands in congratulations. "You must have worked for hours."

"I owe it all to Alex," he said. "He arranged for everything to be purchased and delivered, except the Whistler table. I acquired it on my own."

"Well, it's all quite lovely and I'm sure you'll find the studio—"

"You're wearing white, aren't you?"

"Yes," Emma replied, puzzled by his question.

"I wasn't sure whether it was ivory or white, but in this light I'm certain your dress is white. What else are you wearing?"

"Hardly a question you ask a lady," she said, somewhat flattered by his interest.

"I'm sorry. I'm so rarely honored by the confidences of the opposite sex. I'd like to get a better sense of what fashionable women are wearing these days."

Emma laughed and immediately thought better of it because Linton frowned. "Now, it's I who must apologize. I didn't mean to make fun. It's just such an odd question. My husband would never ask such a thing, but then he can see. . . ."

"I can see and feel."

Suddenly, the painter seemed younger and much more vulnerable than Emma had imagined. She cleared her throat. "Well, I don't dress like Louisa—I'm certainly not that fashionable. I'm wearing a white summer dress that comes up to about mid-calf, white stockings, and black shoes, with a heel that's taller than I usually choose for walking. Which begs the question, may I sit?"

"Of course." Linton led her to the couch and sat beside her. His hand slid to her right calf and then to the front of her leg. "Your stocking has a pattern on it," he said in amazement.

"Yes, they match. Women buy them that way," she said and gently pushed his hand aside.

"And undergarments?" he asked without flinching.

Emma shook her head. "That, for modesty's sake, I will not describe." She laughed again and clutched his hands. "Linton, are you all right?" She caught sight of the sparkle in the pale blue eyes.

He leaned back against the couch and stared at the windows. "I'm perfect. I'm happy you're here—in my studio. My cares dissolve when you're near me."

His happiness cheered her, but gave her pause. When they were together, time was distended, stretched, as if torn from the clock. His touch lingered, his smile shone, and the emotions they invoked were pleasurable. How could this attraction develop so quickly, she kept asking herself. For his part, Linton seemed perfectly happy, as content as Lazarus before the fire on a chilly night. She had to admit she was scared and wondered if she could distance herself enough from Linton to maintain their artistic relationship. That was the only way. No good could come from any other possibility—even though her heart was teetering on the edge of falling in love.

Emma smiled and touched his hand. "I'm glad you're happy." And she knew once the words were spoken she meant them sincerely.

Linton responded with a contented sigh.

"Perhaps we should be serious and get to work," Emma said. "I don't want to waste the afternoon."

"I'm ready. Where would you like me to sit—or stand?"

"Stand, please. Here in front of the couch. I'd like you to face three-quarters toward the windows. I'll start with a sketch. You'll need to hold your right arm out at times. It may be tiring."

Linton rose and took his position as Emma instructed. She made her way to the table, flipped open her sketch pad, and then rummaged through the bag. "I'm sure I put a charcoal pencil in here."

From across the studio, Linton said, "I haven't touched anything."

"I suppose I forgot it, so—" She turned, her words stopping at the sight. Linton stood partially disrobed, his trousers drooping at the waist, shirt dropped like a rag over his shoes. It had been months since she had seen a man—her husband—in any state of undress. Linton's body captivated her; yet, it stoked a hot flush of embarrassment that washed over her.

"Linton . . . Lin . . ."

"I'm sorry. Have I shamed you? If so. . . ." He placed his hands discreetly over his crotch.

"A bit." Emma regained her composure. "Why would you assume I want you to take off your clothes?"

"I studied mythological art in drawing classes. I remember our teacher telling us most images of Narcissus are of a naked youth staring into a pool. If you prefer me in Roman garb, we'll need to get the costuming."

Emma found the pencil, retrieved her sketch pad, walked past him without a look, and sat on the couch. There, she studied the lean muscles of his back, the curve of his buttocks beneath the low-slung pants, the sinewy line of his legs.

"Actually, the image I had in mind was of a young man partially draped. The silks you have in the studio are perfect. I can see some benefit in having the statue naked, except for a well-placed obstruction in the front, perhaps a partial column. Narcissus—naked to the world, absorbed by his own vanity, oblivious to mankind's disasters—it's ideal."

Linton faced her and removed his hands from his groin. "I suppose this was a forward, perhaps sinful, thing for me to do. But I hope you won't think of my nakedness that way. I only do it for your art." He pushed his pants and shorts to the floor and stepped out of them.

For once, his striking face wasn't the sole object of her attention. Linton's chest, belly, and legs were lightly coated with black hair. His penis was uncircumcised, resting below a thatch of dark pubic hair, his chest and abdomen as sculpturally defined as Michelangelo's *David*. Emma sensed the soft fire smoldering in his body. He was as handsome and as erotic as a dark god, so different from Tom, who had approached their sexual relations as if they were clinical studies.

"Linton, I don't think . . ." Emma set her drawing materials on the couch, stood, and walked toward the windows. He quivered as she passed. She placed her hands on the casement, thought for a few moments, and then turned to him. "You're such a beautiful man, but I'm uncertain whether we should go ahead with these sessions." She detected a stirring in his groin.

"Why not?" Linton asked quickly, his brows furrowed.

"It's rather obvious, don't you think? I'm married. You're not. We're working intimately together. Surroundings such as these may lead to temptation." She pointed to him. "I should have *asked* you to disrobe, rather than you taking it for granted. It's not proper."

"I won't surrender to temptation, Emma. This is our art. Remember, you're a sculptress."

Emma returned to the couch. "May I ask you a question?"

Linton nodded.

"Are you a homosexual?" She cringed at her effrontery, but she had to know the truth because of the answer's impact on their relationship.

Linton froze for a moment and then pulled his shorts back up. "My God, not that rumor again. It's hard enough for a man in my position to meet women, to carry on any kind of decent relationship, but . . . that lie has dogged me for years, as it does many male artists. Who told you that?"

"I shan't say. Apparently, it's widely held gossip."

His jaw clinched. "It's Alex's fault. Our association has tainted me. . . ."

"Don't blame Alex," Emma said. "He's been the best mentor and friend you could wish for. Am I right?"

Linton sighed. "Yes, but sometimes guilt lives by association. I have no quarrel with homosexuals, but I'm not one. The only hand I've placed on another man is to shake his." He crept toward the couch as if ashamed of his reputation and sat timidly next to her. "Please. I live for art—it's all I have to keep me going. We can create a beautiful statue. I know it. We can inspire each other to work."

A sense of relief traveled through her, with Linton's admission. *Perhaps there's hope for passion yet, bliss, a child in our lives, if it would work out.* And yet, those thoughts frightened her. She had no right to think of Linton as a lover, no right to break her vows to Tom for an immoral affair that would be the talk of Boston.

She looked at the beautiful man next to her and, buoyed by her sense of right, picked up her pad and pencil. "All right then, there's no time for sitting, Mr. Bower. Please resume your position—but appropriately draped."

Linton dutifully obeyed Emma's request, grabbing the large scarves from the couch, arranging them on his body as she ordered, and turning in a three-quarter profile toward the window.

As the afternoon light flooded the studio, Emma sketched, working and saying little as Linton held his pose perfectly. Only when Narcissus, gazing into the mirror, appeared on the pad fully formed did she stop. As the shadows grew longer, Emma put down her pencil and ended the session, satisfied with her drawing.

She thanked him as he dressed, and looked back at the windows as they left the studio. Steel-blue clouds splotched with crimson covered the city as the sun lowered in the west.

The afternoon had been the most glorious and productive that Emma had known in months. Despite the day's warmth, a chill swept over her as she and Linton walked toward their homes. She thought of Tom and his long hours in the French hospital, operating on wounded and dying men, while she once again enjoyed the passionate vigor of the work she loved. The session with Linton had freed her in a way she had not known since her beginning days at art school.

She marveled at the two extremes in her life—the chance

to work with a man who inflamed her artistic and emotional sensibilities, a conflagration waiting to happen; or an equally fiery end to her marriage. The day was too beautiful to waste on morbidity. For now, she would enjoy the walk with Linton and the joy that nearly swept her off her feet.

The evening air rushed through her studio window. The clop of hooves, the chug of automobiles sounded in her ears like a distant symphony, a reminder that life existed outside the haven of her work.

She sketched other imaginative possibilities for the sculpture using the afternoon's drawing as her guide. Linton's body took form on the page: the triangular cut of the deltoids, the pleasing oval of his calves, drapery added to the figure for effect. Unhappy with the first sketch, she put it aside only to redraw it entirely. Four hours later, she had completed three drawings: those being the front, side, and back of Narcissus. But the muddy face, always shadowed or clouded by impressionistic slashes, never in full profile or face on, dismayed her.

Lazarus's bark jolted her from her work. She rose from the chair and looked out the window. The street noise had ebbed, almost silent, as lightning flared in the distance. She walked softly downstairs to the sitting room. The clock was about to strike midnight; Anne was surely tucked away, fast asleep. The hackles on Lazarus's back rose as he centered his attention on something in the courtyard. Anxious and eager to get out, he wagged his tail and circled her.

Emma opened the French doors, the dog raced into the courtyard, and she cautiously followed. The wind whirled in eddies around her legs, the flashes of the far-off lightning illuminated the zenith.

As Lazarus snuffled in a corner, Emma spotted the object of the dog's concern. A bronze sundial Tom had given her one birthday had toppled in the wind and crashed onto the stone. The sun's smiling face, bent from the blow, felt rough and scarred in her hands like so many of the faces she had drawn.

Emma wiped the moss from the dial and replaced it on top of its marble stand. Moments later, when the rain fell in heavy drops and thunder sounded from the sky, the bronze face looked as if it were crying.

10ᵗʰ June, 1917
My dear Tom:
Last night, the sundial you gave me fell in a storm. It was damaged, and the effect was a bit overwhelming. The accident reminded me of your absence and the distance between us. The rain looked like tears on the sun's face and it nearly made me cry. I admit every now and then I feel blue, but then I remember your strength—a strength that took you away from me. I wonder sometimes if I have that kind of fortitude. If I do, it must be in reserve.

I hope you won't think me too much of a woman (a tiresome little thing who can't make up her mind because you know I'm not!), but I've made no decision about coming to France. I'd like to know more about this doctor and his technique. How does he help these men? What is the process? I have such trouble with faces I'm not certain I'm up to the job. On the other hand, a change from Boston might do me good. I admit the prospect of working with facially disfigured men would be challenging, and, in the end, life must be an adventure, I suppose, or why live it?

I've begun working on my next project, Narcissus. *I found a suitable model for the work—Linton Bower—one of Alex's artists. He is a blind painter, believe it or not, and paints the most extraordinary canvases of bright geometric shapes and colors. And, yet, they have traditional meaning. Perhaps you've met him at some point. Boston is a very small city. Vreland, the* Register *critic, is doing an article on him.*

Well, I'm sorry my letter is short tonight, but I'm tired and must go to bed. Please let me know if you communicate with the Englishman. I shall await your reply.

Anne asks for you constantly, as does Louisa when she is not consumed by some society event. That's a candid, but accurate, assessment of her character. She is a dear friend, but she tries my patience at times. Still, she lifts me up when I need it. I will pat Lazarus for you. He is fine as well, but seems less active since you departed.

Your wife,
Emma

She placed the pen on her studio desk, folded the letter, and wondered whether she shouldn't have written, *Your loving wife.* She hesitated while addressing it to him care of the Red Cross in France because she was aware of her own deception. She had no plans to leave Boston until she could understand the raw, deep emotions stirred by Linton—in the meantime, she had to remain responsible and mature enough to preserve her marriage. However, the painter offered her more than charms and flattery. He was younger than she by four or five years, she surmised, and he was to be admired for so many reasons: his striking features, his talent as an artist, and his attentions paid—Linton's qualities uncovered a buried vein of romance that ran through her and invited him into her heart. But when she carefully considered the relationship, she discovered something else.

She had never consciously thought of Linton as damaged or wounded, but it was clear he looked to her for help, relying on her for emotional support as a blind man, for artistic inspiration, and, worst of all for her, a source of companionship. Her maternal instincts were blossoming, and Linton, in his current state, was hard to resist. An unpleasant choice would have to be made in one direction or the other. Was she to fulfill her marriage with her husband or begin anew with Linton?

As she placed the letter to Tom on top of a stack of books, she pictured Linton standing naked, the perfect model for *Narcissus.*

A few days later, Emma, in a restless mood from sketching all morning, planned to surprise Linton by taking an afternoon walk to his studio. He, instead, surprised her after lunch by arriving at her home in a hansom cab. Anne answered the door as Emma watched from the sitting room. Linton strutted into the hallway like an aristocratic gentleman, as animated in gesture and complexion as Emma had ever seen. He handed Anne his gray woolen jacket and asked her to call for her mistress. Lazarus barked at the surge of activity in the normally placid house.

"She's right down the hall," the young housekeeper said.

Emma was well within earshot. "What a surprise, Linton. I'm coming."

Linton's already wide smile, deepened. He ruffled his right hand through his black hair like a stallion shaking his mane. "It's a perfect afternoon for a ride. I wish I could have obtained a couple of horses, but I hired the next best transportation I could."

Emma peered out the door. A mustachioed driver in top hat, dress pants, and long coat stood next to a silky black horse reined to an equally shiny cab. Linton had spent time and money acquiring the perfect driver and carriage.

"I appreciate the extravagance, Linton, but you . . ."

Linton stopped her with a touch to her arm. "Appreciate the moment, Emma. It's not often I splurge. And I should—I mean, while I have the money. Don't you agree?"

She could only smile at his infectious attitude.

"So, grab a jacket and let's start out. I have the cabman for two hours. The breeze is refreshing, and I'm anxious to see the city." Linton laughed heartily and she joined in at his self-deprecating joke. He retrieved his jacket from the housekeeper as Emma gathered her light spring coat from the hall tree and then said good-bye to Anne and Lazarus.

"I thought you would be working today," Emma said, as the driver offered his arm for support as she climbed into the carriage. Linton made his way around the horse to the other side of the cab as the man again offered his assistance. Linton settled next to her, his right leg achingly close to her left.

"No, the day is too beautiful to waste. You have to take advantage of precious days like these. There's plenty of time for work on a rainy summer day, or through a dreary fall and a cold winter. Besides, we have our project to discuss." He placed his hand upon hers as the driver climbed into the concealed seat elevated behind them.

Emma was tempted to move her hand to her lap but instead kept it in place.

The cabman flicked his riding whip and the horse stepped off at a leisurely walk.

"How is your work coming along?" Linton asked as they moved down the street. The row houses, the sun reflecting off the windows, glided past them.

The late spring air swirled into the cab; the earthy smell of the animal mixed with Linton's soapy, fresh scent. "I'm satisfied with several of the drawings. I think after a few more weeks of working on the sketches, I'll be able to start the maquette. The real modeling sessions will begin then."

He patted her hand. "I'm ready any time."

"And how is your work—and Alex?"

Linton turned away for a moment and looked out the carriage window. The flesh on the back of his neck quivered before he turned back to her, his mouth drawn at the corners. "Honestly, I don't know if the studio was a good idea." He tapped the fingers of his free hand on his thigh. "Don't get me wrong, I love it, but when I'm alone I stare out the windows into the light as if there's something out there I can't reach and must have."

She nodded.

Linton smiled weakly, seeing, or sensing, her movement. He grasped her hand tightly. "Can you understand this? It's as if my success has brought on too much pressure. Now, instead of creating art for my pleasure, my edification, I'm creating to satisfy the public. I feel stifled—in more ways than one."

The cab turned west toward the Charles River. In front of her, snaking lines of pedestrians strolled the Embankment, the river reflecting glittering diamonds of light along its length as it stretched south and west through Cambridge. She inhaled deeply and thought, *This is a chance to be happy!* Now, in this time, she had her best possible chance at happiness. But hadn't she felt the same with Tom before they were married? No! Tom was different—he was security and sensibility. How could she desert her husband and the life they had built—for pleasure—for the vagaries of passion and bliss? In the end, wouldn't the pleasure and intensity of any relationship fade into sameness and the familiarity of failure? How could two artists, with the fluctuations and whimsies of gallery sales, support themselves, especially Emma, who had yet to achieve any kind of fame or self-sufficiency? Linton felt different to her, the bud of romance coming to bloom; but she hadn't sorted through the complexity of her feelings.

She withdrew her hand from his and stared at the sparkling water because she didn't want to look into his eyes. "Tom wants me to come to France."

He seemed to stop breathing, as if life had drained from him. After that, for what seemed an eternity, the only sounds that drifted to her ears were the gentle urges of the cabman to his horse, the clop of hooves, and the rattle of the carriage.

Finally, Linton asked, "Have you decided?"

"No."

He exhaled and her world again seemed on its rightful course.

"I need time to think about what Tom is asking of me," she said. "The thought is tempting—I don't think you know my weaknesses, Linton."

"You have a weakness?" he asked, somewhat bitterly. "I wouldn't have thought so."

"Oh, more than one." She leaned back in the seat as the cab came to a brief stop to let pedestrians cross an intersection. Emma stared at the couples who passed in front of the carriage; a few smiled and chatted, most were captivated by the ground underneath their feet. To go through life staring at the ground, one might as well be dead. Linton was right, the day, the journey, were too precious to waste. She faced him and found him staring at her with his gauzy eyes, waiting to hear of her tribulations. "Well, for one, I have trouble with faces. The critics have always said so. I'd be working with soldiers—making masks to cover their facial injuries. The work would assist me in my art and . . ."

"And?"

"I don't want to sound too noble . . . I'd be doing something for someone else for a change—something good—not just thinking about myself, or my art, or scouring Boston society for patrons."

Linton nodded. "Yes, let Alex, Louisa Markham, and Frances Livingston handle that aspect of the business."

"I know you understand how exciting, but shallow, the whole business can be."

He said nothing, but she knew he agreed. "But there is *our* project. *Narcissus* might keep me in Boston."

"Am I one of your weaknesses?" he asked.

She shifted in the seat and was certain Linton saw, at least felt, her discomfort. *Was* he her weakness? The cab jerked forward past the sleepwalkers staring at their feet and, at that moment, she believed Linton was *more* than a temptation for all the qualities she admired in him. He was a man with whom she could fall deeply, madly in love if she let herself. The question was how far would she go?

As if unwilling to wait for an answer, Linton placed both of his hands on her face.

Emma recoiled as much from the intimacy of his movement as from the vulnerability she felt from public eyes staring into the cab.

She pushed his hands away. "Linton, please!"

He turned crimson and his pale eyes blinked. "I meant no offense. I only wanted to *see* your face. All you are to me now is a whitish blur surrounded by a dark halo of hair. But with my hands I can truly see."

"I understand," Emma said apologetically, and felt ashamed of her rebuff, but still wary of those who might see her with his hands on her face. She lifted the overhead trap and yelled to the cabman, "Driver, could you please take us to the Fenway? I want to see the lush green of the cattails."

"Certainly, ma'am," the driver yelled down.

Emma closed the trap and pressed her back into the soft leather. The cab veered away from the river, heading west, passing several busy streets before taking its place on a road bordered by opulent houses with stately columns and wide verdant lawns. They passed Mrs. Livingston's home before the road narrowed to a lane shaded by tall oaks and cedars. On this part of the journey, her companion had been silent, unmoving, staring through the carriage glass to his left. She wondered what he was seeing, or thinking.

"Linton?" She tapped him on the shoulder, hoping to shake him from his thoughts.

He turned to her and tears glistened in the shaded wells of his eyes.

"Oh," she said. "I'm sorry, I didn't mean—"

"I know you didn't *mean*," he said tersely and swiped a hand across his eyes. "I should be more of a man about it, I suppose. But can you understand how hard it is for me to . . ."

"See?" Emma asked softly, verging on tears herself.

Linton nodded and peered out of the cab.

Emma took his hands, now firmly situated in his lap, and guided them to her face.

He shuddered at her touch and turned.

She placed his right hand on her left cheek. Her facial nerves fluttered at the cool dampness of his fingers against the hot flush of her skin. "*See*," she said.

His body relaxed against hers as his fingertips rested against her cheek for a time. Then, subtly, like a sculptor molding clay, his thumb and forefinger explored her features, at first dimpling them against the hollow of her cheek. He worked his hand upward across her cheekbone, and then cupped it over her left eye, pressing his index finger over the line of her brow. Emma thought her breath would stop as his hand traced lightly over her skin. He followed the line of her hair, leaned over, and then allowed his fingers to drift down the right side of her face, gently contouring the length of her nose. His hand descended toward her jaw; at that point, he brought up both hands and cupped them around her face. In a languid motion, he slid them down until his palms cradled her neck in a gentle embrace. Her pulse throbbed against his hands.

"You are so beautiful," he said after a moment.

Emma placed her hands over his. The cab glided under a dense arch of trees and the shadows deepened.

Linton drew his face toward hers and kissed her.

She swooned under the press of his lips as the city dropped away. How long had it been since she had yielded like this to a man? How long had it been since the sweet sensations of passion had overtaken her? She lost control as the fevered air swept through the cab. Fueled by the humidity of the Fenway's swampy ground, Emma kissed Linton fiercely and he responded by covering her face and neck with his own fervid kisses.

The cab rocked to a stop. The driver's knock on the trap brought her to her senses. Linton pulled away and Emma, flushed, ran her hands across her face and through her hair.

"The road ends here," the driver called out. "Back to town?"

Linton arched his neck, directing his voice through the trap. "Yes, back to the city." He turned to Emma. "We still have an hour left."

Emma smoothed her dress and tried to smile. She wondered whether Linton could discern her discomfort—perhaps by instinct rather than sight. "An hour," she stated in a measured tone. She brushed her hands over her coat. "I'm sorry. I shouldn't have acted so rashly." She expected a quick reply, but none was forthcoming. Linton only stared out of the cab as if focused on some obscure object in the distance.

After the cab had reversed course and begun its journey back, he said, "You didn't act rashly—you acted from your heart."

"Perhaps, but where the heart leads can be dangerous." Emma stared at the distant church steeples that rose above the trees. "We need to step back for a moment—let our intellect rule."

Linton sat stiffly in the seat. The cab passed the resplendent Fenway homes and ventured back to Boston's crowded streets.

Other than polite conversation about the architecture, Emma spoke only briefly. He did the same until they arrived at her home. There he asked the driver to help Emma out of the cab and when she said good-bye, he did likewise, staring at a distant object that seemed visible only to him.

Emma fanned the program in front of her face. Beads of perspiration formed near her hairline and slid toward her temples. Why had Louisa decided to inflict an afternoon of such torture upon her?

The pianist at the front of the church lifted his hands to perform the *Allegro Maestoso* of Mozart's Piano Sonata in A Minor.

Emma wiped her face with her handkerchief as the performer's fingers touched the keyboard. "My God, it's hot in this church," she whispered to Louisa.

"Hot as hell, you might say," her friend whispered back, fanning herself with a carved ivory fan bordered in black Japanese lacquer.

Emma wondered how Louisa could stay so cool in such a formal dress of heavy cotton. She looked out over the rows of dark pews, nearly all occupied by stiffly dressed men and women who had come to enjoy a Sunday concert at the church.

The pianist's hands raced over the keyboard as the afternoon sun burned through a clerestory window. A rectangular pane of blazing yellow light fell on an elderly couple three rows in front. The air grew as suffocating as fingers around her throat as the heat intensified.

"I feel faint," Emma whispered again. "I love Mozart, but I must get some air."

"I loathe Mozart," Louisa replied. "Your need for medical attention is the perfect excuse for an early departure."

"Absolutely," Emma said before Louisa rose from the pew, clutched Emma's hand, and pulled her down the aisle.

Though it was only slightly cooler outside, a moderate breeze cheered Emma and the heat lifted from her cheeks.

"Let's sit for a moment," she said as they crossed Park Street, her arm intertwined with Louisa's. They found an iron bench shaded by an elm's leafy branches. A flock of pigeons pecked and cooed near her feet; two squirrels circled madly around the base of a nearby tree.

"Are you feeling better?" Louisa asked after a few moments. "In the church, you looked like a cherry ready for the picking."

Emma wiped her brow with her handkerchief, watching as couples traversed Tremont Street and, farther to the south, a throng of people crossed Boylston Street. Activity filled the Common on Sunday: children played with hoops, men courted sweethearts, old men smoked and read newspapers. Carriages rolled down Tremont, competing with the trolley for space.

Louisa sighed. "Give me a modern composer any day. Have you heard of Mr. Mahler? He died a few years ago, but *he* was a genius."

"Vaguely," Emma replied, not much in the mood for conversation. "This was your idea. I didn't know you hated Mozart. Why drag us to a recital you disliked?"

"To get *you* out of the house—you've been sequestered so. You might as well be a nun. I had no idea you loved Mozart, but, frankly, it doesn't make much difference, does it?"

"Well, we've learned something new about each other. I like music—I may have heard something of Mr. Mahler's, although most modern compositions strike me as strange."

"Like Linton Bower's paintings?"

"Oh, I see," Emma said, shaking her head. "That's what this outing is about."

"Yes, I wanted a private word with you—away from Anne and Lazarus."

"Lazarus doesn't care about our conversations, and he doesn't tell tales."

Louisa shook her fan at Emma. "Yes, but Anne is a different story. One can never trust the serving class. The walls talk in houses occupied by servants. Besides, what I have to say is rather private." Louisa placed her fan in her lap and folded her hands over it. "Stories are circulating."

"About?"

"You and Linton."

"I see. There's not much to tell."

"It's been said he modeled nude for you, and there's more. Rumor has it you are having an affair with him."

Emma shook her head, drew in a deep breath, and smiled. "And where are these *rumors* coming from?"

"Let's say I heard them from our friends."

"*Your* friends, Louisa. Which brings me to a point—you will not be one of mine if you continue this gossip mongering."

Louisa laughed, her mouth almost curled into a sneer. "Really, Emma, our friendship is too long and too glorious to be ruined by a flock of cackling hens. I only tell you this because I want to protect your name. You know the affectations of Boston society."

"I could do without such society."

Louisa tapped her fan against the bench. "So Linton is not a homosexual?"

"Really, sometimes you astound me. How could you fall into such a trap?" She stopped for a moment to consider what to say next. After a brief, uncomfortable silence, she continued, "He's handsome—and, yes, he has modeled for me—and we've become friends. He's a kind man and a gentleman—but not a homosexual."

Her friend picked at the red cloth tassel hanging from the fan. "You sound quite certain." An arch smile formed on her face. "I'm positive these stories come from Alex. He is the cause, if you need the source. And it only makes sense, what with his jealousy . . . you know Linton is five years younger than you . . . Alex told me so. However, someone we know did see you taking a cab ride with the painter."

"I've had quite enough of this," Emma said, her anger rising. "God knows how, but what if this innuendo got to Tom? He would be furious. I wrote him that Linton was modeling for me, but having an affair is an entirely different story."

A smart young couple passed in front of the bench. The

sight of the loving pair dropped a melancholy veil over Emma. Louisa's assertions were far too uncomfortable. After the carriage ride, she had wondered how far away she was from having an affair. Certainly, it was possible if she wanted it. But Tom's stable voice and steady eyes rushed into her head if thoughts of Linton lingered too long. And it was Tom, she had to admit, who brought her that momentary serenity—a calmness borne of separation and little emotion.

Far down the Common near the intersection of Tremont and Boylston, voices united into a chant. Emma watched as a motor truck, decked out in red, white, and blue bunting, wobbled around the corner and turned north onto Tremont. A group of men and women, some carrying signs, followed the vehicle.

"Peace! We want peace!" the group chanted. "Wilson has betrayed us!" The group continued its protest as the truck rumbled along.

"Oh, for heaven's sakes," Louisa said. "Radicals, probably Socialists."

Emma stiffened. "I understand their thinking completely."

"Then we've learned something else about each other—we are more widely divergent on our musical and political views than I imagined," Louisa replied smugly. "And I thought I knew you so well. . . ."

"Perhaps not," Emma said, rising from the bench. She looked across the Common and found herself flushed with anger. How could Louisa be so callous, her comments so shocking? Could her friend's attitude indicate how superficial their relationship might have been from the start? Her first connection with Louisa was through Tom; then their friendship had been united by a common bond of society parties and art circles. Louisa was always available for a laugh, and a lift if needed, but with Tom gone, their connection was dissipating more quickly than she could have anticipated.

The chanting voices faded as the truck and the marchers passed by.

Emma, followed by Louisa, walked deeper into the Common. Finally, succumbing to the heat and seeing the chance to traverse a street near her home, Emma offered a terse good-bye and left Louisa to fend for herself.

As quickly as spring had turned to summer, the heat was banished by a succession of cool, overcast days. Low gray clouds smothered the city, and often the afternoon was peppered by a fine mist that sometimes lingered throughout the night. The weather precipitated a feeling of dread in Emma, the associated anxiety gnawing at her. She was certain her apprehension sprang from her feelings for Linton and the spreading rumors of their relationship, but even more beastly was the uncertainty about how to cope with a life controlled by forces she couldn't conquer. Her conversations with Louisa had become formal and stilted since they had talked on the Common. Her enthusiasm for *The Narcissus* had dampened because of the gossip, even as she longed to see Linton.

On a day when the afternoon light was dim and bleak, Emma met Linton in the South End. He had telephoned her and asked for a meeting, his constricted voice conveying irritation and worry. As she climbed the stairs to his studio, she wondered what was wrong, her mind channeling her worries in all kinds of strange and bizarre directions.

The studio door was unlocked. Linton, who was stretched across the couch, looked particularly glum.

"Sit by me," he said without giving her a look, even as she drew closer.

In his presence, Emma was aware of the faint smell of her lavender eau de toilette, the sounds she made upon arrival: shoes clicking against the floor, her dress ruffling against her stockings. These sensory offerings were the calling cards she presented to the young artist.

"I knew it was you," Linton said.

"Of course," Emma replied, "you were expecting me."

"I recognized your step on the stairs. When you're near I detect your scent." He held out his hand.

Emma grasped his outstretched fingers. "Pleasant, I hope."

"Your soap is oatmeal, but sometimes you dab on lavender."

He drew up his knees, so Emma could sit. She settled in, somewhat uncomfortably, avoiding brushing against him.

Linton shook slightly underneath his jacket.

"Are you cold?" Emma faced him, bracing herself against the damp air that filled the studio.

"No. Angry."

She turned up the lapels of her jacket. "What happened?"

"I had a row with Alex. *You* know why I'm angry."

"No."

"These damn rumors going around about me—about us," Linton said furiously. "He had no right to start them. He denied it, but I know he talks when he shouldn't . . . he has a few scotches and his mouth flies open. First, I'm a homosexual, and now I'm having an affair with you. It's not fair to either of us. We're artists trying to make a living, doing something we love." He stared at her with eyes as cheerless as the day.

She succumbed to his anguish, tenderness flowing from her, her body arching toward his. "The rumors are troublesome, but . . . oh, Louisa irritates me so because *she's* such a gossip . . . it's what I've come to expect of Boston society. It wouldn't surprise me if she was part of this."

Linton continued his wan stare.

"Do you hear what I'm saying?" she asked. "It's as if I have to make a choice, extricating myself from Louisa—as well as the people who are my patrons. Things haven't been the same since Tom left."

"It's Alex's fault," Linton said. "If I could break my dependence on him, I'd leave his gallery and go somewhere else."

"Please, Linton, you need Alex—for your sake and for your career. He's the only gallery owner in Boston who would take on work like yours. You've been successful with him. He's set you up in this studio. Perhaps he *is* to blame for these rumors—but I can understand why he started them."

Linton flinched. Looking somewhat frail in the dull light,

he got up from the couch and walked toward the windows, his head bowed, his back hunched. He stopped near the panes and leaned against the casement.

Emma remained on the couch, unsure whether to follow. After a moment, she grabbed a blue silk scarf from the seatback, walked to him, and looked out to the street below where a few umbrellas bobbed in the mist.

"Why can you understand the rumors?" Linton asked. "Why?"

She wrapped the scarf around his shoulders and stepped back. "Because you are Linton Bower. If Alex did, it's because he cares for you—not because he's an evil or malicious man. His actions may have been motivated by jealousy, but also . . . love."

"I lied to you, Emma." Linton shuddered and brought his hands to his face, perhaps in shame, perhaps in exasperation. "I deceived you—I did sleep with him, but that's the only lie I've ever told you." Lowering his hands, he removed the scarf slowly from his shoulders and faced her, sadness swimming in the gauzy eyes. "Only a man like me would allow a woman like you to put a silk scarf around his shoulders. Only a man like me would sleep with Alex more than once . . . a few times . . . because I needed representation—because I needed the money. I'm sorry I lied, but it's not something a man reveals to a woman."

"Then, you are a . . . ?"

Linton bunched the scarf in his hands and threw it to the floor. "No! I'm not a homosexual. I'm an *opportunist*. I've been dismissed by men and women alike because of my condition— ignored as the *blind man*."

He swayed toward her and his advance caught her off guard. He reached for her, his arms closing around her, his muscular strength pressing against her body, finally capturing her in his embrace and pressing his lips against hers. As one hand held the back of her head, the other drifted toward her breasts and she knew she should struggle against him, but her resistance faded as Linton's passion increased.

"Linton . . ." she managed to whisper between his kisses. "This isn't right. Not this way."

"Please, Emma," Linton said, guiding her hand to his stomach, his abdomen quivering at her touch. "I adore you. . . ."

She was standing on the edge of the precipice. But as Linton's hands swam over her body, the encroaching intimacy set her on edge rather than fire her passion. The studio's cavernous shadows suddenly took on ominous overtones, with Tom, Louisa, and even Alex standing in the corner, watching them with disapproving eyes. As exciting as making love to Linton might be, she could not go through with it. She was trapped—caught between desire and the stasis of her marriage and conscience. Emma turned away, unable to bear the kisses Linton showered on her neck and face, sliding from his grasp as he undid the buttons on his shirt.

Apparently, neither of them had heard the footsteps on the stairs. The door swung open, followed by words blurted out as if in shock: "Your *Diana* has sold . . . I wanted to be the first to . . ."

An eerie silence fell over them before Linton, his back to the door, gasped and hurriedly tucked his shirt back into his pants.

Emma reeled backward toward the windows.

Louisa, deathly pale, holding a dripping umbrella, stood in the doorway. "Alex told me you might be here—I wanted to give you . . . good news. . . ."

A contorted smile crossed Emma's face before the tears began.

Linton wheeled in a fury. "Get out of my studio! Get out, now!"

Like a phantom, Louisa turned and stepped out the door.

The sound of the closing latch exploded in Emma's ears. She collapsed against the sill.

Linton took her into his arms as she sobbed.

She hurriedly wiped her eyes and drew herself together. "I've got to catch her!" She pushed him away and rushed to the door.

Emma called Louisa's name as she fled down the stairs to the street. Her friend had disappeared in the foggy dampness; the mist had turned to rain. Emma braced herself against the building, uncertain of what to do; but one thought raced through her head as the tears fell: *I will never be able to show my face in this city again.*

Emma tore the sheets one by one from her sketch pad as Anne set the tea service on the sitting room table. Lazarus lay on his back, paws up, against the side of her chair. The courtyard darkened under the evening mist and the fir appeared black and foreboding.

"I'll get wood for the fire," Anne said.

"The evening's chilly for June." Emma wrapped her dressing gown tightly around her and looked at the drawings gathered in her lap. Soon, the fireplace radiated warmth and cheeriness throughout the room.

Emma looked at Tom's picture. Anne had kept it conspicuously clean since she'd issued her instructions. She rose from her chair, knelt before the fireplace with the sketches of *The Narcissus*, and methodically ripped each page in half and tossed the pieces into the flames. The paper whooshed and curled in the fire, and in a few minutes the drawings were reduced to feathery gray ash. She admitted to herself that Linton's revelations had disturbed her. It wasn't so much that he had slept with Alex, but she now questioned his sincerity. Was he an opportunist with her as well?

The drawings were rubbish anyway. How could she have believed such a project could come to fruition?

She stepped away from the fire. The memory of Louisa standing in the doorway, her soggy umbrella in hand, a look of horrific dismay upon her face, floated through Emma's mind. Tomorrow, all of Boston would know. She would be a branded woman.

"Can I do anything else for you, ma'am?" Anne asked. "If not, I'm off to bed."

Emma thought for a moment. "Yes, if it's not too much trouble, could you bring me a pad and pen from upstairs? I'm going to write a letter to my husband."

"No trouble at all."

The seconds ticked away and, briefly, Emma felt warm, comfortable, and safe in the sitting room; but, try as she might, she couldn't shake the thoughts that troubled her: Louisa, Linton, her indifferent relationship with Tom, the city agog with scandal, the persistent specter of the war. All these nagging misfortunes loomed over her like the spirit of melancholia standing behind her chair.

Anne returned with the requested items and said good night. Emma curled in the chair, and put pen to paper.

17th June, 1917
My dear Tom:
I'm sorry it's taken me a while to come to this decision. . . .
Emma stopped writing and studied the sentence. The decision was hers and not one to be taken lightly. Either way, someone would be hurt—either her husband or Linton. And as unsettling as that choice was, she most likely would be hurt as well. She rubbed the pen's nub against the paper and started again.

I'm sorry it's taken me a while to come to this decision—I'm coming to France.

It would be for the best. She owed it to Tom to give the marriage another chance. He was a good man and an excellent provider. Linton would be hurt, but he would get over her. A man of his looks, talent, charm, and youth wouldn't be lonely for long.

My work here isn't going at all well, despite the news today that my Diana has sold. I haven't even talked to Alex about who purchased it. I must confess, my world has been topsy-turvy since you left. Work on my new project has stalled due to my inability to focus upon it. Too many things have been on my mind—including you. I'm following your suggestion and am seeking passage to Paris, where maybe I can do some good

*for the world, as you already are. When I consider it, working
with the brave soldiers is so much more important than anything I could do here at my artist's table. When my itinerary is
confirmed, I will write you with the details.*

*You must believe me, Tom, and know this has not been an
easy decision, or one taken lightly. Giving up my work here
tests all my strength, but there are such good reasons to travel
to France. I trust Anne completely to care for the house. We
can arrange for appropriate compensation. Lazarus considers
her one of the family and, at this point, the dog is probably
closer to her than to me. I'm certain the whole arrangement will
work out for the best.*

*Wish me safe passage. I will post my next letter in all haste.
In the meantime, I send you my love.*

Your wife,

Emma

Thomas Evan Swan.

She studied the black-and-white photograph but imagined
him as if he were standing in front of her. Thinning hair lay in
wisps across the head, eyes of cornflower blue, fair white skin
that reddened easily in the New England summer sun. She tried
to smile. In a short time, they would meet again, and she would
embrace and kiss him because she *wanted* his love—or was it
needed—his body so close to hers, needed so desperately in this
moment of loneliness, this hour of abandonment of a city and a
man she *might* love. Yet, love was so different from passion—
a lesson to relearn with each new romance. Would the flames
blaze again in France?

The fire sputtered and settled beneath the grate. Emma kept
her eyes on the photograph as if charmed by a talisman. Magi-
cally, Tom's face shifted to the darker features of Linton Bower.
And then, yet again, to the man she had opened herself to before
she met Thomas Evan Swan.

Drugged by the elixir of memory, she fell into an uneasy
sleep in her chair.

During the night Lazarus paced between the fireplace and Emma, his keen canine senses aware of the anxiety plaguing her dreams.

Entry: 20th June, 1917

I placed Tom's letter on my studio desk where it sat two days before I mailed it. I was a mass of nerves when I relinquished it to Anne to be posted. My stomach has not settled since. The world seems to have shifted and fate is about to plunge me headlong into a journey I could never have imagined. When I think about the good times of my life—sculpting, the lush green mountains of my girlhood home, the few serene years with Tom—I feel they've passed never to be recaptured.

Half of me is thrilled to make the journey, the other a whimpering child. If I'm honest, I suppose I'm leaving because of Linton. I can't believe what has happened. I never thought another burst of romance would come into my life yet again, and then be dashed. Our last meeting made me keenly aware of the danger that exists between us. My feelings are not skin deep. Linton opens an aching avenue for love and also great trepidation about what might be. He resurrects memories of a passion gone by that were securely buried. Love is a malleable emotion forged by all manner of feelings. One person sees it as strength, courage, and devotion, while another sees it as slavish need and subjugation. Who can say what love truly is?

After Anne returned from mailing the letter, I sat with her in the kitchen. She was baking a pie and the heat was quite overpowering. A sudden compassion for the young woman overcame me—for this waif who left Ireland to make America her home. Her swirling dark hair, her alabaster face highlighted by ruddy cheeks, gave her the appearance of a figure drawn by a master watercolorist. I marveled at the conditions under which she works: the oppressive heat of the basement kitchen, comforting in winter, but hellish in the summer; the labor required to carry wood and coal for fuel, to tote bundles from the deliveryman; and then, after a long day, to climb three stories to her small bedroom, chilled by winter winds and roasted by summer sun. I wish conditions were easier for us all—particularly for Anne.

She settled upon the uneasiness arising from my letter to Tom. "Did something happen, ma'am? Something terrible?" She stopped and wiped her hands on her apron. "I have no right to ask, but if you need someone to talk to . . . I tire of conversing with the dog. You must be waiting for a caller. The house has been strangely quiet. Not a word from Mr. Hippel, or that handsome Mr. Bower, let alone from your friend, Louisa."

I, of course, could say nothing of Linton and my situation. At that moment, I realized Anne would bear a great responsibility when I was gone. She would be the master and mistress of the house. She had already taken it upon herself to gauge my feelings. An unorthodox and radical thought occurred to me. My patroness, Frances Livingston, is having a party. What if I took Anne to the gathering? Frances, an early champion of my work, is pure Boston Brahmin, and a good soul at heart, and it's time Anne meets others outside of her station. I know Louisa will protest, but I cannot be swayed by her objections. Anne is a trusted employee—not a slave. Besides, a night out will do us both good.

When I mentioned the party, Anne, of course, demurred saying she had nothing to wear and she would not fit in. I told her to smile; her face would be her good fortune. If only the faces on my sculptures could be as pleasing as Anne's.

As they rode in the hansom cab, Emma reconsidered her invitation to take Anne to the party. Perhaps her enthusiasm had clouded her judgment. She knew criticism was inevitable, not just for bringing her housekeeper, but of her pending journey abroad as well. The party would be interesting at the very least—Louisa certainly would be there, possibly Alex and Linton, and others of the artistic and social circle who happened to be in Boston and not summering in Lenox or Bar Harbor. Emma would be pleased if Vreland never showed his face, but she suspected the critic was on Mrs. Livingston's guest list.

The horse plodded along in the pleasant June evening. Anne sat looking out the window, as if she were a fairy-tale princess. The fading sunlight sparkled on the Charles like glittering stars patched upon the water, and a rosy hue infused the sky. The cab turned away from the river, the driver directing it toward Mrs. Livingston's Fenway home.

"Oh, ma'am, this is so exciting," Anne said as she peered out. Emma imagined what her housekeeper must be feeling and marveled at the young woman from Ireland who had come to the United States shortly before the war broke out with no job and only a few dollars in her pocket. She had been referred by an acquaintance of Tom's who swore the Irish were to be the saviors of Boston, especially when it came to the serving class. Anne had worked a number of odd jobs and been a bit rough around the edges at first, but Emma and Tom had liked her immediately upon introduction and she had more than shown her worth in the time she had been with them. Emma thought of Anne's solitary journey across the Atlantic, and how the war's disastrous upheaval of the past three years had changed so many lives.

"Yes, it is, and the evening's only begun." Emma patted Anne's hand. The day of the party, Emma had completed what she set out to do. She'd helped with the cooking, walked Lazarus, tucked in Anne's borrowed dress—the black one Emma had worn to the opening at the Fountain—and chose her own attire, a maroon dress purchased several years earlier. It was decidedly out of fashion, ankle length, but she had chosen it with one intention in mind. The color seemed appropriate for all that had transpired the past few weeks. Anne was coming along for the ride—another point to be made. Guilt swept over her briefly. Perhaps it was selfish to use a party as a personal forum, but, upon consideration, no one would misunderstand her implication when she walked into the house dressed as she was.

The evening shadows stretched across the lawn as they arrived at the porte cochere. The driver opened the cab door and Emma withdrew coins from her purse. One electric light blazed above the porch, a beacon against the rations of war. The façade was subdued compared with previous functions Emma had attended: the gas lamps held in the stone lions' paws were cold and dark, no torches lined the walkway, no festive colored lights peppered the shrubs. The house seemed blanched and mute, as if recovering from a long sleep.

Anne sighed as they walked up the steps.

"What's wrong?" Emma asked.

"I can hardly believe people have so much money," Anne said.

"More than any of us can imagine." A doorman awaited them after their climb. "You should have seen it before the war. It's positively dreary as it is now."

A servant greeted them with a nod and directed them past a door studded with leaded crystal and gold gilt. "In the ballroom, Mrs. Swan," the man said stiffly.

A grand marble staircase, carpeted in red, swept up to the right. Violins played down the long hall. She followed the music as Anne trailed behind like a stray puppy. About midway down, Emma turned left into the ballroom. About two dozen of Boston's most well-heeled men and women milled about the room. Some ladies wore their finest gowns, encrusted with jewels real and faux, egret-feathered hats resting upon their heads; others were attired in brown dresses, white blouses, and brown jackets imitating the current fashionable style of the American Expeditionary Force uniform. The most dramatic dresses had been purchased before the war because colored fabrics were in short

supply now. The current muted tones reflected the war's depri-
vations. The gentlemen in attendance wore dark suits or tuxes.

The chatter in the room was hushed compared with the lively
banter Emma had heard at previous parties. A few heads turned
as she and her housekeeper entered.

Mrs. Livingston, attired in an emerald green dress dripping
with silver spangles, rushed toward her.

"Emma, so good of you to come," the socialite gushed. Her
gray hair was piled upon her head, the strands held up in back
by a long Japanese pin, her cheeks flushed with a hearty helping
of rouge, her dancing eyes delicately lined in black. She heartily took Emma's hands in her own, and cast a sly look toward
Anne. "Who is this attractive young lady accompanying you?"

"Frances, this is my housekeeper, Anne," Emma said. "I
rarely entertain at my home, so you've not met her. I asked her
to come tonight because she's never been to a party such as
yours, and I think all of us can use some cheering up during this
difficult time."

Frances smiled at the housekeeper.

"Anne, please say hello to Mrs. Livingston," Emma said with
some embarrassment because her guest stared openmouthed at
the hostess as if she was meeting royalty.

"It's an honor, ma'am," Anne finally said, while attempting
an awkward curtsy.

Frances offered her hand. "You're more than welcome, my
dear."

"I also wanted Anne to be here because . . . I may be leaving Boston for a time. I wanted you to meet the young woman
who'll be taking care of our home and managing our affairs."

Frances frowned. "Leaving? Whatever for?"

Emma saw her hostess's eyes shift toward the door as a man
and woman entered the room.

"Excuse me, my dear . . . I *do* want to know about wherever
it is you're going, but I must greet Mr. and Mrs. Radcliffe." And
she flitted away like a butterfly in the breeze.

Anne took a deep breath and rubbed her hands together.

"She's a grand old dame, really," Emma assured her. "This is a simple party for her. Not a bad bone in her body . . . I can't say that for everyone here." The soft notes of a string trio rose from its position near a long table encrusted with silver platters holding meats and vegetables, as well as steaming chafing dishes. Emma glanced toward the opposite end of the ballroom where wide French doors opened to a garden.

"Isn't that Miss Markham by the door?" Anne asked.

Emma nodded. It was Louisa, holding court with several other women and a man.

A server walked by and offered them a choice of wine. Anne declined, but Emma encouraged her to take a glass, asking, "How often do we experience a night like this?" She walked toward the garden as Anne, after accepting the wine, followed.

Louisa cast a cold glance toward her as she approached.

She recognized the man in Louisa's circle as Everett, the disagreeable gallery patron who had termed Linton's painting "rubbish" and also concluded that women had no business sculpting.

Louisa, her eyes icy and unforgiving, nodded as she arrived. The other women glanced at her as well, and then turned and continued their conversation with the lone gentleman, tittering and carrying on like sparrows about a topic Emma could not discern.

"Good evening, Mrs. Swan," Louisa said. An arch smile crossed her face after the words left her red lips.

"So formal, my zephyr? Has our relationship deteriorated so much since our last meeting?"

"I could hardly call our last encounter a meeting—more an outrage."

Several in the group snickered as if they were secretly listening to their conversation.

"There was no outrage committed, unless you consider intrusion into one's privacy an equivalent violation." She turned to Anne and said mildly, "Take a walk in the garden and enjoy Mrs. Livingston's roses."

Louisa laughed. "Are you concerned word of your indiscretion will get out through your servant? I'm afraid you're too late."

A red flash burst in front of Emma's eyes, blinding her with fury. "Anne is not my servant, and you would do well to remember that fact! She's a woman employed by my family."

"I'll take that walk now, ma'am," her housekeeper said, her eyes wide and the wineglass grasped in her hands as if it were a fragile, precious jewel.

As Anne left for the garden, Louisa blurted out, "Fine company you keep, Emma—bringing your housekeeper to a party like this. How many other domestics do you see here besides those who belong to this house?"

"I'm not responsible for Boston's prejudices. It's amusing that *you* dare question my motives. Who anointed you as the arbiter of my life and relationships?"

"You're the one who will ultimately suffer," Louisa replied firmly. "If Tom knew what was happening. . . ."

Emma retreated based on her friend's threat and motioned for Louisa to step away from the group toward the garden. They stopped a short distance from the French doors, the music and the guests' chatter calming her for a moment. After a time, she said, "Truce. Can't we put this behind us? I think about the fun and laughter we've shared, and how it's come to this."

Her friend turned and inched toward the garden door. Emma wondered if she was considering her peace proposal or was attempting to flee. Overall, she seemed unmoved.

"*I* am willing to forgive and forget, but I'm afraid the damage has been done. I was in such a state after the incident—after what I had seen," Louisa said, her lips curling. "Can you blame me?"

"Nothing happened between Linton and me," Emma countered, knowing she had broken away from Linton's embrace when Louisa entered the studio. She felt compelled to add, "Linton was going to model for me."

"That hardly appeared the case. You can deny your attachment to Linton, but it's clearly obvious to everyone else—

including me." Louisa lowered her head. "But, I suppose, I, too, must be forgiven." She pursed her lips. "Society is not to be trifled with, particularly in Boston. It's a lesson my mother taught me in childhood and I have never forgotten. Society cannot be denied, nor can those who uphold it." A steely resolve filled her friend's eyes. "Perhaps I shouldn't have, but I returned to the Fountain. I felt I had nowhere else to go—to the only person who might understand what I had seen. Alex had begged me to tell him your reaction to the sale of *Diana*. You must believe me, I tried to lie, but he saw through me from the beginning. I sat, overcome with emotion, and shed a few tears. Alex was understandably upset—he had no idea where my grief was coming from—and after much pleading from him, I disclosed what I had witnessed. You must remember that your husband *is* my friend. I swear I told no one else, but the rumor has gotten out. I'm afraid even Tom may know before long."

"I see," Emma said and clasped her hands together. "My intuition about this maroon dress was correct."

Louisa sighed, the corners of her mouth turning down in sadness.

The disagreeable man from the group stepped toward them as a chilly silence took hold. "I'm indeed sorry to interrupt, but I wanted to congratulate you, Mrs. Swan, on your recent sale." Everett offered his hand.

Emma stood stone-faced, not willing to reciprocate to the one who had maligned her.

He withdrew his hand. "I must say, after seeing your statue and reading Monsieur Vreland's review of the opening, I was quite amazed it sold. However, *scandal* has a way of making objects more valuable. Shall we say curiosity overcomes taste?" He laughed, then scowled at her and returned to the group.

Louisa smirked. "See, the rumor has spread. He's a buffoon with no manners and very little breeding. He's attached himself to Vreland like a leech."

"It's worse than I thought," Emma said. "If I don't leave Boston, I'll be run out on a rail."

Frances, arms aflutter, breezed toward them. "Mrs. Gardner and Singer Sargent have arrived," the hostess said. "Please do say hello to them." And then she darted on to her next destination as quickly as she had come.

"I'll be leaving soon for France," Emma said.

"France?" Louisa's brown eyes glittered with skepticism. "So, you've decided?"

"Yes. I'm following Tom's suggestion." Emma looked into the garden. The scene was tranquil, aided by the string trio's soothing music. Anne sat on a white marble bench under a wisteria arbor. Bent with interest and attentive eyes focused on the young lady next to him, a handsome young man in a black tuxedo sat next to her housekeeper.

"Anne seems to be having a good time," Emma said. "I must remember what it was like to sense the first blush of love." She thought better of her words as soon as she said them. "I'm glad she's here." She gripped Louisa's hands and looked into her eyes. "You must promise me that you will stop behaving like a duchess and treat Anne like a human being."

Louisa's eyes narrowed. "She's a domestic—an Irish immigrant."

"You mustn't let her status influence your behavior. If something happened to me and Tom, Anne would be in charge of the household, until the legal arrangements could be straightened out. I'm not so concerned about Tom's parents, but my mother . . . she might put Anne out on the street."

Louisa nodded reluctantly.

Emma looked toward the fireplace where a regal, bearded, middle-aged man in a dark suit stood smoking a cigarette. "Would you like to accompany me? I'd like to reintroduce myself to Mr. Sargent."

"No," Louisa said. She pointed toward the ballroom door where Mrs. Gardner had attracted a flurry of activity. "Mrs. Jack has arrived. I'll see what stories she has to tell. You have more common ground to cover with Sargent than I do—as one artist to another."

"Well," Emma said, "Good-bye for now. This may be our last meeting before I leave."

"Good-bye, then. *Bon voyage.*" Louisa turned quickly and headed toward the crowd gathered around Mrs. Gardner.

For a moment, Emma was left alone at the end of the ballroom. She looked at the ornate crystal chandelier hanging in the middle of the room, the sedate groupings of fashionable women and cigar-smoking men, the domestics who stood like formally attired pawns behind the serving table. All of it seemed like a gauzy dream as she contemplated her move to France and how she would break the news to Linton.

Overcome by apprehension, she walked toward Sargent and the gilt fireplace. A frown crossed his face as Emma headed his way, indicating he'd rather not be bothered. She continued to walk, with reserve, toward the artist, who apparently valued his time with his cigarette. He looked somewhat like a stately grandfather with his high hairline, gray-flecked beard, and thick eyebrows. She greeted him with a firm, "Good evening."

The painter flicked a bit of cigarette paper from his mustache and returned a slight smile.

"I don't know whether you remember me from a brief meeting at the Fountain Gallery long ago," she said. "I'm Emma Lewis Swan, the sculptress."

Sargent tilted his head and his shaded eyes took on an interested glow. "Of course, I remember you, Mrs. Swan. You created the lovely *Diana*, which recently sold."

Emma wondered how he knew of the sale.

"Oh, don't look so puzzled. I make it my business to know what's selling and what's not. You know how easily art falls in and out of fashion. In fact, I had some interest in your sculpture, but Alex Hippel had already promised it to another buyer."

"I'm flattered, Mr. Sargent—a great painter like you interested in my work."

"Your statue was very good—in fact, the best work in the gallery, I believe." He inhaled deeply, arched his neck, and puffed smoke toward the ceiling. A server drifted by and the painter took wine, drank from the glass, and set it on the mantel. "I'm not keen on what's being sold these days. Monet and Renoir I can live with—but Linton Bower? Much too modern for me. Do you know who bought your statue?"

"Actually, I don't. Alex and I haven't spoken recently."

Sargent chuckled. "That's unlike him. Perhaps he wants to keep your money in his clutches. He's constantly gabbing my ear off—'John, you should paint this, and John you should paint that'—as if I needed to sell through him. He doesn't seem to understand that I paint what I want now. I'm well past those abominable society portraits." He laughed at his own good fortune. "What are you working on? Something I might be interested in?"

"I'm not sculpting at the moment. I'm going to France to aid the war effort."

Sargent arched a brow. "Have you been there? Do you know what it's like?"

"No, my mother wanted to take me there when I was a child—"

Sargent cut her off with a wave of his hand. "Mrs. Swan, may I tell you something?"

"Of course."

His forehead furrowed, as if a morbid intensity had seized him and a series of horrifying pictures had formed in his mind. "This war is unlike anything ever conceived by man and can only be the devil's work. If Satan exists, his claws have gouged holes in the earth and left them filled with blood. I've seen it. I've painted it—the death, the destruction, the overwhelming sadness of it all.

"Certainly, it's the good fight, but so many soldiers and innocents have died. And for what? A mile of turf at the Front, only to be pushed back two kilometers, only to repeat the process the next month. The cost has been enormous—hundreds of thousands of lives. If you go, Mrs. Swan, be prepared for horrors you never dreamed possible. The France of your dreams is not the France you will see today . . . nearly every country in Europe has suffered the same fate."

Emma was about to reply when laughter erupted near the ballroom door.

Sargent stared, fascinated by the commotion.

Emma turned to see Alex and Vreland supporting a tipsy Linton Bower.

"So, this is the state of modern art," the painter said. He coughed and the beginnings of a smirk transformed into a quizzical smile.

"Pardon me," Emma said, making her excuses. "I believe this may be the moment to collect my commission."

"An excellent strategy, Mrs. Swan. Good evening. It's been a pleasure seeing you again, and do take care in France." Sargent picked up his wineglass and reached for another cigarette.

Emma looked for Anne. She was in the garden, still fascinated by the young man who had inched closer to her on the marble bench. Then she directed her attention to Linton, Vreland, and Alex, who as a trio walked somewhat unsteadily toward the food table. Mrs. Livingston, always the charming hostess, greeted them discreetly and then brushed past as if Linton's tipsiness was cause for some uneasiness. Emma made her way across the room.

Vreland spotted her first, his slightly drunken smile turning to a sneer.

Emma sensed an uncomfortable condescension flowing from the critic and Alex.

"Mrs. Swan. Care to join us in a drink?" Vreland asked.

"No," Emma replied, "your head start has put me at a disadvantage."

"Oh come now, Emma," Alex said, "we're celebrating Linton's success."

"Success?" she asked.

Vreland lifted the cover of a chafing dish and replaced it quickly after wrinkling his nose. "I don't care for rare beef," he said and turned to Emma. "Yes, since my article about Linton and the Fountain Gallery appeared, Linton has sold . . . how many paintings, Alex?"

"Six more," Alex said proudly. "Eleven in total."

She looked at Linton, who had avoided looking at her since hearing her voice. "Eleven. That's a remarkable achievement—particularly in wartime."

"An excellent point, Mrs. Swan," Vreland said. "I shall have to point that out in my next article: how the Boston art market is prospering thanks to patrons like Mrs. Gardner and Mrs. Livingston—and in no small part, if I do say so myself, to my own efforts to bear the art standard."

"The Pershing of the art world," Emma said.

Linton's filmy eyes fluttered at her sarcasm, and in them she detected a deep sadness.

"Please don't spoil the evening for us . . . for me," he said. "These celebrations are so rare in the life of an artist. Surely you understand that."

Emma moved toward him. "May I speak to you privately?"

Vreland shrugged and Alex reluctantly let go of Linton's arm.

"Don't be long, Linton," the gallerist said. "We have a big night ahead of us."

Linton nodded as Emma took his arm and led him toward the garden.

The sun had set behind the high walls and the crepuscular birds had begun their mournful calls. The shafts of green, the red and yellow early roses, the purple blooms of the rhododendrons glowed in the twilight. The dark beauty of the moment sent chills coursing through Emma's body. Had she the power, she would have frozen time, the evening was so lovely. She guided him past the bench where Anne and the young man talked, onto a white stone path that led deeper into the lilacs and evergreens.

"Why haven't you called on me?" Linton asked as they stopped near a whitewashed rose trellis.

"I could ask the same question," Emma answered.

"Congratulations on the sale of *Diana*."

Indeed, the whole world knew of her sale. "Thank you."

Linton rubbed his eyes and then took hold of Emma's shoulders. He turned her toward the ballroom doors, so he could see into the light that shone from the house into the garden. "You're wearing a red dress—dark, the color of blood."

"Maroon sounds much better."

Linton took her hands and pulled her gently toward him.

"Not here," Emma protested. "We've done enough damage."

"To hell with them," he said. "They don't know anything about me . . . about us . . . they're just a bunch of society busybodies—good-for-nothing sycophants who've never had to earn a real dollar in their lives. I'd be done with the lot of them if I could."

"Linton, you're drunk." Emma pulled away from his grip and walked under the trellis.

"Perhaps, but when I'm near you. . . ." He stumbled toward her.

She caught him in her arms.

"You can't deny it," he said.

Emma pushed him away. "There can be no *us*, Linton. There's an attraction—a schoolboy and schoolgirl crush. We've got to recognize what's going on." Emma attempted to keep her voice down, out of Anne's hearing, but with every attempt to quiet herself she felt herself breaking apart, on the verge of tears. "You are a wonderful man, you are handsome and creative; but I'm a married woman with a husband. Do you realize what we would have to sacrifice to make this relationship work—if it would work at all? I can't take that risk. Can you understand?"

The finality of her question crushed her and her voice verged on a moan as the dark fell around her. She had advanced the same arguments that Karl had used years earlier and she hated herself for it. Any romance with Linton was dead; only the sanctity of her vows and the plodding security of her marriage remained. Her reputation and the only real security she'd ever had in the world would be gone if she pursued Linton. Disgraced, they would have to slink from Boston to another city, living in poverty if their art failed to sell. The shame of her final days with Kurt returned to haunt her again. She was in no position to love another man.

Linton wrapped his hands around the trellis and lowered his head. "I do understand and that's the tragedy of it. We should be . . . that's the only way I can say it, Emma . . . we *should be* together, and because we're not, it's tearing me apart. Another time, another place, and we could be together."

"I'm leaving for France as soon as I can."

His head jerked upright and a look of terror swamped his face.

"To the war?"

"I can do meaningful work in France. Facially disfigured soldiers need me. A doctor in England makes masks for seriously wounded men and I plan to use his techniques in Paris. I'm going to give injured men back their faces and, I hope, their lives."

Linton leaned against the trellis and chuckled through the sadness that filled his voice. "And you, a sculptress, who's afraid of faces. . . ."

"Perhaps I will get better. . . ."

"Giving men back their lives, while taking mine. . . ."

"I'm sorry. I've made my choice." The soft light from the ballroom, the music from the string trio filtered into the garden.

He swayed unsteadily as a tear slid down his cheek. "I'll miss you more than you'll know." With that, he turned, lurching with outstretched arms toward the doors, brushing past Anne and the young man on the bench, stumbling as he reached the steps, falling to his knees on the brick.

Emma, seeing his fall, rushed toward him.

Anne and the young man rose to help.

However, Alex, at the threshold with a ready hand, reached down, grabbed the painter's forearm, and lifted him from the steps.

Emma came upon Linton, but in her shame and sorrow, could offer him no consolation.

"I'll take care of him," Alex said and cradled the distraught man in his arms.

Emma called for Anne, who, after a hasty good-bye to the young admirer, followed her through the chatter and laughter of the ballroom and out the door of Mrs. Livingston's home. They had passed the hostess, Mrs. Gardner, and Sargent without saying a word. They rode home in silence for Emma had nothing in her heart but a bitter sadness.

2nd July, 1917
My Dearest Emma (from somewhere in France):
I'm sorry it's been so long, but correspondence between us has played second fiddle to my work. I do have good news, however. I received your letter and was thrilled to know you are coming to France. As yours crossed the Atlantic, my letter traveled to England to uncover more details about Mr. Harvey, who responded almost immediately. He was a bit skeptical at first, but overall, I believe he's a kind and generous man. With prodding, he shared, as much as he could by letter, the particulars of his amazing therapies. It begins this way. . . .

PART THREE

THE ATLANTIC AND FRANCE
AUGUST 1917

CHAPTER 4

She clutched the iron railing at the ship's bow and looked out over the gently rolling gray sea. The ocean had calmed after several days of squally weather, but the relentless clouds of the North Atlantic retained their stranglehold on the sky. The ship appeared to be sailing into a murky void, where sky and sea melded as one at the horizon. Except for a few officers busy with duties, and several soldiers who craved an early smoke, the deck was ghostly and empty just after dawn.

Emma scanned the leaden waters like a sentinel. Port and starboard, left and right. She had made it her business to learn nautical terms before she boarded the *Catamount*. Off starboard, a cruiser; another troop ship, the *Santa Clara*; and a destroyer sailed toward Europe on the ashen sea. The same configuration steamed off port. A fuel ship chugged safely in the middle of the convoy. The vessels formed an impressive iron triangle of men and weapons bound for France, a tactical response to Germany's unrestricted submarine warfare.

She would not have been on board at all, if not for the efforts of an American Expeditionary Force recruiting officer in Boston. She intended to work in conjunction with the Red Cross, like her husband. Her only goal, after the recent upheavals in her life, was to get to France and begin her education with her new mentor, the surgeon Sir Jonathan Harvey. The AEF officer had been at first uninterested, particularly because she was a woman standing in a line of men offering to serve. As Emma explained her situation, the recruiter's attention shifted from benign to rapt.

"You can help the wounded in that way?" he asked. "I've never heard of such a thing."

"The technique is performed in England," Emma said. "I plan to open a studio in Paris to serve the wounded French and our own troops. All this work is based on the efforts of Sir Harold Gillies and his success in plastic surgery."

The officer pursed his lips and studied her from head to toe, as if he were about to enlist her. "Let me take your information. I know a colonel who knows the commander of the Port of Embarkation . . . you realize there will be paperwork, letters to write, documents to obtain."

Emma gave the recruiter her name, address, and telephone number and thanked him. A few days later she received a call from the colonel asking her to explain her plan in detail. After their conversation, the officer seemed pleased and instructed her to send a letter to him summarizing their talk. If Emma was approved, travel accommodations would be made, the trip dangerous, and the government absolved of any responsibility for her safety. After an agonizing two weeks, during which she lived much like a hermit, avoiding Linton, Louisa, and other friends, she received a telegram giving her clearance to travel to France aboard a troop ship.

Emma accepted the conditions and a flurry of activity began: calls to her mother, who had sold many of the horses and dispensed with Matilda's services, although Charis still lived at the farm; conversations with Tom's parents; arrangements with Anne for running the household and caring for Lazarus; settling last-minute financial matters; distilling her possessions into one large suitcase and a purse. She sent several telegrams to Tom telling him as much as she could—without giving details that would be censored. In the midst of all this, she received her commission check for *Diana*. Alex would only reveal it was purchased by a buyer who wished to remain anonymous.

Emma purposely kept her good-byes to a minimum. She wanted no parties—no forced farewells with Louisa and the rest of Boston society, no tearful scenes with Linton. The night before her departure she dined with Anne in the courtyard. Lazarus lay in the sitting room, his nose poking over the threshold of the French doors. The evening was tranquil and warm and Anne shed a few tears as she cleared the last of the dishes and said farewell to Emma.

On deck, the wind lashed her body, but instead of a stinging force she felt exhilarated, hardly believing she was on a troop ship in the North Atlantic less than three days from France. Her farewell in Boston, the bumpy train ride to New York, the ferry trip from Manhattan to Hoboken, the silent men in spectral columns filing onto the ships, the departure from New Jersey— all seemed a distant memory. But as time passed and the convoy crossed the sea, Emma knew she and the ships would enter even more dangerous waters—those occupied by German submarines.

Several of the men, polite and respectful, questioned Emma about her presence aboard the *Catamount*. One of them, from Kansas, was especially interested in her story.

"Are you a doctor?" he asked, offering her a cigarette. It was evening, before sunset, and the suffocating canopy of clouds had broken temporarily. Threads of yellow light fell like buttery necklaces on the waves. He was a few years younger, with thin light-brown hair streaming back from a high hairline, wire-rimmed spectacles arching across an aquiline nose, and a wide, infectious smile. He was, in his own charming way, handsome.

She refused his offer of a smoke. "No, I'm not a doctor. I'm a sculptress."

"Do you have a beau?" he asked somewhat wistfully after asking her name. She looked down at her naked left hand. She had left her wedding ring in Boston as Tom had done when he departed, the risk of losing them too great. Tom had told her that leaving the ring was "one more reason to come home."

"I'm married. My husband is a doctor with the Red Cross in France."

The soldier's cheeks flushed. "I'm a bachelor. I suppose it's better that way . . . in case something should happen."

Emma shifted uneasily and repositioned the wind-whipped stray curls of hair on her forehead. "Don't be morbid. No good can come from tempting fate."

"Did you see the men as they came aboard? I'm an officer, as most of us are, and I know what my comrades are thinking. Death is behind every man, one hand on the shoulder, guiding us to France. Boarding was like a funeral march rather than a celebration. What are the odds I'll be alive next year? I guess I'm lucky not to have a girl, and certainly better off without a wife and children. My parents will be saddened by my death, but they have my sister to give them grandchildren."

"You sound as if your death is a certainty."

"My father always told me to be prepared 'to meet your Maker.'"

Emma was touched by the officer's frankness; however, the sincerity of his argument troubled her. The war had been far removed from Boston. Even so, many men and women were easily caught up in its fervor. She had avoided the destructive thoughts of what might happen to Tom, or, for that matter, what might happen to the world, much like someone diagnosed with a deadly disease who would throw themselves into life rather than obsessing about the malady. Now, under the conspicuous gaze of the officer, she felt the *possibility* of death. The AEF recruiter in Boston had informed her of the risks, so had the government, but here were men who were fighting for various reasons—freedom, Democracy, a hatred of Germans or the Austro-Hungarians, even serving to earn a living—and willingly sailing to their own extinction. She looked out across the sea, as it darkened in the fading light, and wished the officer had never offered her his attention.

"War isn't as romantic as the world would have us think," she finally said. "'The war to end all wars,' indeed."

"Yes, it was romantic—at first," he replied, "like the day I left Caney station, when I boarded the train, the Stars and Stripes waving wildly in the south wind, the red, white, and blue bunting flapping against the troop cars. The gusts swept away the smoke from the fireworks. As the crowd cheered and my mother dried her tears, I understood strength, bravery, and devotion for the first time. When the train pulled away, she shouted for me to come home soon, that time and God would aid my safe return. But this war isn't about me or any individual soldier . . . I'm just a speck. The strength, bravery, and devotion my family thinks I displayed are carried by the collective forces on these ships. That's what makes the war worth winning. Our men—our nation." The officer inhaled deeply from the stub of his cigarette and then flicked it into the ocean. "Time for lights out," he said. "It's been a pleasure, Mrs. Swan. I hope to see you on deck again. If I can be of service, please ask."

Emma smiled and offered her hand. "Thank you for your kindness. I'll remember your name." She reached for his identity tags. "Lieutenant Stoneman . . . Lieutenant Andrew Stoneman."

After her conversation with the officer, Emma's stomach roiled. She brought a small plate of food from the galley back to her tiny cabin near the captain's quarters. A ship's officer had relinquished his own accommodations when he learned of Emma's passage and offered to bunk with another man. Emma gladly agreed to the arrangement.

The ship pitched and yawed more than usual, in rough seas south of the Irish coast. Emma picked at her bread, beans, and salty pork and then put the plate on the cabin deck. It scraped back and forth as the vessel rolled with the waves. She took a book from her bag and dropped it on her bed; however, as she flipped through the pages, her desire for reading ebbed. She flipped the electric switch and the cabin plunged into utter darkness; the porthole had been blacked out to lessen the chances of an enemy attack. She crawled into bed and pulled the wool blanket over her.

Dreams of Linton modeling for *The Narcissus* were coursing through her head when a *bang* shook her from her sleep. She bolted upright, terrified by the loud noise and its possible ramifications, her hair brushing against an iron beam near the porthole. Frantic curses and shouts filtered into her cabin from the passageway. She peered around the door to see soldiers, most without shirts, pulling on their woolen trousers, scrambling through the narrow enclosure while carrying lanterns, the beams of light bouncing off the bulkheads. She pulled on her robe and stepped into the passage as a wave of officers, scurrying to get from the quarterdeck to the main deck, nearly knocked her over.

"What's going on?" Emma asked a soldier caught in the rush.

"German sub," he said as he hoisted suspenders over his bare shoulders.

"Are we sinking?" Emma asked.

"Don't know yet, ma'am," he replied and pushed on.

Emma was uncertain what to do, but thought of grabbing her bag and heading for a lifeboat. The fates of the *Titanic* and the *Lusitania* were still fresh in the minds of every Atlantic voyager. The prospect of abandoning a troop ship in the dark North Atlantic waters was terrifying; however, doing nothing in her cabin, waiting for the vessel to sink, was an even bleaker prospect.

Her cabin door rocked violently as the ship pitched. Sporadic bursts of light from the corridor flashed into her cabin and then disappeared when the door slammed shut. She fumbled in the dark, grabbing her life preserver, tying her robe securely, opening the door once again, and stepping into the line of soldiers. The men flowed like ants up the ladder, extinguishing their lamps as they rose to the main deck. The ship throttled back as if the engines had been cut and the forward motion of the vessel became less like climbing a mountain and more like a walk over soft, rolling hills.

The wind smacked her face as she stepped on deck, the sky as black as her cabin. She grabbed the cold metal railing at the top of the ladder. The men closest to her looked past the main deck into the inky darkness, none of them speaking. Occasionally, one pointed toward the bow or the stern, the other men turning their heads accordingly. Emma inched toward the bow, clinging to the bulkhead as she walked. No one seemed to notice her.

As she passed the superstructure and emerged, unprotected, on the bow, she marveled at the sight before her. Men swarmed into the triangular point, many half-dressed, seemingly unaware of the gale that swept over them. Emma folded the lapels of her robe around her neck. As her eyes adjusted, she discerned the vague forms of the other ships in the convoy. Some bucked against the strong waves, making frothy ninety degree turns away from the *Catamount*. A breathtaking blast of wind hit her body and she looked toward the sky. Grayish-black clouds streaked overhead while pinpoints of stars sparkled through the broken overcast.

"Enjoying your stroll?"

Emma jumped, startled at the unexpected question. She wheeled to see Lieutenant Stoneman standing behind her.

"My God, you scared the life . . ."

"I'm sorry," he said. "But you do stand out in a crowd—"

A sharp flash cut across the bow, followed by a noise that sounded like a buzz-saw blade whizzing through the air. A hundred yards ahead of the ship, the ocean exploded in white foam. Emma screamed and grabbed the lieutenant's arm. The ship cut its speed again, nearly pitching both of them to the deck. She steadied herself by grabbing the officer's waist. A few seconds later, another volley whizzed in front of them, resulting in an explosive clap and a turbulent geyser of water mushrooming into the air.

An officer ran past. "A destroyer's been hit!"

The men split to port and starboard, searching for the damaged ship.

Emma looked behind Andrew toward the stern.

Lights flickered on what appeared to be a far-off vessel, but they blinked off as quickly as they had come on and the ocean was once again a dark void.

"Have we been hit?" Emma asked.

"I doubt it," the lieutenant said. "We'd feel a shift in the ship's motion and there's been no general alarm. I imagine those volleys were fired at a possible German sub, but there was no secondary explosion below the surface. I think it's safe for you to go back to your cabin. I must say good night, Mrs. Swan." He resumed his push to the bow and disappeared into the swarm of soldiers.

Emma, shivering as the cold wind cut through her robe, lingered on the deck until she was sure it was safe to go below. Men drifted about with no definitive word on the destroyer's fate. Finally, she followed a small group of officers to the ladder and descended, with the aid of lamps, to the passageway that led to her cabin. She said good night to the men and opened the door.

Two fat, squealing, gray rats jumped over the threshold and scurried between her feet. Turning to see what had caused the commotion, the men laughed at her screams and unintended jig. Furious at her timorous display, she slammed the door and made her way back to the bunk, but not before her toes had squished into the plate of unfinished pork and beans that had served as a late-night snack for the rodents.

She struggled to get up the next morning. Judging from the creaking moans of the ship, the seas were rougher than the previous night—if that was possible. She was exhausted from dreams about drowning in an ocean filled with injured men and rats, and her nerves still jangled from the submarine excitement. She dressed and then crossed to the head to wash her face and comb her hair. Picking up the plate in her cabin, disgusting as it was, she carried it to the galley, her body nearly tossed into the bulkhead several times by the vessel's rocking.

A few soldiers sat eating breakfast; others were leaving to

attend to duties. After her inquiry, one man explained that the submarine sighting had been a false alarm and that no convoy ship had been damaged or sunk. A lookout had spotted an unusual wake on the frothy sea and sounded the alarm. Most of the men attributed the wake to a whale or a dolphin pod, not a torpedo. Emma sighed and tried to eat the watery scrambled eggs in front of her, but instead of providing nourishment the food turned her stomach, her head swimming with the ship's motion. The French coast couldn't arrive soon enough.

As she put down her fork, a roar rose from above, echoing down the passageway. Emma shoveled her eggs into the slop bucket and hurried to the top deck with those few men who had remained below. She worked her way to the bow until she could see swells rising like blue hills on the vast ocean. On the undulating horizon, dipping between the waves, like phantoms emerging from the hills, a column of American destroyers bounced into view. The men cheered as the ships bore down upon the *Catamount*, circling the convoy in a wide arc. Soon, the whole assembly, American flags waving in the wind, was in formation and on its way to France.

That evening, the sea calmed.

The excitement and tension created by the voyage had left her feeling alone and bound by her own thoughts. Aboard the ship, she had created artistic and emotional diversions, reading and sketching when she could, pining for Linton many times, particularly at night when she settled into her bunk. She discouraged those thoughts as best she could, relegating them to an uneasy past while looking toward an uncertain future. Often, loneliness shuddered over her when she walked the main deck, gazing out to sea, alone with her musings.

For much of the voyage, the soldiers had been intent on war preparations, duties that required their attention—to her neglect—something she accepted wholeheartedly. Mostly, the men passed by with hardly a glance; some smiled and said hello. A few times she watched their morning drills on the main deck, thinking the soldiers acted more like excited schoolboys rather than men going off to battle. The reality of what they would face in Europe saddened her.

In her cabin, Emma heard steps in the passageway, and recognized the voice of Lt. Stoneman calling for her. At first she was wary of the officer, but after the long days at sea, she looked forward to his company because he was the closest she had to a friend aboard the *Catamount*.

He carried a shore-to-ship message. He sat at the foot of her bunk as Emma read it.

"It's from my husband." She folded the paper and placed it on the blanket between them. "We're less than a day away from France, and I still don't know where he is."

"He could be anywhere, but if I had to guess, I'd say he's serving near Toul," the officer replied.

"Where's that?" She knew something of French geography, but was unfamiliar with the city.

"East of Paris, near Nancy. There's a large troop presence. . . ."

Emma expected more from the officer, but no words came forth.

"I should keep my mouth shut," he finally said, a slight blush rising on his cheeks. "I have to treat everyone—even my own men—as the enemy until marching orders have been given. Fortified locations, troop movements, camps are carefully guarded secrets."

"I understand," Emma said. She leaned back against her thin pillow and studied the officer.

He smiled weakly and fidgeted with his fingers.

"I didn't mean to make you uncomfortable. I only wondered why you think Tom may be at Toul?"

"There's a good chance," he said. "I'm sorry, I've said more than I should have. I must be going."

He shifted, but Emma tapped his arm and smiled. "You have a wonderful face. Would you mind if I sketched you? It would make me happy."

Andrew laughed and stroked the smooth skin of his bare chin. "I guess I could spare a few minutes."

She reached under the bunk and produced a pad and pencil, the only art supplies she brought on the voyage because she planned to buy new materials in Paris.

She said little as she sketched. The lieutenant's glasses masked some of his features—a thin, but finely shaped nose and luminous hazel eyes—but there was more to see through her artist's vision: a wide forehead, thinning brown hair, and a jaw that clenched whenever he smiled.

He seemed intrigued by her talent and watched as her hands skimmed over the page. After several minutes, he asked, "May I look?"

Emma turned her pad toward him.

The officer's reaction was muted; he neither smiled nor frowned. In fact, she thought his mood inscrutable. "Don't you like it?" Her insecurities about faces rose again.

"No, it's not that." He touched the paper and a smudge of charcoal transferred to his finger. "It's quite good. I've never seen a drawing like it, however."

"You know art?" Emma asked, astonished that a man from Kansas would have any knowledge about the subject.

"We're not all farm boys," he said, picking up on her implication. "I attended the University of Kansas in Lawrence for two years. I studied art as well as the classics." He stopped and stared again at his likeness. "I hope you don't mind my saying so, but my face seems odd—I don't know how to describe it—like it's real, but not quite real."

Emma sighed. "You've hit upon the bane of my artistic existence. Have you heard of Winslow Homer, the painter and watercolorist?"

The lieutenant nodded.

Emma turned the pad toward her and continued sketching. "Some critics say he doesn't paint figures well because the human body is his curse. His paintings are full of light, color, and action; yet, his figures are stiff and uncomfortable on the canvas. I've heard the same said about my sculptural faces . . . recently, as a matter of fact."

"I'm sure your sculptures are beautiful . . . the critics must be wrong."

"Thank you, Lieutenant, but there's no need for false praise when you've so clearly identified the problem." She continued sketching.

After a few minutes, the officer said, "I have duties on deck." He stood up, instinctively taking care not to bang his head on the low overhead.

"Wait," Emma said. "I want you to have this." She hurriedly drew a few strokes on the page, tore the sheet from the pad, and handed it to him.

Holding it gingerly in his hands, he inspected it. "I will keep it in my kit as a treasure . . . but there's one problem . . ."

"What's that?" Emma asked, expecting another comment on her artistic ability.

"I want a signed Emma Lewis Swan." He handed her the drawing.

Emma signed it in the lower right-hand corner: *To Lt. Andrew Stoneman, from Emma Lewis Swan.* And on the back she wrote: *August 1917. Somewhere in the Atlantic. To your safe return to the United States. Your loving friend, Emma.* She handed the portrait to him.

The officer read the inscription and smiled. "Here's to *our* safe return. I'll see you when we depart ship." He turned and left the cabin.

The engines chugged below, a constant but sometimes mournful sound, over the calm waters. She fluffed the pillow and the hum of the ship reinforced her solitude, as if she were floating alone on the immense sea. She had little desire for supper, and, as the night wore on, she read for an hour before falling into a sleep deeper than any she'd experienced since leaving Boston.

*   *   *

Early the next morning, Emma stood on the bow with soldiers who cupped their hands to shield their eyes from the eastern sun, their gazes fixed on a hazy spit of land on the horizon. Happy the night had passed uneventfully after the previous night's submarine scare, she craned her neck to see what the men said was the French coast. "Do you know where we're landing?" she asked one of them. No one had told her where the ship would eventually dock.

"I guess it's safe to say," one of the officers said. "We found out this morning. We're docking at Saint-Nazaire."

Emma motioned for him to proceed. The name meant nothing to her.

He continued. "At the mouth of the Loire."

She nodded halfheartedly, attempting to construct a map of France in her head. However, there was no spot on her imagined map for Saint-Nazaire.

The morning was fresh: the wind off the ocean swirled past her face; she inhaled deep draughts of air. It smelled different near the coast than on the high seas; the odor of fish and silt overpowered the crisp salinity of the ocean. The sun glinted in large patches on the green water.

A chorus of whoops and cheers arose from the deck. Emma cupped her right hand over her eyes and looked toward the emerging coastline. Then she saw them—a row of fishing boats cutting madly through the waters toward their convoy, escorts to their already formidable firepower. On the distant vessels, tiny figures scrambled forward, men waving their arms, proudly holding French and American flags. Emma looked across the *Catamount*'s bow, the men crowding as far forward as they could, joyous and smiling in anticipation of the French landing. She marveled at their spirit, living for the moment, unfazed by the hooded specter of death. She steeled herself to be as brave as those men around her and recalled Sargent's words: "Mrs. Swan, be prepared for horrors you never dreamed possible."

The boats circled the convoy and then, like an armada, they

steamed toward the coast. Emma stood on deck, feeling secure as part of the fleet. Someone tapped her shoulder.

The lieutenant smiled at her. "We're not out of danger yet," he said in a low voice.

"Ever the bearer of good news?"

"The Germans patrol the Loire daily. It's more perilous than the open ocean, but we'll be in port soon and then most of the danger will be over . . . if we don't get torpedoed as we dock." He gave her a sly smile.

"Your humor is a bit ghoulish for such a joyous morning," Emma said.

The men gathered on deck broke into a spontaneous chorus of "Over There."

Lieutenant Stoneman mouthed the words and thrust his fist into the air as the men sang, *"That the Yanks are coming, the Yanks are coming."*

Emma listened as the green fields, the sparse trees, and the raking white shore of the coast crept ever closer.

"A New York soldier on board learned this song directly from the composer," he said. "It's spreading like a Kansas wildfire in March." His mood quickly darkened. "God and death watch over us," he continued over the raised voices. "In a war, you can't tell who's calling the shots."

"I vote for God," Emma said. "How long until we dock?"

"An hour or two at most. You might want to gather your things."

"I'll go below, then." Emma smiled and looked up into his face. "I do hope we meet again under more pleasant circumstances." She thrust out her hand.

He shook it lightly. "Perhaps we'll meet again. How will you get to Paris?"

"As best I can. By rail, I hope. If I have to, I'll hire a driver— by car or mule. Then, I'll plan a reunion with my husband at Toul, or wherever he may be."

"Lucky man," he said and kissed her hand. "The pleasure

has been mine." With that he withdrew and left her standing with the soldiers.

"Remember your portrait," she shouted after him.

"For good luck," he shouted back.

"For good luck," Emma whispered as the officer disappeared from view.

The coast of France glided by the convoy; the sun and the breeze buoyed her. At that moment, she had few cares in the world other than how to get to Paris.

She opened a telegram an officer handed her as she disembarked, stopping in the sun near the gangplank. While she read, the soldiers filed into formation on the dock to shouted cadences.

My Dearest Emma:
With all hope and prayers, this should find you well in France. Contact Dr. Harvey, 56 rue de Paul, Paris, for full details.
Your husband,
Tom

The estuary smelled of fish and fuel, unpleasant really, but Emma was happy to have her feet back on the ground—albeit more than three thousand miles from home. Aside from the general commotion of the soldiers and the drill formations, there seemed to be little activity in the port. No brass bands blasted patriotic tunes; no rifle salutes greeted the arriving troops; no French citizens, aside from those on the fishing boats, waved the Tricolor. Emma folded the telegram, placed it in her purse, lifted her suitcase, and strode toward the stone-and-brick buildings that bordered the edge of the harbor.

The city was oddly quiet, as if smothered by the war. Women and children wandered listlessly and the men who remained, all older and not called to service, gathered on the street corners to smoke or sip coffee. Time in Saint-Nazaire seemed measured by bombs and bullets and the deaths that haunted *Breton*, not by the passing hours.

"*Où est la gare?*"

The old man with the pipe stared at Emma as if the Virgin had arisen miraculously from the depths of the estuary. He muttered so quickly in French, between heavy draws on his pipe, that Emma couldn't understand him.

"*Répétez, s'il vous plaît,*" she said.

Her admonition only increased the man's agitation, causing her to be more confused by the lack of connection.

"The train station . . . the train station," Emma repeated loudly as if the emphatic English would have any effect. "I'm trying to find the train station. I'm hoping to get to Paris by the end of the day." Exasperated, she shook her head. "That and a bite to eat."

The man nodded excitedly as if he understood the word "eat." "Le Tonneau," he said, and pointed to a small storefront, with a green sign in the shape of a barrel hanging over the doorway, in the middle of the next block. Emma appreciated the man's recommendation. Hunger gnawed at her stomach, and any spot that served food would be welcome. In the excitement of sighting the French coast and packing for arrival, she had neglected to eat breakfast.

"*Merci, Monsieur,*" she said.

The man waved her toward Le Tonneau in a friendly gesture of encouragement.

A white cat had curled his sleek body into a ball in a sun-splashed chair outside the open door. Red geraniums bloomed in profusion from the window boxes. Inside, the café was considerably lighter and cheerier than Emma had expected from her initial impression.

A thin young woman with dark hair was washing glasses behind the counter. A look of concern flashed in her eyes, an initial distrust that remained unabated when Emma inquired in broken French about the train station and food. The two stood alone in the café.

"Where are you from?" the woman asked in English, a light French accent glazing her words.

"I'm glad you speak English," Emma said with relief. "I was beginning to feel like a stranger in a strange land."

"You are a stranger," the woman responded, neither smiling nor giving any hint of warmth or humor.

Emma was too tired to question her response. "Please, if you could direct me to the train station . . . if I could get something to eat, I'd be most grateful."

"Do you have money?"

Emma drew in a quick breath. Of course, she had dollars—but no francs. The thought of exchanging money had never crossed her mind. Embarrassment rose in her as she blushed from her own naïveté and lack of preparation.

The woman, who had perhaps experienced similar situations with American soldiers, regarded Emma's plight. "The station is up the street, away from the estuary. If you walk straight ahead you'll find it. The stationmaster will exchange your money because he is prepared for such situations. Don't be surprised if he charges you a fee—he earns extra for his family that way."

As the proprietress completed her instructions, a child darted in from the kitchen and ran to the woman. *"Maman, Maman,"* he shouted as he spotted Emma. He clutched his mother's black skirt and stared at the suitcase near Emma's legs.

"Chut," the woman chided him.

The boy grimaced and clenched his jaw. His thick black hair was chopped short in front; so much so, it resembled the points of a pinwheel; his handsome face was marked with reddish circles on olive cheeks. He was an angel living in a time of war. Emma understood the child's anxiety about the strange woman who stood before him, but she knew there were bigger terrors on French soil of concern to his mother.

"Thank you," Emma said to the woman, keeping her eyes off the child. She turned to leave the café.

"Where are you headed?" the woman asked.

"Paris." Emma looked over her shoulder at the pale visage.

The woman parted her lips but didn't smile. "Good luck. I don't think you Americans will be strong enough to win the war—to beat the Boche. I hope so, but I don't believe it. The Germans are invincible. I fear for our lives."

"Please . . . can the child understand? You'll frighten him to death."

"My son? He knows too well what war can do. His Italian father is dead—killed at the Front."

Pain spread over the woman's face, her eyes swelling as the lids reddened with sorrow. The boy called out again for his mother and clutched her skirt in his balled fists. Emma reached to comfort her, but the woman drew away.

"I'm sorry," Emma said, retreating, "I am truly sorry."

The woman composed herself and muttered, *"Bon voyage."*

Emma thanked her and walked out the door, past the napping cat, into the bright sunlight that filled the street like a soothing balm.

The boy's face from the café floated before her as she stared out the train window.

What remained of the watery reeds and willows slid by in a rush of green. She circled a finger against the glass, absorbed by the past, and then erased her hazy smudges with a handkerchief. For the first time in more than a week she was without the company of soldiers.

The branches of a dead tree flashed by the window, the skeletal limbs so close they scratched against the glass, causing Emma to flinch in her seat. A woman across the aisle stared at her for a moment, then averted her eyes and returned to her reading.

The unsettling day, the child, the dead tree, pushed unwanted thoughts into her head. *Faces. Why does everything revolve around the face?* She remembered the boy on the street in Boston who had made fun of the disfigured soldier, her *Diana,* the melting faun, the face of Linton Bower as Narcissus, the drawing of Lieutenant Stoneman, the boy she had encountered only a few hours before. That face had upset her the most.

She clutched her abdomen.

The woman looked up from her book again, eyed Emma suspiciously, and reached for her bag, as if contemplating a move to another compartment.

Emma smiled and removed her hands from her stomach.

The woman shifted warily, but remained in her seat.

Perhaps the brioche she had eaten before boarding had caused an intestinal upset. The stationmaster directed her to an old woman who sold the sweet rolls on the platform. But if she considered the truth, the cause of her upset, a memory that would not die—one that appeared like a phantom—terrified her and then vanished, reopening the wound it had carved years before. The faceless baby shocked her into rigidity, Emma grasping with stiff arms the seat in front of her, her breath rushing in and out of her lungs. Why was the horror, the remorse, so strong now that she was on the verge of working with faces and reuniting with Tom?

She shivered and focused her mind on her husband's picture in Boston, the familiar face comforting her. Soon she would be in Paris to begin a new phase of her life. Perhaps the faces from the past would fade as new ones were introduced.

A wounded French soldier on crutches, his right leg and shoulder swathed in bandages, his face partially covered in gauze, hobbled through the compartment. He turned his head and glanced at Emma, allowing her to see the dark recesses underneath the material, portions of his nose and mouth taken by the war.

The woman across the aisle frowned, waved her hands, and shouted in French above the train's clatter. Emma didn't understand the angry words but she knew the woman wanted nothing to do with the disfigured soldier—she wished him far away from her.

The man shrunk under the woman's withering barrage and lurched away.

Emma turned back to the window.

The train hissed to a stop at a village. The tracks had veered from the river's path and the land sloped higher now, purple hills filling the horizon. At the small wooden station, faces stared up at her from the platform. She turned away and closed her eyes.

Emma lifted the brass knocker at 56 rue de Paul. A sharp metallic ping reverberated through the building as she leaned against the door. The trip had been exhausting, but her excitement about being in Paris had shored up her failing energy somewhat.

Her hands trembled—whether from tiredness from the journey or the anticipation of meeting Dr. Jonathan Harvey, she was uncertain. She rested her suitcase against her leg and longed to be happy, *alive* in the City of Lights, free from Vreland and the faces that haunted her. She pressed her ear against the door and listened for any sign of life in the house.

The carriage ride from the train station had taken her through the Latin Quarter. Along the way, she spotted the massive dome of Montmartre, the airy latticework of the Eiffel Tower and the towering façade of Notre Dame. Like Saint-Nazaire and the villages and towns along the railway, Paris seemed crushed by the weight of the war. The overall mood tempered her excitement as a first-time visitor to the city. Doors and windows were shuttered, and the Parisians moved like phantoms, no small talk or laughter drifting to her ears. Parisian life had been transformed by the war—motorized ambulances, which doubled as troop carriers, rumbled through the city, replacing the clop of horses' hooves. Carts loaded with food sacks, folded tents, and artillery rolled down the streets. The war at the very least had muted Paris, the once lively city aiding and supplying the unfolding battle lines no more than one hundred kilometers away.

Emma sighed and lifted her head. A half moon shone in a milky blue sky as thin horsetails of clouds traced the heavens. At last, footsteps halted behind the door. The latch clicked and the door creaked open, revealing a young nurse in a starched white uniform. She was pretty, with the spark of youth behind her serious purpose. The woman's age, dark hair, and flashing eyes reminded her of Anne.

"*Bonsoir, Madame,*" the nurse said, stepping over the threshold and looking at the sky. "*Il se peut qu'il pleuve demain.*"

"*Pluie?* Rain?" Emma asked, unsure of her French.

"*Oui, demain.*"

"*Parlez-vous anglais?*"

"Of course," the nurse replied. "I must. I work for *Monsieur* Harvey."

"Is he at home? My husband directed me to come here." Emma opened her purse, pulled out the message she had received when the ship docked, and unfolded it for the young woman to see.

"*Oui, rue de Paul.* Monsieur Harvey has just returned from a walk. He's upstairs in the study." She motioned for Emma to enter the apartment. "However, it's not a real study . . . it's make . . . make . . . ?"

"Makeshift?" Emma asked.

"Yes, makeshift . . . office. I have trouble with some words."

Emma lifted her bag and followed the nurse into a hall still warm and humid from the day. Drawings and prints—wispy pencil landscapes of streams and willow trees, and etched still lifes of fruits and vegetables—decorated the whitewashed walls. A vase of yellow roses in full bloom sat on a black lacquer table. Several closed doors sealed off the end of the hall.

The nurse led Emma up a narrow staircase. "My name is Virginie. How was your trip? You are Madame Swan, I suppose. *Sir Jonathan* has been expecting you. Not many strange women show up at *cinquante-six rue de Paul.*"

Emma laughed, more from fatigue than humor. "This is at least the second time today, I've been referred to as 'strange'—well, a 'stranger.' I'm beginning to become quite comfortable with the word."

"*Etrange? Je suis désolée.*"

A voice boomed from a room at the top of the stairs. "Vir-

ginie, will you stop speaking that abominable language? I'm trying to work. How the devil can I concentrate with you clomping
up and down the stairs?"

Virginie stopped at an open door to the left of the landing and
motioned for Emma to enter. "His majesty will see you now."

Emma's throat tensed as though she, like Daniel, was about
to enter the lion's den. A robust man stood up from his chair
and extended his hand. This, Emma presumed, was Sir Jonathan Harvey, the renowned English surgeon and practitioner
of facial reconstruction. He was round and corpulent, wearing
a black jacket, not at all the serious, thin, bespectacled doctor
that Emma had constructed in her mind. She shook his hand as
vigorously as she could despite his crushing grip and wondered
if the doctor was always this cantankerous.

"Good night, *Monsieur,* I am finished for the day . . . thank
Our Lord. I will see you *demain.*" Virginie executed a mock
curtsy.

"Good night, yourself," the doctor replied, dismissing her
with a wave of his hand.

The nurse nodded and disappeared up the stairs to the third
story.

The doctor pointed to a chair across from his desk. Emma
placed her suitcase on the floor and watched as he shuffled his
papers, scattering pens, clips, and folders in the process.

"So, you've arrived at last," he said. He uncovered a cigarette
from under the jumble. "It's about time. I was bloody well ready
to return to England. I must be honest with you, Mrs. Swan,
we don't have much time." He lit the cigarette and smacked
his hand on the desk. "Damn . . . I've told that woman more
than once not to speak French in this house. How will she learn
English if she continually breaks her promise? I've taught her
nearly every word she knows."

"It appears she has more to learn," Emma said dryly.

"Hummmpph. She's obstinate and smart as a whip." The
doctor settled in his chair and stared at Emma. "I can see we
have a long journey ahead of us in a short time. You must be

prepared, Mrs. Swan, to learn as much as you can, as quickly as you can. I will not abide a slovenly or cavalier attitude from you, or from anyone else for that matter."

"You can rest assured that you will have my full attention, Sir Jonathan."

His fleshy mouth turned down at the corners. "Damn her, again. She'll be the death of me." He shook his head. "My name is Jonathan Harvey and I am, indeed, a 'Sir.' However, I am not as old as the Round Table, nor am I a member of the Royal Family. John will do, or Dr. Harvey if you prefer."

"John's a nice name. It has such a pleasant connotation with *Our Lord*," Emma said, hoping her sarcasm drove home the point. "You may call me Emma."

"I am in no way the equivalent of our Savior's baptizer," John said, glaring at her.

Emma smiled. "One doesn't need to attend church to discern that."

John inhaled and puffed smoke at Emma. "I can see we're going to get along famously. How serious are you about this work, Mrs. Swan?"

"Deadly."

He stared at her for a moment, inhaled again, and stiffened his back against the chair. His demeanor shifted from irritation to solemnity as a sudden flatness, as if he was deflated by the topic, spread across his round face. "You will see enough of death, Mrs. Swan, I can guarantee you. Death is easy enough to handle—it ends in cremation or in the ground as rot. It's your commitment to life I question. Can you deal with life?"

"Of course," Emma said, and her response struck her as absurd. *Everyone must deal with life and death. What an idiotic question from a doctor.* Irritated, Emma looked past him to a bookcase crammed with medical volumes and bric-a-brac. A young girl, dark hair curling down from the crown of her head to her temples, stared at her from a photograph, an angelic sweetness infusing her face. All children had that sweetness until they grew older and then were tainted, shunned, or spoiled by life. She shifted her gaze away from the child but just as quickly remembered the boy in Saint-Nazaire whose father had been killed.

"Is something wrong, Mrs. Swan?"

"Who is the girl in the photograph?" Emma asked, trying to disguise her discomfort.

"My niece. Why?"

"She's very pretty."

"Yes." John smiled and then puffed on his cigarette. "I understand your difficulties more than you think. Your husband informed me of your critical reception in Boston—your problem with faces. I know that's one of the reasons you're here—to study, to learn."

Emma nodded. "I would be lying if I told you 'no.'"

"Mrs. Swan, your life in Paris will be very different from your life in Boston. There will be no mucking about with Parisian society. No dainty hours playing with clay or counting the spots on your smock. No gay parties, expensive cigarettes, or champagne."

"I don't smoke and I'm hardly used to—"

"Work, work, and more work. Toil from dawn to the wee hours, until you want to crumble to your knees. Life for these men holds a completely different meaning from the existence you're accustomed to. You must stomach the most pathetic of stories, the most grotesque of faces." He rose from his chair, rummaged in the bookcase behind his desk, took out a black leather-bound volume, and placed it on the desk in front of her. "Go ahead," he said sullenly. "Open it."

Emma knew he was judging her expressions, her ability to be strong.

"Go ahead." He glowered at her, scratched the bald pate running down the center of his scalp, and then stuffed his cigarette into a crystal ashtray brimming with butts. "This is *our* work."

She opened the book and leafed through the pages, each filled with photographs of facially mutilated men. Had she not been prepared, in her own way, she might have been shocked by the pictures. The faces were disturbing: many without noses; some with huge gashes that had torn away cheeks and pieces of the skull; eyes blinded and clouded by the devastation of war; mouths reduced to thin slits or gaping holes; jaws crushed, broken, or grossly distended by grotesque wounds. Each photograph was followed by another showing the repairs the doctor had performed—in many cases the transformation was miraculous, in others the deformities showed through despite the best medical efforts.

"This is *our* work," he repeated. "It's our job to give these men back their lives, their self-respect, and their dignity."

Emma closed the book. "If you'll allow me to speak, Mr. Harvey?"

He nodded.

"I'm not the delicate flower you may have presumed. Perhaps my husband has painted the wrong picture of his wife . . . but that I cannot imagine." John raised his hand to protest, but Emma continued, "I am as dedicated to my art as my husband is to his surgery and saving lives. I have fought for my right to create my own life, free from bad memories, the constraints of critics and certain men for longer than I care to remember; and, my husband, gentleman that he is, has supported me in that endeavor. Still, my life has hardly been an endless round of parties or a vacuous holiday with silly women concerned only with the latest styles of clothes and hair. I have fought for my work, dodging barbs and prejudice along the way, and I will continue to do so regardless of our outcome here.

"However, to say my work in France, and for the war effort, is entirely altruistic would be false. I abhor this war, all who started it, and all that it stands for. But, I'm here to learn and I hope *our* work will make me a better sculptress—one who earns the admiration of critics and my fellow men alike."

"All noble sentiments . . . but we shall see, Mrs. Swan. The task is enormous." He picked up the book, returned it to the case. "Would you care for a drink? I do have a nice brandy knocking about somewhere." He offered his hand.

Emma shook it and nodded. "I could do with something to eat as well."

"I can find my way around a kitchen as competently as Virginia." John smiled and motioned to the door. "I'll show you to your room. Mrs. Clement, the housekeeper, is not here until tomorrow morning. You *are* staying the night, of course, and you are welcome to stay as long as you wish, or until you find your own quarters."

Emma was surprised, but she rose from her chair and lifted her bag. "I'm grateful for your hospitality, John."

They were about to leave the office when they were interrupted by a vigorous knock, which reverberated through the downstairs hallway.

"Damn," he said, "I don't know what I pay that confounded woman for—retired at this hour, while I'm still working. Excuse me, while I see to the door. Your room, at least for tonight, is on the first floor at the back of the house. It's dark, but comfortable. Follow me."

John bounded down the stairs, his jacket flowing around him. Emma was somewhat in awe of his agility despite his size. At the landing, he pointed to a closed door down the hall.

"Let me see who this is. Put away your things and I'll knock when I'm done."

Emma nodded and walked toward the room. Her curiosity about the caller got the better of her and she looked back as the doctor opened the door.

A soldier, clad in a buttoned service jacket, trousers, puttees, and ankle boots stood in the fading light. Fine strands of blond hair fell across his forehead when he removed his service cap. The soldier extended his hand to the doctor in greeting and then stopped as if startled by an apparition, his eyes widening and then shrinking, and as if blinded by something he had seen. He pulled the scarf concealing the bottom half of his face tighter and lowered his head.

The soldier's face unnerved her, leading her to think that perhaps her presence, an unknown woman in a place he had visited before, must have disturbed him. When she reached her room, she looked over her shoulder. The man's eyes bored into her as he followed John up the stairs.

Entry: 19th August, 1917

My journal appears no worse for wear after its voyage across the Atlantic. I suppose I shall open it from time to time to record my thoughts. It has become an old friend—one steadfast and reliable.

I feel sequestered here in John's house. He is a demanding man, but not quite the ogre that Virginie makes him out to be. He can't be all bad; how could he, doing the service he does? I think his jabs are a game. He torments Virginie (and the rest of his staff) in order to make her stronger. War is not for the faint of heart. But underneath John's gruff exterior lies a decent and caring soul. The thought of his return to England frightens me a bit. I will need Virginie's help, along with others, in order for my work to succeed.

I've had little time to think, to rest. John is relentless in his teaching and pushes me each day to learn more. I think of Tom on occasion, but not as often as I should, causing sporadic bursts of guilt. The studio has taken over my life. Of course, I imagine the same is true for Tom—once he was transported here, his surgical duties consumed him. I should be upset he hasn't telephoned me. However, he could say the same. I know his work is as demanding as his devotion to the Hippocratic Oath. Sometimes, I think he's like a boy playing doctor whose world has become violently real. But I'm ashamed when I fault a good man. American doctors are needed in France. I admire his willingness to serve.

My lack of attention to my husband has caused me some guilt. Under John's tutelage, I've remembered the faces I've seen since arriving in France: the child at Le Tonneau, the woman who sat across from me on the train, the injured soldier who struggled to walk on crutches in the compartment, the soldier who appeared at John's front door.

Each of these faces triggers a memory—one I'd rather forget.

"I told you so!" Virginie pounded her fist against the green truck's side panel as the rain pooled above her on the tarpaulin roof. "You have ruined Madame's visit to her husband."

John grimaced. "Hush up and climb in front with us! You'll catch your death." He turned to Emma. "She has *one* talent—predicting the weather. Damn this wretched rain." The tires spun furiously in the mud, sending an ear-piercing whine shrieking through the vehicle.

They were more than three-quarters of the way to Toul when the truck became mired on the muddy road. Emma had fought a case of nerves for most of the trip in anticipation of her meeting with Tom. Would they even recognize each other? Would he be the same person who left her in Boston nearly a half year ago?

"What?" Emma asked. "Are we stuck?" The sound of the tires being sucked into the mud forced her to abandon the prickly questions that disturbed her. Only sodden gray clouds and bent tree branches, laden with dripping leaves, lay ahead on the narrow road. She wondered if they would ever get to Toul.

"Damn it, woman—not you, too," John said to her. "You've been somewhere else this entire trip."

"*Sir* Jonathan!" Virginie yelled from the back, leaning over the luggage tops as she admonished him with a pointed finger. "Use Christian language when speaking to ladies."

"I'll not change the King's English one damn iota to suit you," he shot back. "And I certainly don't consider you a lady. I've never known a nurse who was." He pressed the accelerator, slapped the steering wheel, and cursed again. "I've had enough of her bloody weather prognostications. Her *alleged* clairvoyance is no reason to postpone a trip."

"John, I appreciate your concern in getting me to my husband so soon . . . but I . . . *we* could have—"

"Please don't aggravate me! I am agitated enough as it is. I jumped through hoops to find out where your husband was stationed—let alone commandeer an ambulance for two days." The truck's wheels sunk deeper into the muck. He disengaged the gearbox, opened the door, and stepped into the rain. "Nurse!" he shouted. "Up front and motor this truck. I'll push from the rear. Petrol is too precious to waste."

Emma watched as they sparred over control of the truck.

Virginie, who had been smart enough to wear a raincoat over her uniform, also held an umbrella. John held out his rain-soaked arms and guided the nurse over the tailgate.

She climbed into the driver's seat, her shoes, lower stockings, and the hem of her raincoat coated with mud.

"Carry on!" John shouted. "Full speed ahead. And I do mean *ahead*."

Virginie gripped the steering wheel throttle like a mechanic, her hands wrangling with the lever, her muddy shoe pressing the left pedal. The truck rocked forward by inches as John pushed. In a flurry of movement, she accidentally knocked the ambulance into reverse. The tires squealed in the mud.

"For God's sake, watch out!" John screamed. "Remember me?"

"*Mon Dieu*," Virginie whispered. She clutched the throttle and crammed it forward while lifting her foot from the pedal. "*Maintenant!*"

The truck lurched forward violently, nearly throwing Emma into the windscreen. It sped down the road until Virginie grabbed the floor lever. The ambulance slowed to a stop on an incline strewn with pebbles and rocks. Emma turned and peered through the rainy veil behind the truck.

John, spattered with mud, strode toward them in an angry gait and opened the door. He poked his reddened, grit-covered head inside. "You may drive, nurse. I'll ride the rest of the way in back. Just follow the kilometer posts to Toul."

"I know the road," she replied in a calm voice.

The truck sagged under John's weight as he climbed under the dripping tarp.

The rain relented somewhat as Virginie drove. The nurse dodged the large puddles and sticky mire, maneuvered past the few automobiles on the road, and slipped by slow-moving equine carts. Emma, with occasional shouted comments from John, listened to Virginie recount her hospital experiences, and how lucky John was to find her to work with his *mutilés*. The nurse also made it clear that he was not solely responsible for her command of English. A friend had taught her as well.

John swiped at his muddy clothes with a rag he found tied to a petrol can. Once he had cleaned up a bit, he became more animated, discoursing about his forays into facial reconstruction and mask-making techniques, giving him self-congratulatory pats on the back when needed.

The conversation died when the fortress city of Toul, enveloped in mist, appeared on the horizon.

"My God," Emma said. "A soldier on the ship thought Tom might be here." She turned in her seat and faced John, who hunkered clammy and wet in the truck bed.

He pointed to the east. "And thirty-five kilometers from here, men are dying at the Front—that is if they are fighting at all in this sloppy mess. The hospital isn't far. I've been here a few times."

In front of them, Toul's fortress walls rose from the sodden earth. At the perimeter, a cadre of French soldiers stopped the ambulance. After questioning them and inspecting the truck with the Red Cross emblem on its doors, the soldiers let them pass through the Porte de France. Emma had imagined a more pleasant reception for her reunion with Tom. Instead of a village surrounded by lavender fields, flowering pear trees, and a sunny square filled with fountains, Toul lay dank and desolate under the low, suffocating, sky. The city was quaint enough in its own right, but the streets were empty and water trickled in dark streams down its stone buildings. Here and there an electric lamp burned inside a shop, adding a small degree of cheeriness to the day. Emma thought she smelled sulfur in the air, perhaps the faint odor of spent gunpowder, but then considered her nose might be playing tricks on her.

The truck bounced over the cobblestone streets causing John, with each new jolt, to lambast Virginie's driving.

"Hush," the nurse countered.

John instructed her to turn left, and the street widened a bit. "There," he said, "the building with the flags."

Emma squinted through the grimy windscreen at a solid white structure dripping with French and Red Cross flags.

"*Voilà*," Virginie said. "We have arrived—safe and sound—despite the Germans and your driving, Sir Jonathan."

John elbowed the back of the seat and Virginie flinched.

The nurse attempted to park in a narrow alley next to the hospital, but the lane was crowded with ambulances. She continued down the street and stopped the vehicle in front of a deserted building.

Emma opened the door and stepped into the drizzle. The drive from Paris had taken more than twelve hours.

"Thanks for telephoning Tom last night," Emma said to John, as he shifted his large frame in the truck bed. "I've been so distracted."

John steadied his bulk against the side of the ambulance until his feet touched the street. "I don't know why I feel compelled to play matchmaker. One would think a husband and wife who hadn't seen each other for so long would be in closer contact."

Emma blushed and turned away.

"Tom was quite content when I talked to him—a bit bothered, but otherwise in fine spirits," he continued. "A surgeon is always busy during a war."

Emma led the way to the hospital, a stone building punctuated by a few windows and not as large as she expected. Apart from the word *Hôpital* over the door, one could have passed by it with little hint of the work going on behind the façade.

The nurse sitting behind the front desk greeted Emma with a flat "*Bonjour.*" The room smelled of antiseptic and rubbing alcohol. Several bearded men talked quietly or read a newspaper or book, crutches propped against their chairs. Another sat and rocked in a corner, muttered, and thrust his hands into the air, oblivious to the others around him. The left side of his face and top of his head were swathed in bandages.

Virginie took over the introductions in French. Emma picked out a few words—*d'accord, certainement, allons*—but most of the conversation was beyond her grasp.

"Well?" John interrupted. "Where is he?"

The nurse behind the desk scowled at the doctor.

"She thinks he has just come out of surgery," Virginie said. "Patience, patience. You English are so pushy."

"If the French had been more aggressive, this war would be over."

"You are wet, tired, and in a bad humor," Virginie said, holding back a snarl. "You must choose your words carefully, Sir Jonathan. Others may not be as forgiving as I."

"Please," Emma said, "we're all working for the same outcome—like the situation or not. The world has never seen a war like this."

The hospital nurse rose and climbed a staircase at the back of the room. An uncomfortable silence fell over Emma, Virginie, and John until she reappeared at the landing and motioned for them to come up.

Emma's pulse quickened.

Virginie was first up the stairs. At the top, Emma followed her down a narrow hall. From the adjacent rooms, injured men coughed or moaned. A row of overhead lights cast their dull shadows on a floor scuffed and muddy from the rain. The nurse led them past surgical quarters containing white beds and silver tables laden with bottles, stainless steel cutters, and clamps. In one room, a man lay covered to his neck with a white sheet, blood spreading like a crimson flower across his shoulders. At the end of the hall, the nurse turned right.

When Emma rounded the corner, she saw her husband, his white coat streaked and spattered with blood, talking to another doctor.

Tom spotted the group and a faint smile formed on his lips. He looked thinner, eyes sunken and dark, complexion sallow, his demeanor as fragile as a wounded butterfly, utterly lacking strength, as if a puff of wind might blow him away.

Emma resisted the temptation to rush to him and envelop him in her arms. From her hospital experiences in Boston she knew better—he would worry about the risk of contamination, of infection. Apparently, embracing his long-held apprehension, he walked toward her, passing Virginie and John. Tom bent down and kissed her forehead lightly.

Emma pursed her lips, but no kiss on the lips came.

The hospital nurse and the other doctor departed, leaving the four of them in the hall.

"You look tired," Emma said after Tom had greeted John and Virginie.

"Exhausted."

"Now that we're here, we'll leave you," Virginie said.

"That won't be necessary," Tom said.

"Of course not," John said enthusiastically. "We must discuss the business of Mrs. Swan's eventual control of the studio."

"*Arrêtez*," Virginie demanded. "Later. You can talk business—*ce soir.*"

"*Vous pouvez vous tuer à discuter, elle ne s'avouera pas vaincue pour autant*," Tom said.

"*Oui*," Virginie replied. "There *is* no arguing with me." She grabbed her boss by the sleeve and pulled him down the hall. "We will make our own rounds. *Tout de suite.*"

"But we have no rounds to make," John protested as Virginie led him away.

Tom smiled as the two disappeared, and then looked at Emma. The momentary happiness faded, the smile dropped away, and a melancholy look Emma had seldom seen her husband display blossomed on his face. In fact, the depth of his solemnity shocked her.

Tom pointed to a room across the hall. "My office. I share it with another surgeon, but he's off duty now."

She followed him into a sparsely furnished room where a small window offered a view of a stark building across the street.

Tom pulled the beaded chain on the desk lamp; the bulb crackled and threw out a bleak, dim light. "Toul is not Boston," he said as he closed the door. "Even the electric is suspect." He sat on the edge of his desk and looked at her.

Emma felt as if she were looking back at a stranger, but suppressed her unease and moved toward him.

Tom pointed to his blood-spattered coat and pushed back on the desk.

"Your French seems perfect," Emma said.

"When you use it every day for five months, you learn quite a bit." He tapped his fingers on the desk. "And I have nothing to do off duty but sleep and study the language."

"What's the matter?" she asked. "You don't seem yourself."

"I don't want to get blood on you. Nasty stuff is going round."

"Are you well? I've never seen you so thin."

He sighed. "As well as can be expected. And yourself?"

Emma sank into a chair, stared at her hands, and considered how to reply to his question. Finally, after a time, during which her face reddened and her muscles tensed, she blurted out, "Our troop ship avoided attack by German submarines, I landed in France with only American dollars, managed a train ride to Paris, and now reside with a pedantic English physician who's offered me the companionship of his French nurse and housekeeper, neither of whom can stand *him*. And all you can ask is 'And yourself?'"

Tom groaned and shifted on the desk.

"No, really, Tom, I'm sorry to make you uncomfortable, but I left Boston, traveled three thousand miles for a new life—after you uprooted ours with your generous spirit. Please understand me—your decision was noble. But I've come to France to begin what seems absolutely insane work—and you barely seem pleased I'm here."

He took off his coat and hung it on the back of the door. "I'm sorry, Emma." He pulled a chair in front of hers and grasped her hands. "I'm tired. It's the war. I fight death every day."

"Not even a real kiss," she said.

"All right, a kiss." He leaned toward her, brushed his hands against her neck and shoulders, and then guided her face close to his. His lips felt forced and reserved against hers; an affectation of love devoid of passion.

Could he ever desire me again, or I him? His touch seemed as off-putting and clinical as the hospital office where they sat. Did she want to resurrect the time shortly after their marriage, when he at least attempted to make love? She remembered his fingers, with their perfunctory rush of desire, lingering on her skin. The sexual exchange was barely satisfactory then, their lovemaking as methodical and dull as their home life. As she considered the past, Linton Bower's naked body burst into her head.

Tom broke from her embrace.

"We've both changed," Emma said.

He pushed his chair back and bounced his clenched fist on the desk. "I told you—I'm tired. I live, eat, sleep, and dream death." He stared at her with red-rimmed eyes and then covered his face with his hands, before slowly taking them away. "If only I could stop my mind from working, stop thinking about this damn war. Believe me, there are times I regret this decision and wish I'd never come here. Perhaps I shouldn't have encouraged you to leave Boston—maybe it would have been better if you'd stayed."

"Well, it's too late now," she said, subduing her despair at his suggestion. "I'm staying in Paris. John Harvey needs me . . . I thought *you* needed me, too." She studied his slumped form and a sudden stab of pity pierced her. "We need to sort this out, but first you need to rest."

"Yes, you're right on both counts," he said, his voice tinged with sadness.

Emma looked down at the lint and muddy droplets covering her coat, trying in vain to brush them off. "I'm afraid, Tom."

"Of what?"

"A number of things," she said, looking back at him. She considered the emotional distance between them and thought better of cutting too deep, too fast. "What if I fail on my first day in the studio? What if my masks are a disaster?"

"Men die every day in my hands."

"It's not the same," she said, irritated by the comparison. "Those men would die anyway. You couldn't save them because no doctor could. They were in God's hands. My soldiers are alive and come to me for help. What if I can't give it to them? I can't even sculpt a face properly."

Tom clutched the edge of the desk. "That may be true, but don't wave the white flag until you give it a try. No one will die in your studio."

"That's not the point. Are you so certain our choices have been right? What if they've been wrong?"

"I'm not certain of anything. There are days when the world seems like hell and nothing I've ever done is right." He leaned toward her. "Our individual choices brought us to this place, and perhaps that's the problem. We've always been on our own, even though we're together."

Emma flinched under her coat, knowing the truth of his words.

"You're staying with me tonight?" he asked after a few moments. "We can talk if you're not too tired."

"I assume so, but I'm also at John's beck and call. He mentioned staying with military friends near Toul."

"Stay with me. I can arrange other accommodations for John and Virginie. Are you returning to Paris tomorrow?"

"Yes." Emma studied the gaunt face. Tom's lower lip quivered as she rose from her seat. Trembling, she leaned against him, shutting out the hospital's distractions, breathing in his warmth and the familiar scent of his skin that rose faintly above the odor of antiseptic. She lowered her head, wanting to kiss his hands, but he stopped her with a gentle touch to her shoulder.

"Infections," he reminded her.

Tom walked Emma to the cottage after a late supper with John and Virginie, and then returned to the hospital. Tom had arranged the evening—she would spend the night at his cottage, John and his nurse would stay at the director's home in Toul. In the morning, the three would return to Paris to put together the final plans for the new studio and the completion of Emma's last days of training with her mentor. During supper, John complained about the inconveniences suffered at the hands of a "love-starved husband and wife." He listed his grievances: a forgotten toothbrush, pajamas that needed mending, troubled sleep in an unfamiliar bed. Virginie assured him that he could find a toothbrush at the hospital and that he could sleep in his underwear, or nude in a barn, as far as she was concerned. She was happy to accept the director's hospitality for the night, with or without his company.

As the long hours passed, the cottage the Red Cross had requisitioned for Tom seemed as deserted and lonely as the moon. Memories flashed through her head—from childhood days to the evening's dinner—as her tired brain searched for answers to the questions she and her husband had posed to each other in the afternoon.

She spent much of the night at a small table, drinking from an already opened bottle of wine, musing about Linton, her husband, and the circumstances of war that had brought her to France. Now and then, she rose from her chair and paced the room in the flickering circle of lamplight, taking in, on the surface, the furnishings of Tom's life—so different from their comfortable Boston home at the base of Beacon Hill. An iron bedstead took up most of the space. A bookcase filled one corner near a stone fireplace. The table and two chairs skirted a tin sink to the right of the front door. The only other room in the cottage was a washroom with a hole in the earth for the toilet, and a rust-stained water basin.

The trappings of Tom's profession lay scattered about: books, letters, a stethoscope, soiled clothes. From the disarray, Emma judged that Tom had little time for himself—let alone for anyone else, including her. She resolved to make the best of their reunion and, as difficult as it might be, she would broach the subject of their relationship. She undressed, snuggled under the down comforter, and watched as the fire, at first robust, faded as the night dragged her into sleep.

Wind thumped against the cottage door.

Emma awoke with a start, with no recollection of her whereabouts.

Her husband lay with his back to her, the comforter pulled up to his waist, the upper half of his body covered by an undershirt. Emma moved her arm to touch him, but then reconsidered, and let her hand drop in front of her abdomen. Their talk would have to wait. She muttered a few words of intercession and pushed deeper into her pillow.

Tom quivered in his sleep as rain slashed against the window. The tempest shook the thin panes, keeping her awake and wondering how long the downpour would last. She threw off the comforter, the heat from the fireplace warming her legs. Tom had stoked the fire before going to bed.

He groaned and rolled onto his back. The small clock on the kitchen table struck two, the chimes reverberating in her head.

She rose on her elbow and studied her husband's expression. His face was pale—the skin wan in the mercurial, flashing light, so unlike the healthy New England complexion forged by summer sun and frigid winter winds. His hair, unkempt since his time away from Boston, had thinned, showing streaks of gray, not evident before, at the temples. The biggest change, how-

ever, was in his eyes. Even the sleep-filled lids were purple and
waxen, as if life had been drained from them.

Her eyes wandered down his form, finding it hard not to be
drawn back to his face. She turned away, trying not to awaken
him, placing her feet like cat paws on the floor.

Tom grunted and rolled onto his stomach.

She grabbed a coverlet from the bed, wandered to the table,
sipped a bit of leftover wine, and gazed out the small window.
Down the lane, the dark oak limbs shook in the rain. In the
small garden in front of the cottage, drenched daisies bent their
heads toward the earth. She found herself absorbed in thought
and wished she could write in her diary.

*Sleep comes hard for him. He's exhausted. Sneaking in and
stoking the fire without waking me! The war is killing him. It
makes no difference to me if we make love. It's far more important that we're alive and well, with a chance to get things
settled. . . . Why can't I be honest about why I came to France?
To save my marriage or escape from passion? To work as a
sculptress . . . or to forget the one secret I've never been able
to tell my husband? I hardly know myself why I came. He's
much nobler than I—so determined when he made the decision. He wanted—no, needed—to aid the war effort and the
French doctors. He talked incessantly about the need for quali-
fied surgeons at the Front. I'm not some noble artist come to
save the world or the lives of these disfigured men. I thought
this work would help me become a better sculptress. Maybe,
with time, I'll improve. It seems so deceitful to practice on men
for the sake of my art. It's despicable, really . . . but I shouldn't
think that. This is how the mind works at two in the morning.*

Lightning flashed outside the window and a low growl rumbled within the walled city.

*Thunder. The sound is too long and hollow to be an explod-
ing shell.*

The rain pushed hard against the window, the water sheeting
against the panes. Emma fidgeted in the small wooden chair at
the table and poured more wine.

*If I smoked, I'd have a cigarette. What a day of disasters—
the rain, the drive, even supper with John and Virginie was
awkward. I wanted to be alone with Tom and there they were,
right beside me, John indulging himself with his stories of shattered faces and the marvels of his reconstructions, and Virginie
needling him at every turn. I swear they'll drive me crazy before
he leaves France. John blanched when I displayed a less than
intense interest in my new studio—my distractions getting the
better of me. "Attention must be paid, Mrs. Swan," he kept repeating, as if I couldn't appreciate the magnitude of the work.
Supper isn't the time for a discourse on facial reconstruction
and the techniques of metal mask-making. Later, Sir Jonathan,
when my head is not so full, the studio will have my full attention.*

*And the final tragedy—oh, I call it a tragedy when it really
isn't. How can a man make love to you when he's emotionally and physically exhausted? But you would suppose after
five months the body would be eager, ready for the demands
of the libido. But sex seems so unimportant here with a war
raging and our own emotions overpowering any sexual need.
His body is so familiar to me and yet so strange now—as alien
and distant as my faces. His chest, his arms, his stomach, all
thinner than before, but the whole of him slightly off kilter;
and the feeling, the emotion upon our meeting, vacant as night.
Any pent-up passion in me escaped like a wisp of air—if it was
ever there at all. And, I admit, I was relieved to let it flow away.
The pressure is so much less now that he's asleep. I wonder
what would have occurred if Linton had been lying next to me
instead of Tom?*

Lightning illuminated a stack of mail on the table. She
reached for it.

He's kept my letters.

She flipped through the brown envelopes, realizing there
were more in the pile than she had written: letters from Boston
doctors, correspondence from French surgeons in the American
Expeditionary Force, notes from John.

She replaced the envelopes where she found them, sipped a bit more wine, and stared out the rain-soaked window. As she watched the torrent, a sudden thought chilled her and sent a shiver down her spine. *What if someone from Boston has written to him? What if Tom knows about Linton?*

CHAPTER 5

———◆———

PARIS AND THE FRONT

Late October 1917

"I'm happy he's gone," Virginie said, her voice rising with each word. "*Il est odieux*. Imagine, asking me to work in England. *Jamais!* I hate him. English bully."

"Don't work yourself up so," Emma said. She closed the anatomy book she had been studying. "He's been gone for weeks. I only meant I wish John was around sometimes—after all, he's the one who established this technique for the Royal Army Medical Corps. And, despite what you might think, I don't believe he *hated* you. In fact, I think he admired you for standing up to him. He could never crack you. Consider it a compliment that he chose you as an assistant."

"He upset me and wore me out," Virginie said. "But you are correct—it is no matter now."

"I know." The sun passing behind the clouds cast fleeting shadows across the parquet floor. "We've created the Studio for Facial Masks, and we should be proud of it. I couldn't have done it without you and Madame Clement. On Monday, when we open, I suppose we'll have a line of men waiting for us, if Sir Jonathan's prediction is correct."

Emma walked to the window and placed her hands on the sill where the warm fall light dissolved the chill on her arms.

When she took stock of all they had created, she was satisfied with their work. The studio was as pleasant as she and her assistants could make it. The process had been long and difficult, especially with John and Virginie butting heads at nearly every turn. But Emma recognized their worth as a team: John, as a pedantic teacher; the intelligence and wit of Virginie; and the steady hand of Madame Clement, the housekeeper, who kept them comfortably fed and on schedule.

For a small salary, provided by the Red Cross and bolstered by a few francs from Tom, Virginie and Madame Clement had accepted Emma's invitation to remain at the studio. Virginie was thrilled to be rid of John, who had recruited her and Madame Clement in anticipation of Emma's arrival. Both had suffered tedious demands and rigorous training under him, but his "tyranny" had made the transition easier for Emma. Virginie alone had constructed more than twenty facial masks under John's tutelage.

Emma had worked with the Red Cross to secure the two upper floors of a building in the Latin Quarter near the church of Saint-Étienne-du-Mont. From the studio's arched stone entrance on the rue Monge, a passageway led to a small courtyard and a rear wooden staircase. The courtyard walls were covered with ivy and its square filled with marble and bronze statues purchased by Emma at a flea market.

Madame Clement brought meals daily from her home and shopped for fresh flowers every few days. When the housekeeper warmed her dishes on the small stove, the smells of her delicious cooking filled the studio. She made coq au vin when she could procure a chicken; prepared potatoes in all forms; baked small cakes or cookies, which sometimes graced the table, despite shortages of sugar and flour. The studio became a bastion against the war with its warm light, flowers, decorative posters, French and American flags, homemade dishes, and bottles of wine.

Madame Clement lived nearby in the Quarter, while Emma and Virginie occupied one of two small rooms on the floor above the studio. The garret, with its angled window that looked out across the jumbled Paris skyline, contained a battered oak desk, a chair, two iron bedsteads, and was warmed by an open-hearth fireplace. The space seemed small, even by Boston standards, but Emma knew it would be cozy and warm during the gray winter days to come.

The last of the staff yet to join them before the opening was a tall, fez-wearing Moroccan named Hassan, an olive-skinned man with profuse black hair. He had worked with Virginie at a hospital and inquired about a job with the studio. Emma worked out a small stipend for Hassan after his interview, as well as living quarters in the garret, providing the room across the hall in exchange for his services. Hassan could speak or read little English, but through his intuition and intelligence could interpret a look or a gesture as if someone had spoken to him. He was strong enough to haul supplies despite a slight limp from a leg injury suffered in the war. During their introduction, Emma found he handled the clay-modeling brushes and scrapers, used in creating the masks, with ample dexterity.

Late in the afternoon, after a day of cleaning and organizing in the studio, a repeated loud knock on the door disturbed Emma's brief chance to relax. Soon, Madame Clement, attired in one of the simple housedresses she favored, appeared with a young man in tow. Emma recognized his thin form, the light-brown hair, and distinctively colored amber eyes from a previous meeting. He was a courier from the hospital in Toul who had come with Tom in September to pick up medical supplies in Paris. The courier and her husband had visited briefly at rue de Paul before driving back to the hospital.

Today, Emma sensed something was wrong. The courier lowered his head and whispered to Madame Clement. The housekeeper frowned and then nodded as the courier spoke. The large studio room, one wall hung with the plaster masks of men with missing noses, twisted mouths, and sightless eyes, took on an ominous feel. The masks were used as guides to fill in the flesh lost by injury.

Virginie appeared at the door and asked, "Is everything all right?"

Emma concerned by the courier's tone, countered, "I think the question is, 'What is wrong?'"

"Qu'est-ce qui s'est passé?" Virginie asked Madame Clement. The housekeeper bent toward the nurse and, like the courier, whispered.

"What is going on? Has something happened to Tom?" Emma walked uncertainly toward them, swaying a bit on her feet.

"A moment, Madame," Virginie said to Emma, and cut off Madame Clement from her conversation with the courier and concentrated her attention on the young man. After a brief discussion, the nurse said, "Your husband wishes to speak to you."

"He's here?"

"No, in Toul."

"Is he safe?"

"Yes, but he has an important matter to discuss with you."

"The courier has no idea what this is about?" Emma asked impatiently, clasping her hands in front of her.

The courier and Virginie carried on another conversation.

"He has no idea, but Monsieur Swan apparently is worried—more concerned than the courier has ever seen him."

"I can't stand this," Emma said. "Please have Madame Clement telephone Tom at the hospital. There's no phone at the cottage. It's too late to travel today. Virginie, ask the courier if he wouldn't mind staying the night. We can get an early start in the morning."

Virginie spoke to the courier and then to the housekeeper, who nodded and left the room. The courier took off his hat and bowed slightly to Emma.

"He can stay in Hassan's room since he hasn't arrived yet." She smoothed her dress and stared at the young man, who looked back with equal intent. "I'll make it up." Emma hurried up the stairs, opened the Moroccan's room, and stood trembling by the side of the bed, tears blurring her vision. She blinked them away, fluffed the white pillow, and pulled down the checked blanket to make sure the sheets were fresh. She jabbed the fireplace poker into the hearth and swept some fallen ash into a pail.

Virginie appeared at the door. "Madame Clement is preparing supper for the three of us. She called the hospital. Monsieur Swan is not there. . . ." The nurse blinked, as if searching for the proper words.

"Yes?"

"Your husband is at the Front."

Emma steadied herself against the bed and then sat, bewildered by the news.

At times, caught up in Parisian life, Emma constructed romantic fantasies about her husband despite the awkwardness between them. They could make Paris their home after the war ended, she often thought. It would be their chance to begin again, to return to the days when they appreciated each other, but those thoughts had popped like bubbles in the wind as the reality of the war sunk in.

Emma slept little during the night, imagining Tom plagued by every possible war-related disaster. After a breakfast of oatmeal and pear slices, Emma and the courier climbed into the ambulance. On the chilly street, the first spreading rays of dawn streaked the eastern sky. As they drove away from Paris, the day turned mild with the rising sun. Near noon, they followed a convoy of French army trucks spewing gray exhaust and dust for an hour, until the drivers stopped under a row of spindly birches, the young soldiers spilling out into a field to stretch their legs and eat. Emma and the courier, who spoke to each other in fractured English phrases, agreed they could do without lunch in order to hasten the journey.

They arrived in Toul about seven in the evening.

At the hospital, Emma found a French doctor who spoke English and asked him about Tom. He was a thin, pleasant man by the name of Claude, who, like Tom, suffered from overwork and too little sleep. Thick lines creased his face, but the many wrinkles at his temples led Emma to believe that, even as a doctor, he was able to laugh in this difficult time.

"He was called to the Front because two surgeons are ill with dysentery," Claude said. "Doctors are scarce. He offered to go."

Emma thanked him and turned to walk away.

"Where are you going, Madame?" Claude asked.

"To the Front," she said matter-of-factly.

Claude chuckled and reached for a cigarette in his jacket pocket. "Come with me. I need to smoke." He led Emma down the stairs to the large sitting room, where he plopped into a chair and lit his cigarette. "The Front is thirty-five kilometers away, give or take a few. It is dark. You are a woman."

"A woman? What does my sex have to do with seeing my husband? The courier told me Tom was desperate to see me."

The doctor smiled and pointed the fiery end of his smoke at Emma. "Please understand, Madame Swan, this is not my doing. Both the French and American armies have turned your sex away from the Front—even women who desperately want to fight. They will not allow you through at this hour or perhaps any other hour."

"Then I will go as a man."

Claude snickered. "*C'est la chose la plus insensée que je n'ai jamais entendu.*"

"Did you say I was insane?"

"Oh, pardon, Madame. Not you—the idea."

His sarcastic smile transformed into a knowing look. "*Peut-être* . . . Do you have clothes?"

"Those on my back and a change in my case, but I can make do with Tom's clothes at the cottage."

Claude brushed a few fallen ashes from his pant leg. "No, you need a uniform. I have no American uniforms—only French—from the dead soldiers."

Emma started, but shook off her distaste. "That will do. Do you have one in my size?"

"No matter. Most of them did not fit the man who died in them. The sentries will not know the difference."

Claude stubbed out his cigarette on the floor and then led Emma to a small room underneath the staircase. Piles of army pants, shirts, boots, leggings, and helmets lay stacked on wooden shelves. "Here is the dressing room of the dead," Claude said with a disquieting smile. "Most widows want their husbands to be buried in a suit, not a uniform. Some we return to the army for other soldiers to wear. Most we burn because they cannot be worn."

Emma listened halfheartedly to Claude's comments while she poked through the jumble of clothes. Most were in decent condition, but a few were partially shredded or spotted with the blackish stains of dried blood.

"Here you can create your fashion," Claude said.

As she sorted through the dead men's clothes with the intention of constructing this disguise, the macabre thought of All Hallows' Eve popped into her head. *It's like dressing for some kind of grotesque party. It is insane!* She dismissed it from her mind. "After I'm dressed, will the courier take me to the Front?"

Claude waved his hand. "The courier will take you to the cottage for a good night's sleep. He is a man, not a mule. He is tired from today's drive—as you should be. Gather the clothes and take a little food from the hospital. Richard will escort you to the cottage."

"I can walk from here."

"No," Claude said emphatically. "Richard will escort you. No woman should walk alone in the dark. It isn't right."

Emma sighed. "I've been so self-absorbed. I didn't even ask him his name."

"No matter," Claude said. "He has a medical condition that keeps him from the army—but not from his *jeune femme*." The doctor clicked his tongue.

After she had collected her clothes and food, Emma found Richard. He dropped her off at the cottage after a short drive. He held her clothing in his left hand and made a turning motion with his right when they arrived at the door—he hesitated to open it himself.

She turned the brass knob and the door creaked open.

"You were right," she said, knowing he might not understand her English. "Why would the door be locked? Why would there be theft in a fortified city guarded by troops?"

The courier placed the clothes and her bag on a chair and nodded. *"Bonsoir, Madame. À demain."*

"Merci, Richard. Demain."

Through the small window, she watched as the truck sputtered down the lane until it was out of sight. She took off her coat and cleared a space on the cluttered kitchen table for her supper. The cottage felt familiar; yet, she considered herself a stranger. Little had changed since her time with Tom in August. The table held a jumble of papers and medical books, the bedsheets and blankets were wadded into a ball at its foot. Tom had left in a hurry.

What a change. My tidy Boston husband continues his slovenly ways. She shook her head in wonder, but a prickle of fear raced over her as she thought of any number of calamities that might have befallen him on the battle line.

What does he want to tell me that is so important? I can't carry on about this, or I'll drive myself mad.

She shivered and rubbed her arms to ward off the cold. Needing to start a fire, she opened the door and stood on the walk next to the small garden in front of the cottage. Driven by a chilly northwest wind that pushed against her, gray plumes of clouds soared between her and the stars. The nearby oaks stood black and bare in the autumn night while, in the garden, a few yellow and purple pansies bloomed on long, green stalks. Scattered leaves created a brown patchwork against the sprigs of grass yet untouched by frost. Someone, perhaps Tom, had collected wood and stacked it in an iron rick, which leaned against the stone wall.

Emma carried a few logs inside and positioned them on the fireplace grate. Returning to the garden, she collected dead leaves and dry bark and placed them underneath the logs. A tin match safe rested on the rough wooden mantel above the fireplace. The room soon was filled with a warm, crackling light.

She ate her hastily made supper at a space she'd cleared on the table. At Claude's urging, a nurse had put together a meal—reluctantly, because she had more important duties than to wait upon a doctor's wife—of a few hard biscuits and dried beef tucked into a cloth napkin. Beggars could not be choosers. A sharp pang struck her stomach because it had been hours since breakfast. Her supper, with a glass of wine from a newly opened bottle, tasted good in spite of its simplicity.

Her gaze shifted to the letters on the table. The wind knocked against the window and a draft flowed down the chimney, a few embers sparking from the logs to the wooden floor. She jumped out of the chair to stamp them out, and a scrap of paper, neatly tucked between the mattress and the underlying metal springs, caught her eye as she passed the bed. If not for Tom's messy bed making, she would never have noticed the small white triangle. She reached for it, but then stopped, unsure whether she should violate her husband's privacy in *his* cottage.

I'm his wife. Surely he has nothing to hide.

Linton Bower appeared in a vivid flash before her—the strength of his arms, the muscular curves of his naked back, the fresh, forbidden taste of his lips. A red-hot flush of shame rose to her face, far removed from the effects of the crackling fire.

She lifted the mattress and withdrew the paper: a letter, dated late July 1917, written on finely woven white stationery and folded in half. She opened it:

My dear Tom,
I am sorry to be the one to tell you this, but I know tongues will wag, and sooner or later the truth will come rushing toward you. Better to hear it from me than one of those silly Boston women who do nothing but gossip and slander others for their own benefit.
From the beginning, our friendship has been based on truth,

which we both hold in the highest regard. I treasure your respect for your marriage vows, for your honor and commitment. I suppose that's why you are where you are today, serving unselfishly in a war far from home. But as you serve, others are lax in their duties. Therefore, I feel it my place—nay, my duty—to inform you of occurrences here—so unpleasant and distasteful I hope you will not loathe me for bringing these matters to your attention. But the truth will come out.

Your wife has been seen in the company of a Boston artist, Linton Bower, and unfortunately the pair appears to be more than just companions. I wouldn't tell you this if I hadn't seen this behavior with my own eyes. I'm sure this is distressing to you, Tom, but you must hear out these words. I hope you can understand the pain this letter causes me as well. Writing it was not an easy task.

I believe their first encounter was at the Fountain Gallery. The relationship progressed from there. . . .

The letter ended with a jagged tear across the bottom.

Emma dropped to the bed, shock coursing through her body, the room deathly cold, the fire near yet so small and distant. She clutched her chest and a reservoir of memories rushed toward her.

No, no, no.

Tom's aloofness upon their reunion, his reluctance to make love, his brief September visit to Paris, the urgency of his message to the courier, all of these "actions" suddenly made sense. Emma looked in disbelief at the letter in her hands. She wanted to tear it apart and fling it into the fire, knowing she was fighting a foe that had already made its presence known. And, from the handwriting, she knew her adversary was Louisa Markham.

During the night, the wind stopped its rage against the cottage. Emma pulled the blankets close to her chin and stared at the dying embers. Maybe once an hour, frequently enough to wake her, shells exploded at the Front, sending the troubling rumble into her ears like thunder from a distant storm. She tried to sleep, to brush away the demons prodding her dreams: Linton rushing toward her; Louisa laughing maniacally as Linton stumbles and falls on the steps; the smiling boy she loved in Vermont; and the faceless baby taunting her.

Richard arrived early the next morning, the truck awakening her from a fitful sleep just before dawn. Emma, feeling as if she had fallen asleep only a few minutes before, wrapped herself in a blanket and answered the door, thinking only of the journey ahead. Richard, cheeks shining, smiled and offered her fruit and cold oatmeal.

"*Merci,*" she repeated several times as she began eating. He bowed slightly each time she thanked him. After Emma pointed to an extra chair, Richard pulled it to the table and munched on an apple as she finished her meal.

After breakfast, while Richard smoked outside, she made the bed and discretely returned the letter to its place under the mattress. The soldier's uniform lay on the floor.

"A moment," Emma called out, and picked up the clothes. From his smile, she knew Richard could tell what was coming, perhaps having been informed of her plan by Claude. She walked to the tiny washroom, closed the door, and smacked her elbow against the wall as she struggled to get dressed. If not for the seriousness of the situation, she would have laughed as she viewed herself in the small shaving mirror over the sink. The loose-fitting jacket and pants minimized her breasts and hips. Her hair, piled high upon her head, fit comfortably under the somewhat oversized helmet. She tucked in a few loose strands and pronounced herself ready.

Richard, sitting at the table, laughed when she stepped out of the room, amused by her disguise and predicament.

"*Chut,*" Emma said, but her admonition fell on a broad smile and continued laughter.

"*Non, non,*" Richard repeated as Emma wrapped the leggings around her trousers and then pulled on boots. When he had composed himself, he rose from his chair. "*Nous partons pour le Front.*"

Emma understood and asked, "Do I need anything? Passport? Identification papers?" As soon as the words passed her lips, she realized the ridiculousness of her question. She was attempting to sneak onto a battlefield disguised as a man, her success dependent upon Richard, his guidance, and his knowledge of the Front, not upon documents that showed her to be a woman.

The slight young man shook his head and pointed to the truck, which was parked in the lane. The morning sun shone brightly on the olive green metal.

"It's a splendid day to go to war," Emma said. "*Allons-y.*"

Before closing up the cottage, Emma looked around the room. The tidy bed and the orderly table gave her a momentary sense of serenity. That peace, however, was broken by distant explosions, the first she had heard in hours. After the blasts subsided, Emma listened. The wind pushed through the trees and shook the dead leaves still clinging to the branches, but no birds sang, no animals scurried in the lane. The land was dead, blighted by a war that was close at hand—the morning serving up only the promise of death.

Richard cranked the truck and they drove down the lane, past the hospital, and through the city. The courier waved to the French soldiers as they passed by the gates. "*Poilu,*" Richard said, as the soldiers returned his gesture.

The truck swept eastward, past thickly wooded hills that lined the rutted road. The Front lay more than thirty kilometers ahead. Richard honked at a convoy of ambulances and fuel trucks headed toward Toul. She turned her head as the vehicles passed. Under the tarpaulins and the makeshift metal covers, wounded men lay on gurneys, their arms and legs bouncing limply as the ambulances rumbled over the bumps.

As they neared the Front, they motored past a column of American soldiers. Three gun carriages, hauling artillery and shells, and pulled by horses, lagged behind the lethargically marching troops. Emma thought the men, without helmets, wearing whatever hats they could on their heads, a ragtag bunch. She recalled the woman in Saint-Nazaire who had told her the Americans would not be able to win the war.

"*Les Américains*," Richard said, with a slight edge to his voice. "*Ridicule.*"

"Why?" Emma asked.

"*Parce que*—"

"My French is not very good, as you found out yesterday."

"I speak a little English," he replied, as if quoting from a language textbook.

"Then, tell me, why do you think the Americans are ridiculous?"

"*Nouveau*," he said.

Emma looked past him as he gripped the wheel, wondering if the courier could be right. The American officers on the ship were fresh and inexperienced, but more than prepared to give up their lives. Lt. Andrew Stoneman had assured her of their dedication to the war. She wondered where he was and if he still carried the portrait she had drawn of him.

"Americans are prepared to die for your country," she said.

"*Nos chasseurs. Magnifique.*"

Emma looked at him blankly.

"*Bleu*," he said. "*Le chapeau des Alpes.*"

Emma remembered a group of French soldiers near the Paris studio. They were strikingly attired in dark blue tunics and Alpine hats of the same color. Richard seemed correct in his assumption—the chasseurs appeared, at first glance, to be better and more efficient fighters than the ill-equipped Americans.

"Time will tell," she said. "In war, all men face the same dangers. Bravery and morale count for something."

Richard nodded as if he agreed, but Emma suspected he understood little of what she said, and even less of what she implied.

The truck rolled closer to the Front. Richard pointed to a hill on the horizon. Behind it, columns of smoke flowed into the sky.

"Shells," he said. "Here . . . calm."

"Calm?" Emma asked in astonishment.

"*Oui.*" He thought about his words for a moment before speaking. "The war is quiet here."

"It appears active enough for me."

Abandoned farmhouses, some boarded up, others with sagging roofs and broken timbers, stood like sad apparitions on both sides of the road. A few skinny cows, unattended by man and unrestrained by broken fences, wandered in brown fields. As the truck rolled toward the battle, Emma realized she had no idea what the Front would be like. Her slim knowledge of the war had come from Tom's censored letters and the civilized reporting of Boston newspapers.

Richard suddenly put a finger to his lips. He turned left onto a side road that was nothing more than ruts in a field. The truck bounced through the dead grasses and sparse woods and then slowed in a shallow clearing. About fifty meters east of the clearing a barbed-wire fence stretched in both directions as far as Emma could see. Mounds of dirt, like black earthen temples, rose at various points along the line. Toward the bleak horizon, less than a kilometer past the first row of wire, another elongated length of coiled barbs and dark mounds stretched in a parallel direction. Beyond that, a vast landscape of blasted trees and cratered earth opened like a pox upon the land. Smoke drifted like an unearthly fog over the terrain while the sharp report of machine guns popped in Emma's ears.

"My God," Emma said, as Richard brought the truck to a stop near a group of French soldiers. Concealed by an isolated thicket, they stood chatting and smoking cigarettes.

"*Oui*," Richard said. "*C'est l'enfer.*"

Emma stared at the all-encompassing devastation and concurred, "Yes . . . hell."

The soldiers ignored her. Penetrating the Front was easier than she had anticipated. Part of that ease might have been due to the other activities on the minds of the *Poilu*—cigarettes, cheap wine, and laughter, even as artillery fire and shells shrieked nearby. From what she could judge, these men were ordinary infantry wearing mud-spattered uniforms of light blue—the equivalent of American privates—not an officer among them. The soldiers seemed unconcerned about the fighting around them, instead leaning on their rifles, savoring their cigarettes, drinking their *pinard*, laughing with Richard, and staring at Emma.

Richard asked the soldiers where the American doctor, Thomas Swan, was working. Emma understood at least that much. She also heard the words "woman" and "costume" in French, which solicited more laughter from the soldiers.

"What's going on?" Emma asked him. "You told them I was a woman, didn't you?" She glared at him, irritated by his cavalier attitude toward her situation.

The courier shook his head and pointed to one of the soldiers, a short man with a round belly and a full black beard.

The soldier stepped forward. "I speak English. I studied it in school. I will take you to your husband."

Emma took off her helmet, allowing her hair to fall free. The men stopped their conversation and glanced at her admiringly, causing her to stare at her uniform jacket and trousers, turned a grayish-brown from the ground-in dirt.

"*Oui*," Emma said. "*Je suis une femme.*"

"Officers or police stop women," the soldier said. "We are not officers. Put on your helmet. You'll need it in the trenches."

Emma did as he asked. "Please take me to my husband. It's important I see him."

"Yes, but follow me carefully and watch your head. Let me talk if we are stopped."

"Wait for me," Emma ordered Richard.

"Two hours," he said. "Then I must return to the hospital."

The soldier anticipated Emma's question. "Your husband is at a dressing station in the first trench about a half-kilometer from here."

"*Bonne chance*," Richard said.

"*Au nord*," the soldier said, and led the way along a rutted trail. Emma followed as the soldier picked up his pace, his rifle thrust forward in his hands. A short distance away, a wooden ladder protruded from the top of a mound in the sodden earth. The soldier hitched his rifle, stepped onto the ladder, and descended it like a spider spinning its web. He looked up, urging her to follow. She cringed at the sloppy trench floor, but screwed up her courage, and swung her legs onto the ladder. At the bottom, her boots sank in the muck. The air smelled like stinking, unwashed flesh.

Wires snaked along the dirt ceiling. The soldier led her north to a hole illuminated by hanging lights.

Men slept or sat on crude benches carved into the earthen walls. The soldiers, including an officer, cast stony glances at them but said nothing as they hurried past. They continued through the seemingly endless trench until the soldier turned left into a connecting tunnel.

"We're almost there," he said and pointed to an area obscured in the gloom, leading to another ladder that jutted out of the fetid slime. He climbed up first and Emma followed.

The sunlight, though muted by a small stand of trees, stung Emma's eyes. As her vision adjusted, another clearing appeared. Operating and equipment tables stood under a green tarpaulin covering the dressing station. Soldiers carried or dragged in the wounded as doctors in white aprons worked on the casualties.

Emma spotted Tom hunched over one of the tables. He poked mechanically at a soldier's wound, swabbing with gauze, and prodding the flesh with his forceps. As she approached, he pulled a bullet from the soldier's arm. Tom studied the metal captured in the bloodied forceps for a moment and then dropped it into a tin cup.

Emma tapped his shoulder.

He cast a quick glance behind and said gruffly, "Not now. I'm busy."

"Tom," Emma whispered.

He spun, shock spreading across his face. "Good God, Emma. What are you doing here? How did you get . . . ?"

"You needed to see me—urgently. That's why I'm here." She took off her helmet and put it on the ground.

"Yes . . . yes, that's true, but I didn't want you to come to the Front. You're in danger here."

"As you are."

His tired, dark eyes fixed upon her. "You must wait until I finish with this soldier, then we can talk. Find cover on the other side of the path."

Tom turned back to his patient. Emma picked up her helmet and walked across the clearing, crossing over vehicle tracks partially obscured by weeds. She sat on a grassy slope away from the horse carts and watched as stretcher-bearers disappeared and emerged from the surrounding thickets, passing back and forth in front of her in a chaotic military procession.

"Put on your helmet," a gruff voice commanded. The soldier who had guided Emma plopped down beside her, his backside sliding a little on the grass because of his weight. "Boche snipers are everywhere."

Emma again complied with his request. "How do you do it?"

He pulled at his beard. "Fight?"

"Yes. How do you stand the mud, the cold, the heat, and every atrocity that comes with this war? And face death as well?"

"We have no choice. We must fight or surrender . . . and to surrender is to die."

"Wouldn't it be better to live?"

"What—turn France over to our enemies? The war has dragged on and there have been mutinies, but how could we face ourselves if we allowed the Boche to prevail?"

An unearthly stillness hung in the air after a round of distant blasts. Everyone, including the stretcher-bearers, halted. A few cocked their heads and turned their eyes upward.

The soldier swung his face toward Emma's, his eyes sparkling with terror.

Pressure, like a wave, bore down upon them. Emma's ears crackled as the soldier threw his body over hers.

"Cover your head," he shouted as the shell plummeted toward them. She shielded her face with her arms as his weight knocked the breath out of her.

A concussion pounded in her ears and rippled across her body. The world floated around her.

Out of the corner of her eye, she saw men, horses, carts, and chunks of earth twirl in the air in a slow ballet and then fall carelessly to earth.

After the shock, the world was strangely silent and black.

I am dead.

She stifled a scream. Blood dripped from the mouth of the soldier on top of her and ran warm down her cheek and neck. She pushed the lolling head away, the helmet rolling to the ground, her ears barely hearing the muffled screams around her.

Gradually, more screams and a chorus of moans filtered through the pressure filling her head, as if she was swimming in the depths of a cold lake.

"Tom!" Clutching the soldier's body, she tried to push it away, but his bulk was too much. She struggled, jerking her neck back and forth, in a paroxysm of fright, kicking the man's legs and punching his shoulders, but the weight remained unmoved, as if a heavy slab had been placed upon her.

For a moment, terror filled her—convinced that this *Poilu* would be her sarcophagus. Like a ghost, the face of another *Poilu* floated above her. Blood streaked the side of his tunic, but his legs moved with vigor. He dislodged the soldier with a powerful shove from his booted foot. He leaned over the body, shouted "*mort*," in Emma's ear, and went on his way.

She rose on her elbows and viewed the carnage. The soldier who had saved her lay dead: his bloody legs across hers, his uniform jacket shredded by the clumps of dirt, rocks, and shards of metal protruding from his back. Ten meters to the right of the dressing station where Tom had attended his patient, smoke rose from a newly formed crater surrounded by splintered trees. Not far from her, a dying horse screamed on its back and kicked its legs in the air in anguish. A soldier came to the animal, withdrew his pistol, and fired two shots into its head.

Emma kicked at the soldier's legs, finally freeing herself. She ran to the dressing station to find overturned tables, shattered glass, and operating instruments strewn across the brown earth. Tom's patient lay on the ground, eyes frozen open in death. The soldier's arm, the one that held the bullet, had been ripped from his shoulder.

She stepped over the jumbled equipment and found Tom partially concealed by an operating table and stretcher.

His eyes, at first closed, blinked open. Blood streamed down the side of his face.

Emma lifted the table from him as gently as she could and gasped. An open wound cut across his left thigh and upward toward his stomach, the apron and pants he wore ripped away in pieces.

He reached for her. "Emma, what happened?" His hoarse whisper barely penetrated the ringing in her ears.

She knelt next to him, calling his name, telling him to hold on, praying that help would arrive soon. She grabbed a cloth and pressed it against his thigh to staunch the flow of blood, looking for anything that might act as a tourniquet, crying out for help, but hearing only the moans of the dying in response. She pressed harder on the wound and Tom's eyes rolled back in their sockets.

She was holding the crimson cloth over the laceration and shivering, her hands soaked in blood, when French soldiers emerged from the forest like columns of angry insects.

"Please help my husband," she begged, and collapsed beside him, her own eyes closed in shock.

"How are you?"
Emma shook herself from her lethargy in the Toul hospital lobby. The day, the night, the morning had run together in a blur

of dark trails and trenches that led away from the Front, men speaking maddeningly fast French, an uncomfortable, bouncing, ambulance ride, and a slow, exhaustive, collapse at the hospital. As she twisted in the chair, she couldn't remember the day or the time, or whether she'd had anything to eat or drink.

"Madame? Are you with me?" The lines around Claude's eyes contracted with his piteous look as he stood by her. "You need to rest. Let Richard take you to the cottage."

"No." She massaged the back of her neck.

"Please, Madame," Claude implored, and lit a cigarette as she sank deeper into the chair.

"I want to talk to my husband," she said.

"He is drugged. You need to rest."

"I'm staying here until I can see him. Will he be all right?"

"I'm his doctor," Claude said. "There's no better doctor in Toul, except perhaps for your husband."

He pulled a slip of paper from his laboratory coat. "The desk nurse asked me to deliver this message." He cleared his throat as if to make an important announcement. "You have received calls and telegrams from—it looks like—her handwriting is terrible—Virginie, Madame Clement, a Moroccan named Hassan, and an insufferable Englishman by the name of Harvey. All have inquired about you and your husband's health."

Emma managed a weak smile. "That's very nice. Please tell the desk nurse to give them my regards should they call again."

Claude pulled a chair next to hers, and puffed on his cigarette. "Really, Madame, how are you?"

"Still unsettled. My ears keep popping and I can't believe this has happened. We both knew there were risks. . . . I owe my life to an unknown Frenchman."

Claude bowed his head and gazed at the smoke writhing around his hand like a gray snake. "Yes, perhaps never to know his name. Your husband is lucky. There was a great loss of blood, but he was lucky you were there. You might have saved his life. He will walk. There will be scars to deal with—the ones on the left side of his head, his thigh and stomach . . . but . . ."

Emma stared at him. "Yes . . . go on."

Claude exhaled and coughed. ". . . I worry about one aspect."

Emma stiffened in her chair.

"The shrapnel sliced into his groin as well as his thigh. I can't be certain of the effect on his . . ." Claude looked intently at her for a few moments before continuing. "This is a delicate subject, Madame." He paused and arched an eyebrow allowing Emma to pick up on his inference.

". . . ability to have sexual relations?"

Claude nodded. "I . . . we've tried our best to repair and reconstruct, but the damage may be too much. *Salopards de Boches.*"

"I understand," Emma said, ignoring Claude's pejorative about the Germans. "When can I see him?"

"You can see him now, but he won't talk."

"Fine. I'll sit with him."

Claude extended his hand and led her to an airy room on the second floor filled with wounded men. Tom, covered to his neck by a white sheet, lay in a bed in the far corner. The doctor pulled up a chair for her. "Maybe you will sleep while he sleeps. When he wakes, he may be able to talk." Claude looked at his patient. "Your husband is fortunate. Richard told me the shell was a small one—only a 175 millimeter." An uneasy smile crept across his face.

October 1917

I'm uncertain of the day or time. I know it's after lunch, but the exact date escapes me. So this is what shock does to the body? I've drifted in and out of sleep for endless hours, my head resting on Tom's bed. I begged for a sheet of paper and a pencil from a nurse so I could record my thoughts and translate them later to my diary. Seeing Tom in the hospital, swathed in bandages, has had quite the opposite effect I would have imagined. My com-

*passion is often overpowered by my boiling anger at him
for his blind dedication and my selfish unwillingness and
ignorance about how to be a nurse.*

*Through my hazy thoughts, I ask myself why this hap-
pened! Not only why this has happened to Tom, or even
us, but to me. It's not fair, I keep thinking. Sometimes the
hideous thought that Tom deserves his injuries because of
his bullheaded devotion to medicine slips into my head,
but then I look at my rage and see how displaced it is. I'm
angry because I see the tenuous bond between us disintegrating even further. What if he dies? The thought of
losing him makes me wither in pain. So much unsaid,
so much guilt, and doubt about our lives now and going
forward. This war conspired against us and nothing I can
do will change our situation. And to know that Louisa
has written Tom about Linton—I could throw the letter
in her face and curse her for the damage she's done.*

*I must end because the nurse is eyeing me queerly. She
wants to change Tom's bandages, and for me to move
away from his bed.*

The shell roared toward her, the acidic smell of fear rising
from her skin. Emma struggled with the dead soldier until she
awoke screaming and kicking, gripping the arms of the chair.

Tom, his eyes heavy lidded and nearly closed, looked at her.
The room was dark except for a rectangular slab of white light
that glimmered like a ghost in the doorway.

"You kicked the bed," he whispered.

Emma pried her hands from the chair and leaned toward
him. "I was having a nightmare. The shell was headed . . ." She
picked up a clean cloth from the nightstand and swabbed Tom's
forehead. Patches of blood oozed through the gauze on the left
side of his face. "You're talking. How do you feel?"

"Like a mule kicked me in the gut."

"Tom—"

"Shssssshh, we'll wake the other men."

"You've been dead to the world for nearly two days. I'm happy to hear your voice."

Emma desperately wanted to ask him the question—*Why did you want to see me?*—to inquire about the letter she found at the cottage; but if ever the circumstances were wrong, at this early hour, long past midnight, so soon after his injury, this was the time.

"I'm sorry we didn't get to talk," he said, "but I think it had better wait."

Emma stroked his hand. "It's all right. We can have long conversations when you're well. I'll be here as long as it takes for you to recover."

Tom attempted to lift his head from his pillow, but he groaned in pain and collapsed back upon the bed.

"Don't be silly," Emma said, attempting to quiet him. "You must lie still."

"I can see that," he whispered and then turned his head a bit toward her.

Emma thought she could see, in the semidarkness, a watery film of tears forming in his eyes.

"I'll be fine," he said. "You must return to Paris and go on with your work."

"I'll stay here. Virginie can carry on—she's quite capable of running the studio."

Tom flinched. "No. You must do your work. I insist."

Emma gripped his hand. "Tom, be fair. You have no right to insist. How can you ask me to return to Paris when you're suffering?"

Without hesitating he said, "Because others need you more."

Stunned by his words, Emma released his hand and sagged back in her chair.

"I see," she replied, clasping her hands and fighting against the tears welling in her eyes. "All right, then. I'll leave in the morning. It will be better for both of us."

Tom lifted his hand, but then, as if his arm was weighted by lead, it fell to the bed. "It's the right thing—the injured soldiers need you. Do try to get some rest."

She turned her head to wipe away a tear. When she looked back, he was asleep.

Emma closed her eyes and tried to do the same. A man drifted by her chair in the night; she was uncertain whether he was a soldier or a hospital aide. For all she knew, he could have been a hallucination. The hours slid by in jumpy fits and starts, punctuated by terrifying memories from the Front and the room's lurking shadows. There were ethereal moments when she looked across the sick beds and tried to convince herself she was a participant in a terrible dream. Of course, she knew that wasn't the truth. This was no dream—the world had, in an instant, become much more complicated for her and Tom.

CHAPTER 6

PARIS

December 1917

A bitter wind swept down rue Monge. The wooden door clattered as Emma opened it. Crossing her arms over her chest for warmth, she rushed through the passageway to the courtyard, the air crackling with cold and smelling of snow. Winter in Paris was different from the same season in Boston. The air here was sharp and crisp, not laced with the ocean's salt and humidity. Virginie had predicted the storm the day before, sniffing outside, formulating her forecast.

Looking out over the courtyard, Emma climbed the stairs. The mottled ivy trembled against the stone walls, while the statues, dusted with flakes, stood gray and white in contrast to the muted green leaves.

She fished for the key in her pocket, found it, and opened the door. A sultry warmth, created by the boiling water on the small stove, enveloped her as she stepped inside.

"Snow today, as I said," Virginie called out from the large studio on the front of the building. Hassan grunted in agreement.

"Hello to you, too, Mademoiselle. Did Madame Clement make tea before she left?"

"*Oui, sur la table.*"

The familiar bisque teapot, covered by a white tea cozy, sat on the alcove table. Emma poured a cup and walked to the studio, the room as gray as the snowy clouds visible through the windows. She took off her coat and placed it over a chair. Virginie was busy hanging a facial cast on the wall, while Hassan, attired in a white smock, crimson fez by his side, worked on another. Emma studied him as he etched around an eye socket with a sculpting tool.

"Very nice," Emma said to him.

Hassan nodded. "*Merci, Madame.*"

"How many are we expecting today?" Emma asked Virginie.

"Two. One in the morning. One in the afternoon."

"Not a busy day."

"But the casualties continue to mount," the nurse replied. "I read the death toll in the newspaper this morning. The fighting is heavy near Cambrai. British and German mostly."

"The winter has dragged down the war," Emma said, rubbing her hands together. "We should be grateful we have this haven. But we need to liven up the studio for Christmas. Perhaps Madame Clement can find some holly and holiday candles, or other festive decorations."

"And champagne—*pour une fête*," Virginie added.

Hassan smiled and tipped an imaginary glass with his right arm.

"Yes, I suppose champagne would be appropriate for a toast."

"Did you talk with your husband this morning?" Virginie asked, quite out of the blue.

Bitterness swept over her, and, disliking the feeling, she pushed it away. "No. I decided to take a walk instead. I'm sure nothing has changed since we phoned a few days ago. He's recovering nicely, taking small steps. The doctor expects him to be walking normally by the first of the year. He may even be able to return to work in a limited capacity."

"The news is better and better," Virginie said.

Emma nodded, but her heart was not in her gesture. The letter she'd read in the cottage still weighed on her mind, even though she'd tried to trivialize the memory. "I should prepare for our patient." Emma sipped the last of her tea, picked up her coat, and placed the cup on the alcove table before heading upstairs to her room.

Once there, she tossed the garment on the bed and sat down beside it. The room was chilly under the sunless sky, the heat from below providing only slight warmth. The small fireplace, so cheery when ablaze, held only cold ashes. She sighed, smoothed her cheeks with her hands, and looked at the small desk near the fireplace where two letters from Anne, her housekeeper, rested. Her Boston home now seemed idyllic compared with Paris; such feelings were drawn to the forefront as she read Anne's account of household life and playtime with Lazarus.

Below, a door opened and closed and Emma heard Madame Clement call out to Virginie. Emma rushed down the stairs, happy to the see the housekeeper, who carried a bag of sundry items, a coveted loaf of bread for lunch, and a bouquet of white daisies. Emma had no idea where Madame Clement got her flowers in the winter.

"I can always count on you to brighten our day with blossoms," Emma said, kissing her on the cheek.

"*Bonjour.*" She pulled a letter from her coat pocket and handed it to Emma.

The handwriting was childlike and scrawling, unlike the carefully defined hand of the letter in Tom's cottage. It was postmarked from Boston, the fifteenth of November. Emma ripped it open, studied the writing inside, which was identical to that on the envelope, and read it standing by the stairs.

11th November, 1917
My Dear Emma:
I have exercised considerable restraint in writing before this time—one because of effort, and two because of the frailty of my heart. I know you could take this letter immediately to your husband, but I heard through Alex (who heard a rumor from someone—perhaps a solider from Boston) that Tom is injured

and not with you at the moment. I'm deeply sorry for what you both must be going through. But to the first point—I am not the best writer and I hope you will forgive my poor penmanship. When I was a child, before blindness set in, I learned how to write. My efforts have not progressed much beyond that early point. But if I sit in the direct sun, I can make out the black lines I put on paper. Others might call them scratches, but for me they constitute writing. Alex usually helps me with my spelling and correspondence, but no one, not even he, knows I'm composing this letter.

To the second point—it has been a miserable three months since you left. I think of you every day and wonder, more usually fret, about your safety and well-being. I know you are doing the work you hoped to do, now that you are settled in Paris. I got your address through the Red Cross—please don't be angry with me.

My own work has suffered of late because of my emotional condition. I say this not to blame—you are not at fault; the problem, and the solution, lie squarely upon my shoulders. I should never have allowed myself to engage a married woman in the manner that I did. I was wrong and I hope you can forgive me. Let the matter live and die between us. There can be no good in communicating my afflictions and emotional outpourings to others.

In some respects, I feel we are too late on that account. I heard through Alex that Louisa Markham may have been less than discreet with the unfortunate situation she observed at my studio. Of course, even Alex was shocked to hear the gossip that circulated, I'm afraid so broadly, among Boston circles.

But there is more, my dear Emma, and that is the real reason for my letter. Vreland has hinted to me that all is not well with Tom outside of his injuries. He will only say that something is amiss and, try as I might, I cannot get the point out of him. I am sure this rumor grows like a cancer out of some tale told by Louisa. So protect yourself, my dear sculptress. I know angels guide your work, and they will protect you well, as I cannot be there to do it for them. The wretched war and the Atlantic separate us—as friends.

I have taken too much of your time. I leave your protection to God, your husband, and your own excellent resources.

If you wish, burn this letter so you never have to read its words again or be afraid that it will fall into the wrong hands. I wish so dearly that I could share a moment with you.

Your dearest friend,
Linton Bower

"Madame, are you all right?" Virginie stood before her in the hall. "Your face is white."

"Oh . . . oh, yes, I'm fine." She folded the letter and returned it to the envelope. "When will our patient be here?"

"In less than a half hour."

"I'm ready. Do we have enough plaster?"

Virginie looked at her oddly. "Hassan will prepare the plaster when it is time."

"Good." Emma watched as Madame Clement picked out wilted flowers from the vase in the hall and replaced them with the fresh daisies. Walking to the sculpting room, where Hassan continued his work on the plaster cast, she stopped at the window and watched the stream of Parisians who traversed rue Monge under the leaden sky.

She placed Linton's letter on the sill. There it was—for all to see!

No, I won't burn it!

She picked it up delicately, as if holding a flower, and pressed it against her heart.

A knock alerted Emma to the French soldier wearing a short waistcoat who huddled in silence against the wind-blown snow. She leaned to the left in her chair, far enough to see the man through the door's glass panes. Madame Clement called out that the soldier had arrived and complimented the man on the beautiful crimson-and-blue scarf that covered much of his face. The housekeeper's cheery, repeated *"Bonjour"* sounded like the chirp of an excited bird.

Emma closed the anatomy and physiology book she had been referring to and waited for the soldier. Hassan prepared the plaster and Virginie readied the bandages. Although the reality of her work had toughened her to facial disfigurements, each soldier presented a new and difficult challenge.

Her stomach twitched a bit as the patient approached. His injuries were devastating: a shock of unruly black hair protruded from a stitched scar at the crown of his head; his left jaw and most of his lower face and nose had been blown away, leaving a gaping wound for a mouth and a blunt mound of downturned flesh for a nose. His face resembled the scarred head of an ancient Greek statue pocked and cratered by time.

The devastation to his jaw and tongue was so severe that he could only utter a few unintelligible grunts. The soldier's voice croaked "ahhhhh" and "thhaaahhh" in response to Madame Clement's directions.

Emma smiled and shook the man's hand; several of his fingers were bent and scarred. For those patients without a voice, she kept pen and paper handy when the situation arose. If the man could write, the two could communicate. Writing was much less embarrassing for a soldier than a torturous attempt to decipher words spoken through a mouth destroyed by war.

Even though she had gotten used to the ghastly wounds and mutilations, now and then a soldier appeared who reminded her of someone from her past: the tone of voice, a gesture, a movement often launched a memory. This soldier was no different, sparking a remembrance. Virginie led the man to the reclining chair used for the plaster fittings. Was it the curly dark hair that swirled around the back of his head? Did the texture of his curls remind her of Linton?

Hassan drew the voile sheers over the windows so only soft

winter light filtered into the room. They served another purpose as well: they blocked the soldier's reflection, an image many men couldn't bear. Reflective objects had no place in the studio, either; the only mirror was tucked safely away in a drawer for her personal use. Virginie often covered the "deformed" plaster faces on the wall with cloth to soften the psychological blow to the new visitor.

Emma asked the man to sit. He stared nervously at the chair, exhaled, and then took his seat.

Virginie patted the soldier's hand and explained the casting process in soothing French. Emma fastened a barber's cape around the man's neck and studied his face. The casting process could be uncomfortable and unsettling even for a soldier who, by the time he arrived at the studio, had undergone many hospital stays and painful reconstructive surgeries.

"His left mandible is gone," Emma said to Virginie. "I don't believe I've ever seen such an extreme loss of the septum and upper lip."

"It is tragic," Virginie said, "but what are we to expect from this war?"

Emma turned her attention to the soldier, as Virginie asked him if he was ready to begin the first cast.

His cobalt blue eyes shifted and his brows furrowed, as if he was uncertain. Emma had seen such reactions before—not for the indignities suffered in the casting process, but that the man must endure the process at all.

Hassan stood ready with fresh plaster.

"Tell him, he will have to breathe through his mouth with straws," Emma instructed her. "All right." She dipped an artist's brush into the wet plaster. "Let's begin."

Hassan bent over the soldier and applied a thin coat of lubricant to the injured area. The soldier flinched, but then leaned back against the chair's head brace and relaxed somewhat.

Emma inserted two paper straws between the man's lips. Virginie told him to touch the straws only lightly with his lips so the lack of saliva would keep them from collapsing in his mouth. Emma began by drizzling the plaster onto his left cheek, the nose and upper lip, and then down the disfigured jaw line. Virginie applied cotton bandages to the areas covered with plaster. Emma let the thick, white material cure for fifteen minutes before daubing another coat onto the bandages, building up the injured areas as much as she could, covering them thickly enough to dry into the facial mold.

As Virginie applied the last layer of cotton for strength, the soldier coughed and squirmed in his chair.

"Tell him to relax and breathe normally," Emma instructed the nurse. Virginie complied, and the man, whose face looked as if a partial death masque had been created over the injuries, slumped in his chair.

"Is he all right?" Emma asked.

The soldier's eyes widened as if an electric shock had jolted him. He pointed to his mouth.

"Air," Virginie said. "Perhaps not enough air."

Emma leaned over the man's chest. "He's not breathing."

The solider swiped at his mouth and clumps of wet plaster and bandages flew over Emma and onto the floor.

Virginie shouted as Hassan held down the man's arms.

The soldier kicked at Hassan and writhed in his chair, as if he were being tortured.

"Let him go," Emma shouted.

Hassan released the man's arms and the soldier jumped from the chair, the last of the plaster and cotton mass slipping from his face to the floor. He coughed, sputtered, and clawed at the remaining bits on his face.

Emma reached for him, but he pushed her away.

He grabbed his coat and scarf, hurriedly put them on, and rushed for the door. He turned and cast his gaze toward Emma, a mixture of horror and unspeakable pain glittering in his eyes.

Emma understood his fear and sorrow and knew the solider would never return. He would be like the young man she saw in Boston, wandering the streets with a cup in his hand, his wounds for all to see. She leaned down to pick up bits of plaster. Virginie and Hassan stood over her as she rolled the material into a ball in her hand. Sadness swelled within her.

"A mistake, Madame," Virginie said, attempting to reassure her. "How you say, claustrophobia?"

"Perhaps," Emma said. "I can't save every one of them. I don't know why I try . . . why their faces affect me so. . . ."

The soldier disappeared down the courtyard stairs into the silence of the snow. Forcing a sad smile, Emma looked at Virginie and Hassan, but the man's terror and pain had burrowed into her head.

That evening, in her room, she sketched the soldier's face as it would have looked with the mask had it been completed: from the casts, to the final clay portrait over which the thin copper would be molded. On paper, she filled in the gaping hole of a mouth, the missing nose and jaw, and a young, handsome man appeared in front of her. She pictured the curve of the jawbone, the angle of the nose and how the metal mask, formed over the mold, would fit tightly and cleanly against his face. His new "skin" would have been French Mediterranean in color, with a red blush on the cheeks, a blue sheen stippled on for the shaven beard. That's how he would have looked had the mask been completed. If only he had stayed, she could have transformed his face and restored his life. As she drew, the disappointment of her failure touched her heart.

She sketched in the studio lit by the warm, yellow light of two candles, preferring the flames to the glare of the electric bulb. However, the charcoal drawings seemed more like doodles than studies. She'd thought of sketching Linton from memory but decided against it. Her pencil scratched against the paper— a soothing sound because it connected her to the past: studies at school and sculpting in Boston. She paused and studied the two fresh casts on the wall. Once their masks were finished, the soldiers could rejoin society, walk among the crowd, hold jobs, make love, and have children without fearing the horror precipitated by their faces.

Upstairs, Virginie dragged a log across the bedroom floor to the fireplace. Hassan had already gone to bed in his room. Madame Clement had left hours ago after supper.

The snow Virginie had predicted fell during the day, but only enough to make the streets slick and the air uncomfortably damp. Above the eastern rooftops, and through a broken expanse of pearly clouds, pinpoints of stars glittered like soft diamonds. She opened the window and drew in an exhilarating breath of air. She wondered what Tom, farther to the east, was thinking. What was he doing on this frosty December evening? Was he as alone as she felt?

She gathered a blank piece of paper and a fountain pen, tapping the instrument against the desk to clear the ink before she wrote:

15ᵗʰ December, 1917
My Dear Linton:
I can't tell you how heartened I was to receive your letter. Of course, I'm not angry with you for writing.
To say that the last four months have been an adventure, more often a trial, would be an understatement at best. Yes, Tom has been injured, but I cannot reveal the details because this letter will be censored. You probably already know the details by word of mouth—in other words, gossip provided by a soldier that made its way home.

She dropped her pen on the table and laughed. Had she come to think of Linton so intimately that his blindness had been cured miraculously? Who would read this letter to him, with all its personal detail? Certainly not Louisa Markham or Alex Hippel. Memory carried her back to a night in late May when Anne found her asleep in her Boston studio. She had told her housekeeper she was dreaming of a man in a Greek Temple.

"Was the man your husband?" Anne asked. Emma at once

understood her housekeeper's capacity for passion and longing. Anne would understand now. *She* could be trusted to read the letter to Linton.

Emma picked up the pen.

Tom is recovering, slowly, but his doctor tells me he should be able to return to work soon and live life normally as time goes on.

To your first point—I appreciate your efforts in composing your letter. I had no trouble deciphering your "scratches" as you termed them, and I'm happy you were able to overcome the "frailty" of your heart. A letter from a friend, when you are living in a land of strangers, is always welcome. As important as my work is, I often go through days in Paris with a sense of ennui—no, a feeling of dread that the world has shifted; that this war will never be over, that it will consume us all. And, of course, those of us near the Front fear this the most.

To your second point—the hardest to address—I am sorry your work and life have suffered because of our friendship. I have no control over the rumors spread by a malicious person (you know who she is) but I do have the ability to live my life and conduct my work with pride, without the shame induced by others. At times, I have been bullied and sullied into actions I did not want to take and later regretted, though I must admit my mind was clouded by my own insecurities and adolescence. Some decisions were, in the long run, disastrous for me.

Our time was ours alone and perfect in its innocence.

I'm a branded woman in Boston; first, because of my audacity to be a sculptor (I will use the masculine form here for effect), and second because of the wagging tongue of my so-called friend. You believe she spread a lie after her unfortunate arrival at your studio, and my instincts tell me your assumption is correct. When I return, I will have a chat with her about her predisposition for gossip. That conversation, as you will no doubt guess, may come too late to affect change.

You are also correct in your deduction about Tom. Something is wrong. I'm fairly certain this involves correspondence from my friend, but I can't be sure. The truth will win out in the end.

Please write again. I loved getting your letter. It kept me in touch with Boston—and you.

If the Atlantic were not so dangerous, I would invite you to my studio in the spring. We could sit in the sun in the Luxembourg Gardens and enjoy the tulips and flowering trees. Paris is a most beautiful city, to be savored by lovers and friends, even during a war.

Please take care.

Your friend always,

Emma Lewis Swan

P.S.: I am sending this letter to Anne with instructions to read it to you. She will need to contact you through Alex with utmost discretion. I know she can be trusted to keep our confidences.

The wind clawed its way down rue Monge with fierce talons, sweeping away the gray snow clouds, leaving a sparkling coat of white on the ground and a frosty spray of crystals in the air. The sun shone like a fiery mirror in a flawless blue sky.

The Paris clocks had struck ten on a Sunday morning. Virginie was at church and Hassan was asleep in his room. Madame Clement was off for the day, and Emma guessed she was at church as well. A bit of warmth radiated from the bedroom fireplace and Emma was curled up in bed with a copy of *Madame Bovary*. She had read it in English, but not in French. She lumbered through the pages, writing the words she didn't know on a pad. The story held an uncomfortable fascination for her: a woman who craved love and excitement outside the confines of her bourgeois marriage.

A tentative knock, almost apologetic, sounded on the studio door below. Emma threw off the covers, flung on a robe over her nightclothes, and hurried down the stairs. She caught sight of a man descending the courtyard steps—an American, judging from his uniform.

Emma stepped onto the landing and called out, "May I help you?"

Lt. Andrew Stoneman turned, looked up at her, and smiled.

Emma recognized that contagious grin, the wire-rimmed glasses perched on his thin nose, the sandy hair protruding from under the Montana hat. Holding the railing, he bounced up the steps two at a time in a confident gait, his long wool Army coat flapping in the wind.

Upon reaching the landing, he hugged Emma and kissed her on the cheek. After a second kiss, he said, "The prettiest sight in Paris."

Emma stepped back, flustered by his affection.

"Lieutenant, how are you?" she asked breathlessly, struggling for words.

"I'm sorry," he said, quieting down at the threshold. "Where are my manners? It's so good to see a friendly American face—and a lovely one at that."

Emma blushed and held the door open. "Please, come in."

"Have I caught you at a bad time? Are you well? You're not dressed. It's a beautiful Sunday morning."

"Please, Lieutenant, calm down," she said in response to his barrage of words. "I'm fine. It's wonderful to see you, too. Would you like to sit and have tea?" Emma pointed to an oak chair in the alcove.

Lieutenant Stoneman took off his coat and hat and dropped them on the floor beside the chair. He looked stouter in his tan breeches and tunic than Emma remembered. A holstered black pistol hung from his belt.

"The stove is old," Emma said. "It'll take a moment."

"Don't go to any trouble. We can get tea—or even better, coffee—in Paris on Sunday."

"Yes, at a hotel and pay dearly for it." She clicked on the gas burner and the stove sputtered. Emma struck a match and a blue flame, hissing like a fiery merry-go-round, circled the burner. She took a pan from the cupboard and filled it with water. "We'll have tea in a moment. Now, tell me how you've been."

"I thought you might be at church," the officer said.

"No, Hassan and I are the infidels of the studio. I haven't been in . . . well, too long."

"Hassan?"

"My Moroccan assistant." Emma laughed. "I shouldn't call him an infidel. He's really a kind and gentle man. I must say, he looks a bit fearsome in his fez, and he's always quick to point out that the Moroccans are the fiercest fighters in the war."

"They're like wild men. I can vouch for that."

Emma leaned against the wall and studied the officer as the water began to bubble. She was amazed at how fit and healthy he looked in contrast to the tired and demoralized French troops she'd seen at the Front. "How did you find me? No, let me guess. The Red Cross?"

The officer shook his head.

"No?" She placed a finger on her cheek, unconvinced. "Hummm . . . you *didn't* walk the streets of Paris."

The lieutenant smiled. "I met your husband."

The casualness of his reply caught Emma off guard. "You met Tom?" she asked, trying to mask her uneasy surprise.

"Yes. A wonderful doctor. I was sorry to learn of his injury." He stretched out his legs and crossed them at the ankles. "You see, I've been on what you might call a tour of the Front—from Ypres to Toul. We're still training, but eating better rations now than when we crossed the Atlantic. The French have been great teachers, but they want us in the war now. Pershing doesn't see it that way. He thinks America is an infant when it comes to the battlefield and we should hold back. Still, being near the Front is a good way to get killed."

"Yes, I know," Emma said dryly. The pan rattled on the stove. She turned off the burner, spooned tea into infusers, and lowered them into cups of boiling water, the brew's woody aroma soon filling the alcove.

"Thank you," he said, accepting the cup from Emma. "You've always been kind to me." He smiled again, but this time Emma caught a more affectionate look in his gaze.

"When did you meet Tom?" she asked.

"A few weeks ago. When I was introduced to Dr. Thomas Swan I asked the obvious question."

Emma sipped her tea, hoping the brew might quell the uncomfortable feeling rising in her stomach.

"He's a very lucky man," the officer continued. "To think an overturned operating table may have saved his life. He walks with a limp and he's a little hard of hearing—"

"I know about his injuries," Emma said sullenly. "I've not been in Toul as much as I would like since the—"

"War is hard. Your husband is a brave man."

She leaned forward and placed her cup on the table.

The officer grasped her hand.

She paused, stilled by the gentle touch of his fingers. After a moment, she uncoupled her hand from his.

"I didn't show him this." The lieutenant unbuttoned his tunic and withdrew a folded piece of paper—the portrait she had drawn of him onboard the *Catamount*. He opened it proudly, displaying it for her. "I'm sure its luck has kept me alive on more than one occasion."

"Looks a bit dog-eared," Emma said. "Perhaps I should draw a new one."

He refolded the drawing and replaced it beneath the folds of his tunic. "Not on your life. This portrait is my savior." He patted his chest and straightened in his chair. "Would you like to go for a walk? It's a lovely day."

Emma thought better of it for a moment, but then decided to indulge the officer.

"It would be good to get out. Let me change." She pointed across the hall. "Take a look in the casting room. You can see our work."

When she returned from the bedroom, she found the officer studying the facial casts on the wall.

"My God, I had no idea," he said. "Soldiers with injuries like these are usually dead in the trenches. You must have a strong stomach."

Emma stood by him and pointed to the line of plaster impressions running horizontally across the wall, the multiple casts representing the reconstruction phases of the injured face. She pointed to one in the top row. "This is the face of a French officer, Monsieur Thibault, an early arrival at the studio. Virginie, my nurse assistant, and Hassan, made the first casts. When I returned from Toul I took over."

"Half his face was blasted away," the officer said, incredulously. He ran his hand over the vacant cavity on the right side of Monsieur Thibault's cast.

"It was. He was bent over in anguish and didn't want to look at us when he arrived. Virginie struggled to get him to hold his head up. He couldn't accept that he was a man who terrified children, a man who couldn't stand to be with his wife in daylight, a man who hid every emotion and thought from the world. The light in his eyes was dead." Emma drew the lieutenant's attention to the finished casts. "Look what we've done. We've restored the dead eyes, sculpted the noses and ears, and perfected the mouths until the soldiers' faces appear as they were before the injury. It's chilling, sometimes. In a way, it's like *Frankenstein*, only we're not creating a monster. We're creating a face—restoring a life that's been taken away."

"I never completely understood what you were doing until now." The lieutenant shook his head in admiration. "I'm amazed."

She held up a thin piece of metal resting on the studio table. "This is the new face of Monsieur Thibault." The copper glinted in the winter sun streaming through the studio windows.

"May I take a closer look?" he asked, staring at the oddly shaped form.

"Handle it carefully." Emma gave it to him.

He held the mask in his cupped hands like a baby bird. "This piece of metal will be his face?"

"It will conceal his wounds. In a few more days, he's scheduled for his last fitting. Then we'll put on the finishing touches with paint—matching the skin tone is the most difficult part. The piece is supported by spectacles and conforms to his face."

The officer stared at the molded copper in his hands.

"Perhaps we should go," Emma said. "I have to work after lunch."

"Of course." He held the mask out to her and let it slide gently into her hands.

She withdrew, the obvious affection in his touch making her uneasy. She thought of *Madame Bovary* lying on her bed; and, another consideration: Perhaps the lieutenant knew a secret about Tom which she didn't—one her husband had shared with a genial American officer who liked to talk.

"To the Luxembourg Gardens," she said as she placed the mask back on the table.

Lieutenant Stoneman found an iron bench in the sun and whisked away the thin covering of snow, which fell in fractured white chunks to the ground. Emma, wrapped in her coat, huddled near the scrolled side railing. The officer waited for Emma's invitation to sit and when she offered it, he slid close to her, his body shielding her from the wind. She looked across the snow-covered grass toward the Palais and the marble sculptures that circled the basin. The sun warmed her as she watched a few strollers pass by under the perfect blue sky.

"The gardens must be lovely in the spring," he said and broke her reverie.

She turned to him. "I plan to come here often when the weather warms."

"Perhaps I can join you." He smiled, looking to her for confirmation.

"Who knows? Perhaps the war will be over soon and we'll all be home safe and sound."

The lieutenant sighed and his body, overcome with doubt,

sank against the bench. "Do you ever think about death?" he asked, staring across the wide garden.

Emma nodded, knowing that every day her work affirmed the fragility of life. Only God could know how long their lives would last. "Often, but death isn't my concern at the moment. I'm more interested in healing."

"I understand—but your work must affect you." He looked upon the brown nubs of grass that protruded from the snow.

She followed the direction of his gaze as it shifted across the grounds. "I must admit I came to Paris for selfish reasons, the primary one being the advancement of my career as a sculptress, but there were more important reasons for coming."

He turned to her. "What other reasons?"

Emma wondered whether she should confide in this man when *she* held so much inside: secrets that couldn't be divulged, the emotional fatigue of her work, so little time to work on saving her marriage. No one other than Virginie was privy to her confidences, and those parcels were carefully doled out; yet, the lieutenant's questions made her feel vulnerable and open to conversation—as if she had found someone she could trust.

"I don't want to bother you with my troubles," Emma said. "I don't expect you to care."

"But I'm a friend—and who can predict what the future holds. You can talk freely to me."

"My feelings are my own, and, yes, considering the times we live in, perhaps I should be more open." She paused for a moment considering what to say, staring at the people strolling the gravel paths, some in pairs, some alone, all absorbed in their individual worlds. "I was running away from something in Boston. In fact, I've been running away from something most of my life, but I've only recently recognized how much it's affected me. . . ." The wind scattered a whirlwind of snow around her legs.

"Please, go ahead. Your secrets are safe with me."

Emma believed he was telling the truth. She took a deep

breath. "I was running from someone—from an attraction I wanted desperately to control because I'm married and in love with my husband—at least I'm supposed to be." She lowered her gaze. "Our relationship has been strained for a few years. We're both to blame—partly me, partly him."

"You fell in love with another man?"

"Let's say I could have and a new character would have been added to my life's story; but nothing of significance happened, except for damaging rumors. Another woman, a friend of Tom's and a friend of mine, I thought, found out."

"Oh, I see. Malicious gossip."

Emma patted his arm. "You're very smart, Lieutenant. You'll go far in this world."

He edged away a bit, as if her confession had troubled him. "Please, don't get me wrong. I think of you as a friend—albeit a lovely, talented, and beautiful one. I have no intention of taking advantage now or ever, let alone when you're disturbed."

She tugged on his arm, urging him to slide closer. "There's no chance of that. Right now, I need you as a windscreen."

He laughed and then touched her cheek with his gloved fingers.

She smiled, moved his hand away, and shivered. "No, Lieutenant, I have a husband and work to do. It's been nice in the garden, but it's very cold." She rubbed her hands together to stave off the chill. "We're having a Christmas Eve party at the studio if you'd like to come. We've invited all our patients. Most said they'd be happy to attend for a sip of brandy and an excuse to get out of Mass." Emma stood and then brushed the snow from her coat. "I shouldn't joke. Most of these men are devout and thank God daily for their lives. Maybe the war will stop for Christmas and death will take a holiday."

"I don't know if I'll be in Paris on the date, but if I am, I'd love to attend."

She held out her hand. The officer grasped it and got up from the bench. As they circled the Palais, Emma stopped near one of the white statues, which loomed like a colossus over the promenade, and ran her fingers over a delicately veined marble leg. "Sculpture was all I was interested in for so long." She looked up. "This face . . . do you realize how important the face is, Lieutenant Stoneman? From the moment we're born, people judge us by our faces. But I want to create more than that; I want to create real life and love—not live through a statue." The horrible dream from the doctor's office in Pittsfield jumped into her head. "And, if I could, I'd bring back the dead."

"I hope you get your wish."

They walked arm in arm, until they were a short distance from the studio. The sun was lowering in the sky, casting deep, black shadows across rue Monge. The anonymous pedestrians, in their heavy coats, moved in lines down the street. However, Emma knew they were human beings, rich and poor, soldier and civilian, with needs and wants, not just studies for her art. As she said good-bye to the lieutenant, she wished that the war and the dark winter would disappear, and that peace and warmth would take their places.

If I could, I'd bring back the dead.

As the officer walked away, she realized how hard it would be to love Tom, or any man, until she forgave herself for the action taken so long ago.

Virginie whistled a merry tune as she hung holly and mistletoe over the doors and laced their frames with paper Tricolors. Emma explained the significance of mistletoe to her nurse; it was, after all, Christmas Eve, a night for peace and love. Virginie giggled and told Emma she had never been fortunate enough to participate in such a custom.

Madame Clement dried the last of the champagne glasses while Hassan carried a few more bottles to the courtyard to chill in the freezing air. The afternoon sky had faded from an inky blue to black and the evening gleamed luminously with a nearly full moon, only the brightest of stars daring to compete with the orb's radiance.

Emma raced from room to room inspecting the decorations;

she wanted the festivities to be perfect for the soldiers. Aromas from holly, evergreen boughs, and strong black coffee wafted through the studio. Madame Clement had managed to buy cookies and a frosted white cake from a baker who hoarded flour and sugar. Emma offered to pay for the desserts, but Madame Clement refused.

The housekeeper also surprised Emma by having her son, and a soldier, haul a Pathé phonograph up the stairs. They placed the machine, with its sound trumpet shaped like a giant green petunia, on the casting room table. Hassan was the first to try it. He selected several marches from a box of records, cranked the handle, positioned the needle, and tapped his feet to the stirring rhythms. After Madame Clement chose a waltz, Hassan grabbed Virginie by the waist and attempted, unsuccessfully, to coax her to dance.

A few minutes after six, the first of the soldiers arrived, and by seven, the studio was filled with guests.

Lieutenant Stoneman, looking relaxed and handsome, arrived a short time later. "From the street, it sounds as if you're having a raucous party," he told Emma as she took his coat. He waved his leave pass at her.

"You can hear our celebration from below?"

"Yes, laughter and phonograph music. You'd hardly know a war was going on if you didn't know better. Maybe it's as you said the other day—death will take a holiday, like it did on Christmas Day 1914." He leaned over and kissed her on the cheek.

He smelled of soap and citrus cologne.

"We've only a few cookies and one slice of cake left," she said as they stood near the alcove.

"That's all right. I've already eaten." The officer spotted the mistletoe above the doorway. "Merry Christmas," he said and kissed her quickly on the lips.

She gave him a peck on the cheek, and thought briefly of Tom and what he might be doing at this hour. She had promised herself to call him tomorrow, on Christmas Day.

She led the officer to the casting room where the soldiers were posing for a picture. Some stood, others sat cross-legged on the floor, their faces covered with bandages and eye patches; others with wounds exposed or wearing newly completed masks. The few who could drink comfortably held champagne glasses. One soldier, Monsieur Thibault, the right side of his face swathed in white strips of cotton, posed with his rifle.

Hassan waved his hands for quiet. The group hushed as the Moroccan readied a tripod camera; then, signaling three, two, one with his fingers, he pressed the shutter cable with his thumb. The magnesium flash powder exploded in a puff of smoke, sending a white, acrid haze ballooning into the air. As the fumes rose and dissipated, laughter and coughs echoed in the room. Soon, glasses clinked and conversations began anew.

Emma was overjoyed at the soldiers' good spirits.

The lieutenant looked toward the wall of plaster casts, again hidden by the white sheet. "You've covered them," he said to Emma.

"For our patients' well-being. Virginie draped the casts this afternoon. Some men have gone insane over their reflections. The soldiers don't need to be reminded of their injuries, especially on Christmas Eve."

"I understand. God knows, these men have been through enough."

During the next half hour, Virginie, Hassan, and Madame Clement all breezed by Emma and the officer. The housekeeper, attired in her best black dress, swayed a little as she approached them, apparently a victim of too many glasses of champagne. The creases around her eyes deepened as she stared at the American; then, she laughed, patted him on the shoulder, and shouted in a somewhat slurred voice, "*Joyeux Noël.*"

"Would you like to dance?" the lieutenant asked Emma as Virginie put a record on the phonograph.

"Only if you ask Virginie and Madame Clement first," Emma replied.

"Well, I can see asking Virginie, but Madame Clement is another story. . . ."

Emma slapped his arm.

"No, I don't mean she's too ugly or infirm. She's had too much to drink. What if she falls from my arms?"

"It appears one of our soldiers has saved you from your dilemma." Emma and the officer watched as Monsieur Thibault approached the housekeeper and asked her to dance. A wide smile swept across her face; then, she gulped a last swig of champagne before the soldier led her to the dance floor created in the middle of the room.

"So, I *must* dance with Virginie?" the lieutenant asked, as he spotted the attractive, young nurse in her white uniform.

Emma nodded.

"I think I can make the sacrifice." He ambled across the room and pointed to the dance floor.

Virginie smiled in surprise and looked to Emma for approval.

Emma nodded and the couple began to dance, the officer leading Virginie slowly around the floor, picking up the pace as they meshed as partners. Lieutenant Stoneman's booted feet waltzed in unison to the music as he held the nurse's hand high in his.

From the corner of her eye, Emma spotted a flash through the curtains. *Probably fireworks, or someone shooting a rifle from the rooftop in celebration.* In an instant, the flash brought back the disturbing memory of the shelling at the Front and the nights spent at Tom's bedside. *What is he doing now? Is he thinking of me, or of someone else?*

Another flash split the sky and a nearly imperceptible rumble reached her ears.

Is the city being shelled?

Lieutenant Stoneman broke away from Virginie and hurried to the windows.

Emma, her heart pounding, followed.

The officer threw back the curtain, exposing the glass, and peered out.

"What do you think it is?" Emma asked.

He stared intently out the window. "An aerial bombardment or Big Bertha."

"No . . . not even the Germans . . . on Christmas Eve."

The officer's head jerked left as yet another flash lit the sky.

"That was farther away," Emma said.

"Yes, I saw it." He seemed relieved as he held back the curtain. "A pyrotechnic shell."

A shadow fell across the window.

Madame Clement gasped.

Emma wheeled to find the room's occupants frozen like figures in a painting. The phonograph needle slipped into a repetitious *clack . . . clack . . . clack* at the end of the record. Everyone stared at Monsieur Thibault, who had deserted the startled Madame Clement in the midst of the dance.

The French soldier, his right arm extended, stood in front of Emma, pointing a pistol at her, but seemingly looking through her body into the night beyond the window pane.

Emma sensed that Lieutenant Stoneman was about to move toward the armed soldier.

Monsieur Thibault suspected the officer's actions as well and waved his pistol at the American, a deathly signal not to move.

Emma grabbed Lieutenant Stoneman's arm and pulled him back to her side.

"*Arrêtez la guerre*," the French soldier whispered gruffly through his deformed mouth.

"What did he say?" the lieutenant asked Emma.

"Stop the war."

The officer whispered, "Is he crazy?"

"Be quiet, he might understand English," Emma ordered. "He's seen his reflection in the window. We mustn't upset him." She forced a smile and took a step toward him. "Monsieur Thibault . . . this is a Christmas party. Put down your gun. Virginie, tell Monsieur Thibault we understand his sorrow and we want to help him. Tell him that's why he came to the studio in the first place—to reclaim a normal life."

Virginie, her brown eyes wide with fear, recited Emma's instructions.

Monsieur Thibault moved closer to Emma and the lieutenant. "*Tuez les Boches*," he commanded.

"The Germans are not here," Emma said.

From the other side of the room, Hassan crept toward the soldier.

Emma signaled for the Moroccan to stop.

Monsieur Thibault again waved the pistol at Emma and the officer. At his order, they moved in front of a bookcase in the corner.

The soldier walked toward the window as if stalking the enemy and aimed the pistol directly at his reflection. "*Mon Dieu, mon Dieu*," he said like a sad prayer and unwrapped the bandage that covered the right side of his head. When he was done, he dropped the dressing on the floor and stared, as if looking into a mirror, at the cavity that was his face.

Emma reached for the soldier.

"*Arrêtez!*" he yelled and jammed the gun's barrel into his right temple.

Virginie cried out. Some of the soldiers brought their hands to their faces to wipe away tears while others stared in disbelief at their comrade.

"Monsieur Thibault," Emma pleaded, "put down the gun. Think of your family."

The soldier turned to Emma. Tears slid down from his left eye and a piteous smile emerged from the ravaged mouth.

Then, he pulled the trigger.

The injured soldier's smile contorted into an agonizing twist as the room exploded in a flash, a deafening report, and a cacophony of screams.

Blood splattered across Emma's white dress.

Drift away, drift away to sleep, perhaps nothingness, on the night of the Child's birth.

The police arrived first; a few minutes later, an ambulance.

The medical workers carted Monsieur Thibault's body down the stairs and through the passageway, their breaths ballooning from their mouths, the dead man's legs and arms splayed across their shoulders.

After the corpse had been removed, Virginie donned an apron and scrubbed the casting room floor with towels, swiping at the wood like a mad washerwoman.

After helping the nurse, Madame Clement, through teary eyes, packed up her records and player and wished Emma and the lieutenant a joyous Christmas. She stared at the blood-stained floor as her son and another man, carrying the phonograph, coaxed her from the room.

The other soldiers, like lost children, straggled down the stairs.

Christmas Eve is a dream. I want no part of it. The war is a dream. I should have been prepared for something like this. I was too wrapped up in the holiday—too wrapped up in my own idea of the perfect party for these soldiers. How stupid of me, not to see this coming. If only the flashes hadn't happened and Andrew hadn't pulled the curtain. I saw Monsieur's rifle, but I never suspected he had a gun. So many kill themselves during the happy times.

Virginie tossed a blood-soaked bandage into a bucket and sobbed.

Lieutenant Stoneman knelt, placing his hands on the nurse's shoulders, wiping the tears from her cheeks, saying in a steady voice, "Everything will be all right."

"I can take no more," Virginie said, wrenching herself away from him. "I'm going to a friend's house for the holiday." She stared at her red fingers and the bloodstains streaking her apron.

"Wash up and go to your friend's," Emma said. "Hassan and I will finish cleaning up."

Virginie nodded and rushed from the room.

The remaining three—Emma, Hassan, and the officer—washed the floor until it was cleansed of blood and human tissue; then, they moved the furniture back into place and extinguished the candles. Except for the mistletoe and a few decorations, there was no indication a party had ever taken place.

Hassan said good night and trudged up the stairs.

Emma walked with the lieutenant to the alcove to retrieve the officer's coat.

His hand lingered on the door. "Are you sure you'll be all right?"

Emma looked into eyes filled with concern. "Yes." She held his hands and studied the thin, elegant fingers. They were red-tipped also, stained by Monsieur Thibault's blood.

"I can stay with you," he said.

"I'll do better alone." Emma hesitated before speaking again. "It's not a good idea for you to stay." She walked back to the casting room and withdrew the drape covering the masks. Her body sank, crestfallen at the sight. "His mask was nearly done."

The lieutenant followed and then embraced her in his warm arms; the steely odor of adrenaline still clinging to his skin.

She gazed at his face, an invitation to intimacy, her fingers lingering on his chest, feeling the strong beat of his heart.

His eyes shifted in anticipation, drifting toward the ceiling and her bedroom above.

"No," she said.

He smiled slightly, released her, and returned to the alcove for his coat. He wrote down a telephone number on a piece of paper and handed it to Emma. "I'll call tomorrow, if you wish. Please telephone if you need me—I mean it sincerely—in the best possible way. Good night, Mrs. Swan. I wish you a Merry Christmas." He opened the door and descended the stairs.

She walked upstairs alone. Virginie had already left, her bedspread creased with the signs of a hasty departure: Hassan's door was closed.

Emma lit a fire and the light, warm and cheery, flickered against the walls of the garret. The moon, following its path, oblivious to the turmoil of the evening, still masked the brightness of the stars.

She undressed, shivered in her distress all the way to bed,

and ached with sorrow for Monsieur Thibault. Despite her pain, she imagined what it would have been like to invite Lieutenant Stoneman upstairs to her bed for comfort and, perhaps, make love to him; but her thoughts turned to Linton as well, and then her husband. The world seemed as cold and lonely on this Christmas Eve as she could remember and love never farther away from her heart.

Late in the night, the fire died, the moon waned, and a silvery veil of stars shone through the window. Emma listened to the silence, stared into the starry deep, and cried as quietly as she could.

PART FOUR

---·-·---

PARIS
JULY 1918

CHAPTER 7

———— ◆ ————

"So you haven't stopped working, have you?" John Harvey smiled at her from across the studio desk. "Do you have an ashtray in this bloody facility?"

"Virginie?" Emma called out. "Could you get John an ashtray from the alcove?"

Virginie peered around the door. "Yes . . . anything for his lordship."

John snickered. "Obnoxious leopards never change their spots. I'm happy to see Virginia is her usual cranky self." He struck a match and puffed on his cigar, taking in one deep breath as the tobacco fired red. "I've switched from cigarettes to cigars. Better for your health, I believe."

"Virginie is only cranky when you're here, John."

"Bah, she's a pain in the—"

"She's a treasure." Emma chuckled. "I don't know what I would do without her. In fact, what I would do without my whole staff. Hassan has become quite expert at modeling, and Madame Clement takes care of us like a grandmother."

The nurse entered and placed a metal ashtray on the desk in front of John.

"Thank you, *Virginia*," John said. "What a pleasure it's been to see you again."

"You should visit more often," she responded. "The Germans still sink ships in the Channel."

"Well, fortunately for you I've arrived in one piece, saved from torpedoes; otherwise, you would be deprived of my company." He blew smoke in lazy rings toward her.

Virginie coughed and waved her hands. "I must be going. I don't like cigar smoke."

"Too bad," John said. "Perhaps I'll see you again on my next visit."

"I'll be in my room," Virginie said.

"*Au revoir*," John said.

"*Pitre*," Virginie muttered as she left the room.

"What did she say?" John asked. "I didn't catch it."

"She wished you a good day," Emma said, knowing that the nurse had branded him a "clown."

John rested his cigar on the ashtray. "Highly unlikely."

Emma slid a few books away from the middle of her desk and leaned toward him. "So why are you here, John? I'm almost certain this isn't a social visit."

He lowered his head a bit and stared intently at the edge of the desk. "I'm afraid I can't say."

"Can't say? That's very unlike you."

He shifted the cigar between his fingers. "I don't mean to be evasive—let's just say I was well protected during the Channel crossing. The entire German Navy wouldn't have had a blighter's chance against the convoy I was traveling in. Doctors sometimes get involved in wartime projects that are out of line with their normal duties."

"You don't have to explain."

He nodded, flicked his cigar ash, and without hesitation asked, "How's Tom?"

"He's fine," she said under the uncomfortable scrutiny of his penetrating gaze.

"He's fine? That's all? Now who's being evasive?"

"I've been to Toul twice since Christmas for short visits—both times I planned the trip. The first time, in January, I helped Tom get comfortable in his cottage—straightened it up and cleaned for him. The second visit, in May, he was back to work fully and we barely had time to speak. It was just after the battle at Cantigny."

"So you know about the American forces?"

"Word filtered down . . . even in Toul."

He had not taken his eyes off her while positioning the cigar in the ashtray. "I must say, if you were one of my patients, I'd be treating you for malaise."

Emma stared back indignantly. "Malaise? I have more work than my staff and I can handle. New patients arrive every day—all of them wanting some semblance of their lives back. If you treat me for anything it should be exhaustion."

He pointed to the casts on the wall. "I see your work is going well. You have a reputation, Emma. I've even heard word of it in Porton Down. The French love you. They say you work miracles and talk about the wonders of your masks."

"I'm glad to hear it. I'm flattered."

He paused. "But they love Tom as well. They say he is a great surgeon."

Emma picked up a pen and rubbed it between her fingers absentmindedly. "We do very different work. We're very different people."

John sighed. "As a friend to both you and Tom—and I know it's not my affair—and may I say, you *are* very different people . . . but you're married. Neither of you act like it."

"Rather obvious, isn't it."

"Painfully so. I talked with Tom two weeks ago by telephone and I told him I was coming to Paris. I asked him to tell you about my trip and give you my regards. He said *I* would probably see you before he talked with you. I can't believe this silence is just about your busy schedules."

She leaned back in her chair. "To be honest, it's not about our work. It's about us."

"I'm going to see Tom the day after tomorrow. I'll be spending quite a bit of time in Toul. Is there anything you'd like me to do—anything you want me to say?"

"Thank you for the offer, but no." Emma laughed.

"What's so humorous?" John asked.

"I was going to ask you to tell Tom that I love him, but that's rather ridiculous, isn't it?"

John picked up the cigar and puffed on it. "It's only ridiculous if it's not true."

Emma considered his words as smoke drifted through the room. Finally, she said, "I do love him. We're both having a difficult time at the moment."

"I'll tell him you love him." He ground his cigar tip into the ashtray and dusted the excess ash off with his finger. "It's getting late—at least for me. I'm in Paris through tomorrow if you require my services. The Hotel Charles." He opened his jacket's breast pocket and dropped the cigar inside. "Please deliver my good-byes to Virginia and your staff. I'm very pleased the Studio for Facial Masks is doing so well." Emma escorted him to the door. "Remember, there is more to life than work."

"You're one to talk."

"Precisely." Before he closed the door, he added, "I don't have a wife, Emma. I have nothing but England, this war, and my work. You have so much more than I do."

He bobbed like a cork down the staircase and crossed the courtyard to the tunnel. Then his footsteps disappeared into the sounds of rue Monge echoing through the walkway—chattering pedestrians, the clop of hooves, the "uh-ugah" of a distant automobile horn. On impulse, she ran to the casting room window and looked out on the street. The plump body and bald pate turned left toward the hotel. The street lay in shadow, but the sun, still heavy and warm in the July sky, made its presence known as it settled in the west. It was after nine in the evening and daylight would linger for another hour. There was time, before she trundled off to bed, to read a book, think about what John had said, and consider why love had deserted her.

The night, soft and languorous, drifted through the window like a secret lover. Virginie was fast asleep, her face turned away from Emma toward the wall. The silky July air stole across her body, caressed her skin like warm fingers. In the dark, Emma shifted restlessly on her bed and remembered a day long ago at her parents' Berkshires farm near summer's end when the air blew warm and soft through the window as well.

In the July heat, the sky flashed over Paris. The thunder's low rumble assured her the threat was only rain, not a German attack. She rose from bed and watched as the clouds descended in dark veils over rue Monge. The rain began as soft sprinkles, but soon curtains of water lashed the street and cascaded down the gutters.

A deep sadness enshrouded her, when she remembered the melting faun in her Boston courtyard. But the memory of the faun shifted into an image much more unsettling—and her anger rose, despite the cooling rain, because she knew, as a woman, she had had no other choice. Much of her soul died that day.

Emma had tossed and turned, thinking about when American soldiers might arrive at the Studio for Facial Masks. The doughboys were increasingly involved in the war, but it was too early for Americans to appear on her doorstep, she concluded in restless musings before dawn. The Yanks fought their first battle at Cantigny during the last days of May, and Emma knew American soldiers would eventually need the studio's services. However, months, possibly years, of hospitalization and operations lay ahead of a soldier before he could make his way to the studio.

Regardless, Emma was unsure about the nationality of the man who arrived one day after her disquieting thoughts. The soldier, attired in a Canadian uniform, had healed from his last round of surgeries. At first glance, she thought his recovery, accented by a splotchy redness of the skin, might be too soon for the mask. He was tall, blond, with a thin frame like her husband, and couldn't speak, or chose not to, because of his injuries. The whole of his lower jaw was obliterated on both sides, as if someone had taken a knife and scooped out his face below the nose, like melon from the rind. However, something about him touched Emma: the way he regarded her with his eyes, the only part of his face, it appeared, unaffected by his injuries.

He sat in the alcove and curiously stared at her as she continued to work in the casting room. Virginie hovered over the man, asking questions in her best English, smiling and laughing in her natural role as nurse to the afflicted. Emma observed her interactions with the soldier as judiciously as she could. Her assistant asked questions and the soldier penned the answers on paper, using the alcove table as a writing desk. After one particular question, the soldier shook his head and scribbled violently across the page. Virginie nodded and walked into the studio.

"He wants to begin," Virginie said. "His stomach is upset. He thinks he may be sick." She thrust out the paper so Emma could read the scrawled writing.

"Show him to the washroom before we get started," Emma said. "I have questions for him as well."

Virginie nodded, returned to the alcove, and led the soldier down the hall.

Emma picked up the medical file the nurse had left on the desk. The soldier's name was Ronald Darser, a native of Chicago, an American, but assigned to the 7th Canadian Infantry Brigade. The notes from the field hospital read: *Mouth shot away from gunshot wound to chin. Fractured mandible with large loss of bone in symphysis region. Tongue extracted.* The soldier had been injured at the Third Battle of Ypres, the Battle of Passchendaele, in April 1917. The file described an extensive list of surgeries, including a pedicle tube from his chest to chin to replace the missing portion of the chin, skin grafts, more pedicles, enlarging of the mouth and extraction of teeth. A difficult case, not only because of the disfigurement, but because the soldier had no hope of ever speaking again.

After a few minutes, the soldier reappeared in the hall, Virginie following him to Emma's desk in the casting room. The man stood stiffly in front of her until she asked him to sit down.

"From your file, I've studied the nature of your injuries, Private Darser," she said in a soft voice to allay any fears the soldier might have. "I'd like to ask you a few questions before we start the first cast. Is that all right with you?"

The soldier nodded.

"If you would be so kind," Emma continued, "please write your answers on this paper so I can include them in your file." She pushed a clean sheet across her desk and handed him a pen. "Do you have any allergies to dust or plaster?"

The soldier shook his head and wrote, *No,* holding the pen tightly in his right hand.

"How about allergies to metals, copper in particular?"

He looked at Emma intensely and wrote, *Surgical steel, perhaps.*

Emma studied the soldier quizzically. She thought the answer odd, but instead of questioning him decided to offer sympathy instead. "I can understand your aversion to surgery after having gone through so many operations. The whole ordeal has been very painful, I'm sure."

He stared at her with his unflinching gaze. The strange color of his eyes, like the pale turquoise of thick winter ice, unsettled her. She shifted in her chair and rubbed her fingertips against the oak grain of the desk.

He wrote: *You have no idea how painful this war has been for me. I appreciate your sacrifice, the work you do for me and others like me, but, suffice it to say, you have it easy. You sit here in Paris, in relative safety, while the bombs and the bullets of the world's armies rend their terrible destruction. My life is destroyed and I can never get it back.* He shoved the paper across the desk to her.

Emma took it gingerly. As she read his words, thoughts of the Christmas party—and Monsieur Thibault's suicide—raced through her mind. Fearing this soldier might explode as well, Emma attempted to calm him. "Private Darser, our studio can help. I know you understand our work, and we can help you recover your face and life. You'll be able to enjoy the company of your wife and friends again and be able to hold a job, if you wish, without fear of ridicule or laughter."

He snatched the paper from Emma and scrawled the words in capital letters: *I AM SILENCED FOREVER. HAVE YOU EVER BEEN SILENCED, MRS. SWAN? I SUSPECT YOU HAVE. I CANNOT SPEAK; BUT, FAR WORSE, I HAVE NO ONE TO SHARE MY SILENCE.*

The soldier dropped his head, and his shoulders trembled as he fought back sobs.

Emma touched his hand.

As she did so, he threaded his fingers through hers and grasped them tightly.

Emma flinched, but made no effort to withdraw. "I know silence," she said, "a terrible, cold silence that fills the body, and when you think it's released its frigid grip, it returns stronger and more deadly than ever. Yes, I've walked hand in hand with lonely silence—and suffered from its constant companionship, the suffocating withdrawal from pain. Suffocation can be as horrendous as loneliness." Emma stopped, quieted by her thoughts. "Are you married, Private Darser? It was wrong of me to make such an assumption."

He looked up and shook his head, his eyes softening a bit as he released her hand to write. *Never—there was a girl once, but we came to a bitter end. She was quite beautiful and I loved her in my way, but she couldn't understand my affection and I couldn't convey it. I was younger then—if I had the chance today, I would be stronger and more forgiving. But she has moved on, and now I am mute.*

"I understand, but you're not mute. You're talking with me now."

He brought his hands to his face and covered his eyes for a moment. When he removed them, he wrote: *Words, when spoken, last only seconds, but can change lives forever. How I wish I could correct the harm I've caused. How I wish she could forgive me for all that we went through. I could rest in peace if she would tell me that all was forgiven.*

"I'm certain she would." For a time, they studied each other from their respective viewpoints, until Emma spoke again. "Are you ready to begin? Virginie, I'm sure, has explained our work: the casts, the sculpting process, how we reconstruct the face as it existed before the injury, and finally the making of the mask. When the mask is painted, fitted, and ready, you will have—"

He placed his left hand over hers to quiet her. *Dr. Harvey has explained everything. I am ready to begin.*

With a start, Emma recognized the solider—he was the one who had arrived at John Harvey's her first night in Paris.

Through the summer, the sweet perfume of yellow roses drifted through the house as Madame Clement continued her self-imposed task of finding flowers. More than anything, the housekeeper wanted to brighten the studio and make sure the casting room was filled each day with blooms. Monsieur Thibault's suicide had affected her deeply, making her even more cognizant of the soldiers. Now, she offered each a cheery greeting, despite her own mood, and offered them food or drink before they had the chance to ask.

One evening in August, the exhaust, the smell of horses, lifted from the street into Emma's bedroom and overtook the odor of the fragrant roses. She sat on her bed and leafed through the few letters she had received from Linton Bower. The last was dated July 23rd, 1918. She opened it gently as if it were an expensive gift. The paper smelled like the paint in Linton's studio. It was his mark; his imprint upon the world he shared especially with her. The writing was his: choppy and scrawled across the page. There was no mistaking his hand; a few letters had arrived written by Anne on Linton's behalf. They had been more formal, less revealing than when Linton desired an intimate message.

Emma stretched across her bed.

My Dearest Emma,
I'm so happy we've been able to write to each other. You will, of course, excuse my handwriting. I didn't want Anne to

transcribe these words, although I'm having her address the envelope for fear of the letter not making it to Paris because of my bad hand.

By the way, Anne and Lazarus are fine. I believe you were quite correct in your assumptions about her—unlike Louisa's assessment—she is the perfect housekeeper and organizer of your affairs, and she dotes on Lazarus, who seems, to me, to have become a very pampered and lazy animal, but still as kind and faithful a companion as one could ever require.

As you and I have corresponded, the connection between Anne and me has grown stronger. She's been kind enough to ask me over for dinner. I think she truly enjoys having company—the house must get lonely at times—and my social calendar isn't overflowing. One can attend only so many art openings and exhibits. Only Alex keeps me entertained on that account.

Anne has a beau, a young man she met the night of Fran Livingston's party shortly before you left for France. But don't concern yourself. I believe it's just a flirtatious crush. Anne is too firmly rooted in Catholicism to allow any indiscretion. At first, I believed the young man was part of the Livingston circle, but then I discovered he is a protégé of Singer Sargent's and is probably poorer than I am in bank account. Apparently, he is studying to be a painter, a questionable profession at best, as we both know.

It is difficult for me to express my true feelings in this letter. I've avoided them long enough by writing about Anne, her friend, and Lazarus, but I am acutely aware, as you have always claimed, that your first devotion is to your husband.

But dare I say it, in our recent correspondence, I detected a change. You've written only of your work and the soldiers who have come to your studio. I get the sense, even across the miles of ocean that separate us, a chasm has developed between you and Tom. I wonder if his injuries have somehow come between you, or if there is an emotional wound as well, which you alluded to in your last letter.

And that, my dear Emma, is the purpose of my writing on

this glorious July day. The sun is bright enough I can see as clearly as I could ever hope to, and the sea breeze has swept away the heat from my door. I sit in front of the open window, grateful for the light and wish I could touch your face. What comfort that would give me since the pleasures of paint and canvas have begun to fail me. I wonder how you spend your days. Do you ever pine for me, as I long for you? But whenever our next meeting, you understand I am always here for you and always will be despite what happens between now and that glorious reunion.

I pray that our meeting will come soon—that this war will end and you and your husband and the soldiers will return safely to our soil. I write these words with my heart and no regard for the censors. Let them think what they will.

I've gone on for too long and the strain of writing has tired my eyes. I must rest and say good-bye. As it is, there will be no painting today, and tomorrow is questionable.

My thoughts are with you always.
Your dearest friend,
Linton Bower

Sometime after ten that night, the bedroom door opened. Virginie, who had spent the evening with a friend, said hello and sat on her bed. Emma was surprised to find she had dozed off while dreaming of meeting Linton again in Boston. The pages of his letter were scattered across the sheet.

The face of Private Darser took shape as Emma molded clay into the cavity left by the wound. She worked on the cast without assistance—a strange feeling coming over her as she sculpted. Across the studio, Hassan smoothed fresh plaster on another cast while Virginie stippled paint on a mask.

"This reconstruction is one of the most difficult I've worked on," Emma said to Virginie and Hassan as she worked clay into the chin, "because there is so little left of Private Darser's jaw and mouth. There is no mirror, no left and right, to gauge the reflection. I don't know whether to make the chin with a cleft, or whether to make it weak or strong."

"A man always likes a strong chin," Virginie said.

Hassan nodded in agreement.

"Yes, but I will ask him," Emma said. "I can picture his chin in my mind. . . ." Emma put the wooden sculpting tool down.

Madame Clement appeared at the door. "Private Darser is here for his appointment," she said, her English coated with her usual French accent.

"Show him in," Emma tugged at her jacket and took a quick glance at her own reflection before she pulled the studio curtains. Rather than put on a dress, she had opted for attire similar to a woman's Army uniform. The jacket was severe and matriarchal, and she preferred to work in a dress, but Private Darser, in his formality, had influenced her, and she had come to realize how much of an effect, subtle at first, he had on her. Her choice of clothing was a result from their meetings, but she found herself, of late, thinking of him more and more because he was an American. When the sun flashed upon trees a certain way, or the air carried a damp sweetness, he entered her mind at the most unusual times and reminded her of New England.

He appeared without Madame Clement, stopping for a moment in the doorway, standing motionless, his starched shirt and scarf wrapped high and loose about his neck and face, covering the greater part of his injury. The light in the alcove behind him framed him in a diffuse glow.

"Please come in," Emma said, struck by his austere and commanding presence.

As if energized by her words, the soldier strode toward her, withdrawing a pad and pencil from his pocket, handing her the pad on which he had written: *There is no need to draw the curtains. I love the sunlight and summer is almost over. We should enjoy the beautiful weather while we can.*

Emma looked at the note. "I understand your wishes, however—"

He waved his hand in front of her and wrote: *I know of your unfortunate suicide. I have no wish to die. Please open the curtains.*

Emma acquiesced to his request. Light flooded the room. "Better?"

He nodded.

Virginie patted the soldier on the arm. "We admire your courage."

He wrote, *Thank you*, and added, *Can we begin?*

"I'd like to make another cast today. The first wasn't to my liking." She held up the form she had been working on. "Can you tell me if this chin is similar . . . ?" Emma paused, somewhat embarrassed by the indelicacy of her statement.

You want to know if it looks like my face?

"Yes, does it look like your face? I have no way of knowing."

Private Darser looked at the cast, but wrote nothing.

"No opinion?"

Make my chin, my face, any way you wish. You are the sculptress, the artist, and I'm at your mercy. You may do with me whatever you like.

A shock raced up her spine, prickling her back. After a moment, when she had recovered, she said, "I'm not sure I understand."

Of course, you understand. You have always understood your power. You are the sculptress and you may mold me as you wish.

"I see," Emma said, cupping her hands together, wishing to move past his words. "Hassan, bring fresh plaster for another cast. We must work on Private Darser."

Hassan lifted a pail and brought it to the chair. Emma covered the soldier's clothes with an apron, drizzled the plaster over his face, and worked on the injured area gently, and as she did, the soldier responded to her fingers, shuddering as she applied the wet substance to his face, as if she had touched a raw and open wound.

*   *   *

The brown daisies, petunias, and marigolds continued to bloom in the Paris gardens, but Emma sensed a shift in the season. The sun had lost its warmth, the sky, more often than not, displayed a rich, autumnal, blue rather than the haze of summer. Gooseflesh broke out on her arms in the chilly dawn or at sunset.

At her studio desk, she gazed at the rows of casts hung upon the wall, focusing on one row in particular, those taken of Private Darser. She opened the medical history of the soldier who was now solely under her charge and reread the recent note clipped inside the folder.

What is it about this man? He is unlike the others. Perhaps it's because I am used to working with French soldiers—and this man is so different he's gotten under my skin. I find myself consumed with his case to the detriment of others. I snapped at Virginie the other day, when I found her fussing with Darser's final cast. She was taken aback when I told her that Private Darser was my case and that I was quite capable of handling him. I had never spoken to her like an underling—I apologized later in the day, but the damage was done. She was quite cool to me the rest of the week. When I attempted to convey the importance of the case to the studio, I found myself struggling for words—there was no real reason, other than my own infatuation with his face.

Emma studied the thin sheet of hammered copper. The mask—the lower half of Private Darser's face—began below the eyes, and descended past the cheeks to the chin. When completed, the mask would attach to his ears with glasses and conceal the wound. A smile had formed on the lips—not an intentional effect, but one Emma decided was an optical illusion. The chin, full, but without a cleft, looked lumpish in form—another unintended flaw that needed correction.

At the end of the counter, Emma searched through the human hair samples. She picked a slightly darker shade than Private Darser's blond, twisted it into a mustache and positioned it above the upper lip. The effect was handsome, but wrong. Private Darser wouldn't wear a mustache, she knew intuitively, and wondered how she could be so certain in her assessment.

Darkness fell upon the city.

She picked up her pad and pencil, turned on the desk lamp, and then sketched Private Darser's head, starting first with the hair and forehead, taken from a photograph Hassan had snapped of the soldier. She worked on the top half of the portrait, getting the details in place—the ears, the blue eyes, still vibrant in black and white, the thin wisps of hair—until she no longer had to refer to the photo.

She placed the completed sketch, the top half of Darser's face, in front of her.

She lifted the mask and imagined what paint was needed to match Private Darser's skin. Keeping that image in mind, she placed the mask so it aligned perfectly with the bottom of the sketch.

She stared at the face in front of her.

It can't be . . . it simply can't be.

The face on her worktable never had a cleft in the chin or a mustache; her memory lucid, crystalline in its recognition. Yes, the face was older, but it was as recognizable as a longtime friend who had returned after an absence of many years.

The face of the boy, now a man, she loved so long ago in Vermont stared up at her.

CHAPTER 8

PARIS AND TOUL

October 1918

"How was your visit to the Front?" Emma asked John Harvey.

"I'll tell you as much as I can," he said and puffed on a cigarette.

"I thought you had given up cigarettes for cigars." Emma settled into her chair, restraining herself from gloating about his change of smoking habits. John, like many intelligent men, hardly seemed the type to stick to routine; he thrived on variation.

"You can't imagine how difficult and expensive it can be to finagle a cigar at the Front. But you didn't telephone me to talk about smoking. Why the urgency?"

"Two reasons," Emma said, as the waiter arrived to take their order. John had been kind enough to invite her to the Hotel Charles for dinner. She kept her voice hushed in the dining room; it was morgue-like except for the occasional clink of glasses. Emma sipped her wine and put the glass down. "I'd like to know how Tom is faring, and I have a personal favor to ask."

"Any favor, within reason, will be honored for you, my dear." He stubbed out his cigarette into an ashtray.

Emma placed her hands in her lap, smoothed her dress, and waited for an answer to her question about Tom.

John looked around the room as if it were infiltrated by spies.

The few other couples in the dining room were elderly and French. After a sigh, he said, "Tom seems to be doing jolly well, despite the war, his injuries, and the influenza outbreaks. I do believe he's put on weight since last you saw him. He inquired about you."

Emma straightened a bit in her chair. "I'm glad to hear it, considering the extent of the conversations we've had over the past several months. 'Hello' and 'How are you?' Not exactly the stuff of romance."

"Don't be absurd," John said. "Romance? Balderdash when it comes to the essence of a relationship." He planted his hands firmly on the table. "Emma, if you learn one thing in this life, let it be that a good man and a good woman are bound together by vows and duty, not by some cock-and-bull notion of the romantic."

"I've ignored romance for duty too many times," she said. "I'll take the stuff of romance."

"Why are women attracted to such tragic folly?" John asked without a hint of humor. "Flaubert pointed out the absurdity of romantic love years ago in *Madame Bovary*."

"I think that depends on your interpretation of the novel," Emma said. "Why are men so obstinate? Can't you see the tragedy of it all?"

"No, we are unassailable in our masculine predispositions and assumptions."

"Really? I thought better of Englishmen . . . 'this scepter'd isle' may be more backward than I imagined."

John sputtered with a "tut, tut" and then added, "There's no call to slander a nation."

They stared at each other, as if at an impasse, while the waiter delivered a watery potato soup. They picked up their spoons and, after a few sips, laughed aloud simultaneously. The glint in John's eye faded with the laughter and he replaced his spoon on the white tablecloth. "I have one impression, though, to tell you. Something is afoot, and I wasn't able to ascertain the nature of the problem. I was very, very close to discovering the cause—like a barb had pierced Tom's heart—but my French companion, from the project I'm working on, interrupted our conversation at a most inopportune time. Damn the bloody French—they never quite seem to get it right."

"So, something *is* wrong—I've known it for a while now. It's not just the injury. There's never been a good time to broach the subject."

John scowled. "It's clear it's tearing him up inside."

Emma sighed. "This can't go on. I postponed talking to him because of his recovery. Then I got absorbed in my work and, frankly, didn't want to deal with it. But now, I'll force the issue. I'll telephone and say I'm coming to Toul. We have to talk. When my work slows. . . ."

"I believe that's the only sensible course of action." John spooned soup into his mouth. "Nasty stuff." He dropped the utensil on the table. "I thought the French were experts at potato soup."

"Onion soup . . . you know very well the war has affected cooking supplies. We're lucky to have this."

"That's what I like about you, Emma—grateful for small favors. Speaking of. . . ."

"Oh, yes, my favor. Do you have any contacts in the Canadian forces?"

John looked at her oddly, gauging her intention. "Not directly, but I can make inquiries if you wish. I've worked with some Canadian soldiers."

"I'd like to find out information about one of my cases— a Private Ronald Darser assigned to the Seventh Canadian Infantry Brigade. I have his medical file, but I believe the information has been falsified."

He shook his head. "Falsified? I have no recollection of the name."

"Possibly forged."

"Why would medical information about disfigurement be—"

"That's all I can tell you. You have your secret project— I have mine."

John raised an eyebrow. "I'll do what I can, but don't expect miracles. If the information is indeed falsified, finding the truth may be harder than you suspect. I assume what you are looking for is the true identity of the man in question?"

"Yes. I believe the soldier may be hiding behind a false name."

John tweaked his chin and looked around the dining room. "I will say the cultured French know how to dress, particularly those of a mature age. Do you see how refined, how quiet the world can be even during a war? Look at that couple." John pointed to a man and woman, both elegantly attired and eating calmly, a few tables away. "I could never be as thin as either one of them. His suit is impeccable compared to the rags I have on. It gives one hope, doesn't it, that the world will go on; and, somehow there are people worth a damn. People worth saving. Unfortunate, that—how you and I work with men so distraught they cannot face themselves, but ultimately, I suppose, are worth our time."

"You know the French word for them—*mutilés*," Emma said.

"I could give a hang what the French call them," John said. "God, I wish this war were over and I could get back to England. The project I'm working on is an abomination. It only heightens the potential for more death and destruction." He patted the table. "There, I've said it—much more than I should. The King will have me executed for treason. Where in God's name is our food?"

"The Americans are advancing. More Germans are being captured every day." Consumed with the thoughts of war, Emma looked at the soup in front of her.

"No more mincing words, my dear. You must talk with your husband as soon as possible. There's more to the world than work and war, as hard as it might be to believe."

John was about to unleash another barrage upon her when the waiter arrived with the chicken they had both ordered.

"Tell me, why do I always feel like I'm talking to my father when we chat?"

"Probably because I'm older, and the most sensible man you've ever met." He grabbed the waiter's arm just as he was about to leave the table. "Another glass of wine, and remain here while I try this dish."

The waiter, aghast, swiped John's arm away as Emma translated in French as best she could. The man glared at his customer, and stood next to the table with crossed arms.

John lifted his fork, stabbed a bit of chicken, tasted it, and asked the waiter in a reproachful voice, "You call this *poulet*?"

Emma shook her head. "Of course, the first word you've ever spoken in French would come out as an insult."

John scowled.

"Please don't fidget." Emma hoped she could still the anxiety that lay underneath her command. Her stomach had rumbled all morning in anticipation of Private Darser's appointment. "You must hold still or the paint will smear."

He, as calm as an August summer night, sat in a wicker chair as she daubed paint on the mask. She had matched the skin tone at a previous fitting; the mask would be complete after applying the final touches to the beard, lips, and the chin. Soft morning light flooded the studio.

As she worked, many thoughts coursed through her mind. One was born from John's telegram from England that had arrived in Paris two days before. It read: *No Ronald Darser in 7th Canadian. Further inquiries required. Papa.*

She concentrated as much as she could on the painting, her gaze locking onto the fully formed face she had created, her hand trembling as she worked the brush near the left cheekbone.

The soldier noticed her unease and waved his hands for Emma to stop. He took his pad and pencil from his tunic pocket. *What's wrong? You seem anxious today. Does my face disturb you?*

He knows. Oh, God, he knows. Why has he come here? She walked to the studio table, placed her paintbrush in its holder, turned away, and looked out the window. Below, life went on as always: the parade of pedestrians, the leaves turning gold and brown, the chill of fall in the air. After a moment, she said, "Your face is perfect. In fact, it's so perfect it brings back memories. Sometimes the strain of the job . . ." She turned to him.

He was seated, statue-like, in his chair, his eyes piercing her.

"Sometimes the strain is difficult," she continued. "Getting the skin color right . . . I want the mask to be perfect. It's only fair, considering what you've endured."

He blinked, his eyes red and swollen beneath the lids.

The studio air felt oddly close. Emma heard the rustle of Virginie's hands as she pulled books from a shelf; the scrape of Hassan's modeling tool sounded in her ears. "Could you leave us for a moment?" Emma asked her assistants.

Virginie placed the books on the table and Hassan wiped the clay from his hands. They both looked somewhat shocked by Emma's abrupt command, but they complied with her request.

"Shut the door when you leave," Emma ordered. She kept near the window until the door closed, then, her anger flaring, she strode toward him, her voice rising, "Why are you here? What *right* do you have to do this to me? I *know* who you are."

The soldier rose from his chair, approaching her in measured steps.

She retreated until she could go no farther, the windowsill blocking her escape. She looked for a weapon. The broom in the corner caught her eye.

The soldier stopped near her and stared out the window across rue Monge.

He could see himself in the glass—the bright sun heightened his reflection. Emma stood rigid until the soldier looked at her.

He took out his pad and pencil. *Do you have a mirror?*

Emma nodded, inched away from him, walked to her desk, and retrieved the looking glass from a drawer where it had been stored for her use, not the soldiers'.

Private Darser looked into it, studying his reflection, touching his left temple and the glasses' earpiece.

Emma knew he also wanted to touch the mask, but she

stopped him with a firm "No." He was fascinated by his own image, like the Narcissus she had wanted to create with Linton. "Don't touch it," she added. "It's fragile." Even as she admonished him, she was filled with an odd thrill in her accomplishment. She had restored a man's face through her art; her skills would allow him to live free of fear and rejection. Some might see, if they looked closely, the nearly imperceptible line between his skin and the mask, the demarcation that marked the marriage of flesh and metal, but most would go about their self-absorbed business, seeing the face like any other, never giving notice to the man who might walk among them with slightly bowed head or upturned collar against the wind, avoiding the looks of horror, sneers, or, worst of all, the laughter.

On the other hand, she was repelled by the soldier who gazed into the mirror. He was the one who had caused her the deepest pain after she had surrendered her young, obsessive self to him. And now she had recreated him.

Finally, he wrote: *You've done a superb job. How can I ever repay you?*

"You know very well how you can repay me," Emma demanded. "You can tell me the truth."

He returned to his chair, still carrying the mirror, seemingly pleased with himself now that his sorrow had abated. *Your work is done and I must return to Canada. I will not be returning to the Front.*

"I know who you are," Emma said. "The least you can do is admit it. How long has it been—ten years since you abandoned me?"

I don't know what you're talking about.

"Your face! You were the father of my child."

His unwavering stare cut through her. For a moment, Emma considered she was going mad—the strain of the war, working with disfigured men, the stress of her relationship with Tom. No, that wasn't the case! *He* sat in front of her, manipulating her again for his benefit.

He wrote for a long while and then handed the pad to Emma. *I am not the father of your child. I would never make any pre-sumption of such knowledge—before God or before you. It's clear you have suffered some indignity in your past—one that has caused tragedy in your life—but I'm not the cause. I told you to construct the mask as you wished and you have done so. I'm what you've created, Mrs. Swan! You've made me in the image you desired. I'm real in that respect, but in no other, despite your imagination. The war tries the strongest of men. Perhaps, like those men, you are no match for the horrors it unleashes.*

Emma stared at the words in disbelief. Was she going insane? What if she had somehow recreated the face of a man she once loved and now scorned? She dropped the pad on the desk and sat in her chair. The studio door creaked open.

"Are you all right, Madame?" Virginie asked. It had been ages since her assistant had addressed her as Madame.

"Yes, thank you," she responded. "You and Hassan may re-turn to your work. Private Darser is leaving."

He wrote: *Thank you again, Mrs. Swan. I suppose this will be our last meeting.*

"You may be right, but I've captured your face in my mem-ory, and, perhaps, when we meet again you can look me in the eye and speak the truth."

The soldier again stared into the mirror. When he lowered the glass, a sad smile had formed on the mask.

Such a smile was impossible, but her emotional percep-tion was real. Could he atone for his desertion when she had needed him the most? Could he help her banish the memory that haunted her?

Private Darser found his coat, nodded to Emma, and walked out the door. His firm steps echoed down the courtyard stairs and through the tunnel. She ran to the window to see him, but he had already disappeared down rue Monge as if he'd never existed.

*   *   *

"I hear rumors about the war," Virginie said, opening the studio door. She and Emma circled the teakettle like children waiting for candy.

"*Fermez la porte,*" Emma said. "It's foggy and cold and I'm in no mood to catch pneumonia this morning."

The sun, as it journeyed south, had grown feeble in the late October sky. The lovely warmth earlier in the month had been quelled by a series of dreary and bone-chilling days, damp and overcast, a portent of November and approaching winter.

"We need air," Virginie said. "I'm sick of plaster dust and the smell of clay and the smoke from Hassan's terrible cigarettes."

"I don't care," Emma insisted. "Close the door. Sometimes you're as cranky as John says you are." She looked at Virginie. The young nurse had aged during the year they'd worked together. The sprite-like attitude and youthful looks, which Emma initially compared to her Boston housekeeper, Anne, had diminished as the war dragged on.

Emma also had taken stock of herself that morning and counted a few gray hairs spreading backward from her temples. The rich blackness of her hair was disappearing with her youth. She could easily blame aging on the war, but other factors had contributed to the lines now creasing her face. She and Virginie were growing older together while Anne, in her memory; Hassan, as most men seemed to do; and the ageless Madame Clement crossed the swiftly flowing current of time with ease.

"What have you heard about the war?" Emma asked. "I haven't looked at a newspaper in ages."

Delaying her response, Virginie closed the door reluctantly. "More battles along the Front. Many dead along the Meuse and the Moselle. The dead are everywhere—even near Toul."

"Yes," Emma said, remembering the uniforms at the Toul hospital that had been taken from the deceased soldiers. "We can only pray the war will be over soon."

"The Americans are fighting . . . how you say . . . fee . . . ?"

Emma thought for a moment. "Fiercely?"

"*Oui*, fiercely. They surprise even our French boys."

The kettle whistled. Emma turned off the burner, poured the steaming water, and dropped the previous day's infuser into Virginie's cup and then dipped it into hers, watching as thin reddish filaments streamed through the water. She looked at Virginie. "Waste not, want not in wartime. I think we're all tired. Perhaps we need to close the studio for a week and take a rest."

"A magnificent idea," Virginie said, "but what about the soldiers?"

"Well, we'll have to plan our vacation and catch up with as much work as we can before we go. . . ."

Emma started. Two voices, both speaking French, rose from the stairs. She recognized one as Madame Clement's; the other she was unsure about until he appeared at the studio door. It was Richard, the driver from the hospital. Madame Clement opened the door.

A smiling Richard followed. "*Bonjour*, Virginie," he said, taking in the nurse's figure with obvious delight. Turning to Emma, as an afterthought, he added, "*Bonjour*, Madame Swan."

Her heart raced, hoping Richard had only good news to bear. After Tom's injury, Richard had visited the studio several times, but his visits had fallen off recently. The courier appeared as vigorous as ever, his scruffy, sandy beard making him appear older; however, the facial hair only enhanced the rakish attitude and figure he cut.

Virginie apparently noticed as well and offered her cheek for a kiss.

Richard willingly complied. "Monsieur Swan asks you to return to Toul," he told Emma, his voice earnest and brassy.

"Is something wrong?" She dreaded his answer.

"No. He requests your company."

"He said nothing about coming to Toul when we last talked," Emma said to Virginie.

"You must go," Virginie said. "The trip will do you good. Hassan and I will conduct business."

"We have three appointments today," Emma said, apologetically. "I have nothing packed."

Richard spoke in French to Madame Clement and the housekeeper chuckled.

"What did he say?" Emma asked Virginie.

"He said women are too, too . . ."

"Too what?"

"Like a statue."

"Stone-like . . . rigid?"

"*Oui.*"

"It's like Tom to issue a challenge, when I'm not in the mood for one. Tell Richard I'll be ready in a half hour. We'll talk about a holiday when I get back." Emma rushed up the stairs as Virginie, Madame Clement, and Richard chatted in the alcove. She gathered a few toiletries and clothes, pushed them into a bag, brushed her hair, grabbed her coat, and was downstairs in ten minutes.

Emma said her good-byes and Richard escorted her from the studio. The courtyard slept lifeless and gray under the fog, the statues black with mist, the ivy clinging to the walls with their dark tentacles.

Entering the tunnel, Emma saw the back of the ambulance parked on rue Monge. A soldier in a greatcoat rushed past the truck. He turned his head for a moment and Emma thought she saw Private Darser grinning at her. As quickly as the man appeared he was gone. She realized the soldier couldn't be Darser— his mask had no smile. The lips had to be neutral, pleasantly full, and slightly open; otherwise, the mouth would appear fixed in a disquieting expression. She recalled the sad smile she thought she had seen on his mask at their final meeting.

She said nothing to Richard about the soldier, and climbed into the truck. They said little as Richard drove east through the Paris streets. When the city finally dropped behind them and the ambulance had traveled far along a country road, Emma relaxed enough to strike up a conversation.

"*Ça va, Richard?*" she asked as they putted through a village. It was the only small talk she could think of—his health. She remembered his arm injury—the one mentioned by Claude, Tom's doctor in Toul. Emma looked at the shop windows, which appeared dismal and forlorn in the enveloping gray mist. It swirled around the ambulance and Richard switched on the headlights.

"*Très bien*," Richard said.

"How's your English? My French could be better."

Richard cleared his throat and pronounced each word slowly, "Your . . . husband . . . is teaching . . . me." He turned to her and smiled. "I thank him . . . each day."

"Well, you're making remarkable progress. Where did you stay last night? You know you are always welcome at the studio. We can put a cot in the casting room."

"No, thank you," he said firmly. "The masks are too frightening."

Emma laughed. "They *can* be a bit scary in the dark."

"I stay with my sister. She lives in Saint-Denis." He paused for a moment and then asked, "How did you meet?"

Emma turned to him, confused by the abrupt change in subject.

"My husband?" she asked, knowing Tom was the object of his question.

"Yes."

"In Boston. Tom was studying medicine. I was getting ready to attend art school. We met through a mutual friend—Louisa Markham." Emma stopped, realizing Richard may not have understood her. "I'm sorry. Was I going too fast? Can you understand me?"

Richard nodded. "Most, yes." He peered through the windscreen as intermittent drops of rain splattered against the glass. "Was he always so sad?"

His question seemed casual, as if sadness was normal for Tom, but his inquiry unsettled her and a queasy sensation fluttered through her stomach. "So, you think Tom's depressed . . . sad?"

Richard stared blankly at the road.

"I can't speak for Tom, but the war has been difficult for both of us," Emma continued. "I would expect he might be depressed after his injury at the Front, and his continual work with injured and dying men. I've never been able to understand how doctors keep their sanity."

"When we met . . ." Richard considered carefully his next words. "He was happy . . . happy to be a doctor."

Emma slumped in her seat, guilt momentarily overpowering her. Was Richard attacking her, and not the war, as the cause of their problems? Certainly, she had done nothing inherently wrong, other than form a relationship with a Boston painter who had demonstrated affection for her and sparked her own reciprocal feelings. She embraced the thought. After all, how could innocent fondness be so misconstrued compared to the world's ongoing horrors? But was her relationship so innocent? What of her fantasies about Linton?

"When Tom and I met we were both overly optimistic, I think. The war hadn't begun and we were filled with joy and life. When fighting broke out, Tom grew anxious. He was eager to do something—anything he could to help. That's why he volunteered to work with the Red Cross in France. He saw the need, and, in the beginning, I know he was happy to be here. I could tell from his letters." She stopped, unsure of how much of her conversation Richard had understood.

"The village is small," Richard said. "People talk. Americans are watched."

"What are you getting at?"

"I have no proof. People say he walks."

"Walks?" A prickle of fear rose in her chest.

"Yes, at night."

Emma chuckled, more from anxiety than humor. "Well, I'm certain Tom isn't a vampire. He loves to take walks—we both do. If that's what you're talking about?"

"You will ask him. That's all I know. *Le bruit court que* . . ."

"*Pardon?*"

"How do you say . . . stories about people?"

"Rumors?"

Richard nodded. "*Oui*, rumors."

"I'll be sure to ask him." Emma settled in her seat and looked out at the dull sky. As the truck rolled on, she was certain she heard shells exploding in the distance. It was too cold for a thunderstorm.

By the time they reached Tom's cottage, night had fallen and the camouflaged city lamps fought weakly against the overarching power of darkness. The night spread a dreary cloak over Emma, which lifted only briefly when Tom limped past the damp garden and brushed his lips against her cheek. Her husband thanked Richard, and the ambulance disappeared down the lane in a spray of mist.

"Have you had anything to eat?" he asked after they had entered the cottage. "Please, sit down." He pointed to a chair at the kitchen table. "Let me take your bag." He reached for it, but she held on to the straps. Rebuffed, he sighed, and walked to the fireplace, knelt, and threw a birch log into the fire. The flames roared and several red embers popped and sputtered to the floor. He swiped at them with his hand.

The clutter Emma had so carefully put in its place earlier in the year had reappeared: papers were strewn about the table, the bookcase was crammed with volumes, clothes were scattered across the bed, the messy behavior so unlike his fastidiousness in Boston. The cottage's chaos added to the chill embracing her heart.

"It's cold tonight," he said, still kneeling in front of the fire.

Emma stared at him—acutely aware of the changes in her husband. He had gained a little weight since her last visit to Toul, although his wool sweater and pants still hung on his frame, his eyes were hazier perhaps, his hair a shade darker but combed differently, swept down to disguise his thinning hairline, the mustache spreading below his upper lip. Emotionally, the person in front of her was someone unfamiliar. The connection between them had sagged under their separation. He might as well have been a man she met on the street, a man who could have piqued her interest, but ultimately left her cold and searching for warmth.

"Cold, indeed," she said, scooting her bag underneath the chair. "Some cheese would be nice. A glass of wine, I suppose." A half-empty bottle sat on the table.

Tom rose. "I made a plate for you. I hoped you would come, Emma."

"Was there ever a doubt?"

He limped to the cupboard, opened it, lifted a white plate from the shelf, and brought it to her. It held dried meat, a wedge of cheese, and apple slices. He poured the wine.

"How is your leg?" she asked.

Tom sat next to her and looked out the window spotted with mist.

"My left leg needs patching up, but my limp is excellent." He smiled and poured a glass for himself. "I've had too much to drink of late—it's a habit I'm not happy about, but alcohol helps pass the time and ease the pain." He picked up the glass and drained nearly half of it. "My leg has taken longer to heal than Claude anticipated. . . ."

"Why didn't you tell me?" Emma asked. "You never mentioned that when we talked."

"Frankly, half the time I don't remember talking at all." He gulped the rest of the wine. "Morphine. The drug douses the pain, but leaves me in a fog. It's addictive, hard to get off it."

Emma frowned. "There hasn't been much to remember for a long time." She took a bite of cheese, the food leaving a warm, salty taste in her mouth. "How are you otherwise?"

"My stomach hurts from the wound. Hell, on bad days it hurts to take a piss. Some parts of me have recovered, some parts haven't." He turned and looked into her eyes. "I have a lot to say to you, Emma—some of it isn't very pleasant."

Emma steeled herself and sipped her wine. "I know what you're referring to. I found the letter when I stayed over, the night before you were injured."

His eyes widened, but the expression was one of resignation rather than shock. "The letter? Which one?"

"How many did you receive from my so-called friend?"

"A few." Tom turned his attention to the glass again. "After a while, the letters became more flowery—her affection toward me unwarranted and unwanted. She was gleeful in her recounting of the situation between you and Linton Bower."

Emma was no longer hungry. She took her glass and stood by the fire, the crackling heat warming her legs. She placed the wine upon the mantel and watched the flames lick and sputter and then vanish into swirling vapor. After a time, she sat on the bed nearly on top of the spot where she had found the letter tucked under the mattress.

"I guess the time for cat and mouse is over," she said.

Tom nodded.

"I found it a year ago when you called me to the Front. I supposed then that the letter was the reason you wanted to talk."

"Yes," Tom said, and turned his chair in her direction.

"I saw it, quite by accident, under the mattress. The name had been torn off, but I knew it was from Louisa. I was prepared to face the consequences of her—what should I call it? Betrayal? Treachery? But a German shell ended that the next day. . . ."

"I wanted to talk," Tom said. "I wanted to hear your side of the story, but I have to admit I was scared that I had already lost you to a lover."

Emma laughed and leaned back on the bed. "Life is funny, Tom. You hadn't lost me. I was prepared to tell you the truth, but after your injury we both had so much to deal with—your recovery—I didn't want to upset you when you were ill; then the studio took all my time. Oddly enough, I *was* yours until I felt *us* slipping away. You seemed so distant, your calls and letters infrequent. I believed you didn't want to talk to me."

"I assumed we were already on the outs."

"Nothing could be further from the truth. Nothing happened between me and—"

"Linton Bower? Then why would Louisa lie about your relationship?"

Emma resisted the urge to fight with him; however, her defensive instincts clawed at her to get out. "Perhaps Linton and I got closer than we should have. I have to admit he is an attractive man and I was terribly lonely after you left."

Tom winced.

She could have gone on and cut more deeply. She could have told Tom about the carriage ride and the thrill she felt sitting next to Linton, the excitement she'd experienced in his studio when he posed for her, but she reined herself in. In a way, she wanted to smirk and blame her husband for their troubles, but she knew she was just as much at fault. There was one point she couldn't resist, however. "Why would Louisa lie? Surely, you aren't that naïve, Tom." She'd hit a nerve; Tom's eyes flashed in distress. "Louisa has always loved you, even though she brought us together. Her intentions were always directed at you. After our marriage, I was *her* friend so she could get to you. After you left, she talked endlessly about you. Any hint of indiscretion was an excuse to attack me. I think that was her plan from the beginning and it's been more successful than she could have imagined. That's what I think."

Tom lowered his head. "So, nothing happened?"

"Linton is my friend. One time, he showed more affection toward me than he should have. Louisa was a witness to that unfortunate display. But, honestly . . ." She paused, assessing the truth of her confession, knowing she was holding back the true extent of her feelings.

"Yes?"

"Honestly, he does care for me and I do care for him. But I made my decision—I came to France."

Tom got up and walked to the bookcase.

Emma watched as he created a cleft between two books and pulled a sheet of paper from the opening.

Tom studied it. "I worked on an American soldier last week. I couldn't save him." A bright pain crossed his face. "I thought you would want this." He handed her the creased paper. "I know you cared for him, too."

Emma stared in horror at the drawing. The delicate lines of the portrait were spattered with splotches of dried, brownish blood; the face was shredded in several places from shrapnel, giving the drawing the appearance of a facially mutilated soldier. Despite its condition, she knew the subject immediately. Only bits of writing were legible because of the stain, but Emma remembered the words: *To Lt. Andrew Stoneman, from Emma Lewis Swan. To your safe return . . .*

"I did care for him—as a friend," Emma said. "He was a kind man, a good man."

"I first met him last fall. He was with you when the Frenchman committed suicide?"

"Yes," Emma said. "Lieutenant Stoneman was very brave." She stopped and ran her finger over the portrait. "But from the moment I met him on the ship, I think he knew he was going to die."

Tom placed his hands gently on her shoulders and Emma recoiled, the strength of her revulsion surprising her. The last thing she wanted was sympathy from her husband. She retrieved her bag from under the chair. "I'm exhausted from the trip. I should go to bed."

Tom followed her to the table and poured more wine into his glass. "Yes, I understand." He stuttered a bit and then said, "I have more to tell you." He sat, his tall frame towering in the small chair.

"Tomorrow." She placed her bag on the bed and stared at him. "Where is Lieutenant Stoneman buried?"

"A few kilometers from here, near a small village."

"I want to visit his grave."

Tom nodded. "Richard can take you."

She put the portrait in her bag and slid it under the bed. Fighting back tears, she walked to the toilet, looked into Tom's shaving mirror, and fought back the sobs that threatened to overwhelm her.

*   *   *

The dead leaves rustled on the oak. Bare branches jutted from the tree, creating weblike shadows across the freshly turned grave. Rows of white wooden crosses rose from the ground and stretched as far as the brown hills that surrounded the village. The number of new graves staggered her.

Emma pulled the lapels of her coat together—it was colder than she had anticipated despite the brilliant sun. Still, it was one of the few bright days she could remember in the countryside near Toul. She stood among the graves, blinking into the light, thinking how alone and foreign she felt, walking the muddy, narrow lanes searching for Andrew Stoneman. In the northeast corner, close to a scrawny leafless tree, she found him, his last name scrawled upon the cross.

She looked back across the graves toward the iron entrance gate coated with rust. Richard sat in the passenger seat of the ambulance, door open, enjoying the sunshine, smoking a cigarette. He waved and Emma politely returned the gesture. She turned and knelt beside the grave.

"So, this is how it ends, Lieutenant Andrew Stoneman," Emma said over the spaded earth. Tom had told her British and American soldiers were buried in the village graveyards, next to the French. There was no time to ship the bodies home. A quick military funeral where the soldier died had to suffice.

"Time and God would aid your safe return, you said." Emma stared at the white wood jutting from the damp earth. A ghostly breath of wind passed over her and she shook from a sudden chill. "I remember how you said it was best you didn't have a sweetheart, a wife, or children, and how you said the war wasn't about you—that you were just a speck in the scheme of things." Emma let her tears fall. "You were correct, of course, but your mother and father in Kansas will miss you, and I'm deeply sorry you won't be going home. . . ."

She remembered their walk in the Luxembourg Gardens and how brave the officer had been at the Christmas party when Monsieur Thibault committed suicide. That night, he had offered to stay with her and she had refused. It would have been easy, even mystical, to have slept with him that Christmas Eve, as she watched the moon and the stars slip by her window, but she was too sad, and he too much of a gentleman to take advantage of her vulnerability.

I can stay with you. She remembered his words and then she sobbed—not for herself, but for all the faceless men and women and defenseless creatures of the world who died alone.

"I do this for you." She reached into her coat pocket and withdrew the portrait. "You wanted an Emma Lewis Swan and you shall have it for eternity." She tore the drawing into tiny pieces, dropping them like snowflakes upon the grave, looking back after she walked away. The pieces were already turning black on the moist earth.

Richard lit another cigarette when she arrived at the ambulance.

"Take me to the hospital," she told him. "I have a few words to say to my husband."

He turned the vehicle toward Toul. As they departed, the graves swept past Emma and, in the far corner, she saw the slender tree and imagined Lieutenant Stoneman next to it, waving to her, as alive as he had been on the Atlantic crossing.

As the graves receded, Emma knew this was the last time she would ever visit the officer. And in that instant, a thrill washed over her body and she turned in her seat to see a doughboy standing by the tree, his right hand covering his mouth as if to blow a kiss.

"I have the feeling you don't believe me," Emma said. "I only drew the portrait as a favor for him." She struggled to control the emotions surging through her, and sat stiffly in the chair across from Tom, her fists clenched in her lap.

Tom brushed his hand through his unkempt hair. Lately, he always looked as if he had just gotten up. If she was an emotional wreck, Tom was her equivalent on the physical spectrum.

His hospital office was dingy and crowded, and pity filled her briefly for all he had been through. However, what she really wanted was to be on her way back to Paris with Richard. Lieutenant Stoneman's death angered her, and her husband's implied accusation of a betrayal disturbed her—because of its inaccuracy, and because of its possibility.

Tom was about to answer Emma when Claude stuck his head round the edge of the door.

"*Bonjour, Madame Swan*," he said with genuine joy. He lifted Emma's hand and kissed it. "*Ça va?*"

"*Comme si, comme ça,*" Emma replied. Although she liked the French doctor, she wished he had come at another time for she had more important issues to discuss than social pleasantries.

"It's been so long," Claude said. "Too long a time." He cocked his head toward Tom.

Tom returned the look with a scowl.

"A patient with an urgent request . . . needs to see you," Claude continued.

"Is it an emergency?" Tom asked, leaning forward in his chair, his annoyance diminishing with Claude's request.

"No."

"Well then, please do me a favor and take over."

"The patient is not a man," Claude said.

Emma caught the sparkle in the French doctor's eyes.

"I see," Tom said stiffly. "Tell her I'll be with her shortly."

"Pardon, Madame Swan, women can be demanding," Claude said.

"I've been told," Emma said, the hairs on the nape of her neck rising.

"Please, Claude, Emma and I really need this time together."

"Of course." He ducked out of sight as quickly as he had come in.

Tom looked resigned, creases etching his face. "I do believe you drew the portrait out of kindness . . ." His words trailed off, as if the certainty of his argument eluded him.

"I've been faithful," Emma said.

"How many times must I repeat . . ." A deep sadness welled

in his eyes. "Oh, I've been such a fool. I was overtaken by the urge to be the good doctor, and in my obsession I've ruined our lives. I was so happy you were coming to France—to make a difference. Then Louisa's letters began, along with relentless death."

She reached for him. He drew back a little, not out of refusal, she considered, but from contrition. Perhaps there was hope after all. "What's been taken can be replaced; what's been broken can be repaired. I haven't been a saint, Tom—I've been as standoffish as you. Of course, if Louisa hadn't written those letters—her friendship, after you left, was relentlessly Lucrezia Borgia. She was a beast to Anne. I should never have underestimated her capacity for duplicity."

"Such a fool . . . such a fool. . . ." He rubbed his forehead and then placed his hands on the desk. "It was so odd, after the letters arrived, how my life changed . . . you became this gray, faceless thing . . . it was as if you didn't exist, as if our marriage was part of a different universe in a lost time. I got carried away with my work here. France was all that mattered. I belonged here and you weren't part of that arrangement. I *couldn't* answer Louisa. I never wrote back. . . ."

"You never responded?" Emma asked with astonishment.

"Never. I was too concerned she would take my inquiries the wrong way. I didn't want to exacerbate the situation, and, frankly, I didn't have the time. After a few months, the letters stopped. I assumed my feelings toward her had been made quite clear. Louisa was always my friend and I will be forever grateful for our introduction, but never beyond that. I was unaware of the depth of her feeling, or her jealousy. By the time her letters ended, the damage had been done."

Emma got up and walked behind him. She looked through the grimy window into the deep shadows that lined the street. The sun would be setting soon. She was in Toul for another night.

She placed her hands on Tom's shoulders and gently rubbed his neck, and, for a moment, she rested her chin on the top of his head. His warmth, his scent, drifted up to her and the smell reminded her of the intimate moments they had spent together. "Do you think we can put all this behind us?" she asked and draped her arms around his neck.

He clasped her hands in his and squeezed.

Emma warmed to his touch, but the feeling was like that of an old friend rather than a lover. Despite that, the loneliness that had been so much a part of her life lifted slightly.

"I'm afraid it's too late," Tom answered.

She withdrew from his grasp and returned to her chair. "Why?" Her voice quivered as she struggled to maintain her composure. "Why is it too late?"

"The trust between us . . . it's gone."

She stared at him, the melancholy sadness she had seen so often of late reappearing in his eyes.

"Doctor," Claude's voice called from down the hall, "your patient is hysterical."

"I must go," Tom said. "I'll be on duty tonight and, most likely, getting home late. Richard will take you to the cottage."

"I must return to Paris tomorrow."

"I know. I promise I'll be there for a visit soon. Too much work gets on one's nerves." He rose, leaned across the table, and kissed her cheek.

"I'll walk to the cottage," Emma said. "I don't want to bother Richard."

Tom sank into his chair and picked up a folder on his desk.

Emma's heels clicked on the tile as she walked down the stark, white hall, once again amplifying the loneliness that settled inside her. As she descended the steps to the lobby, she spotted Claude hunched over a chair where soldiers normally sat. However, instead of a man, a darkly beautiful woman in a cream-colored overcoat sat weeping into her cupped hands. As Emma approached, the woman looked up and the color drained from her face. She lowered her hands and stared at Emma with tear-stained eyes.

Claude bowed slightly and said, "*Bonsoir, Madame.*"

The woman said nothing, but her eyes followed Emma.

She walked past the nurse's station, opened the door, and nearly stumbled over Richard, who sat on the steps smoking a cigarette. He said hello and smiled rather sardonically.

Emma swept past him into the street, where the dark had already invaded the shop doors and alleyways in the faltering light. She veered to the right, looking ahead, searching for the lane that led to Tom's cottage, blocking from her mind the face of the woman who so urgently needed him.

The memory of their conversation about trust and marriage burst as Emma searched the cleft in the bookcase where Tom had concealed the drawing of Lieutenant Stoneman. She pulled a few volumes from the case and several letters dropped to the floor. The light from the fireplace rose and fell with the burning logs; however, Emma could make out the handwriting. They were indeed from Louisa Markham. These, unlike the letter she found tucked under the mattress, were in envelopes. Oddly, there was no return address on them, only a flowing LM in script in the upper left-hand corner. The first letter was dated August of 1917. They continued, broken by the passing of months, until they ended in the following spring.

She lit an oil lamp and settled on the bed, reading the letters carefully, dissecting each word for hidden meaning. Most of them were pleasantly pedestrian and made little reference to Linton or Emma directly, but the underlying meaning was apparent—*I, Louisa Markham, am good and noble, while your wife, Emma Lewis Swan, is* persona non grata *to the whole of Boston society because of her affair of the heart.*

The fire had waned when Emma heard the cottage door open. She squirmed under the covers, knowing she had fallen asleep with the letters draped across the bed. One of them fluttered to the floor.

"I see you've found them," Tom said.

Emma nodded, unsure what to say.

Tom shook his head. "Now you understand what I mean about trust?"

She gathered the letters and placed them on the nightstand. She thought of lifting her arms toward him, using affection as reconciliation, but then dismissed the idea. Now was not the time. Tom was right—she had taken advantage of his trust.

He made no movement toward her and instead undressed slowly in the pale light. He removed his shirt and walked to the fireplace where he stirred the embers and added another log to the fire. Soon, the room was filled with flickering warmth.

He stood by the bed, so Emma could see him fully. He unbuttoned his trousers and pushed them to the floor. He swayed a bit and then dropped his underwear as well.

Emma gasped.

The shrapnel wound had left a red gash across his left leg and stomach. All that remained below the brown thatch of pubic hair was the dark stub of a penis. He had been castrated as well.

"Now, you know," he said wearily and crawled into bed. "I'm no longer a man."

Emma moaned, then touched his hand. "Claude warned me, but I never knew. Why didn't you tell me?"

He stared at the ceiling and said, "Timing, my love. When you lose your manhood, it's a bit of a shock, to say the least. It's taken months for me to even look at myself in the mirror. Claude's been a wonderful doctor."

Emma clutched the sheet and an unexpected wave of anger washed over her. "You should have told me. I had a *right* to know. I could have helped."

Tom turned to her, took her hands, and pressed them against his chest. "What could you do? Once the surgery was over, only I could lift myself from the pain, with Claude's help. I didn't want anyone else to know about the extent of my injuries. I thought it didn't matter to you because of the letters. That's why I wanted you to go back to Paris and your work. I'm back to normal now—as normal as I can be—and when the war is over, as it eventually will be . . ."

Emma, in the flickering light, detected the sorrow building in his eyes. "Yes?"

"We can never have our own children." A tear rolled down his cheek and onto the pillow.

A chilly sadness swallowed her. She withdrew from his grasp and turned away.

"I understand how you must feel," he said. "You have every right to be angry."

"Word got out in Boston that you were injured. I don't know how they came to find out."

"In the hospital . . . there was a soldier from Boston. We talked about the shelling, and I suppose he could tell from my wounds what was going on. He must have written home or told others. Who told you?"

"Linton . . . and Anne. They hinted . . . even Vreland knew, of all people, that something deeper was going on with you. Is there?"

He didn't answer, only sobbed as Emma stared at the dark wall across the room, her body wracked from the emotions that filled her: anger, sadness, confusion. What was to become of their life together? The fact that she could not have a child with Tom made her feel as if no part of her would go forward in time. Only blackness lay ahead.

An infant floated through the cottage shadows, a faceless thing with no mouth and eyes. It soared like a ghost toward Emma while she balanced on the edge of a scream. She covered her mouth with her hands and the baby disappeared. In its place, the disfigured faces of Private Darser, Monsieur Thibault, and other soldiers hung in the air above her, speaking nightmarish gibberish until they faded as well. As she tried again to lose herself to sleep, the sad injury to her now impotent husband swirled through her mind. Her life had become an endurance test. She was no closer to banishing the memory of the infant than when she arrived in France. *What hope do I have?* She was uncertain of the answer. One overarching thought came into her head:

I would do anything to bring back the child I conceived.

CHAPTER 9

PARIS

November 1918

"The war is ending," Virginie said. "I know it in my heart."

"I hope you have firm evidence for your statement—not a whim based on your weather forecasting abilities," Emma countered. Their morning camaraderie was pleasant, made all the more so by sharing tea and biscuits at the large casting room table. She was happy to see Virginie, Hassan, and Madame Clement again after her time in Toul. A solid overcast darkened the room, but Emma's spirits remained cheerful despite the somber day.

"My friends tell me, the Americans are making great strides along the Meuse," Virginie continued. "The Boche are melting like butter in the summer sun. The war may end in a matter of days."

"We've gone through this before and have always been disappointed," Emma said.

Hassan and Madame Clement nodded, although Emma wasn't sure if they were agreeing with her viewpoint or simply being polite.

"*Tout va mal.*" Madame Clement smiled while she held up the teapot.

"Yes, but things could be worse," Emma said. "We're alive and we have our families and friends."

"Worse . . . ? Yes, that reminds me," Virginie said. "A telegram arrived from John Harvey. He is visiting Paris again—much too soon as far as I'm concerned."

"On what business?" Emma asked. "Did he say?"

"No. Only that he will be here. He is of no concern to me."

"Virginie, you should really bury the hatchet with John. We say that in America. Do you know the expression?"

"Yes, and I would be happy to bury the hatchet—in his head."

Emma and Virginie laughed. Hassan and Madame Clement looked at each other and then joined in because of the contagious mood.

Emma suppressed a final chuckle and said, "You should be kind to John. He's a great resource, and could be a wonderful reference for us all, regardless of where we end up."

"What do you mean?" Madame Clement asked.

Emma thought for a moment and said, "Well, Virginie might aid John with research in England. You and Hassan might join him."

"*Jamais,*" Madame Clement and Virginie said in unison. They all laughed again, but the levity was broken by Madame Clement nodding at Virginie.

"*Maintenant?*" Virginie asked.

"*Oui,*" Madame Clement answered.

"There is one thing," Virginie said. "Since you left . . ."

Emma looked at her assistant, waiting for the news.

". . . Madame Clement has asked me to tell you—she's seen Private Darser on rue Monge. He pretends not to see her, but he appears to be watching us."

Emma remembered the soldier she'd seen briefly as she and Richard were leaving for Toul, whom she'd suspected might be Private Darser.

"Is she certain?" Emma asked.

Virginie nodded and drank her tea.

"Why would he be spying on us?"

"There was bitterness between you," Virginie said. "I remember—when he arrived for the final fitting."

Virginie was correct about the tense meeting with the soldier: the accusation Emma levied that he had abandoned her years ago; his blithe denial.

"Perhaps I'll take a walk at lunch," Emma said.

Madame Clement shook her head. "*Non*," she objected, "*dans la nuit.*"

"He walks at night," Virginie said.

Emma put her teacup on the table. "Have you been talking to Richard?"

"*Madame?*" Virginie looked down, as a blush spread across her half-concealed face.

"Richard used the same words when he drove me to Toul. He was speaking of another business entirely."

"Richard and I are friends," Virginie said, "but, no, we have not spoken of Private Darser—"

"Or of anyone else?" Emma asked.

"*Non, Madame,*" Virginie said emphatically. "I never speak of our patients. Private Darser walks in the dark because he has something to hide."

A shiver skittered over her. *Something to hide? Some injured soldiers work at night because their faces are less noticeable. Perhaps he's such a soldier—not as brusque or confident as he seems. All swagger, but little else. He's so full of himself.* But then another thought struck her. *What about Tom? What other secrets has he hidden from me? Why does he "walk at night"?*

"Then I'll take a walk after our appointments—after the sun has set," Emma said. "I'll watch for our friend."

That night, Emma bundled up in her coat, scarf, and gloves, and buttressing herself against the chill turned onto rue Monge. Approaching winter had diminished the Parisian activities of spring and summer. Most shops, except for a few, were closed because of shortages and the early nightfall. Few people were on the street, most were on their way home from work. Two businessmen passed her, tipping their hats and muttering, "*Bonsoir.*" Emma nodded and continued her stroll down the street.

She walked at a moderate pace until she neared the towering church of Saint-Étienne-du-Mont. To her right, the Pantheon's columned dome, like an immense bell, jutted into the sky. However, the cathedral's dark stones were nearer, looming over her, the solemn façade forcing its heavy weight upon her. The church's windows absorbed the darkness—no light, electric or candle, escaped the structure. Hounded by the night air, Emma stepped inside, a safer and warmer sanctuary than the street, her first visit to a Paris church since her arrival, a thought not lost upon her as she pulled on the heavy wooden doors.

The cathedral lay shrouded in darkness except for the few votives that flickered in a side chapel. She peered into the depths of the nave. As she stood, hands cupped over her eyes, the latticework stairwells of the choir and the gothic vaults of the ceiling gradually came into view. She sat in a chair near the doors where the votives offered the most light. Nothing stirred as she meditated upon the journey that had led her to this strange outing. Occasionally, a creak or pop reverberated in the sanctuary like a distant echo.

She bowed her head and a profound melancholy flowed through her. She had little propensity for religious feeling these days, her experiences with the church mostly relegated to childhood, but her morose feelings tonight threatened to swamp her. She had come dangerously close to falling in love with another man; her marriage was in tatters; her emotional and physical life with Tom would never be the same; and her best friend had betrayed her.

Could it hurt to pray? *No.* She bowed her head.

My dear Lady, it's been years since I've been in church. I've not felt worthy of your love, your goodness, your kindness,

*and grace. I know I've sinned, and my greatest sin of all has
kept me away from you for many years. I feel awkward and
ashamed, coming to you at this time of war, when so many are
dead, wounded, and suffering; but I, like the rest of the world,
need your forgiveness and help. Because it's been so long and
I'm not a Roman, my prayer should be simple—a plea for absolution, and the benefit of your loving guidance. For years, I've
struggled with my past. How different my life would have been
had I listened to my heart instead of the urgings of a man. If
only I'd had the courage then. I pray for—*

The door creaked behind her.

She opened her eyes and turned.

A man in a long Army coat, his face obscured by darkness,
stood in the shadowy entrance. She returned her gaze to the
front of the church for a moment; when she looked back again
the man had disappeared. She wondered if she had imagined
the dusky figure—a phantom rather than a creation of flesh and
blood. The hair prickled on the back of her neck and she cocked
her head in attention. A chair scraped the floor to her left.

She rose and called out, "*Hallo.*"

No one answered.

She calmed herself, hoping a priest had entered for vespers
instead of some supernatural creature conjured by her imagination.

A candle flickered and floated in the darkness to her left, the
light rising and falling like a wave, coming ever closer, until she
could see the illuminated hands and face of the carrier.

The man she was seeking held the votive. He sat down a few
feet away and placed the candle on a chair between them.

She flinched, but quickly regained her composure and stared
at the face illuminated by the flickering light. "Why are you
spying on my staff?" Her anger echoed throughout the church.
"Why have you followed me here?"

Private Darser, unmoving, locked his eyes onto Emma's.

"I asked you a question," she said. "I've seen you on the
street. You must leave us alone."

The soldier calmly withdrew his pad, wrote, and held it to the candlelight: *I am still silenced, Mrs. Swan, but I've finally come to ask your forgiveness. That is, if you will forgive me?*

Emma looked at the soldier blankly. Had she not just prayed for forgiveness?

The man dropped his writing instruments near the candle and reached for Emma's arm.

She jerked away, but the soldier, nearly knocking over his chair, caught her at the elbow and held onto her with a fiery grip until she stopped struggling. Then, he caressed her arm as she sat erect and unforgiving.

"What do you want? Do you need money? Food?"

The soldier grunted.

Her hand constricting in pain, she quieted herself as best she could while hoping to escape from his grip.

He pulled up her sleeve, removed her glove, turned her arm over, and exposed the small scar on her left index finger—the wound she had inflicted on herself in Vermont shone silver in the candlelight.

He ran a finger over it, squeezed her hand, and then released her arm.

She recoiled, but even in the gloomy light she understood the expression in Private Darser's eyes; he was pleading with her to stay by his side.

He picked up his pencil and pad. *I know the horrors you've seen. I should have been a good father to our baby, but I couldn't. I was too selfish and all-knowing. Life has taught me differently.*

Emma shivered and rolled down her sleeve. "What do you want from me?"

Forgive me.

The awful memories of the last days with Kurt flooded her, and she rocked silently in the chair as those thoughts consumed her. She covered her face with her hands, before she had the courage to take them away and speak. "What you ask I considered years ago, but I could never find it in my heart."

Private Darser eyed her forlornly and her anger subsided somewhat.

"However, I have prayed for peace—and forgiveness—and my prayers are still unanswered. You come to me like the devil you are." She rose from her chair, approaching him. "I *hated* you for deserting me. You left me alone, with a baby I couldn't have—then I *hated* myself." In a sudden fury, she slammed her fists against his chest. "Why now?"

He shook his head and lowered his gaze as he wrote. *Because of your reputation as a sculptress—an artist who makes soldiers whole again. I was told of your work in Paris. It wasn't hard to track you down.*

"So you found me and assumed I would forgive you. You believed the simple act of asking could wipe out all my suffering."

Private Darser scribbled on the page. *No!*

"I would never have agreed to take you at the studio if I had known. And tonight, you think I can absolve your guilt because you sought me out in a house of God?" Emma stopped, her hands shaking with anger.

Since our last meeting, I've thought of nothing else. I wanted to disappear, never revealing the truth, but I couldn't. I understand now how pain can devour you—eat you alive. I'm not the monster you think I am. I know you loved me and you still have the power to love. I know you can forgive me.

Tears crept into her eyes. "Oh God, I loved you so much." She went to his chair and gently touched his shoulders.

He slipped into her arms.

Emma cradled his head against her waist. "The baby was there and then it was gone. It haunts me nearly every day, and I suppose it will for the rest of my life."

He drew away. *I learned about your husband's injury. I have friends stationed near Toul.*

"You know about Tom?"

Yes.

He rose from his chair and faced her, exposing her to the face she had sculpted. The mask, showing darker than the flesh in the dim light, added to the soldier's unnatural appearance. A few dents pocked the cheeks, bits of paint had chipped near the chin and earpieces; however, the depth of expression in Private Darser's eyes remained unchanged. He truly sought her forgiveness.

He wrote again and turned the pad toward her. *I have no face, but I can give you a child. I can undo the wrong I created.*

"No," she said, shrinking from the preposterous thought. "You can't expect me to accept such an offer. It's obscene. Don't even think it."

He underlined the words: *I can give you a child. I can undo the wrong I created.*

Emma backed away until she reached the church doors, the soldier following as she pushed them open and scurried to the street. A dim figure stood under a blacked-out streetlamp to her right. She ran toward the man, plunging into Hassan's arms.

"*Madame, ça va?*" he asked with concern while holding her close. "We worry . . . seek, *pour toi*. . . ."

"I'm fine," Emma said, and held on to the Moroccan. "However, I'm very happy to see you. Let's go home."

Emma looked back at the church several times as they walked away arm in arm. Only shadows draped the stones of Saint-Étienne-du-Mont, one of them shifting almost imperceptibly as she and Hassan stepped briskly around a corner, leaving the cathedral behind.

She reached under her bed and retrieved a stack of letters secured by a red ribbon. Dust had settled on them. She blew across the ribbon and motes floated like miniature snowflakes in the sunlight.

Emma searched for the last one she had received from Linton Bower, and found it—dated August 31st, 1918, the scrawled writing confirming the authorship. Unlike his previous letters, Linton's words were perfunctory, with little personal connection, romantic or otherwise, uninspired, and so different from the tone Emma had come to know. He wrote of the weather, a walk through the Museum of Fine Arts (although he found he could see only the brightest objects), scribbled a few terse lines about Alex and then said good-bye without his usual, *Your dearest friend.* He wrote only, *Linton.*

She hoped that he was well and not suffering.

Earlier in the day, out of that concern, Emma had asked Madame Clement whether any of Linton's letters might have been accidentally lost or misplaced. The housekeeper put down her dust rag, picked absentmindedly at the bun knotted in her gray hair, and shook her head defiantly, offended by the suggestion that she would lose important mail.

Emma found a letter from Anne, delivered only a few days before. The handwriting was young and sure.

15th October, 1918
My Dear Ma'am:
All is well here. I've managed to avoid the terrible influenza.
I thank the Lord every day for you and Mr. Swan. You have changed my life with your generosity and for that I will be forever grateful. At times, I wish I could be with you in France, but then I know Europe is not a place for anyone these days. I hope the war will be over soon. God knows, Boston is better than Ireland.
The bills have been light. I've kept household expenses low. They should be when it's only Lazarus and me to feed!
I have a friend who comes to call once a week. His name is Robert Merriweather and he studies at the Boston School. He knows Mr. Sargent and other painters. He's so smart and so handsome, but I am playing coy with him. I wonder what he sees in me. And, God forgive me, I often wonder if I will have the name Anne Merriweather, but any such occurrence is on the far side of the mountain as far as I'm concerned.
Robert doesn't like Mr. Bower's painting. He calls it "extreme." I would be wondering what has happened to Mr.

Bower? I know you are friends (and I have told not a soul about your correspondence). Has he written to you? I have not seen him in nearly two months.

I happened on Miss Louisa Markham on Charles Street last week. I was as civil as could be considering the circumstances. She inquired politely about you and Mr. Swan. I told her I hadn't heard from you in several months—which was the truth, I swear. She also asked about Mr. Bower. Ma'am, I thought she seemed sad. It must be hard for one in her position to be sad, what with all her parties and money and all, but I swear it was so.

Wouldn't it be wonderful if this war was over by our Lord's Day in December? I will say all my prayers at Mass on Sunday and I will keep you and Mr. Swan in my heart.

Love to you,
Anne

Emma placed the letter on the bed. Light blinked across the floor as silvery clouds blocked the feeble sun, reminding her that winter was coming. She took her diary from the desk.

Entry: 6ᵗʰ November, 1918
The approaching winter chills my soul. A strange feeling has encased my heart and I'm not quite sure what to do about it. My life is as unsettled as it has ever been, the bad seeming to outweigh the good. Tom is a mystery, and I feel he is hiding something, although I can't be certain what secret he bears. Linton's letters have stopped and Anne has not seen him in two months. Lieutenant Stoneman is dead. My work has led me in a new direction, but not the one I expected. I can create masks, but I've had no time for sculpting since I came to France. Who knows whether I can still make art at all?

But most troubling is Private Darser. Is he Kurt? So much time has passed, but the memories linger. He seems to be, but I can't—don't want to—believe it. Does he truly seek my forgiveness? That's a hard bargain for me. I have never forgiven his desertion, leaving me with no choice but to accept the consequences of our immature behavior. His proposal at the church bordered on madness; yet, I can't forget his words: "I can undo the wrong I created." Can I atone for my past? Could I bear another child with him? The thought is hideous yet comforting as I contemplate my future.

Virginie has arrived and I must cease writing. I share some confidences with her, but I would prefer she not be a party to the turmoil raging inside me.

Two French soldiers shared a cigarette on the courtyard stairs while a third sat in the alcove, admiring Virginie as she washed her hands in the sink.

"It seems we have a full house today," Emma said. The soldier inside relaxed in his chair and a smile erupted through his eyes as he followed Virginie's every move.

Her assistant nodded slowly with pursed lips, and wiped her hands on a towel, her hunched attitude decidedly different from her usual confident self.

"Are you sick?" Emma asked.

"I am tired, Madame. I want this war to end, but I feel something bad will happen before it does."

"Nonsense," Emma replied, annoyed by the pessimism. "You're a good predictor of weather but not much else." Virginie's words had touched a nerve, sending a tingle through her; things were not looking bright anywhere in France.

"We've made masks for so many soldiers—wishing all comfort and peace," the young woman said. "I can't help but think about Monsieur Thibault and his family. It's been nearly a year now."

Emma looked at the man in the alcove, lowered her voice, and then asked Virginie, "Are you worried about another suicide?"

The nurse shook her head, and whispered, "No, I fear Private Darser . . . and I fear you will move away—return to America."

"You mustn't worry about that now or Private Darser. I'm sure he'll leave us in peace now that I've confronted him."

"He only wanted to thank you?" Virginie asked, the skin around her eyes crinkling with the question.

Emma nodded, having made up her mind to keep her conversation at Saint-Étienne-du-Mont a private matter. "And as far as leaving you—yes, our work together will eventually end, but you are capable of running the studio yourself. Why, you practically do it now. We'll cross that bridge—"

Virginie muttered a short cry and tears filled her eyes.

The soldier rose from his chair and offered a crisp white handkerchief to the nurse, who blubbered something in French and waved the soldier away.

Not understanding, Emma followed the nurse into the casting room where Hassan was molding a mask over a clay model.

Virginie slammed her fist on the table. "I won't work with the man! *Jamais!* But I have no other job."

"I know he's been horrid at times. But in the future, if it comes to that, John Harvey will be kind. I promise. I'll see to it." Emma embraced Virginie and wiped the tears away with her sleeve. "Come, now, let's get to work and waste no more time on sad possibilities."

Madame Clement entered the room and motioned to Emma. "A young woman to see you, Madame."

Emma turned. "I don't recall an appointment with a woman. Did she say what she wanted?"

"Only to speak with you. Richard is here, too."

"Richard?" The woman had come from Toul! She brushed past Madame Clement and hurried to the alcove where the French soldier still sat in his chair. He had wrapped his scarf around his face up to his eyes, self-conscious about the two strangers in the room.

"*Bonjour, Madame,*" Richard said with gusto.

Emma thought he looked pleased, as if he carried a great secret from the walled city, along with his human cargo. Emma stood for a time, looking at the pair. Richard had shaved his scruffy beard, and only a sharply trimmed mustache remained. He looked fit and well for someone with an injury so severe he could not fight.

The other guest, clad in a blue dress and cream-colored shawl, kept her face lowered until Richard finished speaking. When she raised her head, Emma recognized her as the woman who had been waiting for Tom at the hospital. Her startling beauty filled the room—the rich ebony color of her hair, the liquid fire burning in her brown eyes. She posed defiantly, her stance rigid and unforgiving, arms by her side, as if daring Emma to speak.

"Madame Swan . . . Madame Constance Bouchard," Richard said after an uncomfortable silence. "Madame Bouchard has accompanied me from Toul."

"What can I do for Madame?" Emma asked. "There must be good reason for one to travel so far."

The woman nodded stiffly, throwing the end of the shawl defiantly over her right shoulder, asking in a slight French accent, "May we talk privately?"

"Of course . . . in the casting room." Before turning away, Emma said, "Help Virginie with the soldiers—make yourself useful."

"*Avec plaisir,*" Richard said.

"I thought you'd be willing to lend a hand. Hassan will help as well."

Richard's smile turned to a frown at the thought of the tall Moroccan acting as a chaperone.

Emma showed Madame Bouchard into the casting room and instructed Virginie and Hassan to assist the waiting soldiers. She closed the door and took a seat behind her desk.

The woman studied the facial casts on the wall. "I've heard what you do."

Emma detected a touch of jealousy in the woman's voice.

"Thank you," Emma said, puzzled by the statement. "Did you come to discuss my work or do you have something else on your mind?"

The woman gestured to a chair in front of the desk and Emma responded with an invitation to sit.

"My husband is dead." Madame Bouchard sat erect, her eyes cutting through her. "Killed two years ago in a worthless battle in the north of France, shot in the head in a struggle over a half-kilometer's worth of land. The Germans recaptured it three months later." She let out a small laugh filled more with bitterness than humor.

"I'm sorry," Emma said.

"You needn't be. Our marriage was a farce from the beginning. I was pregnant, but he decided to marry me rather than walk away. But, in death, he only left me a small amount of money and what little love we shared went with him to the grave." She looked past Emma to the disfigured faces on the wall. "So these are the lucky ones—the ones who get a second chance."

"Some believe so. We are proud of our work. . . ."

"You see, I am from Spain, but I was raised by an English nanny. So, after my husband's death, it was easy to strike up a conversation with Thomas."

"You're referring to my husband?" Emma asked, knowing the answer to her question.

"Yes, after what your husband and I have shared together, I wanted to meet the sculptress Emma Lewis Swan—the woman Thomas married and still loves."

Emma sat stone-faced and silent.

"Toul is a small village," the woman continued. "Gossip can be nasty. I'm surprised you haven't heard of Constance Bouchard before." She smiled. "Thomas was angry when he met me. It was a chance encounter on the street in front of the Mad Café—certainly not planned. I was a widow of one year and Tom was frantic—disturbed by letters he had received from a woman in Boston. He drank too much that evening. It was weeks before he told me his wife had deceived him. He was in need . . . and so was I."

Emma's pulse rose in her throat and she clutched the arms of her chair, as if she were slipping away from the world. "What do you want?"

Madame Bouchard's dark eyes bored into her. "To meet the woman Tom says he will never leave—even for his child."

The room grew cold. Madame Bouchard's eyes flickered, her mouth moved, but Emma could hear no words. She placed her hands in her lap and bowed her head, unable to look at the woman as a frigid silence enveloped her.

"Are you listening to me?" Madame Bouchard demanded. "In your case, a proclamation of innocence is unnecessary. Thomas has feelings! He acted as any man would have done when faced with infidelity."

"Get out," Emma said. "Leave me and my husband alone."

"I expected as much from you," the woman said, remaining calm against Emma's anger. "If you had nothing to hide—no sins to bear—you would have stated your innocence plainly. Your actions still trouble you."

"You have no right to make judgments." Emma rose from her chair and walked to the door.

"Before you have me removed, I have one request."

"What is it?" Emma replied, iciness frosting her voice.

"We have a beautiful boy who is six months old." Madame Bouchard stood and moved toward Emma. "He was conceived before Thomas's injury. I should thank you for my second child; after all, you bear some responsibility. However, I cannot convince Thomas to stay in France. He will return to America to be with you, but our baby . . . he will remain here with me." She paused and her defiance lightened. "I may need financial help to raise my son—in case Thomas forgets. It can be very difficult to raise children without a father."

Emma studied the woman who stood so proudly before her, knowing the truth of her words, but doubting the necessity. Madame Bouchard's dress was of blue silk and she wore it elegantly. The cream shawl that draped her body was woven of freshly dyed wool. Her fine shoes gave the impression they had never strolled a village street. The woman appeared quite capable of supporting herself and her children; however, Emma was struck by the similarities to her past—when she was alone and faced life with a fatherless child.

After a moment, she said, "I'll leave my address with Virginie when I return to Boston. If you need funds, wire me your request. I make my living as an artist. I don't have a great deal of money, but I'll do what I can—"

"You needn't say more. I know you will honor your word."

Emma opened the studio door and Madame Bouchard strode past her into the hallway. Her staff and Richard, laughing and smiling over some French joke, were huddled around the soldiers. The soldiers, despite their injuries, joined in with muted laughter and pats on the back.

Richard eyed Emma as she stood near the alcove entrance. His sly smile affirmed that he knew Madame Bouchard's story; yet, the softness in his eyes revealed his sympathy for Emma's plight. He opened a tin of cigarettes and waited for her to speak.

"Madame Bouchard and Richard are leaving," Emma said to the group. "It's time to get back to work."

Virginie and Hassan directed the first man to the casting room, while Madame Clement headed upstairs.

Madame Bouchard stood near the door, her hand clutching the knob as she waited for Richard.

"Only a few hours in Paris and we must return to Toul?" Richard asked Madame Bouchard.

"Nonsense," the woman replied. "We'll stay overnight at the best hotel we can afford."

Richard winked at Emma.

"In separate rooms, of course," Madame Bouchard said, gauging Richard's reaction.

"A safe trip, Richard," Emma said. She looked directly at Madame Bouchard as she spoke. "Please convey my best wishes to my husband."

"Now you understand," Richard said to her in a voice barely above a whisper. "*Il marche dans la nuit.*"

Emma nodded and watched as the two descended the steps to the courtyard.

After they departed, Emma picked up the studio phone, barely aware of Virginie, Hassan, and the soldier in the casting room. It seemed to slip from her hands, but finally the operator connected her to the hospital in Toul. *Courage . . . courage to talk to Tom. We no longer have the luxury of time.* The call went through.

"*Docteur Swan,*" Emma said when the connection was made.

"*Un moment.*" Emma recognized the voice of the nurse who usually sat at the front desk. The woman put the phone down and it seemed hours before another voice came on the line.

"Thomas Swan."

Emma hesitated, her throat constricting with emotion.

"I know about . . ." she finally managed to say.

"Emma?"

"Yes."

A long silence reinforced the gulf between them.

"You were right about trust," Emma said.

"What do you mean?" he asked, concern rising in his voice.

"Madame Bouchard. The child. Everything."

"Oh, God. You saw her?"

"She came to me."

Before Tom spoke, silence flowed between them like battering waves. "Emma, please understand . . ."

"At the moment, understanding is beyond my reach."

"Let me explain. Don't be hasty."

"Time . . . I need time to think . . . please don't call or come to Paris."

"Emma . . . ?"

She placed the phone gently in the cradle, cutting off their conversation, and bowed her head. After a time, the room re-emerged around her.

The soldier shifted uncomfortably in his chair as Hassan

smoothed plaster over the wounded face. Virginie flicked her brush against the mask she was painting.

Emma left her desk and walked to the window. The finality of her conversation with Tom—the painful truth—forced her to remember why she had never told anyone, not even her husband, about the loss she'd endured years before.

CHAPTER 10

PARIS

November 11, 1918

"We came very close to extinction," John Harvey said.

They stood at the studio window and looked down upon the revelers who congregated on rue Monge. To Emma they seemed like ants scattered by a careless footstep. Men and women waved the Tricolor, but there were other colors as well—foreign flags hoisted on banners, nations celebrating together after four years of war. Emma knew very little about these other people and nations, but shared in their relief that the war finally had come to a close. From their vantage point at the window, Emma and John heard the sharp reports of fireworks and shots fired into the air from celebrations breaking out across the city. Even an overcast sky, sometimes punctuated by blue breaks in the clouds, failed to dampen the crowd's enthusiasm. Men hugged, women cried, both sexes laughed and kissed on the street below. Emma looked at the clock; it was just after noon.

"Do you believe in the afterlife?" John asked, pulling a chair near the window. He lit a cigarette and positioned it in the ashtray he held. The gray smoke drifted toward the window and blended with the heavy sky over Paris.

Emma turned to him and smiled. "An afterlife? What an odd question to ask considering the day," she said casually. A disquieting emptiness filled her despite the rejoicing outside.

"Not at all; in fact, I think it's quite appropriate." He reached for the cigarette. "We all evaded death—even Tom. That's something to be thankful for. Had we not, who knows where we would be." He laughed at his own sardonic joke.

"I believe in what we have now," Emma said. "There's nothing more. This war has convinced me of that."

"I've seen many corpses, Emma. And judging from the view, I'd have to agree with you. When you see a dead man with hands reaching for the heavens, his stomach bloated in death, the face gripped with terror, frozen for eternity, you have every right to wonder whether there is a God." He paused and flicked off an ash. "I suppose I can tell you now. Bloody hell, what are they going to do? Hang me? The project at Porton Down, had it come to fruition, would have ended the war—possibly even mankind. We were developing a weapon—a gas so hideous its deployment would have killed hundreds of thousands more— perhaps millions."

"Millions murdered by this war and we should count ourselves lucky," Emma said.

"Not murder. Government-sanctioned genocide." He stubbed out his cigarette and looked at her. "You're behaving strangely. You should be happy . . . celebrating like Hassan, Madame Clement, and that obnoxious assistant of yours. They're out roaming the streets of Paris with champagne in hand. A thought is an unsatisfactory substitute for the experience. . . ." John made a fist and tipped it toward his mouth.

"Not a bottle in the house unless there happens to be a stray in the alcove," Emma said.

"Please, do us a favor and give it a good looking over."

"Why not?" she asked, walking away. The cabinet over the sink held tea, crackers, a tin of cookies, and Madame Clement's freshly washed dishes. A few rumpled dishtowels and a box of soap powder lay under the basin. However, she found what she was looking for in a small cupboard on the opposite wall. Emma grabbed a bottle and two glasses and returned to the casting room. John shifted his ample body in the chair and propped his feet on the windowsill.

"No more champagne," Emma said, "but I found a half-full bottle of Irish whiskey. I imagine one of the soldiers left it— perhaps from Christmas."

John smacked his lips. "Irish whiskey. Even better."

Emma poured two glasses, handing one to her guest as the fruity odor of the liquor washed over them.

John raised his glass and clinked it against Emma's. "Here's to the end of hell."

"Or possibly the beginning," Emma replied, thinking about all that remained unfinished in her life.

Before he drank, John said, "Seriously, I'm concerned about you."

She turned her back to the crowd below and leaned against the sill. "Things have taken a turn for the worse. I thought matters between Tom and me were on the mend, but I was wrong." She strained to hold back tears. "I won't bore you with details."

"It's been a while since I've seen Tom. I was headed to the Front when we got wind of the armistice. I only made it as far as Paris, damn the luck. I was certain I'd be far away from your assistant when the war ended." He raised his glass again. "Here's to both you and Tom. I'm sorry things are so rough."

Emma raised her glass, feeling strangely complacent, not at all joyous the war was over, despite the cheering crowds and exploding fireworks. "Yes, so am I, but I suppose we have to work it out—if it can be worked out."

John drained his glass and put it on the floor. "Well, enough of a celebration. I've enjoyed our little talk, but I must be on my way. I don't want to get so drunk I can't navigate back to the hotel." He removed his feet from the sill, gathered his coat, and withdrew a note from its pocket. "I nearly forgot. I have information for you about your Private Darser. I believe I know who he is." He handed it to Emma. "It's the strangest thing—I treated him under his birth name here in Paris. That's why Darser meant nothing to me. You may have even seen him when we first met. I never would have found out the deception if he had kept his mouth shut . . . well, I mean to say, if he hadn't written things down after his injury. He adopted a new name, and a few of his buddies caught wind of it from his bragging. He never said why. His comrades thought it was battle fatigue setting in—a mental lapse—a soldier going slightly crackers from a horrible wound."

"Thank you, but I know who he is," Emma said. "An old acquaintance."

"Old acquaintance? Why would he hide so? Seems a bit murky . . . but for all my efforts I should at least get a hand-shake."

Emma gave him a peck on the cheek. "It's a long story—too long and depressing to go into today."

"Yes, indeed," John said. "An American who joined the Ca-nadian Army, injured at Passchendaele, in and out of hospitals, and then to Paris for treatment. I believe he's still in the city. His address is on the paper." When he reached the alcove door, he said, "Good-bye, Emma. I don't know if we shall meet again."

She followed him. "One favor, John. I have a wonderful staff here. If you could see your way clear to give them a reference, or perhaps a job after the soldiers stop coming. . . ."

He laughed. "You want me to find work for your nurse—the former bane of my existence?"

"Yes, that would be kind of you."

He grasped her hands. "The studio's done wonderful work, Emma. The soldiers will never forget you."

"Virginie, Hassan, and Madame Clement have contributed to the success we've achieved—especially Virginie."

"There are wounds yet to be healed. Masks to be made. Virginie can follow in your footsteps. The studio's legacy will live on."

"John?"

"I can't promise anything . . . keep me in your thoughts, my dear." He closed the door and descended the stairs.

His cheery whistle echoed through the courtyard, the tune fading to nothing as he entered the tunnel, until Emma heard only the clatter of the crowd.

The evening lights came on early and shone brightly in the city. She sat alone, at her desk, the studio muted in comparison to the Paris streets. Emma unfolded the note John had given her and positioned it squarely in front of her. Finding a pencil from her desk, she wrote the first name in block lettering on the paper.

KURT LARSEN

And underneath she wrote the name of Private Darser.

RON DARSER

She studied both names, then altered the first name by adding dashes and erasing certain lines. After the changes were complete, the deception appeared plainly before her.

KURT LARSEN

John had written the address, 36 rue de la Victoire, on the paper. Emma checked a map book of Paris and found the street located on the east end of the Ile Saint-Louis. It took her only a moment to decide to leave the studio and find Kurt Larsen's apartment.

Emma snaked her way through the crowds on rue Monge to the Boulevard Saint-Germain until she found the Quai and smelled the muddy wash of the Seine. Many of the Parisian revelers were in the death throes of their celebration despite the early hour of seven. A few men, coats unbuttoned, shirts open at the neck, exchanged kisses with their ladies while leaning against whatever would support them: a tree, a building, a lamppost. Across the river, the buttresses of Notre Dame arched like spider's legs in the night. In a few more minutes, she reached Pont de Sully, the stone bridge that stretched across the river to Ile Saint-Louis. The crowd that meandered along the riverbank was large, but more contemplative than those gathered in the street. Everyone seemed transfixed by the flowing water and thankful that, like the eternal river, the City of Light and their lives would be spared the war's carnage.

After crossing the bridge, Emma turned left on the Quai de Bethune and then right on rue de Bretonvilliers. In the dimly lit streets, she searched for the entrance to rue de la Victoire. She found it, marked by white paint on the side of a limestone building. The narrow lane led to several row houses, half the size and not nearly as grand as the six-story structures that surrounded it. A few lights peppered the windows, but the illumination was not enough to prevent Emma from stumbling over a cobblestone before she found the door to thirty-six. As far as she could tell there were three apartments: Floors two and three were populated by tenants bearing French surnames; the first-floor nameplate sat empty.

Emma knocked twice and waited. A short time later, a soldier wearing a mask opened the door. As it swung open, his eyes widened.

"Kurt," Emma said, keeping her voice low. "I'd like to come in."

At first, he stood motionless under the hazy hall light.

Emma considered that he might slam the door in her face. On the other hand, the soldier had presented an offer at Saint-Étienne-du-Mont; perhaps he'd expected her to accept his proposal.

He propped his hands against the door, steadied himself, and then stared at her.

The sour smell of sweat and liquor rose from Kurt's body. The sculpted mouth from which his breath escaped had transformed into a leer. Even in the dim light, Emma could see the mask was damaged—the paint had flecked off, dents pocked the chin, the copper was torn across the right cheek.

"I've considered your offer," Emma said. "May I come in?"

He stepped away, steadying himself against the wall.

She entered the hall and he closed the door. The musty odor of a two-hundred-year-old building filled her nostrils with a dry itchiness. The wooden floors creaked underneath her shoes as she brushed past the faded rococo wallpaper of men and women cavorting on swings, which was peeling away in thin strips.

Kurt's apartment, only a room, was open. Emma stepped inside.

He stumbled after her and closed the door.

It contained a single bed, a rickety bureau holding a white ceramic washbasin, a chair, and a wooden stand upon which a single candle burned. The flickering light triggered a memory, and, for an instant, she was transported back to the bedroom in Vermont with its fiery dappled blaze. Emma settled into the chair, her nerves taut with anticipation.

Kurt nestled a pillow against the wall and dropped carelessly onto the bed. The mask nearly slipped from his face, but he managed to secure the earpieces with his hands.

"You must listen," Emma said. "Don't bother to write—I won't read it. I know who you are. I've known since I drew your face, but I didn't want to believe the truth." She unbuttoned her coat, revealing her legs. "You lied to me. You lied to me from the beginning."

Kurt shifted uneasily on the bed.

"We conceived a child and then I killed the one precious gift you ever gave me. I threw away a life because you and I were too selfish, too absorbed, to see past our own self-centeredness. We've both paid the price in our ways."

Kurt shook his head and reached for the notepad on his bed.

Emma slapped it from his hands. "No! Pay attention to me! I'm through listening to you. Since I saw you at the cathedral, I've hardly thought of anything else. I wondered whether I should go through with your offer. You have no idea how I've suffered because of my action—one you pushed me to take. I should have stood up to you and my mother, but I wasn't strong enough to face her. I knew she would never forgive my pregnancy. For all I knew, she would have thrown me to the street, branded as a whore.

"You were silenced by the war, but I've been silent even longer. I've longed for this day—when I could take back what

I did. We created a life and I extinguished it. Today, I've been liberated along with the world, and I'm free to do with you as I wish, free from my husband, free from a nightmare that haunts me." Emma drew in a sharp breath. "Death has followed us, but life has given us another chance—one that will complete my emancipation." Her voice brimmed with anger. "I've never been able to rid myself of that black stain on my soul. It holds my guilt and I've carried it for too many years. I'm going to exorcise it with the man who conceived it."

She took off her coat, rose from the chair, and sat on the edge of the bed, staring at Kurt, who shrank from her like a wounded dog.

He groaned under the mask and reached again for the pad, but Emma seized it and threw it to the floor.

She grabbed his wrists and, with all her strength, forced them flat on the bed.

His head lolled against the pillow, his body wriggling like a snake in the talons of a hawk, but his struggle subsided after a few moments, the resistance draining from his body until his eyes appeared as lifeless as pale moons.

Emma released her grip, hooked her fingers through the thin metal earpieces, and lifted the mask, exposing the face with its mouth and jaw ripped away.

He instinctively reached to cover his injuries.

Emma tugged at his hands. At first he fought against her, but when she guided them to her breasts, he shook violently on the bed and his grip slackened.

"I want our child back," Emma said, positioning her body over his, kissing his forehead, her anger lessening as her passion for absolution rose. She caressed the scarred tissue around the cavity that was his mouth, felt the jagged bone beneath the skin. Even as she touched him, she remembered Kurt as he was in Vermont, consummating this sexual act, an act of atonement for herself and the child she had lost. She had to remind herself it was so; otherwise, her actions were too intolerable to bear.

He weakened under her touch and soon he was lifting his body to meet hers.

She met his thrusts with her own, covering the wounded face with kisses, tugging at the buttons of his shirt.

He pulled her to his chest, pressing his pelvis against hers, his hardness jabbing against her thighs.

She quivered at the touch of his erection, and lifted herself gently from him, slid off the bed, and watched as he unzipped his trousers and pushed them down to his knees. He was exposed to her once again and she recalled the contours of his body, the smooth skin, the downy hair surrounding the clefts and mound of his pubic area, the deep brown circle of the circumcision scar, the shape of his sex. He existed in his body as he always had, except for the face, and she remembered.

Emma unbuttoned her dress, slipping out of it, letting it fall to the floor.

His chest rose and fell with his quick breaths.

She stripped away her shoes, stockings, and undergarments, and climbed on top of him, pressing her vagina against him, loosening up, for she was tight with emotion. She cried out when he entered her, but soon moved in unison with him, meeting every thrust with an equally intense motion and pleasure. Her hands massaged his chest and she caught sight of the scar on her finger with its flash of silvery skin.

Emma stopped her thrusts.

His hardness tensed.

She squeezed in response and held him tightly inside her.

Lifting the mask from the bed, she ran her finger over the cleft in the metal and then peeled back one half of the tear, exposing the jagged edge. Holding Kurt's left arm, she positioned the mask against his wrist and prepared to slash the metal across the blue vein rising from the white skin.

Kurt shut his eyes in anticipation of the cut Emma was poised to deliver.

Instead she swung the mask above his hand, purposely missing the flesh, dropping it to the floor where it fell upon his notepad.

His eyes flashed open, sexual fury boiling in them.

"You wanted me to cut you, just as I cut myself," Emma said. She looked down at the man who lay with his arms thrust over his head, his body as rigid as stone. "I won't give you that satisfaction." She reached behind her, nearly collapsing on his chest, massaging his testicles as he thrust in-and-out of her in rapid strokes. Within moments, he came in violent spasms and their bodies shook in unison, his slickness combining with hers. She held him inside until his penis slipped from her and lay limply against her buttocks. Emma rolled off and tightened her groin to keep the fluid inside. When she finally climbed off the bed, she accidentally stepped on the mask. It crunched like a dead leaf underneath her feet.

Kurt yowled like a wounded animal.

The mask lay flat upon the wooden floor.

"I'm sorry," Emma said, despite the thrill of revenge that crept over her. "Come to the studio. I'll make another."

Kurt never moved, but stared at her with desolate eyes, as she dressed and slipped out of the apartment.

The night air invigorated her as she walked back to the studio, her senses heightened, the broad sweep of the city electrifying her. She spent the night alone in the bedroom thinking of what she had done—the others at rue Monge were wrapped up in their own celebrations of the war's end. As the night grew long, the dream of the faceless infant gradually receded from her memory.

The next day she saw Kurt again at his apartment. He wrote: *I am lonely.*

She wrote back: *I want our child.*

Emma made love to him several times before she left Paris. Each successive time, her revulsion about her sexual liaisons lessened. She only had to think of a child growing inside her to erase the guilt.

Many days, she lay in her bed until Virginie called her to work. The fall and winter dragged on and their chilly depths depressed her. Even Christmas was cheerless and dull for she still wanted no contact with her husband. Despite the war's end, Emma found it difficult to be joyful. Thoughts of Tom and Kurt quickly erased any sense of happiness. More often than not, she found herself thinking of Linton and the love he offered—the true affection she had foresworn for France. The memory of his face lifted her briefly when no other joy could be found.

The year drew to a close, but Kurt never returned to the studio for another mask.

PART FIVE

BOSTON
JANUARY 1919

CHAPTER 11

———◆———

19ᵗʰ January, 1919
Dear Virginie,
Hello, my dear one.
In life one often runs squarely into the obvious—sometimes at great cost. Writers are told to avoid clichés, but I must take exception and reiterate how profoundly my life changed in France and how much I miss you and the staff.

When I left the studio that morning after the New Year, I avoided a look back at the staircase. I couldn't stand to see you or Madame Clement weeping at the door—God knows, even Hassan shed a few tears over my departure. However, I sleep peacefully in Boston knowing the studio is in your prosperous hands. I have the greatest confidence in your abilities and I'm certain you will carry on our work to the great benefit of your country and all soldiers in need. Be forewarned, I know John Harvey will figure later in your life somehow. Please, be gracious and welcome him with open arms. He really is a good soul at heart, and I think every one of you may benefit from any kindness he displays.

My trip home on the USS Manchuria was uneventful—if sailing on a ship loaded with American doughboys can be described in such a conventional manner. They were a gay crowd and carried on much longer into the night than I cared to, but these are men who deserve to celebrate every minute that life allows them. Even those hampered by crutches or arm slings held their heads high. But despite the congeniality onboard, I couldn't help but think of Lieutenant Stoneman and my voyage to France, filled with my fears of German submarines and the unknown fates that lay beyond. I suffered none of those concerns on my return trip.

My arrival in Boston was tearful as well—exhausted as I was after the sea journey and the rail trip from New York. Anne and Lazarus met me at the door—Anne with a smile, hugs, and tears, and Lazarus with a subdued wag of his tail. I think he has forgotten me over the past year and a half of my absence and has grown fonder of Anne. My God, can it be that long! It's taken me longer to re-adjust than I imagined. The winter wind in Boston cuts through you in a way unknown in Paris. Oh, it's all so different: the city, the light (the war seems a distant memory here); the Bostonians, except for the perceived hardships of rationing, are hardly aware that millions were slaughtered an ocean away.

I asked Anne to keep my arrival somewhat of a secret. I still have to renew acquaintances with several friends. I needed time to think, to study, to read, to sit in the living room in front of the fireplace with a cup of tea while Lazarus warms my feet. This solitude, even though my art has suffered, has been the best homecoming for me. Anne graciously spoils me with delicious meals and regal touches that make me feel like a pampered queen.

So, Virginie, I will keep you from your work no longer. I wish you all happiness in life as I do for Madame Clement, Hassan, and, yes, even John.

I must end this letter on a sad note. Although I never talked to you explicitly about my troubles with my husband, I'm sure you were aware of their existence. If he takes the time to call or visit Paris in concern for my health, please let him know that I am safe in Boston. I didn't inform him of my decision to leave France, fearing more emotional trauma. Tom has his own life at the moment—and I mine. It remains to be seen whether the two of us will reunite.

Thank you for your efforts and dedication to our task. The world is better for our work and I know we can be proud. Please write often and tell me what has transpired with our creation.

Yours always,
Emma Lewis Swan

"Oh, my dear, I am so happy to see you." Mrs. Frances Livingston raised her crystal champagne glass and tapped it against Emma's. "I'm so glad you could come. When I heard you were in town, my excitement bubbled over."

"I'm very happy to be here," Emma said. "I'm quite surprised you knew of my return. No one really does, except my mother."

"Boston society, my dear. Nothing escapes the eyes and ears of our circle."

Emma lifted the glass to her lips and tasted the golden, frothy liquid, which tickled the inside of her nose. She was happy to be here, surrounded by luxury. The arched marble fireplace crackled with warmth. A servant, stiffly clad in day attire, stood prepared if Emma finished her drink. She rubbed the arms of her gold-gilt chair and was reminded that her life and the life of Frances Livingston were very different. The drawing room was filled with art—portraits and sculpture—many of the pieces purchased from Alex Hippel, the owner of the Fountain Gallery. A life-size portrait of Frances, opulent in its gold frame, hung on the wall opposite the hearth. Emma immediately recognized it as a painting by Singer Sargent, a masterwork composed in his sweeping brushstrokes. Impressionistic landscapes in brilliant blues and greens also graced the walls.

To her left, Emma looked into the immense ballroom with its gleaming French doors. Past those doors lay the garden steps, now dusted with snow, where Linton had fallen in his effort to escape the pain of her decision to leave Boston. She had not set foot in the house since that party so long ago.

"More champagne?" Frances asked. Her forehead crinkled a bit as if she had more on her mind than libations. "Aren't you thrilled the horrid war is over? You must tell me all about your travels and troubles in France—when we have the time."

"Yes, Frances, when we have the time, and I feel up to it." Emma sighed and settled against the chair's formidable back. Despite its plush red-silk upholstery, the seat was barely comfortable. Emma wriggled, attempting to relax into an agreeable position.

"Is something wrong, my dear? The moment you walked in the door, I felt you were out of sorts. I hope you didn't contract something in France or on that squalid voyage home. Imagine, using the *Manchuria* as a troopship. I once sailed on her to Italy."

"I'm fine, Frances . . . a bit tired, but I think that's to be expected considering what I've been through for nearly two years."

"And that's what I want to find out—when we have the time—but today, I have a surprise that will erase all those awful memories." Frances raised her nearly empty glass and the servant stepped quickly to her side and poured more champagne.

"What's that?" Emma had no idea what Frances might have in store.

"I've invited a guest. Louisa Markham!"

Emma flinched.

Frances's eyes sparkled. "I knew you'd be pleased. When I spoke with Louisa, she didn't even know you were home. I kept our meeting today a secret, so this reunion will be a surprise for both of you."

"Oh, Frances, you shouldn't have. I really can't impose on your hospitality. Anne is—"

"No excuses, dear. Two old friends shouldn't be deprived of each other's company." Frances looked at her gold watch.

Emma, realizing Frances's plan had been intricately constructed, twisted in her chair when a knock at the front door echoed through the hall. An elderly maid traversed the hall like a pallbearer. The massive door creaked open and then closed as the maid welcomed the visitor with a gentle, "Good afternoon, Miss Markham."

She steeled herself for Louisa's entrance.

Her friend entered the room oblivious to Emma. Perhaps Louisa thought an acquaintance of Frances's, unknown to her, had been invited for afternoon champagne, or perhaps the reality of Emma sitting squarely in front of her was too much to bear. Louisa finally let out a small cry of recognition, her eyes lighting up under the brim of her black hat, her long ermine coat billowing as she strode to her side. Without saying a word, she offered her hand.

Emma took the gloved hand tepidly.

Louisa shed her coat into the maid's waiting arms and slid gracefully into the chair across from Frances.

Emma looked at the hostess. Frances beamed and then looked at them both before she spoke. "Isn't it wonderful to have two old friends reunited." The hostess raised her glass. "Here's to friendship and the end of the war."

The servant hurriedly brought champagne to Louisa.

"I shouldn't drink," Emma said and placed her glass on the marble-center table.

"Nonsense, Emma," Frances said. "The afternoon's hardly begun and I have plenty on reserve. I've been saving my special bottles since the war began; but no more. The time for abstinence has passed." She chuckled.

"That's very kind of you, Frances, but I've lost my taste for champagne." Emma crossed her arms and stared at the fire.

Louisa took a sip and settled into her chair.

"Well, I can understand your reluctance, my dear," Frances said sweetly and leaned forward, trying to make the best of Emma's sour mood. "I'm sure my reserve isn't nearly as grand as the champagne you drank in France."

Emma resisted the urge to snap at her hostess. "I *rarely* had time to celebrate. In fact, I can only remember drinking champagne once and that was at a Christmas party where a soldier . . ."

Frances's eyebrows bunched together.

"Another time," Emma said. "That story isn't fit for company."

Frances smiled, determined to save her get-together, and then turned her attention to Louisa. "Don't you look well, my dear. Don't you think Louisa looks well, Emma?"

She reluctantly admitted to herself that Louisa had retained her looks through the war, uncertain the same could be said for her own appearance. The cold weather had added a rosy blush to Louisa's cheeks, yet her face remained nearly alabaster, contrasting dramatically with her dark hair. Her svelte black dress was cinched at the waist by a white sash, which added to her fashionable appearance.

"I feel positively dowdy," Emma said.

"You do yourself an injustice," Louisa said. "The gray in your hair is significantly less than I imagined it would be—and you've only added a few more lines to your face. But that's understandable, given the war."

Emma leaned forward and smirked at her friend. "The Germans weren't the only ones shelling France. Volleys were lobbed from Boston as well."

Louisa sipped her champagne.

Frances scooted forward in her seat, as if she were about to witness a cataclysm that might tear the room in half.

"I'm sure I have no idea what you're talking about," Louisa said perfunctorily.

"You know perfectly well, you do."

"More champagne?" Frances asked.

"No thank you, *Frances*," Emma said. "If your maid will get my coat, I'll be on my way, for I really must be going. Thank you so much for your hospitality . . . I look forward to the day when we can continue our conversation—*alone*."

The maid, aware of the tension in the room, retrieved Emma's coat promptly. "Good day," Emma said, as the woman assisted her. "Please don't end your party on my account."

The maid walked as fast as she could ahead of Emma and held the door open. A hansom cab waited down the street. Hearing footsteps behind her, Emma turned to see Louisa hurtling down the hall toward her.

"How *dare* you insult me in front of Frances," Louisa said, cutting in front of the maid and slamming the door behind her.

"Careful," Emma said. "It's cold out—you'll catch your death and that would be an unmitigated tragedy."

"What have I possibly done to deserve such treatment?" A tempest arose in Louisa's eyes. "I've respected all your wishes. I've been kind to Anne—as much as I could without kowtowing to a domestic. I've taken your side in the onslaught of criticism against your foolhardy venture in Paris. I even extolled your art—let it be known what a great sculptress you are, despite your abject failure with faces."

Emma swung her hand, striking Louisa hard on her left cheek.

Louisa gasped and reeled backward, clutching her face.

Emma swayed on her feet. The slap, a furious, instinctive reaction, shocked her as much as it did Louisa.

"My God, Emma," Louisa said, when she recovered enough to speak. "We *are* through." She turned and placed her hand on the door.

"How could you destroy my marriage?" Emma asked, her voice quaking with anger.

Smirking, Louisa took her hand off the latch. "*Destroy* your marriage? I had no hand in destroying your marriage—you're quite capable of managing that task by yourself."

"I'm talking about your letters to Tom."

"What do you mean?"

"You wrote Tom about my relationship with Linton."

The fury in Louisa's eyes subsided. "Yes, I wrote Tom, but I never mentioned Linton. I only mentioned the most innocuous subjects—Boston and our friendships—I wanted to lift him up from the troubles of war."

"I don't believe you. I saw your letters. You wrote Tom because you're still in love with him and you desperately wanted to break us apart."

Louisa laughed and steadied herself against the doorframe. "You poor fool. You don't believe me? Well, you will someday . . . when it's too late for you and Tom." She paused and looked at her with disdain. "You're correct. I do love Tom, but I would never break you apart. It's not something I would ever think of doing to a friend. Your *zephyr* would never betray her best friend."

Emma stepped toward her.

"Stop," Louisa ordered. "There's no reason to continue this conversation. I'm the one who will still have friends and the chance of marrying a man—a good husband who will love me and provide a happy home. I pity you."

The door shut gently and Emma stood alone on the porch. As she walked down the steps and hailed the cab, she wondered whether she would ever see Louisa or Frances again. The ride home seemed as cold and lonely as the January day. Emma shivered in the seat and thrust her hands in her coat pockets. As the horse's hooves clopped on the cobblestones, a thought, at first as dim as a distant star in the night sky, filled her head until she could ignore it no longer. It spoke maddeningly and threatened: *Listen to her—she's telling the truth!*

"Have you heard from Mr. Bower?" Emma asked her housekeeper.

Anne, who was slicing potatoes and dropping them into a pot of boiling water, stopped her hands in mid-cut. "No, ma'am, not a word in months. It's very strange. He seems to have disappeared—like the goblins took him overnight."

"Yes, it is strange." Emma sat at the kitchen table and watched as Anne continued her work. "In his last letter to me, he told me he would like to . . . oh, I shouldn't bother you with such details."

Anne smiled, clearly eager to hear more. "Ma'am, do continue."

"Please, stop. Ever since my return you've insisted on addressing me as 'ma'am.' We came to a decision about that salutation weeks ago." Emma returned Anne's smile. "You're part of the family now—at least part of my family. You've been wonderful to me—guarding my heart so closely. There *are* good people in the world, Anne. You're one. Virginie, Hassan, and Madame Clement are good, too. Virginie reminds me of you in so many ways—I think you would be quite good friends."

"And your husband?"

Emma paused. "Would you be good friends with my husband?"

Anne laughed. "No—I love Dr. Swan, but he wasn't on your list. *Is* your husband a good person?"

Emma lowered her gaze, taken aback by her housekeeper's perceptive question. After a time, she said, "Yes, he is . . . I think we both lost our way." Emma rubbed her hands together. "But let's not talk of that. I'll have an attack of melancholy and that won't do for this evening. I have other plans."

"I see."

"No, you don't see," Emma said in jest. "Although you're part of the family, I still have my secrets. By the way, how is that young man of yours? Mr. Merriweather?"

A blush flowered on Anne's cheeks. "He's a fine gentleman and talented, too. He doesn't like Mr. Bower's art, but he certainly appreciates the skill and dedication it takes to be an artist."

"Yes, we all do."

"And even a starving artist at that."

Emma nodded, all too familiar with the vagaries of making a living as a sculptress. "I'll confess point-blank to remove that devil from your eye. After dinner, I'm taking a walk. I'm hoping to inquire about Mr. Bower before I visit him. One man, above all others, can tell me what I want to know, and I've avoided him."

"The man who introduced you to Mr. Bower," Anne said matter-of-factly.

Emma smiled, knowing her housekeeper was no simpleton.

Emma confirmed Alex Hippel's address from a previous letter and, after eating, set out to find his apartment. In all her dealings with him, she had never been to his home. All their business had been conducted in Emma's studio or at the Fountain Gallery. Unless he had moved recently, Alex would still reside on Fairfield Street between Boylston and Newbury.

The night was cold, but not bitter by Boston standards. Emma enjoyed the walk down Boylston, past the imposing façade of the Public Library, and the towering Romanesque steeple of Old South Church. The wind brushed against her face and she breathed deeply, drawing the fresh air into her lungs. In her estimation, the city lights seemed brighter now that the war was over, and she was certain more people were on the streets, gaiety blossoming on the faces she passed. The number of motorcars had increased, and the overall mood was lighter, the air charged with mechanical energy. And strangely, she walked with a quicker and lighter step—a consequence of her confrontation with Louisa at Frances's. Now that her feud was out in the open, she no longer feared venturing from her home. The gauntlet had been thrown.

Emma arrived at the address to find the name *Alex Hippel* floating in flowing script on the brass nameplate. She rang the adjacent buzzer and soon heard footsteps on the stairs. The door swung open, and, Alex, clad only in loose trousers, stood in front of her, his eyes forming wide circles of surprise.

"My Lord . . . Emma . . . Emma . . ."

She grinned at his sputtering and held out her hand.

He closed the door halfway and positioned his body behind it. "I'm sorry, I was expecting someone else."

"Clearly," Emma said, suppressing a laugh. "May I come in? Boston is a bit chilly this time of year."

"Of course. Pardon my manners and my nakedness."

Emma stepped into the hall and Alex closed the door. As

soon as it latched, he sprinted up the stairs. Emma followed, taking each step in slow measure, giving him time to dress. When she reached the second-floor landing, Alex stood in the doorway, pulling on a white shirt. He reached for her hand—cordially, she thought—and motioned for her to come inside.

"It's such a surprise to see you. I heard a rumor you might be in town, but I never expected to see you. Well, I don't suppose you know—or do you?"

Alex's apartment was in disarray. Paintings, many only on stretchers, were slanted like dominoes against the walls, packing crates stood like monoliths in the center of the room, and mountains of paper rose in front of crammed bookcases.

Emma spotted a lone chair between a desk and the crates and sat down despite not having an invitation.

Alex's brows lifted, anticipating a question. "Would you like something to drink? I only have scotch."

"No thank you. Do I know what?"

Alex fiddled with the buttons on his shirt. "I made the decision to close the gallery. Last August."

"Oh, I'm so—"

"Don't bother to feel sorry for me," he said abruptly. "I knew it was coming, despite my optimism. Boston was never a city for the avant-garde; it's like a small town, really. I reduced the hours, conducted a few private sales, but I've spent most of the last five months disengaging from the business. I attempted to keep the closing a guarded secret, at least from Frances and Louisa—you understand how one can feel like a failure, especially from their viewpoints—but it was useless really. Word travels. The unrelenting war sealed the coffin—the war and Vreland." He stood by the desk, lit a cigarette, and poured liquor into a tumbler. "As hard as I tried, I could never get him to understand my artists or the purpose of my gallery. The only ploy I didn't try was sleeping with him."

"Every critic has his price."

"Not Vreland. If I remember correctly, he wrote that your statue had the 'soul of an icicle.' That criticism alone laid bare *his* foul soul." Alex sipped the scotch, then tilted the glass toward Emma. "But, what do I care now. I survived the war without a scratch. I can thank my mother for giving birth to me when she did—making me just old enough not to be drafted." His mouth puckered as if he had said something distasteful. "I'm seeing a wonderful man and we're moving to New York. . . ." He set his drink amid the books and papers on his desk and fidgeted with his cigarette, acting as if he had revealed too much.

Emma nodded, signaling him that she understood his concern. "I'm truly sorry about the gallery, but I'm happy that the Fountain exhibited my work, and equally pleased that you sold my *Diana*. But that's not why I ventured out tonight. I came to ask you a question."

Alex leaned against the desk. "I'm sure I know the question and the answer—I haven't seen Linton for months. I don't even know where he lives. I think he moved to a smaller apartment somewhere—because he couldn't afford . . ."

Emma sat silently, uncertain what to say.

Alex reached for his glass. "We had a falling out . . . to put it politely." He poured another shot of scotch and gulped it. "Shortly after I made my decision to close, Linton left the gallery in a rage. I held out for my artists as long as I could, but I couldn't keep pouring money into it forever. Sales had slowed, including Linton's work. I didn't know the war would be over so quickly after reaching my conclusion. The war wasn't the only reason, however. You were a cause as well. Are you sure you wouldn't like a drink?"

Emma shook her head.

"We argued about you," Alex continued. "Linton said he was in love with you and could never be in love with me . . . or a man at all. I held on to the fantasy of a life with him for a time, even after Louisa told me about the two of you in his studio."

Pain swirled in his eyes.

"But, I finally said enough was enough. Every fixation . . . obsession, if you will . . . has a precipice where one falls into madness. I think you might understand what I mean . . ."

Emma nodded.

"Fortunately, I recognized our personal relationship was over and stepped back—our business dealings as well—because the gallery was dead. Linton stormed out after I told him, more hurt and frustrated than angry, I think, and that was that. I shipped his paintings to his studio the next day along with the money I owed him. A few weeks later, I saw him on the street, looking haggard and depressed, like he'd lost his last friend. It nearly broke my heart. I didn't want to see him—don't want to see him, until I can bear the pain of my . . . 'unrequited' love. I suppose that's selfish, but it's how I protect myself."

"You don't know whether he's well or not?" Emma asked.

A flush spread across his face. "No. I'm sorry. I love—rather loved—him too much. I hope you understand—it's not healthy for me to see him."

She understood all too well.

Alex jumped at the electric buzz that filled the room. "That'll be . . . at the door. Oh, you could give a damn."

"I do, but I must get home." Emma got up from the chair. "Does Linton still have his studio?"

Alex grimaced. "Not unless he found someone to bankroll him, but that would be a happy ending to a sad story. Let's go down. I'm sorry to cut our visit short, but my friend is here . . . I didn't know you were coming."

"I wanted it to be a surprise."

"It certainly was," Alex said as they descended the stairs. He opened the door and a handsome young man doffed his hat, brushed past Emma without a word, and headed up to the apartment.

"Ah, the manners of youth," Alex said. "At the very least, he's discreet."

"Good-bye, Alex," Emma said and kissed him on the cheek. "I hope life works out well for you in New York . . . I hope life works out well for both of us."

"We shall see. Perhaps New York will be kinder to me than Boston. Good-bye, Emma." He closed the door, leaving her on the cold landing.

*   *   *

Anne's footsteps padded on the stairs, preparing Emma for the knock on her studio door.

Gray light filtered through the window. She closed the cover on a sketch pad she hadn't touched in more than two years. In it were some of the first drawings of *The Narcissus*. The flowing lines brought back memories of her time with Linton, but the sketch depicting the face was off—too formal, too stilted, with little regard for human feeling.

Why does everything revolve around the face?

"Emma," her housekeeper said awkwardly, still uncomfortable with addressing her by her first name, "it's Miss Markham to see you."

"Really?" Emma asked, surprised that Louisa would call.

"Yes, I told her you weren't to be disturbed, but she insisted on discussing 'a matter of importance.'"

"Well, the topic must be important for Louisa to come here. Send her up, please."

In a few moments, Emma heard the click of her guest's heels on the stairs. She glanced away from her desk when Louisa arrived, but the flash of color was too much to ignore. Attired in a scarlet coat, matching dress, and black sash, Louisa entered like an exotic bird, her lips on the verge of a sneer. At least she appeared that way in Emma's eyes.

"I've come for an apology," her guest announced with perfectly nuanced haughtiness, "and the chance to clear my name."

Emma pointed to the chair across from her desk.

Louisa took off her coat and draped it across the seatback.

"Louisa, I—"

"Please, this pains me more than you . . . but in the interest of *veritas*." She placed her hands in her lap and looked directly into Emma's eyes. "I never wrote those incriminating letters to Tom, but I believe I've uncovered the culprit. It was positively evil on their part."

Emma attempted to speak, but Louisa held up her hand. "I

told you I would never betray you and you must accept that statement on trust. If you don't, we might as well end all aspects of our friendship as of this moment; be done with it, and never strive to revive it again. But let me tell you, my dear Emma, all would be fair game then. I would avoid you like the plague. Your name would be anathema to me." Louisa arched her eyebrows threateningly. "I might even make a play for your husband."

"Don't be a ninny," Emma finally managed to get in. "Neither of us are silly schoolgirls. Tom might have something to say about the matter as well." She locked eyes with Louisa. "I have a confession to make—when I left you at Frances's, the thought did occur to me that you might be telling the truth. Assumptions were made by Tom and me, and they made sense at the time. I'm sorry I acted as I did at Frances's. I had no right to strike you. I'm ashamed and deeply sorry for my sudden temper."

Louisa puffed up in her chair. "No, you didn't have the right. I certainly expected an apology today and I'm glad you gave one. You can't imagine how hurt and mortified I was—to go back into Fran's and make small talk after that scene. She was like a bloodhound on the scent, wanting to sniff out every gory detail. Thanks to me, you're still in her good graces, but it was an effort—believe me, an effort. It took all I had. My silence was worth its weight in gold for your reputation. Later, when I had time to compose myself and think, I thought too much water had passed under the bridge to give up on us entirely, despite what insane thoughts might fill your head."

"If what you say about the letters is true, do you have proof?"

"Not yet, but soon. You'll be the first to know."

A chilly silence rode between them until Louisa said, "I have other news for you as well. . . ."

Emma stopped fiddling with her pencil in anticipation of Louisa's revelation.

"I know where Linton Bower lives."

She stiffened, trying hard not to show her interest. "Oh? Alex didn't know—or didn't want to say."

"I'm sure you still harbor affection for the man," Louisa said with some distaste in her voice. "A certain Boston art critic we both know tracked him down."

Emma allowed the depth of her emotion to flow freely, her nerves feeling as if they were being stretched under her skin, her pulse accelerating. "Please, Louisa, I must talk to Linton."

"I know. Alex told me you had inquired."

"Alex should keep private conversations to himself."

"I'm afraid Alex's propensity for gossip may have caused this muddle in the first place. He was the only one I told about you and Linton."

"I wish I could say this whole affair was over and done with, but the damage has been significant to all involved."

Louisa leaned toward her. "I know, and that's another reason I came. I'm not the heartless soul you think I am. I do bear some responsibility for this . . . misunderstanding." She stopped and withdrew a paper from her coat pocket. "Linton's address is on this slip. It's not far from here—in the West End. But if you go, be prepared for what you might find. I think Linton has had a tough time of it. I've not seen him since the Fountain closed. I don't think he ever got over your leaving."

Emma rose and offered her hand.

Louisa shook it gently.

"Thank you for coming," Emma said. "I appreciate your concern . . . and friendship."

"I will clear my name. Mark my words." She put on her coat and turned toward the door. "Good luck with Linton."

When Emma heard Anne latch the door, she picked up her sketch pad once again and opened the cover. There, in another drawing, were the muscular back and legs of Linton Bower, his face, unfinished, turned toward an unknown horizon.

Entry: 29th January, 1919

I've resumed this diary because the winter has undone me. I never fancied myself as a writer—always an artist—but I find myself secluded with my thoughts on these cold days, with no one to confide in except Anne and Lazarus. Both must tire of my ramblings. Cold, cold, and more cold, plus an unrelenting parade of gray clouds that hangs on for days, as if the sun were captured and bound, and, like a prisoner, allowed only a brief respite outdoors. I can only hope that spring will come early this year with its promise of change.

I dreamed of Tom last night and the awful explosion at the Front. I woke up screaming because I rushed to him and he had no face. The shell had wiped it clean away leaving only a bloody pulp. The dream has taken other victims, all reduced to ashen, faceless figures. But Kurt and Tom seem to appear most frequently in these nightmares. I haven't heard from my husband and, at this point, I don't know if I will. Our forced separation is creeping into divorce.

Also, I have attempted, since Louisa's visit, to keep my thoughts about Linton to a mild distraction. I did take a walk one day through the snow, to his studio, only to find the door bolted and the second story looking particularly empty—the intuitive feeling one often gets when a building has been deserted.

My only hope of seeing Linton will be to go to the address Louisa gave me. I suppose that's what I'll do when I gather up the nerve; my emotions are still raw from Paris. Louisa's warning about his condition has tempered my enthusiasm; but, since my return, I've overlooked the ache in my heart. The memory of Linton's affections, which pushed me to France, has returned. Suddenly, it's as though I have that insane choice to make between Tom and Linton. Is the ache in my heart from the possibility of what Linton and I could have had—as he pointed out in our last conversation at the Livingstons'?

The war and France have changed me. How can one do the work I did and not be altered? Life is more precious to me than it has ever been, though I lack the love

I desire. If I had to make the choice between Tom and Linton, I fear it would tear me apart.

Lazarus has nosed open my studio door in order to find me. He has been overly affectionate the past few weeks, especially since he's gotten used to me being here again. But I believe there is another reason for his attentions. He is protective through his own instinct, and knows by his senses—as I do as well—that my body carries another human being. And as the child grows, the haunting dream dissolves. I used Kurt for my own advantage, but I have no remorse. How could I live with this hideous dream for the rest of my days?

CHAPTER 12

BOSTON

February 1919

A brilliant powdery blue sky covered Boston. The air was cold enough for snow, but the sun shone without clouds for company. The morning passed with Emma bent over the toilet bowl; however, the queasy sickness had faded by noon when she managed to eat a bowl of oatmeal for lunch.

After the bout with her stomach had cleared, feeling well enough for a walk, she'd decided to find Linton, knowing she could no longer put off the inevitable. *Time waits for no man— or woman.*

She traversed the narrow streets of the West End where the row houses, in their congested and endless line of brick fronts, depressed her. The deeper she descended, the closer she came to the address she sought, the worse the houses became. Many of them stood derelict, their windows broken or shuttered with yellowed newspaper, the wooden steps rotting from the damp. In the dark shadows that covered some of the façades, Emma spotted candles burning through the windows—a piteous source of heat on a frigid day.

She shuddered upon reaching the address Louisa had given her, lifting the note from the shadows into the sunlight to make sure she had arrived at the right building—but there was no mistake. She stared at the house and struggled to contain her revulsion. The third-floor windows were broken, the frames twisted like branches into the air. Pigeons cooed and fluttered in the openings. A filthy sheet covered the second-story windows and behind the makeshift scrim, the figure of a heavyset man moved in shadowy outline. The first-floor windows were sealed against all light, heavy maroon drapes hanging against them like ornamental swags adorning a tomb.

She gathered her courage and forced herself to knock on the door. Curses rose from above, followed by the heavy clomp of feet down the stairs. The door flew open and Emma faced a man larger than John Harvey, balls of yellow spittle clinging to his mustache, the warm odor of beer floating on his breath.

"What do ya want?" he asked in a brogue laced with hostility.

"I'm looking for Mr. Linton Bower," Emma said, trying to maintain her composure.

"He ain't 'ere," the man replied, "and no decent woman would go looking for 'im in this neighborhood."

"Are you sure he isn't here? This is the address I was given."

"Quite," he replied with mock civility. "Now, go about yer business elsewhere."

Emma was about to leave when she heard a raspy voice call out from the first-floor apartment, "Terry, who's there? Is it a visitor for me?"

"Shut up and mind yer business," the man spit back. "Yer not fit for guests."

"Is that Mr. Bower?" Emma poked her head past the doorway.

"Did you 'ear me? I said begone."

"Terry?" the voice asked again, this time with more force.

"Go back to bed," Terry shouted at the door and then turned on Emma. "This ain't none of yer concern!"

"If it is Mr. Bower, it is definitely my concern—and his."

"I knew it," the man said. "Yer after money, too. Well, the bugger ain't paid his rent for two months, and he ain't gettin' out of here scot free."

Emma looked past Terry as the inside door inched open. Through the crack, the face of a man appeared, although she wasn't at all sure the features belonged to Linton. Filmy eyes sank deep into ashen sockets; the man's black hair lay matted against his scalp. He wore trousers but no shirt, his shoulders and chest wrapped loosely in a gray blanket.

"Linton?" Emma asked, barely containing her horror.

The tenant's face twisted toward the door; then, his head tilted back in recognition.

"Emma?" His voice barely rose above a whisper.

"It is you!" She ran into Terry, who blocked the doorway with his girth. "Please, let me past."

Linton lowered his head and said, "You should leave. It isn't safe—it isn't right."

"Are ya deaf?" Terry asked. "He's told ya to get out."

"I have money. I'll give you twenty dollars if you let me pass."

Terry's eyes lit up.

Emma withdrew two bills from her coat pocket and pushed them into his outstretched palm.

He bowed slightly and let her pass.

She rushed toward the door.

Linton attempted to close it in front of her, but she pushed back, staring through the gap between them. His legs buckling, his strength failing to sustain the resistance, he clutched the doorknob before collapsing.

"My God," Emma said. "You need help."

"He needs more 'an help," Terry called back as he headed up the stairs. Then he laughed and shut his door with a thump.

Emma lifted Linton by his arms and dragged him toward a small bed pushed against the inside wall of the tiny room.

He collapsed on the dilapidated mattress, shivering and moaning as he wrapped a soiled sheet over the blanket.

Emma found another covering under the bed and placed it over him. Kneeling by his side, she put her hand to his forehead feeling the fiery skin, clammy to the touch, yet beaded with sweat.

"I'm burning up," Linton whispered, his voice scratchy and hoarse.

Emma withdrew her hand, suddenly terrified of the possibility of influenza. "How long have you been like this?"

"Going on the third day, maybe more, I can't remember," Linton said, his voice rattling as he gasped for breath.

"I'm taking you out of here." Emma looked around the room, in the scattered light, seeing only a chair and Linton's soiled clothes piled in a corner. The apartment smelled of an oily sickness—of sweat and disease that emanated from the lungs and skin. "You're burning up and freezing to death at the same time. You need to see a doctor."

"I can't—I owe Terry rent. I don't have money for medicine."

"To hell with Terry. I'll pay him and get you to the hospital." She wanted to stroke his clothed leg and kiss his pale cheeks, but as a doctor's wife she was aware of the infectious diseases that might harm her and the unborn child.

A weak smile formed on his lips. "I'm glad you're here. I thought I'd die before I could touch your face again."

"Don't talk nonsense. You'll be fine. I'm calling for a cab. Does Terry have a telephone?"

Linton suppressed a laugh, which only caused him to hold his chest and wince in pain. When he could breathe again, he said, "Terry lives as sparsely as I do. A telephone is a luxury."

Emma opened the door. "I'll be back shortly. Can you walk?"

"If you help me."

"You know I will." She stood by the bed, wishing she could touch him. "You must be calm and wait for me no matter what happens."

Linton nodded.

As she shut the apartment door, Terry's rough voice boomed down the stairs. "Had enough, 'ave ya? I said he was no good—not fit for a piece. I 'ear he was a fine specimen once, even though he's sightless." His head appeared over the railing.

"How much does he owe you?" Emma said coldly.

"Well, if ya count the twenty ya gave me—which I shouldn't—as being a fee to enter this fine establishment . . . I suppose I could let him go for another twenty as long as he swabs his room for the next tenant."

"I'll be back with forty—lock the door and keep his things as they are."

"Lock the door?" Terry guffawed in response to Emma's request. "He ain't got nothin' to steal—a few worthless paintings and some grubby old clothes. Who'd want 'em?"

"If you destroy his work, I'll personally come after you."

"I'm shakin'," Terry said, puffing out his eyes. "Come back with the money." He spat on the floor.

Emma found a cab at the edge of the West End. She instructed the driver to take her home and then return to Linton's address. Anne helped her gather a nurse's mask, gloves, a couple of handkerchiefs, and one of Tom's left-behind winter coats. She washed her hands and returned to Linton's wearing the mask and gloves. She found him, soaked in sweat, dressed in trousers and a shirt and sitting on the bed. She held out Tom's coat and guided Linton's arms into it, led him into the hall, and closed the door. She felt Terry staring at her and, saying nothing, dropped the forty dollars on the mucky wooden floor.

"Boston General," Emma told the cabdriver, who looked at Linton with suspicion, keeping as far away as he could from the sick man.

A few blocks away, Linton's head swayed onto Emma's shoulder.

She placed one of the handkerchiefs under his head and looked at his ashen face.

A thin line of blood trickled from his nose.

Emma felt it too risky to return to Linton's apartment that day to get his paintings. She assumed Terry would wait a few more days before ignoring her order to keep the soiled clothes and the artwork, and thought of hiring a workman to retrieve his belongings.

The day after Linton was admitted, Emma walked to Boston

General. The admission process the day before had not been easy. Linton had no money or family to support him. The staff, who knew Emma on sight because of Tom, welcomed her, but, overall, seemed more interested in her story in Paris than they were in the patient. After a half hour of getting little accomplished, she finally called for the director, a venerable Boston gentleman with years of experience as a surgeon. Once she talked with him, Linton was admitted to a ward with other influenza patients. The director assured Emma that his new patient would have the finest care and that she could visit any time if she was willing to take proper precautions.

Despite the previous day's drawbacks, Emma knew that Boston General was opulent compared to the hospital in Toul and that Linton would be well looked after. The corridors were spacious and the floors gleamed white, unlike the cramped facility in France. Here, the doctors and nurses walked in their starched uniforms down well-lit halls.

When she arrived, the front-desk nurse greeted her cheerily and called for an orderly. The young man led Emma to a sparkling white room where she pulled on a smock over her clothes, positioned a fresh cotton mask over her mouth and nose, and put on gloves. He then directed her to the ward.

"How is Mr. Bower?" she asked a nurse who stood outside the door.

The woman smiled and said, "He's holding his own. So many young men are sick. We're concerned about the pneumonia."

"Pneumonia?" Emma asked, shocked by the diagnosis. "He has it?"

"Unfortunately, yes."

"May I see him?"

"The director has asked me to make an exception for you, but please don't touch him and don't take too much time. He's very weak. He's in bed ten, near the window."

Emma thanked the nurse and walked into the rectangular room full of patients, mostly men, some wearing masks. She spotted Linton near a corner, enveloped in a pool of sun from a window behind his head. As she approached, he lifted his head from the pillow. The pallid face showed slightly more color than the day before; still, his overall complexion remained ghastly. Emma started to touch his shoulder but relented, and instead stood close to the bed.

"I knew you would come," Linton said.

"Of course."

Linton studied her with watery eyes. "Another time, another place," he said in a strained voice and managed a smile.

She backed into the sunlight so he could see her better.

"I recognized you today, just as I did when you came to my studio. That day, you smelled of oatmeal soap and I ran my hands over your stockings."

"I remember," Emma said. "But don't talk—you must save your energy."

"The doctor says I have pneumonia."

"Yes."

He shook his head. "If I hadn't been so blind, I would have whisked you away."

Emma held a finger to her lips, before drawing up a chair and sitting beside his bed. "Let me talk, Linton."

He turned his head toward her.

"I have something to tell you . . . I want to thank you for your letters. They meant so much to me, I saved them in Paris and brought them back to Boston. They've traveled thousands of miles and now they're home. I was worried when your letters stopped, but now I understand what happened."

Linton's eyes, gauzy and pale, gazed past her into the ward.

"I've spent much of my life running away . . . from my past . . . from you. But I've stopped running. I returned to Boston because I had to. I've struggled with numerous difficulties over the past two years and I've faced them in my own way. The day Alex introduced us and we walked to your studio, I knew I could love you. I'm sorry there couldn't have been more days, but my marriage, my work . . . you understand. I've been a coward many times in my life. You were right when you said, 'another time, another place,' at Frances's party. In such a world our love would have been reserved for each other."

"But if you and Tom aren't . . . ? Don't we have time?"

Emma leaned as close to him as she dared and lowered her voice, "I don't think so. This is so difficult for me to say . . ."

Tears welling in his eyes, Linton turned away, anticipating the worst, and stared at the ceiling.

"I'm going to have a baby."

Linton swung his head toward her, his face turning into the sun. He tried to lift his arm to cover his eyes but failed, and dropped it stiffly by his side.

"There's no time to explain," Emma pleaded. "Please believe me when I say that my affection and respect for you never faltered."

"You shouldn't be here," he said, choking back tears. "Your baby shouldn't be exposed to sick people." His voice sputtered and a cough wracked him so violently he shook in bed.

Emma grabbed a clean white cloth from the bedside table and dropped it over his mouth and nose. Soon, crimson streaked the fabric.

"I'm sorry," Emma said. "You must hate me."

Linton turned toward her again, the cloth falling from his face, tears streaking his cheeks. "I could never hate you, and I'll never stop loving you. Your child will be my child as well. . . ." He tried to lift himself up on his elbows, but couldn't. Groaning, he fell back on the pillow.

He began again after catching his breath. "I'm not afraid of dying, Emma. I'm afraid of never *seeing* the world again, of leaving behind all this beauty. I'll never be able to touch your child—our child—or be there when it takes its first step. I'll never be able to walk with you through a meadow, smell a rose, feel the warmth of the sun, know the turn of the seasons, or watch the bright day fade into night. I'll never have that again."

She wept.

"You will see beauty again, wherever you may be," she said after composing herself. She stood, leaned over the bed, and kissed him lightly on the forehead through her mask, his love melting any fear of danger. For once, she wasn't afraid to show her affection.

Linton put his arms around her neck and pulled her gently toward him.

She felt his breath in her hair, and stayed in his embrace, enraptured, until a hand tapped her shoulder. She looked back to see the ward nurse.

"That isn't wise," the woman said. "Please . . . move away, he's contagious."

Emma disengaged herself from Linton's arms. "You're right, but I would have held him just the same."

"You must think of your own health—not just the patient's," the nurse said.

"You must go," Linton said. "I'm tired and they need to take care of me."

"You can visit again, but you *must* obey the rules or you'll be removed," the nurse told her.

"Tomorrow." Emma stood in the sun and blew him a kiss.

He pursed his lips in a kiss.

The nurse escorted her to the door. "Please observe our rules, Mrs. Swan," the woman said in a reproachful tone. "I'm sorry to be so strict, but these patients are seriously ill. We don't want more deaths."

Emma nodded, slipped off the mask, gloves, and gown, and handed them to the nurse. She was glad to be out of the ward, away from the sickness and the painful emotions Linton stirred within her, feelings that would require the balm of time to heal. She chided herself for not having the nerve to tell him who had fathered her child, but that story would have to wait until he recovered.

On her way out, Emma spotted Alex at the bottom of the hospital steps. He leaped up them, stopping near her, a frantic grimace on his lips. "A friend told me Linton is here."

"He has pneumonia," Emma said. "You might not be able to see him."

"Oh, God." Alex drew in a sharp breath and closed his eyes, but only a moment passed before he said good-bye and rushed to the hospital doors.

From her chair near the sitting room fireplace, Emma watched the snow fall in soft, lazy circles. Winter had arrived full blown in her dark world. The courtyard worktable, nearly obscured by the drifting flakes, was covered in a layer of glistening white. Lazarus stretched on his back in front of her, his limbs sprawled akimbo.

Anne brought a steaming pot of tea and placed it on the table next to her. "I'll be going to bed now. Is there anything else you need?"

Emma shook her head and sniffled.

"Drink your tea. It will make your head feel better."

"It's just a cold," Emma said, hoping her self-diagnosis was correct. She had stayed away from the hospital for three days because of her illness, and called the nurses' station to relay her get-well messages to Linton.

Emma sipped her tea and opened her diary. The fireplace crackled and a damp log hissed and popped on the hearth. Startled, she shifted in her chair. The reports reminded her of rifle fire at the Front and the fireworks the night Monsieur Thibault committed suicide. She took a deep breath while holding the warm cup in her hands. After a time, she lifted her pen.

Entry: 14ᵗʰ February, 1919

Today is Valentine's Day and here I sit, like a lump, on the evening of love. If a Gypsy had foretold my fortune for this day, my laughter would have echoed down Charles Street. I've rather made a mess of life and prospects don't seem to be getting better. Who knows, soon I may be a single mother in Boston—not unlike the woman I met in Saint-Nazaire who lost her husband in the war, or Madame Bouchard—if Tom does return to Boston. When my baby is born I will exorcise many memories.

Despite my demons, I know my love for this child will extend beyond my own concerns.

Neither Tom nor Madame Bouchard have written, telephoned, or sent telegrams. Madame Bouchard would be looking for money. I haven't the faintest idea what Tom's been up to. Sometimes I feel him in the house, looking into the studio, shaving in the bathroom, sitting in the courtyard, and I do miss him. He was always strong in ways I wasn't. It's not that I pine for him; however, I see his picture on the mantel and I realize we're still married despite our trials. Honestly, Tom is an anchor for me— not a man who thrilled me like Kurt with his sense of the forbidden, or like Linton with his unbridled romance. Tom is kind and strong and always present like a faithful friend. But where was the spark, the fire, in that friendship? I ask myself that question too often. Yet, after he left for France, without him for an anchor, I drifted.

I worry so about Linton. When he recovers, we must settle into our roles as friends. I don't know if that will be possible for either of us. Sometimes separation is the only option when love causes so much pain. It will take time for us to adjust. There's so much to be done with the baby and Tom I can't think about it now. The thoughts of a divorce and settlements, relocation, the disapproving looks and the telling "I knew you'd disappoint me" from my mother sends me into spasms of anxiety. Many times, like this evening in front of the fire, I wish my life could have been different. That's when I yearn for a world with Linton that I know is just a dream.

I've received no word from Louisa about Tom's letters. Perhaps she is concocting the perfect alibi to prove her innocence.

I did get a letter from John Harvey, telling me he might have a staff opening in London for Virginie. I wonder if she will take my advice and follow a lead I'm sure would benefit her career. A note, I'm certain, is already on its

way from Paris to me, and knowing Virginie, she will ac-
cept the position, but protest all the way to London.

I have written enough for one evening. There's a full
lover's moon tonight, but the snow continues to fall and
obscure its cold beauty. Tomorrow promises to be windy
and cold. This lump must lift herself from her chair, dis-
turb Lazarus, tend the fire, and crawl into bed—alone,
but warm, this Valentine's night.

The knock on the door, the bustle on the stairs and downstairs hall was followed by a deathly silence. Her bedroom clock
ticked forlornly as she strained to see its face, the dial partially
obscured in shadow. It was a few minutes after two in the morning. She sat up in bed, uncertain, in the haze of sleep, of the
sounds below. Soon, hurried steps pattered up toward her bedroom.

Anne called from the hall. "Ma'am . . . Emma . . . ?"

Heart pounding, she jumped from her bed, and opened the
door.

Anne stood trembling, a single candle illuminating her wan
face. "A man from the hospital is downstairs. . . ."

"Yes?" Emma asked, fearing the worst.

"Mr. Bower died just before midnight."

Emma reached for the door but instead stumbled backward.
Anne captured her in her arms and silently guided her to bed.

"I am so sorry, ma'am," Anne whispered as they sat, holding
hands.

Emma could only look at the young woman beside her and
think about a future swallowed by death, before she burst into
sobs that clawed at her throat.

Entry: 18ᵗʰ February, 1919

I'm not much in the mood to write. We buried Linton
this morning. When I say we—I mean, Alex, Anne, my-
self, and the funeral staff. We were the only people who
bothered to attend his burial in Mt. Auburn. I arranged

and paid for it, although Alex offered to help. Linton had no living relatives as far as Alex and I could tell. So, we buried him in a lovely plot, under large trees on a snowy hilltop. Alex said a few words and I attempted to, but I couldn't keep my composure. I wanted the whole affair to be over as quickly as possible, and I think Alex did as well. Poor man, I believe he loved Linton as much as I did, if not more.

From there, Alex drove Anne and me to Linton's apartment in the West End. Fortunately, the second-floor landlord was a bit more obliging than last time, considering the money I had paid him previously. He hadn't touched the apartment, but was glad to be rid of Linton's belongings. The three of us, dressed in masks and gloves, disposed of Linton's clothes and gathered the rest of what he owned, which was insignificant except for three small paintings, which were buried under the soiled garments. As Anne and Alex got into the car, I searched the apartment one final time, looking for any correspondence or personal items that might have escaped our eyes. I found nothing. We brought the paintings back to the house. Alex told me to keep the artwork—which I had hoped to keep anyway—as a remembrance of Linton's life.

Anne prepared tea for us and Alex left early that afternoon. Once again, I was left with Anne, and my thoughts, and the reminder of Linton as I looked at the paintings stacked against my studio wall. This evening, after dinner, I will collapse into bed. My body feels empty, as if a light has been extinguished in my soul.

CHAPTER 13

———◆———

BOSTON

May 1919

The driver offered the stability of his extended arm to Emma as she arrived at Frances Livingston's home. Disembarking from the carriage, she leaned on him just as she had when the cab arrived to collect her. She was obviously pregnant to any observer now, her belly distended underneath her dress.

She walked up the steps, conscious of the extra weight she carried. Under the warm play of sunlight, Frances's stately home looked as resplendent as Emma had ever seen it. The spring flowers were in bloom, the trees in fresh green leaf. She never tired of Boston's May tulips, their radiant beauty, and today was no exception. The east garden, extending to the high stone fence bordering the property, burst with vibrant hues of maroon, yellow, purple, and white, those wide rows interspersed with trimmed evergreens and leafy bushes. The sky was like blue silk and the warm air touched her body in a soft and thrilling way. Emma shed her light jacket and reveled in the sunshine. The regenerated earth and the pleasant sun filled her with a sense of wonder and life she hadn't felt in months. Her memory of the war and Linton hadn't faded, but the beauty of the day did much to lessen the sting.

"I'm so glad you and Louisa are friends again," Frances said as she directed Emma to the garden table, which was set for three. "The whole business between you seemed so nasty. I was very concerned."

Emma nodded as she sat. "Thank you. The affair was disagreeable, and it all came down to one man who forged Louisa's handwriting . . . but she can tell you about that."

"But I'm dying to know who perpetrated such a foul deed," Frances said. "I can tell you, my dear, there is nothing nearer and dearer to my heart than protecting those in our circle."

"Frances, really, you embarrass me sometimes. I'm hardly in your 'circle.' I have neither the wealth, the social status, nor—"

"Nonsense. Never underestimate yourself. Think what you have done. Most of the women in the world will never achieve what you have. Money is just part of our circle. I shudder to think what life would have been like if Mr. Livingston had not admired your work before he died." She paused to pick up her wineglass. "Oh, I wish you could partake. You could join me in a toast to your success and your new baby. Tom must be so proud . . . when is he coming home?"

"Yes, we're both immensely proud," Emma said, skirting the truth. "The baby is due in four months. I'm not sure Tom will be home by then. He's still involved with the French hospital."

"Well, he needs to come home to Boston and be a proper father. Let the hospital rot."

She was about to reply when Louisa appeared at the garden doors. She was attired in a white unbuttoned cape-coat, a pale blue dress with matching brimmed hat, her lean figure accented by a single strand of ivory pearls that fell to her waist. As always, she looked the epitome of fashion.

"Good afternoon," Louisa said and then kissed them both on the cheek. "I'm sorry I'm late but I was detained at the dressmaker's." She took her seat next to Frances.

"Another fortune spent on clothes, my dear?" Frances asked.

Emma laughed. "But for a good cause."

"Certainly," Louisa said. "There's no better cause than a single woman who needs a husband."

"I'm sure a proposal will come along any day now," Frances said.

"You're always so positive about my matrimonial chances, Frances. I wish I could be so certain." Louisa doffed her cape and asked Emma, "How is the baby?"

"I'm long over morning sickness and the doctor says it's coming along fine. I think it must be a boy—the way he kicks."

"Are you hoping for a boy or a girl?" Frances asked.

"A boy," Emma said without hesitation.

"Tom must be happy," Louisa said.

Emma nodded, implicating her husband again in the fabrication.

"Yes, I'm sure he is, but I do want to hear the story about the letters," Frances said to Louisa. "You've withheld it from me for so long, I'm nearly ready to burst."

"The whole episode is so dreary," Louisa said. "I'm sure Emma would like us to talk about more uplifting subjects."

"No, it's fine," Emma said. "One more time in the telling, then I'm sure we can leave the subject behind, never to be mentioned again."

"All right, once more for you, Frances," Louisa said. The sun glanced off the brim of her hat as she turned. "Do you remember a man—I believe his name is Everett as near as I can recall—a very disagreeable fellow who attended your parties and attempted to ensconce himself in your circle?"

"Oh, yes," Frances replied. "Mr. Everett, a confidant of Vreland. He went off to war, I believe . . . I haven't seen or heard of him since."

"I don't believe he went off to anything as noble as war," Louisa said. "I'm certain he's in prison."

Frances gasped. "Prison?"

"He's a forger," Louisa said, "the primary reason he remained a protégé of Vreland's. What better way to access art than through a critic? He copied the artists' techniques, created fakes, and then sold them as if he'd acquired them as originals."

"An incendiary man," Emma said. "I had my run-ins with

him. At my opening at the Fountain, he termed Linton Bower's work 'rubbish' and then declared I had 'no place in the male world of sculpture.'" She preferred not to mention that the man had later congratulated her at Frances's party on the sale of *Diana*—the sole reason for the purchase, he theorized, being the scandalous rumors surrounding her and Linton.

"Cretin," Frances huffed. "A certified brute with no morals or breeding."

"I'm certain Mr. Everett obtained a thank-you note or a letter I'd sent to Alex, studied my handwriting, and forged a series of letters to Tom." Louisa paused and sipped her wine. "I needn't go into details—it was a private matter between Emma, Tom, and . . . another party."

"We all understand your meaning, my dear," Frances said. "Mr. Everett's actions were despicable on all counts."

"When Tom got the first letter, he assumed I'd written it, and so did Emma when she saw it. Thus, the trap was set."

"But why would Mr. Everett do such a thing—for what purpose?" Frances asked.

"To ruin my reputation and marriage by scandal, and destroy my chance of making a living as a sculptress," Emma replied. "Perhaps he fixated on me because I'm not primarily a painter; it's difficult to forge a sculpture. He's a childish, *misogynistic* crook who caused more trouble than he'll ever know. By all accounts he's an intelligent but destructively evil man who can't stand to see women succeed."

"And, of course," Louisa said, "the whole conceit would have collapsed if Tom had written back to me. But Tom, being the gentleman he is, banished such crass thoughts from his mind and never gave them a second thought. Of course, even if Tom had responded to me, the damage would already have been done. The seed of doubt would have been planted. Nefarious . . . isn't that right, Emma?"

"Positively diabolical," Frances said before Emma could answer.

Emma looked toward the garden and the brilliant tulips,

placed her hands on her rounded belly, and waited for the maid to serve. After a luncheon plate was placed in front of her, Emma, knowing that Tom had indeed given the letters more than a second thought, said, "Damage occurs in layers. A shell explodes and a man is disfigured. My work in France masked the painful physical injuries of the war, but could do little to soothe emotions, and, as I've come to find out, in life other dangers exist besides shells and bullets. A simple letter can injure with the same explosive force, the physical and emotional wounds lingering much longer than the words."

Louisa lowered her head so the brim of her hat covered her eyes.

"You mustn't fuss, my dear, not in your condition," Frances said. "You need to throw yourself back into your work—something less challenging than sculpting, of course—drawing, or painting, perhaps. A diversion—good, solid work—that's what you need."

Emma smiled and took a bite of her fish. She stared at the garden's brilliant colors, thinking how wonderful it would be to capture its hues in sculpture, just as Linton did in his painting. "As always, Frances, you have the best interests of your friends at heart. Work may be just what I need."

A few days later the sun retreated, leaving the city cool and humid under a thick layer of clouds. Emma drew in her studio—she had started several new sketches of *Narcissus Rising*, her planned new work, but the drawings left her as cold and dissatisfied as the weather. She crumpled the papers and threw them on the floor by her desk. Lazarus noted her displeasure and sniffed the detritus that collected around his front paws.

She would hardly have given the knock downstairs a second thought had it not been for Lazarus's reaction. His ears pointed straight up and a sudden fire, a dog's expression of joy, coursed through his eyes. Then, he sprang up on all fours, pranced in a circle, and barked wildly at her closed studio door.

"What's gotten into you?" Emma asked. He responded by

nipping playfully at her hand. She opened the door and Lazarus, his tail wagging furiously, raced down the stairs.

"Anne?" Emma called out.

An audible gasp rose from the hall below.

"Anne!"

When her housekeeper didn't respond, Emma walked downstairs as quickly as she could, clutching the railing along the way. At the bottom she turned and saw Tom. Her housekeeper was plastered against the door as if confronted by a ghost. A woman stood behind him.

Lazarus jumped on his master and barked with joy.

Tom kneeled to pet the wriggling dog and smiled at Emma, a gesture that faded as soon as he recognized the change that had occurred in her body since they'd last met.

"Lazarus, come into the kitchen," Anne said. She grabbed the dog by the collar and tugged.

Tom rose and kissed Anne on the cheek. "Thank you for taking care of him, the house, and . . . my wife."

"It's so good to see you again, sir," Anne said. "It's been so long."

"Yes, it has. Anne, I'd like you to meet Madame Bouchard and her son, Charles."

The woman stepped from behind Tom and Emma immediately recognized the brooding features of the French woman, who stood with a young boy cradled against her shoulder. Madame Bouchard looked at Emma in much the same manner as Tom and then surveyed the surroundings.

"May we come in?" Tom asked as he lifted the boy from Madame Bouchard.

"Come now, Lazarus, let's go for a treat," Anne said and closed the door while holding onto the dog. She tugged him toward the kitchen as Lazarus dug his claws into the floor.

Emma pointed to the sitting room, acutely aware of the trappings of *their* home. Tom's picture still looked out from its place on the fireplace mantel. Emma sat in her favorite chair opposite the hearth while Tom and Madame Bouchard took seats on either side. Emma turned on a lamp to chase away the afternoon gloom.

Tom jostled the child when he sat and the boy uttered a short cry.

"You must be gentle with your son," Madame Bouchard said. She smoothed the wrinkles on her dress with her strong fingers. "He, like the rest of us, is tired from the trip."

"I'm not used to handling little ones anymore," Tom said. "I participated in very few deliveries in Toul. Wounded men and the dying—those were the players on my stage."

Emma stared at them, uncertain what to say. Madame Bouchard wore a navy dress that drained the color from her face. The woman was agitated, unsure what to do with her hands, her gaze flitting around the room. Tom looked as if he had gained a little weight—he was always too thin—and had shaved off his mustache, giving him a younger appearance. The new look unsettled Emma because now he reminded her again of Kurt when they had met in Vermont.

"You have something to tell us," Madame Bouchard said through an ironic smile.

"*I'll* explain *my* pregnancy *to Tom*—if that's what you mean."

Madame Bouchard huffed and turned her attention to the objects in the room.

"We won't keep you long," Tom said, "but I felt we needed to talk."

Madame Bouchard nodded reluctantly.

"We've come to a decision," Tom continued. "Charles and I are staying in Boston. Madame Bouchard has decided to remain in France with her other son."

The woman smiled somewhat haughtily, and said, "You must have known this would come to pass. Your husband would not desert you . . . I told you so in Paris. It is hard to raise children without a father. But Thomas is kind and I know he will help with our provisions. My other son is French through and through—and I have become so. He needs to know the ways of our country. I only came to provide milk and make sure that Charles would find a good home."

"She is returning to France in a few days. She has no desire to stay, or to bring her other son to live here."

"Where will you live?" Emma asked Tom.

"I haven't figured that out yet. We're staying at a hotel at the moment. I hoped I could talk to you about an arrangement." His blue eyes deepened in intensity. "I see circumstances have changed on both our parts."

"She has gotten even with you," Madame Bouchard said.

The hackles rose on Emma's neck. "My baby was not a question of getting even. My pregnancy was necessary—I need not explain it to you. Not even Tom knows my reason."

"I must say it's a bit of a shock," he said and patted the boy in his arms. "But then, who am I to talk about shocks?"

"Could we talk in the courtyard?" Emma asked him.

He rose with the boy and Emma opened the French doors.

"Don't be long, Thomas," Madame Bouchard said. "Charles needs to be fed soon."

Tom gave an approving look and stepped past the doors.

Emma looked at the bricks, as the space, damp and mossy, closed around her. The tender, green fir shoots were outlined against the walls. While she was gone, an ivy had taken root in one corner; now, its feelers, cross-hatched by variegated leaves, streamed up the stones and reminded her of the courtyard in Paris.

"She's a most disagreeable woman," Emma said after closing the doors.

"Beautiful, but disagreeable."

"She is that. . . ."

"I was very needy at the time, Emma, and I hope that's something you can understand. Solace for one evening was all I sought and our relationship grew from there. To be honest with you, I'm happy I have a son since I won't be able to have a child again." He looked down at Charles, whose head and dark locks were partially covered by a blanket.

Emma pulled back the cover and looked at the smooth, young face. The boy was dozing, and quite handsome in his slumber. "He's beautiful as well. He has your features, but her hair and eyes," she said stroking the abundant black hair covering the boy's head. The child's eyes fluttered, revealing his dusky gaze for a moment, before he drifted back to sleep.

Tom laughed. "I don't think he'll go bald at an early age, like his father."

"She told me in Paris you would come back to me. I didn't know what to believe at the time. Is this really what you and she want?"

Tom sat on the edge of the table and rested the boy in his lap. "She would never admit it, but she wants Charles to grow up here. I think she's afraid of another war to come."

"Then why not come to America and live with you and her other son?"

"She's a proud woman, fiercely nationalistic, who loves her country. She loved her first husband, a Frenchman, deeply, but he wasn't kind to her. He and their son are the touchstones of another life—one she's intent on preserving. She doesn't want to leave her home." Tom looked down at his child. "Charles and I were afterthoughts in her plan of life. Not that she's cruel . . . she isn't. I would call her 'pragmatic,' somewhat like Louisa. Constance and I were both looking for comfort."

"And she for money," Emma offered. "She's a business-woman and as independent as can be."

"Perhaps. Like another woman I know . . . and love."

A blush rose in Emma and the feeling shocked her. Why should it be so hard to accept such a confession from a man she knew so intimately? "I don't know about that," she said.

"After much consideration, she decided to give up Charles," Tom continued. "It took months, but I've been granted formal adoption. We Americans are quite the heroes now. I think the French bureaucracy looked more favorably upon my application because of my role in the war. I have all the necessary papers— so Charles can stay."

"So," Emma said, pondering the question. "You've come home?"

"I thought coming home might be a possibility until I saw you. Is it Linton's child?"

"No." Emma struggled with the words. "Linton's dead."

Tom's eyes narrowed, dazed by her revelation.

"Influenza . . . with complications. When I returned I didn't see him for weeks, and when I found him it was too late."

"I'm sorry. I know you cared for him."

Emma nodded, unwilling to reveal more of her feelings.

Tom looked at her expectantly.

"You don't know the father," Emma said. "Someday, I'll tell you."

"You didn't know Charles's mother, either. The world is full of surprises." The boy squirmed in Tom's lap and began to cry. "Remember when I told you at the hospital that the trust between us was gone? I meant for both of us—not just me." He stroked the boy's head. "I think he's hungry and soon to be cranky. We should be going."

"How can I reach you?"

"At the Copley Plaza. Room 405. I hope you'll telephone me."

"I need time to think."

Emma opened the French doors and Tom stepped inside, the boy clutching at his shirt.

Madame Bouchard sat in her chair, a newspaper across her lap. "I heard him fuss. He's hungry."

Emma imagined Charles suckling against her breast, feeding on her own milk.

"Did you reach an agreement?" Madame Bouchard asked.

"Of sorts," Tom said.

Madame Bouchard took the child from Tom. "I am entrusting my son to you, Mrs. Swan. You must be certain he receives the finest care and attention. You are a strong woman. I know my son can depend on you." She stopped and kissed the boy's forehead. "I will miss him, but I know he will be happy here with his father." She extended her hand to Emma. "Thank you for your hospitality. I doubt we will ever meet again—unless you allow me a future visit."

Emma shook her hand and said nothing.

"Good-bye, Emma," Tom said.

"Good-bye," she said and led them to the door.

After it closed, Anne, breathless, raced out of the kitchen. Lazarus, equally fast, followed, snuffling at the door and wagging his tail in quick, jerky strokes.

"Who was that woman?" Anne asked, trying to control her excitement.

"One I doubt you will see anytime soon."

"And the child?"

Emma trudged down the hall, her feet plodding as if weighted with lead.

Anne overtook her, brushing against Emma's back.

Emma sat in her chair and stared into the courtyard. Only minutes before, Tom had been sitting on that table with *his* child.

Anne stood by the chair, awaiting an answer.

A thousand memories flashed through her mind before she said, "The story will have to wait for another time. I need to think . . . because I honestly don't know what I'm going to do, and, right now, I don't have the strength to struggle."

When the telephone jangled two days later, Emma believed Tom was calling. She had spent a restless and miserable two nights thinking about him and his adopted son. A decision would not be easy. On one hand, she wanted Tom, and his son, to be happy. On the other, she was uncertain whether she loved him enough to ask him back into her life. On balance, she considered, perhaps the most important question to answer about their relationship was one of happiness and not of love. In that case, her decision would be easier.

Anne answered the phone, then handed the receiver to Emma. "It's Mr. Hippel."

Alex greeted her, his voice sounding the cheeriest of any person she had spoken to in weeks with the possible exception of
her housekeeper.

"Finally . . . I'm leaving for New York today," Alex said.
"Everything is packed and already on its way. My friend and I
are traveling by train this afternoon."

"Congratulations," Emma said. "I hope everything turns out
well for you."

There was silence on the other end, as if Alex was measuring
his words. "I'm sorry about this whole affair with Linton," he
finally said. "I'm sorry he couldn't love me. In the beginning, I
really believed it was possible."

"I know, Alex. We all loved Linton."

"Yes, I'll never forget him. It was never really any of my
business—what happened between you—but you must believe
me when I say that I'm sorry you and Linton couldn't have
shared more in life. You're right—we all loved Linton."

Silence captured the line again, until Alex's voice returned to
its chipper form. "I do have something for you."

"A surprise?"

"One from Linton and me. It should arrive within the hour.
Good-bye, Emma, and do call upon us if you're in New York. If
you begin sculpting again, let me know. Who knows, if I don't
have a gallery myself, I'm sure one of my friends will. I can't stay
too far removed from the art world."

Emma said good-bye to Alex and for the next hour paced
about the house, annoying Anne and Lazarus with her nervous
anticipation. She opened the French doors to let in the fresh
May air. The sun shone around puffy clouds and the warm
spring breeze tickled her skin. After treading the same floor for
too long, she walked about the house, moving pictures and bric-
a-brac to suit her mood.

A large crate, loaded on a horse cart, arrived just before
noon. The driver held the animal in check as a strapping young
man struggled with the heavy load at the door.

"I wonder what it could be?" Emma asked the youth.

"I don't know, ma'am, but it's heavy," he said. "Is there a man who can lift it for you?"

"No," Emma said. "Anne, have him put it on the outside table."

"Let me help you," Anne said. "My mistress is with child."

While the young man grunted, Anne grabbed one side of the crate and guided it through the hall and sitting room to the courtyard. With the housekeeper's help, he slid the crate onto the table and then sighed with relief. "That's going nowhere for a long time," he said, doffing his cap to Anne. "Thank you for your aid."

"Please give him some money," Emma said. She studied the crate as Anne and the worker left. Alex had marked it with stamps from the Fountain Gallery. Its top was secured with two-penny nails, but was loose enough that Emma could pry off the lid with her hands. She pushed back the cloth that covered the object inside.

It dropped away to reveal her *Diana.*

Two envelopes lay next to the bronze, which glinted in the sunlight. One was marked from Alex; the other was unsigned.

Emma opened the letter from Alex.

24ᵗʰ May, 1919

My Dear Emma:

Near the end, I paid the rent on Linton's studio because his money was beginning to run out. Some months after I ended the relationship, the studio's landlord (whom I know) asked me to remove Linton's belongings. I had stopped footing the bill and the landlord hadn't seen his tenant in a long time. I found Diana *concealed by a cloth at the bottom of the bookcase. The shelves had been taken out to make room for it. Linton was in such a state after the Fountain closed, I think he went quite mad. He never wanted me to tell you he had purchased your statue with funds from the sale of his paintings and made me swear that I would uphold his secret. Initially, I advised against the purchase, telling him he needed to save his money for living expenses, and let wealthy art patrons like Fran Livingston buy the work. He wouldn't hear of it. He said so many of his finger-prints were upon it, it was practically his anyway. So, I reluc-tantly agreed to sell it to him. He kept it hidden from you . . . well, you know the rest. I've had time to grieve since Linton's death and I think it only fair that the statue returns to you along with a letter I found underneath it. I won't lie to you and say I didn't read it, but it belongs to you. It's from his heart.*

Yours truly,
Alex

Emma, her heart beating furiously, opened the undated let-ter. She immediately recognized it as Linton's scrawling hand.

My Dearest Emma,
The war has raged on far beyond comprehension and I de-spair of ever holding you close to me again, ever smelling your skin, feeling your touch. Today, I'm in one of those moods. The sky is bright and blue enough I can write as the sunlight comes pouring through my studio window. But I doubt whether I will ever have the nerve to send this letter because I fear it may fall into the wrong hands, even though I trust Anne implicitly.

My God, how I miss you. I think of nothing else but you and I wonder how you are and what you are doing in Paris. Are you asleep when I'm awake? Do you touch your body and wish it was my hand upon you instead of your own? Do you feel, as I do, that I have missed my one chance at true love?

The memory of the night I fell at Frances Livingston's runs over and over in my head. I should have begged you to stay—to leave Tom and never go to France—so we could start our lives together. But those were the ravings of an infatuated and con-fused mind—one desperate with passion and love for you. The longing in my soul cuts through me like a knife. Sometimes in the middle of the night, I shoot upright in bed because my mind screams your name. And then I must calm my heart and wipe the tears from my eyes.

I want to touch you. A man with his full senses has no idea how lucky he is. How many men go through the world oblivious to what is around them? If only they could be blinded for a day and not see the women they supposedly hold in high regard. I'm sure the world would change overnight.

My relationship with Alex is deteriorating and I despair of ever seeing you again. My life seems to be sinking into a morass and I cannot think, cannot paint, cannot speak, but only endeavor to hold you in my heart.

When you do return, I fear you will have changed while I sat frozen in my world in Boston. But know this, my dear Emma, whatever happens between us, I will love you forever. I make no apologies for that love. No matter the time or day we meet again, or if we meet again at all, you must never make any apology for our love—I for you and you for me. I want you to love, Emma, and be happy—you deserve so much in your life. And if the choice comes down to Tom or me, I know you will make the hard decision. Whatever happens I will respect that choice because, in the end, my love for you is greater than my selfishness.

The sun is leaving the room and I can write no more. When the light disappears I am thrust into that dark world once more. I have only my heart and my love for you to spread light and warmth.

And with that, good night, dear Emma.

My love is for you. Always.

Linton

Struggling to catch her breath, Emma dropped the letter, watching as its pages fluttered to the brick. She cupped her hands over her face and cried out as Anne stepped into the courtyard.

Emma retrieved her pad and drew with a fervor she hadn't felt in years, the lines coming furiously from her pencil. *Narcis-*

sus Rising took shape, in all forms and dimensions. The muscular torso was Linton's—she knew it and was happy to see his body reappear before her. In one of the sketches, a frontal nude, she had drawn his face and was pleased with the outcome. Linton's handsome features peered out from the page, the lines flowing, human and filled with love.

Lazarus curled around her feet. The French doors were flung open. The sun had drifted far past the courtyard walls. Anne had released *Diana* from the confines of its crate and the bronze sat on the table, a silent testament to Linton, his fingerprints still smudging the metal.

The room was growing dark when Anne brought tea. "You need a lamp. You'll ruin your eyes drawing in this light."

Emma put down her pencil, brushing off her housekeeper's concern. "After the baby is born, I want to work again."

"Sculpting?" Anne asked.

"Yes. This will be my first project." She flipped the pages of her pad so Anne could view the drawings.

"They're very nice," Anne said modestly. "They're of Mr. Bower, aren't they?"

Emma nodded. "The faces are very good, don't you think? I think they're the best I've ever drawn."

"I would say they're perfect. Would you like something to eat?"

"No," Emma replied, "but could you do something for me?"

"Of course."

"Tomorrow morning, arrange a cab. After breakfast, I'm going to the Copley Plaza to visit Dr. Swan. I want to meet with him—on my terms. I have many things to discuss—and to share a secret I've been holding far too long."

Anne touched Emma's shoulder.

She grasped Anne's fingers and looked at the pad in her lap.

The face of Linton Bower smiled at her from eternity.

AUTHOR'S NOTE

The inspiration for *The Sculptress* came from Gustave Flaubert's seminal work of realist fiction, *Madame Bovary*. I was immediately taken with Emma Bovary's story upon reading the book, which, like a few other classics, I read later in life.

Flaubert was born in Rouen, France, in 1821, and as he grew older developed friendships with many in the Parisian literary world. According to Francis Steegmuller, the translator of my favorite edition of the novel, *Madame Bovary* was "not only the most 'realistic' novel of its age . . . it was also the most 'psychological.'" My fascination with Emma Bovary drew from just that—the psychological. How this seemingly provincial woman could drive herself to madness was the question that enthralled me and kept me turning the pages. As dated as the novel may be by today's social standards, its plot, building tensions, and depiction of unrequited love are, to me, as dramatic today as the day they were written.

Flaubert took five years to write the novel, which appeared serially in a Paris magazine beginning in 1856. The work was met with charges of "offenses against morality and religion" almost immediately. The author stood trial but was acquitted with a reprimand. Many years ago, in Boston, I read passages from *Madame Bovary* as part of Banned Books Week, an annual event that celebrates censored and banned books. The particular passage I selected still gives me chills to this day.

The last thing I will point out about the novel is a thought that the author had as he envisioned his words on provincial life: "One likes to imagine some, deep, great, intimate story being lived here amid these peaceful dwellings, a passion like a sickness, lasting until death." (Quoted from the 1992 Modern Library introduction.) Flaubert's words capture the theme of *Madame Bovary* perfectly—a woman driven by her own desires and wishes who had no choice, much like Emma Lewis Swan.

The Sculptress also was inspired by actual events during "The War to End All Wars." The work of my heroine, Emma Lewis Swan, was modeled on the similar vocation of Boston sculptress Anna Coleman Ladd; however, the reader should refrain from making comparisons between the two. The life of Mrs. Ladd bears no resemblance to the fictional drama created for the title character of the novel. The other characters in the book, including Thomas Evan Swan and John Harvey, are likewise fictional characters and should not be substituted for human beings, dead or alive. This book, if I may be so bold, is the most romantic, the most "psychological" of all the historical novels I've written for Kensington. I hope I've succeeded in my task.

A number of sources were consulted during the writing of this book. They include, but are not limited to, primary source documents, books, and internet sites. In particular, I would like to thank Paddy Hartley, and his collaborators at Project Facade, for their generous help with the research of facial reconstruction techniques. Various processes were used during World War I and the technique used by Emma Swan in the novel is an amalgamation of several and not intended to be the actual process. I would direct the interested reader to the Project Facade archive on Paddy's website, and these articles for more information about facial reconstruction and the making of facial masks:

- "Faces of War," by Caroline Alexander, *The Smithsonian*, February, 2007
- "Anna Ladd's Masks, Mending WWI's Scars," by

Jack El-Hai, *The History Channel Magazine*, July/
August 2005

These internet sites were particularly helpful for reconstructing historical events:

- www.paddyhartley.com
- www.firstworldwar.com
- The National World War I Museum and Memorial
  at www.theworldwar.org. The museum, located at
  the Liberty Memorial in Kansas City, Missouri, is a
  treasure trove of war-related artifacts.

Nonfiction books and novels consulted, but not limited to:

- *Memoirs of My Services in the World War, 1917–
  1918*, by George C. Marshall, Houghton Mifflin,
  1976
- *US Doughboy, 1916–1919*, by Thomas A. Hoff,
  Osprey Publishing Ltd., 2005
- *World War I Day by Day*, by Ian Westwell, MBI
  Publishing Company, 2004
- *Life Class*, by Pat Barker, Doubleday, 2008
- *Suite Française*, by Irène Némirovsky, Knopf, 2006
- *Madame Bovary*, by Gustave Flaubert, Modern
  Library Edition, Random House, 1992. Translated by
  Francis Steegmuller

Thanks also must be given to Julien Sanchez and the Toul
Visitors Bureau for their timely and important research on their
historic and lovely town during World War I; to Jean-Marie Jacqueme for his French translation skills. Also, as a reminder to
the reader, the Red Cross is an internationally recognized trademarked symbol used during times of war and natural disaster.

This book could not have been written and edited without
the exceptional skills of my beta readers, Scott Colella, Ricardo

DeFrutos, Michael Grenier, Robert Pinsky, and my wonderful writing colleague who is now sadly missed, Leslie Lombino Schultz. All, in their way, contributed to the final creation of *The Sculptress*. I also have relied upon a community of writers, from the members of Florida Romance Writers in South Florida, to the equally inspiring members of the Writers' Room of Boston. Special thanks go out to Karen Kendall, Kathleen Catalano, and Traci E. Hall for their sage advice and unwavering support.

Writing is never easy, but the process is one of the most gratifying in the world. I love it, even though it often drives me to insanity. I shudder to think what my life would have been like had I not immersed myself in the world of books as a child. This novel, my fifth for Kensington, was written nearly twelve years ago and has undergone extensive revision since the initial draft.

I write about women who have taken a stand in history—sometimes they are overwhelmed by their fictional circumstances, but their struggle is always real, always worth fighting for. A reader told me a few years back that I must have had a "strong" mother to write such heroines. I did. I thank my mother, Gretchen, for giving me the fortitude and discipline necessary to undertake such a daunting task as the creation of a novel. I would also be remiss if I didn't mention my former writing partner, and still wonderful friend, Jenifer Otwell, who provided a huge stepping-stone on this journey.

As always, thanks go to my astute editor, John Scognamiglio, for his faith in this book; and to my steadfast agent, Evan S. Marshall, for his business and literary acumen.

THE SCULPTRESS

V. S. Alexander

ABOUT THIS GUIDE

The suggested questions are included
to enhance your group's reading of
V. S. Alexander's *The Sculptress*

DISCUSSION QUESTIONS

1. The inspiration for *The Sculptress* came from Flaubert's novel *Madame Bovary*. Do you see parallels between the two books? If so, what are they?

2. Emma from *Madame Bovary* and Emma from *The Sculptress* have two decidedly different character endings. Do you believe this was because societal roles for women had softened from 1856 (*Bovary*'s publication date) to World War I?

3. Are the issues that Emma struggled with in the book still prevalent today?

4. "The War to End All Wars" became a common catchphrase for World War I. How did the war change women's lives, including their fashions?

5. The war was also supposed to "make the world safe for democracy." Do you believe that happened?

6. If the book were set in contemporary time, how would Emma have reacted to her circumstances? Her pregnancy? Her relationships with Linton, Andrew Stoneman, and Tom?

7. Would you have liked to see Emma and Linton come together as a couple?

8. Who was the most likable character in the book?

9. Besides Everett, who do you believe was the least likable character in the book?

10. The book closes with Emma seeing Linton's face on the drawing pad. Do you believe she and Tom get back together?

Connect with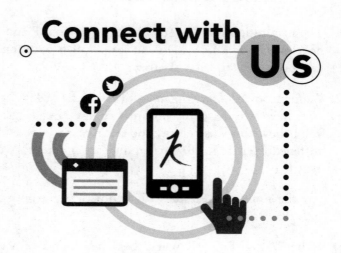
Us

Visit us online at
KensingtonBooks.com
to read more from your favorite authors, see books
by series, view reading group guides, and more.

Join us on social media

for sneak peeks, chances to win books and prize packs,
and to share your thoughts with other readers.

facebook.com/kensingtonpublishing
twitter.com/kensingtonbooks

Tell us what you think!

To share your thoughts, submit a review,
or sign up for our eNewsletters, please visit:
KensingtonBooks.com/TellUs.